Cartel Prince

The Cartel Brotherhood

Sabine Barclay

All rights reserved.

No part of this publication may be sold, copied, distributed, reproduced or transmitted in any form or by any means, mechanical or digital, including photocopying and recording or by any information storage and retrieval system without the prior written permission of both the publisher, Oliver Heber Books and the author, Sabine Barclay, except in the case of brief quotations embodied in critical articles and reviews.

NO AI TRAINING: Without in any way limiting the author's [and publisher's] exclusive rights under copyright, any use of this publication to "train" generative artificial intelligence (AI) technologies and/or large language models to generate text, or any other medium, is expressly prohibited. The author reserves all rights to license uses of this work for the training and development of any generative AI and/or large language models.

PUBLISHER'S NOTE: This is a work of fiction. Names, characters, places, and incidents either are the product of the author's imagination or are used fictitiously. Any resemblance to actual persons, living or dead, business establishments, events, or locales is entirely coincidental.

Cartel Prince Copyright © 2025 by Sabine Barclay.

Cover art by Dar Albert at Wicked Smart Designs

Published by Oliver Heber Books

0 9 8 7 6 5 4 3 2 1

May every queen find her Prince Charming.

Find me writing Historical Romance as
Celeste Barclay.

Happy reading,
Sabine

Subscribe to Sabine's Newsletter

Subscribe to Sabine's bimonthly newsletter to receive exclusive insider perks.

Have you read *The Syndicate Wars?* This FREE origin story novella is available to all new subscribers to Sabine's monthly newsletter. Subscribe on her website. www.sabinebarclay.com

Sabine also writes Historical Romance as Celeste Barclay. Discover her Highlander, Regency, Viking, and Pirate Romances. www.celestebarclay.com

The Cartel Brotherhood

Cartel King

Cartel Viper

Cartel Prince

Cartel Rose (Coming 2025)

Cartel Protector (Coming 2026)

Cartel Devil (Coming 2026)

Chapter One

Pablo

"I swear by all that's holy, *Tío* Humberto, if you don't get your shit together and get me what I came for, this will be *la gota que rebosará una copa ya casi llena*." The drop which will cause an already nearly full cup to overflow.

It's the Spanish version of the straw that broke the camel's back. My *tío abuelo*—great-uncle—is pissing me off to a level he never has before. It's taking everything I can muster not to wrap my hands around his bloated neck and squeeze.

Squeeze until his jowls turn purple.

Squeeze until his eyes bulge.

Squeeze until he's no longer a pain in all our asses.

"You've always been so melodramatic, Pablo."

I could slap that smirk right off his face. No one—not a single person ever—would describe me as melodramatic. Just the opposite. Most people wonder if I possess any emotions.

"You've always been a disappointment."

The woman sitting at the table with her laptop glances

toward me, and I struggle not to shift in my chair. She does something to me. To my dick. But her expression is a mixture of disdain, shock, and warning. Her eyes betray her thoughts even if the rest of her face remains neutral. She believes I tread a fine line.

I draw that line.

And it's Humberto—I only use the honorific *Tío* when I'm speaking aloud—who's teetering on it.

She's supposedly my *tío abuelo's* newest assistant, but I get the distinct impression it's something more. She doesn't strike me as the type to let him paw her in exchange for access to his wealth. Or more often than not, access to *Tío* Enrique—the *jefe de jefes* of all the Colombian cartels. In reality, he's the *jefe de jefes* of all the Latin American cartels. Nothing happens in this hemisphere—Southern or Western—without his approval. Fuck the bratva, Mafia, and mob at home in NYC.

I can't see her computer screen, but I don't think she's managing his social calendar. Something about her gives me the feeling she's far overqualified for this position. I want to know who she is and why she'd subject herself to his company if she's not after money or social status. But what do I know at this point? Maybe she is his mistress, and this is all for appearances to justify the lavish lifestyle she's enjoying at my family's largesse. If she can tolerate fucking him just for nice clothes and jewelry, all the power to her.

"Did my nephew send you here as his little bitch messenger?"

I sit back in my chair and inhale. It broadens my chest and shoulders, showcasing—if you will—the full breadth of my frame. I'm nearly fifty years younger than him and in far better shape than he ever was in his prime.

"If I were, how do you think my *tío* would respond if I told him you said that?"

Doubt settles in his gaze, and he knows he's seconds away from pushing me too far. The last thing he needs is for me to actually tell *Tío* Enrique what a douche he's being. But I know he's stalling, hoping to distract me.

"*Tío*, you have a choice. It's a simple one. Get me the product before tomorrow night or prove you're entirely useless and serve no purpose. What happened to Ignacio Kimura will look like a mercy kill."

Tío Enrique's always said the moment his *tío* no longer serves a purpose, he'd be dead. I'll happily be the one who swipes the knife across this *viejo's*—old man's—throat. *Tío* Enrique's been looking for a reason to be done with him. Nearly forty years of house arrest hasn't dulled Humberto's arrogance. Now he's not doing his job.

Ignacio Kimura was a Brazilian regional boss who fucked around and found out. My *tía*—*Tío* Enrique's wife—has a history that's one of the world's best-kept secrets. Let's just say she made sure dead men can't tell tales. There were eight men at the table that night, and only one walked away. My cousin Alejandro.

Sweat beads across Humberto's face as the color drains from it. I notice his left hand trembles before he shifts in his chair. He doesn't know who carried out the hit, but he knows it was violent. Worse than that, it was so fast no one could react. It was over before Ignacio, his son, or their men knew what was happening. Alejandro said it was unlike anything he'd ever seen, and he's been in our Cartel since before his birth, and he's now in his thirties like me.

We're legacies—kinda like rich kids who get into an elite college without trying, just because they're born into a family that's always gone there. Same thing for our Cartel.

"I told you, *sobrino*, someone stole the shipment." Nephew.

"And I told you that's bullshit, and I know it. Where the fuck is the product?"

He fights the instinct to look toward the woman, and she's suddenly far more interested in her computer than she was a moment ago when she looked at me.

"It wasn't the finished product that got stolen."

Why's he hedging?

"So, you never got as far as making the shipment you owe us?"

"It's the new *pozolero*. They left the lab, and someone broke into it."

Pozolero—soap maker. It's the chemist who creates the formula for Colombia's number one illegal export.

I appear focused on Humberto, but I'm still observing the woman. She doesn't care for that excuse. Why?

"It's not like the lab is in some building in the worst part of Bogotá. It's in the middle of the fucking Amazon. It's difficult to find on purpose. Your security is shit if someone followed your *pozolero* there or someone stumbled upon it."

No one fucking stumbles upon our labs. They're purposely hidden in the most obscure, nearly impossible-to-reach parts of the rainforest. And why the hell did he say "they?" Humberto isn't a forward-thinking man. This isn't gender-neutral language. He doesn't want me to know the new scientist he hired is a woman. That only raises my suspicions about the one at the table.

Our enterprise is massive, and we're the leading suppliers of the world's third-most-popular substance. The fine white powder—*cocaine? What cocaine?*—is a chemical compound requiring true science to formulate. There are plenty who think mixing the various parts together will create something worth selling. If it doesn't kill the user, it's such inferior quality that it's not worth the money spent to make it.

How do I know beyond being a leading purveyor? I have an undergrad degree in chemistry and biology from Harvard. I did a semester abroad at Cambridge. I have a grad degree in chem from MIT. Short of a PhD, there are few better educated than me in the field.

"Excuses, *Tío*. You know you're responsible for overseeing our trade deals down here. Alejandro has plenty of proof that this shitstorm is your fault."

My cousin is the second coming of Houdini. He slips in and out of places with no one knowing. He can disappear while you're practically looking at him. He's been like that since we were kids. He was always in the thick of the trouble all of us got in, but he was gone before the adults could catch him. He escaped punishment until our mutual cousins and I doled out our own. He never feared us as much as his mom.

He's our leading spy when we need to know what's really going on. He brought home plenty of intel to support our suspicions that Humberto is falling down on the job.

My *tío abuelo's* face reddens. He didn't know Alejandro'd been down here.

I rest my elbows on the armrests and steeple my fingers. It makes my suit coat's sleeves strain around my biceps. That gets the woman's attention. Her gaze is slow to meet mine. Then she smirks.

Fucking smirks.

That doesn't bruise my male ego at all.

La reina—the queen.

Her self-assuredness.

Her imperious stare.

Her entire bearing screams a woman not easily intimidated and usually in control.

It's fucking hot.

"What do your records show, *señorita?* How much did these thieves take? It must be in your notes somewhere."

My *tío abuelo* is an utter *idiota* and actually writes shit down. Fortunately, it's in code. But he still keeps records. No one in my immediate family—we barely acknowledge he's related to us by blood—can get him to stop because no one lives down here. We all live in New York or New Jersey. When the cats are away, this mouse will play.

Too bad he's just found himself in a trap.

"Um..."

The woman peers over at me before shifting her attention to Humberto. She's waiting for him to intercede on her behalf, but he won't say shit. He'll let her take the fall. He'll blame her crappy record keeping for not knowing how things stand, that somehow, she's to blame for it happening.

"*Señorita*, what's your name?"

Oh!

She definitely doesn't like that question.

She probably thinks I'm going to find where she lives and have her whacked in the middle of the night. Her eyes are practically shooting fiery arrows at me. I feel scorched at how intense her gaze has become.

It's fucking hot.

It's doing way more to my dick than it should, especially if she's his latest conquest. I cross my legs to make sure she can't tell. Thank God for boxer briefs that have little room for my cock to stand out. I definitely don't need Humberto to know I'm attracted to her. He'll be a prick toward her, and then I'll really have to kill him.

I cock an eyebrow as I wait for her to respond. I watch her jaw set before our gazes meet, and her defiance is a challenge I'd accept if I thought it was an offer.

"Florencia Aguilar Bautista."

My gaze flies to my uncle.

What the ever-loving fuck?!

I stand and lean over the coffee table that separates us.

"Forget tonight. You have two hours to fix this before I put a bullet between your eyes. We will *never* forgive you."

I'm around the end of the table in a flash as I flick open the knife I keep in my right pocket whenever I'm down here. It's a larger blade than the ones I carry in NYC. I've carried at least one every day of my life since I was twelve.

Fucked-up tradition. All of us boys in the Four Families—*los Diaz*, the Mancinellis, the O'Rourkes, and the Kutsenkos—plus their Andreyev cousins—got them for our twelfth birthdays. It's a rite of passage.

This one has a blade thick enough to do the job. I stand to the side and grab Humberto's right wrist and yank his hand off his thigh and pin it against the armrest. I bring the knife down and sever the pinky with one slice. He howls, and I grin. He tugs at his hand, but I refuse to let go. Instead, I put pressure on it, making his finger stump geyser.

"You lost the other one forty years ago when you betrayed your brother. *Tio* Enrique warned you it was a reminder of what you did to my *abuelo*. He could've done far more. He could've killed you. Instead, he made you his bitch. Now you can remember you're my bitch. Two hours."

I don't look at the woman because she can't help who her family is. But I'm not sticking around to find out whether she knows what a tremendous error she made working for Humberto. If she knows, I'll destroy her.

I left Humberto's house before I lost all my shit. I'm still seething, but at least I'm doing it in private. I switched cars with one of my guards. Instead of being in a luxury vehicle with a driver, I'm in a subcompact that blends in. It's allowed me to watch Humberto's estate with no one noticing.

Tío Enrique's allowed him to exist in a mansion that makes Pablo Escobar's house look like a shack. But for all its grandeur, it's been his cell for forty years. He hasn't stepped foot outside his front door since the day my *tío* interred him there. There are armed guards who patrol the grounds. Unlike our homes in New York and New Jersey, they're there to keep him inside rather than keep anyone outside. Sure, they've shot men who've attempted to breach the estate, but Humberto knows he's dead the moment he passes through the door. He can go in the backyard, but that's it.

Now I'm turning on the car and pulling out of the spot I've been waiting in for the last hour. Florencia just left, and I want to know where the fuck she's headed. I want to know who the fuck she speaks to next. I want to know what the fuck is going on.

We navigate through the city until we get to a decent neighborhood that's safer than most but hardly wealthy. She parks in front of a pharmacy and gets out. I have parking karma and find a spot half a block before hers. I reverse and parallel park like a pro. I observe her go inside and count to twenty before I get out of the car.

I glance back at my guard, who's prepared to follow me. I shake my head, and he falls back. He'll be unobtrusive but at the ready. I sweep my gaze over my surroundings again before I walk to the door. As I open it, I peek over my shoulder before scanning the interior. There are six customers—a woman and her toddler son, an old man with a cane who's with his equally elderly wife, a man in his forties, and a woman in her twenties by the counter.

He's the only one who could present a problem since he

appears reasonably in shape. He turns toward me, and his eyes widen. He puts the box of antacids back on the shelf and looks around for a way out that doesn't require him to pass me. I'm certain I don't know him, but he clearly knows me. I step aside, and he practically bolts.

The others notice his hasty retreat and discover me still near the door. The couple look at the woman as she scoops up her child. I'd never attack any of them, but my reputation isn't one of benevolence, and I'm sure as shit not Santa. I can't blame them for not trusting I won't hurt them. The little boy waves to me as he and his mother approach. I waggle my eyebrows at him and return his wave. He giggles, and his mother reaches for his hand until she looks at me. She's unprepared for me to make funny faces at her son. She's rushing, but no longer practically running to get out of the shop.

I turn toward the pharmacy counter, wondering where Florencia went. I'm tall enough that I can see she isn't in any of the aisles, and there are only six of them. It surprises me to find her in a white lab coat. It looks crisp and starched.

A perfectionist?

If she is, it must chap her ass that something's gone wrong with the shipment, or that Humberto would indirectly blame her if he's at fault.

I observe her as she speaks to the last customer in the store. She hasn't looked in my direction, but I sense she's aware something's changed. It's not until the woman turns away, medicine in hand, that Florencia glowers at me. I nod to the customer as I walk past. Before I can open my mouth, she greets me.

"You can fuck all the way off."

Chapter Two

Flora

One of these days, my mouth is going to get me killed. Telling *El Tigre* to fuck off certainly wasn't my wisest choice. What the fuck was I thinking?

He may be smoking hot—like I'd strip to my skin right here if I thought he'd fuck me—but he's looking at me like I'm a bullet ant that he wants to crush. A wonderful little Colombian creature whose bite feels like you've been shot.

Pablo Diaz—"The Tiger"—is the second most powerful Latino in the world. He's heir to the Diaz empire. He's second-in-command to his uncle, but he's in charge of more than just what happens in New York City. His father is the most terrifying man in Colombia. Luis Diaz is known as *el Espíritu Santo*—the Holy Spirit—because you know you're about to meet your maker if he comes to visit. Luis's older brother, the *jefe de jefes*, sends him to remind people that what Enrique giveth, he can taketh away. Enrique Diaz may not be God, but you'll be praying to him for divine intervention if Luis shows up.

Right now, Pablo appears like the second coming of *el Espíritu Santo* because he's a mirror image of his father. His glower threatens to send me up in smoke. I'd rather be anywhere but here. I definitely didn't set the tone for an amicable chat.

"Hello to you too, *Señorita—Aguilar.*"

He stresses my last name like he might choke on it. Like he's spitting out the most disgusting thing he's ever tasted. Like he hates hearing it, let alone saying it.

I'm not frozen in place, but I don't move more muscles than I need to breathe. I don't look away as he approaches the counter. This pharmacy carries narcotic medications that more than one person's tried to steal, so I have a gun beneath the counter. I doubt I could get it fast enough.

"How can I help you?"

Remembering my customer service does me little good when it sounds mocking after that greeting.

"You can tell me how long you've been fucking that *pedazo de mierda.*" Piece of shit.

My chin jerks back as I fight not to curl my nose in disgust.

"Don't enjoy being spoken to like that? You must not have been working for my *tío abuelo* long. He'll say far worse."

He's not wrong. There's no HR department to report sexual harassment to. Humberto says whatever fucked-up thing he wants. He does it to get a rise out of me. I know his cock gets a rise out of it. But I refuse to respond to him, and I refuse to respond to Pablo. I merely stare at him. He grins. His parents clearly got him braces, and he probably spends a fortune on teeth whitening. He could be on a toothpaste commercial. His white teeth contrast against his tanned cheeks, making them practically dazzle.

Fucking hell, Florencia. Fucking think about something other than those teeth biting your nipples.

"Ah, he already has. *Quelle surprise.*" His mocking "what a surprise" makes me want to grind my teeth.

"Can I help you find anything? Perhaps something for constipation? Or is it diarrhea?"

He chuckles, but it's not filled with humor like it was when he laughed at the little boy who made faces at him.

"People say my eyes must be brown because I'm so full of shit. Or did you think I had diarrhea of the mouth when I warned Humberto what I would do?"

He's laughing at me, not with me.

I'm fighting not to be the one who's insulted.

"You can help me understand why you're working for Humberto. You clearly already have a job selling pharmaceuticals."

Legal drugs is what he means, but he's silently reminding me of what he and Humberto sell.

I shrug as I answer. "I needed a second job to help pay off my American student loans."

That's a benefit but not the reason.

"Working for a narco-trafficker is the best second job you could find?"

Still mocking me.

If it weren't at my expense, and if his words were genuine, he could appear charming. His handsome face and what I'm certain is an exquisite body beneath his custom-tailored suit are distracting. I can't ignore the simmering anger, though.

I didn't bat an eye at the violence I witnessed earlier. It was tame compared to shit I've seen before. But he wasn't looming over me then. Even with the counter between us and a step up to get behind it, he still towers over me. He's even broader than he appeared in the chair.

"It pays well."

"What's the going rate for being a mistress these days?"

"Leave."

"It's an honest question. Why not give an honest answer?"

"You're insulting me and trying to humiliate me. I have nothing to say to you."

"That's fine because I have plenty to say to you. You can listen while I talk."

I shift and reach beneath the counter, but he's faster than I am. He reaches across and wraps his fingers around my wrist. He doesn't manhandle me like he did Humberto. His hold is gentle as though he's mindful of not crushing my bones, which I'm certain he could.

"*Señorita*, we're just talking whether or not you like what I say. You really don't want to pull that gun on me. You won't get a shot off, but you are likely to get hurt while you try."

He allows my arm enough movement for me to bring my hand back up to the counter. I place both on the surface. He immediately lets go. This wasn't how I'd hoped he'd restrain my wrists. Kinky sex is likely the furthest thing from his mind right now.

"*Señorita*, you are more than just his assistant." He sweeps his gaze over the prescriptions behind me before he meets my gaze again. "If you aren't his mistress, then you're even more foolish than I thought."

"So now you're only insulting me. Leave, Pablo."

He leans farther across the counter and practically purrs in my ear. "Say that again. The last bit."

"You need to leave."

"Say my name, *chiquita*."

"You might think I'm fucking your uncle, but I'm not a whore. You obviously know who I'm related to. This is the last time I'll say this. Leave."

He doesn't move away from me, but his expression becomes

deadly serious. His voice is just as low as it was a moment ago, but there's an edge to it.

"I never thought you were, and I'd kill anyone who called you that, *chiquita*."

Our gazes lock, and a shiver vibrates up and down my spine. I struggle not to shift and let him see how he affects me. His intensity is wholly attractive, but I remind myself he's already tried to embarrass me.

"Remember that the next time you regret having anything to do with Humberto."

My brow furrows. Is he offering his protection?

"Have a good day, *señorita*."

He steps back and turns around. He's so confident I won't shoot him in the back that he walks straight down the aisle in front of me. He's a clear target for the gun he knows I have hidden. All I do is stare.

"*Mamá*, you can't avoid telling me forever. I'm not a child anymore."

But Pablo did call me little girl earlier. It was the sexiest thing I've ever heard. The way it rolled off his tongue. It did things to me. It did things to my pussy.

"Your father was a good man, and they murdered him for it."

That doesn't match the rumors I've heard my entire life.

"If he was so good, then why would *los Diaz* want him dead?"

"They want anyone who isn't one of them dead. They're murderers. All of them. Even their women. His mother's killed more than once."

I've heard that story. It's the stuff of legends. Apparently, Pablo was like two, and his younger brother was a baby. Some men tried to stop the convoy of cars headed to the family's estate on San Andrés. She was going to meet Luis and his mother. Roadside bombs blew up the lead and last cars. Not realizing her family customized her vehicle in NYC and smuggled it here, men opened fire. It was a tank. Completely bullet-proof with metal plates to protect the undercarriage. Despite the tires being shot, it kept moving.

From what I've heard, in the chaos that ensued, she put her sons on the floor—Juan wasn't old enough to go anywhere, and I guess Pablo obeyed his mother—then she climbed into the trunk while the SUV continued moving. She opened a small window over the rear quarter panel. There was an arsenal back there, and she took out the men who flooded onto the street behind her SUV. Picked them off one by one.

She got out and tossed the rifle that had no bullets left on the ground. When the man in charge approached her, he assumed she gave in because she realized her attackers outnumbered her entourage. He thought she'd beg for mercy for her sons, for herself.

Instead, she drew a knife and stuck it in the guy's aorta and dragged it across his throat before stabbing him in the eye. It covered her in blood. Like the fucking chick in the movie *Carrie*.

She challenged any man to come near her children and see if they could best her. No one did. People now whisper the name she earned. *Huitaca*. She was the Muisca goddess who represented art, music, and dance—and witchcraft and sexual liberation. The one who rebelled against the patriarchal god Bochica. She's not exactly revered, but no one wants to test whether she has mythical powers.

"*Mamá*, we're not discussing Margherita. Deflecting and

distracting might have worked when I was little, but it won't work now. You need to tell me the truth that no one else will. *Abuela* refuses to talk about *Papá*. She always bursts into tears if anyone says his name. *Abuelo* just starts swearing. I didn't ask to work for Humberto, and now whatever *Papá* did before I was even born is likely to get me killed too."

I don't think for a moment Pablo will kill me. After how light his touch was this morning, I don't think he'd hurt me either. But that doesn't mean I couldn't get caught in the crossfire.

"Stop stirring up trouble where none exists, Florencia."

"*Mamá*, you've done everything you can to protect me my entire life. But you can't protect me now that *Abuelo* forced me to work for Humberto. I need to know exactly what he got me into. I think it's a lot more than either of you told me."

My mother watches me before she nods. She looks at her right hand and the sapphire ring she often wears. It was a gift from my father.

"Your *papá* told me from the start he would never marry me. I knew he wouldn't, but he was so handsome and charming."

Sounds a lot like Pablo.

"He was already engaged to Luciana Diaz when we got together. I knew he was going to marry her. Or, at least, he was supposed to until Esteban Cardenas barged into their lives. Esteban discovered your *papá* was working for Humberto. Your *papá* got himself into some gambling debts with Humberto, and to pay them off, Humberto made a deal with your *abuelo*. It was the only way to save your *papá's* life. He had to spy on Josue, Enrique's father, and report back to Humberto."

"I know this part, *Mamá*. Humberto decided after thirty years to resurrect that debt. Paying it off is how I wound up working for him. *Abuelo* sold me off just like he did *Papá*."

"No, *niña*. Your *abuelo* protected you just like he did your *papá*. Humberto would've killed both of you if your *abuelo* didn't intervene."

This is as far into the story as we ever get. *Mamá* never explains why Humberto still holds a grudge thirty-something years later. She never explains why I must make up for the sins of a father I never met. The man died before I was born. What I know is what I've pieced together over the years. He played a role in Pablo's *abuelo's* death, and their family never forgave him. I don't know how he was involved, but he was.

It was Pablo's *tío* who assassinated my father—murdered him in cold blood, according to my family. Esteban wanted retribution for my father convincing Luciana Diaz, Pablo's *tía* and Enrique and Luis's youngest sister, to marry him. I guess Esteban wanted her, then took her despite her being engaged to my father. He forced her to marry him—at least, so the story seems to go. I've always questioned that. Esteban killed my father to remove a rival.

"*Mamá*, I deserve to know what those debts were. It had to be more than gambling. *Abuelo* would've paid those off if it were just about money."

"Why're you dredging up old, painful memories?"

"They're your memories. I have none of my own, so I need you to explain why I have to work for Humberto. I agreed because you guilted me into it after *Abuelo* threatened to disown me and give my cousins my inheritance. He said I'm only in his will out of his own generosity since I'm illegitimate."

That was an unpleasant conversation.

"Then you shouldn't rock the boat."

I'm getting nowhere with this. Round and round we go. Where we'll stop this bullshit, nobody knows.

"Fine."

I give up—for now. Something about the way Pablo looks at

me tells me he knows far more than I do about my life. That irks me to no end. I hate being at a disadvantage in general. Something about him particularly pisses me off. It's not just his arrogance—which he has in spades. It's like he sees through me, and yet, I can tell nothing about him. I've been around cartel men my entire life thanks to my *abuelo*, so I recognize I won't know what Pablo is thinking unless he wants me to.

But besides superiority, I can't tell if the man feels anything. He certainly thinks he's superior to both Humberto and me. I don't think it was anger toward Humberto earlier. I don't think it was even impatience. His swift reaction was a flex. A reminder that Humberto is at the bottom of the Diaz hierarchy. That a man half Humberto's age ranks higher than him. That Pablo will inherit, making the succession skip Humberto by yet another generation.

"Florencia." *Mamá* reaches for my hand as I stand from the sofa.

"I'm going to go. I have laundry to do when I get home. I got ink on my lab coat I need to get off before work tomorrow. I also have an early meeting with Humberto. I want to go to bed early."

All of that is true, but I'd originally planned to have dinner with my mother. Now, I'm exhausted and just want my own space.

"Your grandfather shouldn't have said what he did. He didn't mean it."

"He most definitely meant to manipulate me."

"True. But he won't disinherit you. He loves you just as much as your cousins. There are more moving parts than even I know."

"Then he explained at least some of this to you. You know it's more than a thirty-odd-year-old set of gambling debts. Is it even about *Papá*, or did something else happen?"

She hesitates, and that's its own answer. It doesn't matter if she says anything. There's little she can say now to make it better.

"*Mija*, I heard Pablo is in town. Be careful. The man has no soul."

Chapter Three

Pablo

I barely slept last night. After meeting Humberto and Florencia, which already had me thinking, I watched the surveillance video from Humberto's place. My cousin Joaquin is our intel gatherer. He sent me five hours of recordings from while I flew down here. Turns out, Humberto met with a potential rival from Medellín. That pisses me off. It's the family that's trying to oust my dead *tío's* brother. The Cardenas family has dominated the poppy industry in Colombia for four generations. They started out as flower sellers and moved on to something far more lucrative.

That meeting's problematic.

I'm giving Humberto time to stew in his fear since I let the two-hour window expire without striking. He knows I didn't forget or back down. He knows I'm plotting.

I need to go north to the second largest city in Colombia tomorrow to deal with the fucker Humberto's plotting with.

The trip means encountering additional risks I'd prefer to avoid. It's dangerous to travel there, so I'll fly. It's dangerous to move around Medellín when you come from the family that dominates Latin America and has connections to the head family in that city.

I'm not my cousin Alejandro. He's a fucking ghost, I swear. He slips in and out of spaces that should be far too narrow for someone with shoulders as broad as his. He moves on silent feet, and despite being the most attractive man in our family, he blends into crowds. I'm sly, but I've never been like him. It means people will find out I'm there.

I'm distracted from planning my trip when my computer pops up a notification that Humberto's making a call. Not only do we have cameras all over his property, we also tap his phones. He knows about some cameras and wiretaps. He thinks he's sly and skirts our surveillance, but we have shit he'll never find strategically placed all around his house and yards. The men who patrol his property are loyal to *Tío* Enrique, not that *pedazo de mierda*.

I'd call him other things—son of a bitch, motherfucker—but they'd insult my *bisabuela*—great-grandmother. Apparently, she was a lovely woman. Humberto was just a mistake from the start.

I don't recognize the number that appears on the notification, so I'm unprepared to hear Florencia's voice on the line.

"I expect to see you here in two hours."

Prick.

He called her and didn't bother to greet her when she said hello.

"I know." She sounds less than thrilled to have him on the other end of this call.

"Be on time."

"I always am."

Her responses are clipped. She doesn't sound like she's interested in humoring his bullshit this morning. I don't know her, but she sounds tired compared to yesterday at the pharmacy.

"Late night, *hermosa*? At your club again?" Beautiful.

Not at a club.

Your club.

Is she into...

Does she belong to...

Holy hell.

The idea that she might be into BDSM makes my dick jump to attention.

Florencia doesn't respond. Silence hangs between them, and I know Humberto will fill the void. He loves the sound of his own voice, and he hates protracted periods of silence. It makes him feel out of control, so he thinks talking makes him dominate the conversation. He usually just makes himself sound like a *gilipollas*. Asshole.

"Bring the sample."

"No."

"What the fuck did you just say? You don't refuse me."

She remains quiet again.

Once again, she reminds me of a queen. A woman who bows to no one.

Reina.

It just seems to fit.

"You must need more sleep because you're being difficult this morning. Maybe if you were better rested, you'd understand why that's not a good idea."

"I don't have the sample."

"Why not?"

He sounds like he's about to rip into her. That angers me in a way I'm unprepared for.

"It wasn't delivered."

"You told me yesterday you tested the formula last week, and it was pure. It should be here by now."

If I had any doubts she's his newest *pozolero*, they're gone now.

"'Should' doesn't matter since it didn't happen. *You* employ the courier. *You* didn't pay him for the last job. *You* put a bullet in his shoulder instead. He can't drive his motorcycle because his arm is still immobile. He can't get to the drop-off point in a car, and it's too far for him to walk. Even if he could, how would he carry the shipment with one arm?"

"Take your tight little ass to the lab and get it yourself."

"No."

If I didn't want to admit we listen to his conversations, I'd fuck Humberto up for insulting Florencia. Part of me feels a twinge of pride for her standing up to him, but more of me worries she'll piss him off. His imminent tantrum is likely to result in her dying.

"Florencia, you don't seem to understand that 'no' isn't an option."

"I have a job. I can't just take off for the three days it'll take me to get out and back."

"This job is worth far more than working at some shitty little store."

"It's the only job that pays the bills."

He doesn't pay her?

"And if you want to keep it, you'll do as you're told. I'll have you out on the streets before noon if you don't fucking cooperate. You'll have nowhere to turn but back to me."

"For how long?"

"Until I tell you you're done."

"So, I'm your indentured servant? I didn't agree to that."

"No one gave you a choice about working for me, so there was nothing for you to agree or disagree to."

"And if I go to Luis the next time he's here? I'll take my chances with him."

Fucking hell. She's playing with fire.

Her voice doesn't waver. She sounds confident with an edge of defiance. If I didn't know how volatile Humberto can be, I'd be proud of her self-confidence.

"You'll obey me, or it won't just be your job you lose. Your *mamá* will spend the rest of her life chained to my fucking bed. I'll fucking kill your *abuelo* and all your *primos*."

He's not just threatening her, he's moved on to her mother, grandfather, and male cousins. This is escalating fast. I pull my phone from my pocket and fire off texts to four men I trust more than anyone else in Colombia.

Tío Esteban was super close to his cousin Alicia. She was his first childhood friend, and he said she was his conscience before he met *Tía* Luciana. She has four sons I've known my whole life. I'd play with them and my cousins Jorge, Javier, and Joaquin—*Tres J's*—when I came down here with my parents. They'll know whether Humberto's threats are credible or just hot air he's blowing in Florencia's direction to intimidate her.

"And I know where the lab is, but you don't."

"My men are loyal to me, not you."

I snort. Good thing neither of them can hear me.

The men who work for Humberto are loyal—but not to him. They work for *Tío* Enrique, but they're assigned to Humberto. It appears like a shit assignment, but the men know it's an honor. It means we trust them more than most because Humberto hasn't successfully left his property in the thirty-six years since I was born.

Florencia remains quiet. Her refusal to agree, concede, or

even contradict him speaks louder than anything she could say. She's the first to break the silence this time, but she isn't giving in.

"*El patrón*, labs are dangerous places. So many chemicals known to ignite fires. All that smoke would draw attention to its location. It would be a shame if that happened because then you wouldn't have the product or the money you owe your nephew. At least some of it has to go to *el jefe* in New York. You'd also have to explain destroying part of the jungle. It wouldn't take much to connect you to a cocaine lab. No one but me knows how to get to and from the site. I drove the workers and guards who were bound, gagged, and blindfolded. They can't leave without getting lost in the Amazon. It means they can't lead anyone there. You wouldn't provide me guards while I scouted the area—or any of the other times I've been out there."

Hearing that last part pisses me off more than anything I've heard so far. She could've already died each time she went out there. Between man and nature, she's been far too close to death already. There are still indigenous tribes who don't like trespassers, and there are rival syndicates with labs. We allow it because it's the price of peace for us. The price they pay is death if they think to overreach.

I listen as Florencia continues to issue her thinly veiled threats.

"Since I take the food and supplies to the workers and the guards assigned there, they won't work if they starve. If anything happens to my family, ka-boom. If anything happens to me, the forest will simply swallow it. Maybe the men would figure out how to navigate out of the jungle, but most likely not. If you want me to cooperate, then you agree my service is done when this shipment goes out. You can keep the recipe."

I won't name names or even use pronouns even though our texts are encrypted. There's always the possibility someone could hack them. If I weren't listening to this conversation, I would talk to *Tío* Enrique. We have jammers and scramblers, so making a call would be more secure.

I put my phone aside as I focus on the conversation between Florencia and Humberto.

"If you really want me to cooperate, then answer some questions. What was my father's debt to you? What was so significant that I'm paying it off thirty-odd years later?"

I know he's considering his answer. I suspect I know, but I'm curious how he explains it.

"Your father had a job to do, and he failed."

"What was the job?"

"He didn't marry that bitch."

My fists clench. He'll pay for that.

"Luciana Diaz?"

"Yes. He let that *puta de madre* seduce her." Motherfucker.

"I thought Esteban took Luciana. Forced her to marry him."

Humberto grunts. I don't know who told Florencia that crock of crap, but that is *not* how it happened.

"I take it my father was your spy. He was supposed to marry her and bring back information from her father."

"He was supposed to do a fuck ton more than that. He had more than one chance to kill Enrique and Luis. He even had the chance after I had Josue killed. Instead, he failed. Enrique lived and had the U.S. government extradite me here. He paid a fucking fortune to relegate me to this fucking shithole he refuses to allow me to repair. It's falling down around my ears."

Rage fills me.

Mamá was pregnant with me when Humberto had his own brother murdered. She was nearly three months, so it was early enough that she and *Papá* had told no one. My *abuelo* died before he learned he'd be a grandfather.

Humberto had the *huevos*—balls—to call *Tío* Enrique and deliver the news that his father was dead. He didn't admit he ordered the hit, but it was obvious he had. He was always so fucking jealous of his older brother. Now he's jealous of my *tío*, *Papá*, my cousins, and me.

Tío and *Papá* went on a rampage after *Abuelo* died. They made sure everyone in Colombia understood what it meant to defy *los Diaz*. Their retribution was swift and devastating. Within days of their arrival from NYC, anyone even remotely connected to Humberto died slow, excruciating deaths. *Tío* imprisoned Humberto in his marble mausoleum because the sack of shit wouldn't suffer if he was dead.

Instead, Humberto can see freedom from his bedroom window. He can hear voices on the other side of his wall but knows he'll never walk free. He watches cars drive by but knows he'll die where he lives rather than escape his imprisonment.

Once a month, *Tío* reminds Humberto that he lives because *Tío* allows it. He comes down here to punish Humberto in person. The man permanently has at least one broken bone. When he fucks things up, *Tío* Enrique's vengeance is swift and merciless. He makes sure Humberto sees him walk out the gate simply because he can.

"So, I'm paying the price because my father didn't kill the most powerful man in Latin America?"

If I showed emotional reactions, I'd flinch. Reminding Humberto he isn't the man he wants to be—that my *tío* is—won't win Florencia a reprieve from Humberto's temper.

"No. You're paying for your father getting killed. It ruined my chance to have someone inside Enrique's family and for being stuck in a house that once rivaled Pablo Escobar's but is now a decrepit pile of shit."

"It's not like he asked Esteban Cardenas to murder him even though he'd already stolen Luciana."

I hear her temper finally flare.

"Stole? You really believe that, don't you? Your *mamá* has filled your head with bullshit. Esteban didn't have to steal Luciana. She never loved your father, but she would've married him out of duty. She and Esteban loved each other more than you could ever understand. Your father died for trying to kill Luciana after she rejected him. The night Luciana left your worthless father for Esteban, he shot at the car she was in. Then he thought he could force himself on her. She nearly slit his throat and would have if Esteban hadn't stopped her. That would've been too quick a death. Esteban tortured your father for his sins before he killed him. No one but your mother misses him. She was dumb enough to fall in love with a man who enjoyed fucking her until he found out she got knocked up. He dumped your mother and claimed she was a whore, said you could've been anyone's. If you didn't look like him, people might've believed him. Too bad he died a month before you were born. He never got to see God's sense of humor."

Humberto vomits the story at Florencia, and my heart

aches for her. It's an unfamiliar sensation when it's for anyone outside my family. But I feel horrible. She didn't deserve to learn the truth with such vitriol and disdain.

"Luciana went with Esteban willingly?"

"Ran away with him and never looked back. She killed three men who worked with your father when they finally got retribution for your father's death. Only took the dumbasses eight years. She proved Enrique and Luis are pussies when it comes to torture. She taught her brothers some shit. She's why your *abuelo's* never gotten his dick up since he ordered the Hierro brothers to kill her husband and leave her children fatherless. She fucking gelded him. Cut one of his fucking balls off and sent it to your *abuela* in a box with a bow. Wrote a note that said if she couldn't have her man, then your *abuela* wouldn't have hers either. The only reason he survived when the Hierro brothers didn't is because Enrique already had your *abuelo's* dick in a vise. He was already indebted to Josue before my brother died. Enrique still owns him. You need me for protection now that Pablo knows your *abuelo* indentured you to me. Don't doubt he's figured out you're repayment."

The conversation I listened to yesterday still bothers me. It ended with Florencia agreeing to get the samples to Humberto before the end of the week. She convinced him she can't get to the lab before that. If she misses work, her boss will demand answers since she already took off two weeks while she was at the lab. She needs the job to maintain the appearance that she's just a typical woman with a career that pays her bills. Losing her job would draw attention from friends and extended family. Humberto bought it.

I keep replaying her initial refusal to follow Humberto's

commands, then her subdued response to learning my *tío* and *tía* loved each other. My *tía* will never remarry. She'll never love anyone else. She's been a widow longer than she was a wife, but she's never looked in another man's direction.

Just the opposite, she's blinded men for looking in hers. She's killed men for getting too close. Having to defend herself and my cousins one too many times in Bogotá convinced the rest of my family she and *Tres J's* needed to move to the States.

I push my thoughts aside as I step out of the SUV and smile at my dead *tío's* brother in the early morning light. I can see *Tío* Esteban's father sitting in a chair near the window. He's in his early nineties. He's still one of the smartest men I've met, but rheumatoid arthritis makes it difficult for him to get around the poppy fields like he once did. *Tío* Esteban's younger brother now runs the family's business.

"*Me alegro de verte, Pablo.*" It's good to see you, Pablo.

"*Gracias por dedicarme tiempo, Fausto.*" Thanks for making time for me, Fausto.

"*Siempre.*" Always.

Just like all the conversations I've had or listened to since arriving, we continue in Spanish.

"Do you have bad news for me?"

"Unfortunately, yes."

"How much did we lose?"

Both Medellín and Bogotá get frequent hailstorms during their rainy season because of their elevation. Both cities are technically in the Northern Hemisphere since the equator runs through southern Colombia. However, Colombia's weather believes it's fully in the Southern Hemisphere. It's summer right now, so it's supposed to be drier in January. That didn't stop Mother Nature from raining down a nasty unseasonable one last night.

I dread hearing what Fausto says since the poppy seeds

they harvest make us millions. It's what's kept their rival at bay so far, but more weather like this risks the Cardenas family's monopoly. The money's in opiates made here in Colombia and the seed exports to Asia. It matters little to us that production has decreased over the past few decades. International law enforcement doesn't consider Colombia a major player in the heroin market like it is cocaine. However, they still earn us more as opiates than they would in lemon poppyseed muffins.

"Half. We brought in the first half of the harvest at the end of last week. The last ten fields weren't ready yet, but yesterday morning, the farm manager said they were."

"*¡Mierda!*" Shit.

"At least we've already extracted the gum."

Workers split the seedpods with a multiblade tool, releasing a gummy ooze the workers collect with a curved spatula-looking tool. Frequent rain, even in summer, prevents poppy farmers from using open wood boxes to dry the milky fluid like they do in other parts of the world. The liquid opium is mixed with hot water, then left to dry. As long as they've done that to half the crop, then we can still make a healthy profit.

This won't be bad enough to give our rival any leverage. It'll just piss off our buyers that we don't have everything we promised. But no one can control the weather despite what conspiracy theorists say.

"That's a relief. When will it be ready to roll up?"

Workers can roll or bag the semi-dry resin.

"If the weather stays like today, then about a week."

It's a gorgeous day. Bright blue skies and not a cloud in sight. You'd never guess frozen boulders fell from the sky not even eight hours ago. Last night's weather fit my mood much better than today's. The issue with the poppies is only a fraction of what's causing my irritation.

Being here fills me with bittersweet memories. It reminds me of the role Humberto played in *Tío* Esteban's death. What he didn't tell Florencia was that Humberto paid Domingo's father—her *abuelo*—who paid the Hierro brothers to murder my *tío*. Her *abuelo*—Ernesto—was only too happy to take the money to fund his revenge. Ernesto begged for the cash and further indebted *los Aguilar* to Humberto.

We used to come here during winter in New York, escaping the snow, wind, and ice for the weather we have today. Raúl—*Tío* Esteban and Fausto's father—used to let me ride the horses. He taught my brother, cousins, and me to ride. Javier took to it as much as I did, but he wanted to learn to play polo. He'd skip around with a polo mallet bigger than him, pretending to ride a horse as he swung it.

I learned to milk the cows and collect eggs from the coop. I learned what the term breed like rabbits means from first-hand observation. The animals just fascinated me. I wanted to be a vet until I realized that wasn't realistic because of the position I would one day inherit.

It wasn't until I was in my teens that it became obvious it was unlikely *Tío* Enrique would have a son. His first marriage was an utter failure, so as the oldest nephew, I became his successor. My compromise for giving up being a vet was still pursuing my love of science. I double majored in undergrad then went straight to studying chem in grad school. Recalling what I studied and why I became a trained chemist makes me think of Florencia all over again. It sours my memories once more.

"We'll salvage what we can, but it may not be much. We can always visit *los Aguilar*."

I smirk, cock an eyebrow, and shrug. That's as close to an official agreement I give when Fausto suggests they steal from

Ernesto. Fuck that family from now until eternity. It's unfortunate Florencia is one of them, but just because I want to fuck her doesn't mean I'll forgive her family.

"*Sí.*"

"*El Tigre*, you need to get back here."

It's barely mid-morning, and I'm already on the way to the airfield when the call comes in. It's *Tres J's* second cousin on *Tío* Esteban's side. He's one of the guys I contacted to check out how much of a threat Humberto poses to Florencia. Being greeted like this...Antonio is about to tell me something unpleasant.

I left the Cardenas farm after chatting with Raúl. He made me laugh until my sides hurt, and it was like when I was a kid. He slipped me the equivalent of twenty U.S. dollars in Colombian pesos. It's a tradition that started when I was eight and thought that was a fortune. It's continued every time I see him. The nostalgia moved me since I suspect that might've been my last visit with him. I was happy to retreat to the relative privacy of my SUV's back seat.

"What happened?"

"Humberto's put out a quarter-million-dollar hit on *Señorita* Aguilar. At least six mercenaries have picked up the hit."

¡Joder el infierno! Fucking hell!

"Watch her, but do nothing unless someone makes a move. We're about to take off."

It's a little less than an hour flight. It feels like an eternity. Like I could've flown to at least Europe for how long it feels. When we touch down, I'm waiting at the door for the single flight attendant to lower the steps. There's a town car already there for me. I'm across the tarmac at a full sprint.

My intuition tells me this isn't something to downplay. Florencia pushed too hard, and now Humberto's ego's bruised. He might not know someone heard the entire conversation, but it was still enough to piss him off.

My driver slows as we approach the address the guy gave me over the phone. Anyone with an untrained eye wouldn't notice the four men staked out around Florencia's apartment. But I know what I'm looking for, and I spot all of them.

"Let me out here."

My driver glances back at me, and I know he wants to disagree. He's not just a chauffeur; he's also my guard. He won't contradict me, but he doesn't approve. I don't give a shit. I don't want these men scared away. I want them eliminated. I don't need a shootout, which is what will happen if any of them think they're being cornered. I turn away from Florencia's building and go around the block to fully survey the scene. When I'm satisfied there isn't anyone else lying in wait, I circle back around.

The gun I carry has a silencer. I pick off one guy after another until the current threat is gone. It gives me stealth despite being a guy who stands over six feet tall and looks like a lean American football offensive lineman.

I enter Florencia's building and creep up the stairs. I want to be sure no one else is lurking. I'm glad I do because I shoot a man through the back of his skull as I pass the mail room. I recognize him as someone my family's hired in the past. The only loyalty mercenaries have is to their bank accounts. One day, they're working for you. The next, they're ready to kill you.

When I find her apartment, it tempts me to knock. I decide against making any extra noise. I've spied no one else, but that doesn't mean the sound against the door wouldn't draw someone out. I pull the lock picking set from my pocket. They're illegal in New York, but I carry it anyway. It's laughable to think I wouldn't carry it here.

I ease the door open.

"Get the fuck out."

Chapter Four

Flora

I heard someone at my door before Pablo opened it. I live alone, so no one should be fiddling with the doorknob. I knew it wasn't my mother, who's the only other person with a key to my place. She would've knocked. I suspect men followed me here from work, so hearing the lock turn freaked me the fuck out. I grabbed my gun and aimed for where I figured a man's chest would be.

To say I'm pissed to see Pablo break into my home would be a half-truth. It pisses me off that he believes he has the right to enter here whenever the fuck he wants. That he can barge in because the mood struck him. But he's so fucking hot looming in the doorway.

My brain is seriously twisted.

"You have the sweetest way of welcoming me, *chiquita*."

He enters and shuts the door behind him. I should freak all the way out when he locks us in. But somehow having him between me and the outside world is actually reassuring.

My brain is seriously extra twisted.

"Get out of my home. You have no right to be here."

He raises his hands where I can see them after putting the lock picking kit on the table beside the door—right next to my keys. It's as though he's dropping his next to mine.

Honey, I'm home.

He could reach for his own gun, but he doesn't. He could reach for however many knives I'm certain he carries, but he doesn't. It's as though his sheer aura can command me to give in.

Nope.

"Flora, whe—"

"We are not friends."

"Florencia, whether or not you come with me, you need to get out of here. There were men watching your place."

"Were? You killed them."

I don't know why the first part was a question since the second part proves I already know the answer.

"Would you have preferred they kill you? You didn't shoot me the moment I opened the door. If I'd wanted you dead, I would've shot you before you knew who was on the other side. They would have too."

Rather than respond, I lift my arms to aim the gun at his forehead rather than his heart. I flip the safety off. His hands drop as he shakes his head.

"*Chiquita,* that safety should've been off the moment you heard the doorknob twist."

Rather than believe I'm one step closer to killing him, he steps toward me. I wrap my finger tighter around the trigger without squeezing it. He takes another step.

"You have more confidence in yourself than you should, Pablo. No matter how fast you can draw your gun or flick open your knife, I'll still be quicker."

"Put the gun down, Flora, before you hurt yourself. I will take it from you, but that risks you getting shot."

"More likely I'll shoot you if you take another step toward me."

"And then what? The men in my family won't kill you, but the women will. If you're as smart as I believe you are, you'll understand how much worse that will be than facing my *tíos*, *papá*, or *primos*. *Mamá* and my *tías* will hunt you to the ends of the Earth, drag you back to their den, then feast on you like a pack of she-wolves. It won't be a quick kill. *Mamá's* always been overprotective."

The story about how Margherita defended her sons comes to mind. Getting a hint of what his *tía* Luciana did to the men who carried out the hit on her husband doesn't ease the sudden bolt of fear that courses through me. I know nothing about his *tía* Catalina, but I'm certain she must be like her sister Luciana. I've heard speculation that his newest *tía*—Enrique's wife—is the worst of them all. That her family is Mafia in America and that she's been a gun for hire before. It could just be a rumor, but something Humberto said a few weeks ago makes me think it's not just conjecture.

"You're considering what I said. You know your life is forfeit if you move a single hair on my head. Put the gun down, Flora."

"I didn't invite you into my home. You don't give me orders. Leave."

"*Chiquita*, pack what you need for the next week. If you don't have somewhere safe to go, I will find you somewhere."

"And why should I believe you? Why should I think you're any more trustworthy than your *tío abuelo*?"

A wall drops between us, even if I can't see it or touch it. I sense when it slams to the ground. I've deeply insulted him by comparing him to Humberto. While his outward demeanor doesn't shift, I know I've made a grave error.

"Choose, Flora. Get your stuff and walk out of here on your own, or refuse me, and I'll carry you over my shoulder. If I have to do that, I'll spank you."

"You are unreal. No."

No one calls me Flora, yet he insists upon it as though we're friends.

He moves faster than I expect. He surges toward me, and I raise the gun on instinct rather than shoot him. Any other man outside my family, and I'm confident I would've pulled the trigger. I have no fear of taking someone's life. I haven't done it, but I've come close.

I don't want to shoot Pablo.

He disarms me and flips the safety back on before dropping the weapon onto the sofa. While one hand gains control of the gun, his other arm wraps around me and pulls me against his body. It's all hard muscle and bone. He's so much bigger than me—bigger than I realized from a distance. I can't help but brace myself with my hands on his chest. My palms itch to slide down to the rock-hard abdomen I feel pressed against my tits.

"OW!"

I'm utterly unprepared for his hand to land across my ass.

"Pablo! Stop! OW!"

"It may have been hot as fuck watching you during that meeting and when I went to the pharmacy, but your obstinance isn't attractive. You are going to get yourself killed if you don't listen to me. If you won't agree to my help on your own, then I won't give you a choice."

"I don't give a flying fuck if I'm attractive to you. Let go."

"My spanks might push your hips toward me, but you're pressing the rest of your body against mine on your own. You give a fuck."

His hand lands across my ass over and over. It burns like a motherfucker, but he isn't wrong. I may want him to stop because it hurts, but I'm not pushing away from him. I'm not truly rejecting this spanking. I feel safe despite him being a virtual stranger. He's doing it because I turned down his offer for protection. Because we both know I'm cutting off my nose to spite my face.

But I'm not ready to agree to his offer. I don't trust him entirely.

"You'd knock me over if I didn't use you to brace myself. I don't consent to this. Stop."

His arm drops from around my waist immediately. He stops spanking me and steps back. As he observes me, it's as though he's surprised by his own actions. He looks at me as though he's not sure what to make of me, as though he's confused.

"*Chiquita—*"

"Why do you insist upon calling me that?"

"I don't know." His answer is swift, and from his still befuddled expression, I believe him.

"Pablo, I'm not going anywhere with you or anyone else."

That snaps him back to reality as his eyes narrow. He glowers at me, and I'm certain this look has made plenty cower before him. I lift my chin and lock gazes with him. He cups my chin, but he's gentle even though he holds it in place when I attempt to pull away.

"Your stubbornness will get you killed. Humberto's put a quarter-million-dollar bounty on you. I heard your conversation with him yesterday."

"How—Did you tap his phone or mine?"

Confusion gives way to anger.

"His. I didn't like how he spoke to you, and I definitely won't allow you to go back into the Amazon on your own. Do you have any clue how lucky you are that you're alive? No one —not me nor any of the men in my family—travels there alone. We'd lose our ever-loving shit if any woman in our family even suggested doing it. You sure as hell aren't going."

"You don't dictate to me, and you shouldn't have listened to any of my conversations."

"You weren't the reason I listened, but I learned plenty. I also know Humberto far better than you."

When he cocks his eyebrow at me, I bare my teeth. I try to shove him away.

"I've never fucked him. How dare you even hint that I have?"

I struggle to get free of him for real. He lets go just as fast as he did when I said I didn't consent to the spanking. He has boundaries even he won't cross. That's reassuring in a fucked-up kind of way.

"Then you should believe me when I tell you that your unwillingness to follow his orders pissed him off. He can't stand it when anyone defies him, but he's limited in what he can do since he can't leave his home. He can't come here to intimidate you—"

"But you can."

"You don't fear me, *chica*."

"I don't fear him either."

"Then you're as foolish as you are beautiful. I would never hurt you, and I'll kill my *tío abuelo* for trying. But *he will* have you killed and not suffer a moment's doubt. You need to go somewhere safe. It can't be to your mother or grandparents. That's too predictable. You need to get away from Bogotá."

"I'll take my chances—"

"No, you will not. You will not endanger yourself. I won't allow it."

"You don't get to decide. Why does it even matter to you?"

"I don't need your death on my conscience, *chiquita.*"

"I'm not your problem, Pablo. I don't matter to you. You're just worried it'll be bad for business. You'll have to find someone new to develop the product, and that'll cost you."

I take a step toward him, closing the gap he made when he let go of me. I don't realize I'm doing it until the tips of our shoes touch. We stare at each other for a moment before his hand fists my hair, and his arm wraps around my waist. He pulls me against him, and I clutch his shirt. His mouth crashes down on mine, and I open to him without resistance.

What the fuck, Florencia?

One moment, you're refusing to consider the common sense he speaks, and the next you want to jump his fucking bones.

I'm completely consumed by the kiss as his tongue slides into my mouth. I open wider to him, and his hand glides down to my ass. He squeezes hard enough to bring me onto my toes. I press my pussy against his dick, and I want to rub when I feel how hard and long he is. His other hand continues to hold my head in place, but rather than fist my hair, he cradles my skull.

As the kiss draws on, that hand eases down my neck to my breast. He cups it, and I arch my back with a moan. His lips follow the same path his hand took as he kisses behind my ear and down my neck before traveling back to where he started.

"Now I'm definitely not letting you decide."

Before I know what he's doing, he hoists me over his shoulder.

"Pablo!"

I try to kick my legs, but he wraps his arm around the back of my thighs. I liked it far more when it was around my waist. I slap his back before pushing up to grab a handful of his hair. I don't mean it to be erotic as fuck like it was when he had his hand in my hair. I pull hard, and all I get is another three spanks across my ass. He carries me into my bedroom and dumps me on my bed.

"Unless you want me to pack for you, pick what you need for the next week."

"You're insane if you think I'm going anywhere with you. I don't know you, but I know your reputation."

"The one I've justly earned. I warned you, *chiquita*. I will kill my *tío abuelo* if he hurts you. Do you want his death on your conscience? You want the death of any more mercenaries on your shoulders? I've killed for you already, and I'll keep doing it. If you want me to stop, then you come with me to a safe house where no one can find you."

"I didn't ask you to kill anyone!"

"You don't strike me as being ready to die, so stop refusing help when it's offered."

"I don't trust you. How do I know you won't do worse to me than Humberto?"

"Because I don't rape women or allow my men to. Because I don't torture or kill women. Because I'm not my fucking *tío abuelo*."

He's pissed I compared him to Humberto again. He takes it as a slight against his honor. It's not just anger; it's hurt I see. I get that now. He may bully me, but he doesn't want me to see him the same way I do Humberto. He's doing it because he wants to protect me and because I am being stubborn. Humberto does it to silence me and demean me.

"Pablo, breaking into my apartment and barking orders doesn't make me trust you, even if you aren't like him. Where will you send me? How long do I have to be there? Why does it matter to you? How can I be certain your offer will keep me safer than going to my family? How do I know you won't do something to me, even if it isn't rape, torture, or murder? I don't know you. I'm not going anywhere with a stranger."

He leans forward, and his hands bracket my hips. I lean back, but we're still nose to nose. I don't stop him when his lips press to mine. This isn't like the kiss from a couple of minutes ago. It's gentle. I don't resist this any more than I did the last one.

How can I trust him to touch me?

Why would I have sex with him right now if I could, yet I refuse to believe he's here to help me? Because you don't believe he's above seducing you to get what he wants. You might enjoy fucking him, but you won't give in to his demands.

You wouldn't give in even if he said please. You'd be batshit bonkers to go anywhere with him voluntarily.

"Florencia, please. There were five men here when I arrived. I recognized all of them. They were all mercenaries. I know Humberto put the bounty out for you. There will only be more, and it may not just be men. Many women might try, assuming you'll lower your guard around them. That you'd be likely to trust them and be an easy mark."

"Your family left here because they don't have a record for surviv—"

"Do not finish that thought." His voice is a gravelly whisper.

He's back to being entirely walled off. He isn't the gentle man from a moment ago or even the passionate one. He's the man without a soul my mother warned me about. His eyes appear devoid of any feeling. I only know how badly I overstepped from the harshness in his voice.

I know I was being a bitch, but it's true. His grandfather and uncle died here, and the rest of his family left Colombia because it was safer in the States.

"You heard part of the story from Humberto, but you didn't hear all of it. Obviously, whoever's told you about the past didn't tell you a fraction of the truth. My *abuelo* ruled Latin

America for nearly twenty years before his brother had him killed. My *tío* has ruled for more than thirty. He doesn't live in the U.S. because he's afraid to live here. He lives there because he has more power and influence in this hemisphere than any other man alive. He controls more from there than he could here. When Humberto's hired gun killed my *abuelo*, my father and *tío* came down here. I've seen the photos of the destruction they left behind. The Mexican cartels didn't come up with the idea of leaving bodies to litter the streets to remind their neighbors who runs their country. Thirty-six years later, buildings remain rubble and ash. My uncle won't let anyone—not private citizens nor the government—rebuild them. That's the control he has here. If you've known Humberto for more than a month, then you know he's had different bones broken every few weeks. *Tío* Enrique makes sure that *pedazo de mierda* can never forget he breathes because my *tío* allows it. If he hurts you, *I* will make sure he knows how badly he fucked up right before I kill him."

When I met Humberto, he had bandages wrapped around his right hand. I discovered he had broken bones in the center of his hand. I didn't know why and couldn't figure it out. Right now, he's limping. He has to wear sandals because three of his toes are swollen and taped together. I can tell they're broken. I didn't know what happened to them either. I can guess it was Enrique who did it, or someone he sent. Maybe one of his other nephews.

"While that's chivalrous, your uncle killed my father."

How I let that slip my mind until now is beyond me.

"You should count yourself lucky I don't hold your family or your name against you. Your father tried to kill *Tío* Enrique and my father. When he failed at that, he tried to kidnap *Tía* Luciana. She won't repeat the vile threats he made to her, but I'm certain he planned to rape her then kill her. He cornered her outside the grocery store and wrapped his hand around her throat. He punched her in the face. When he tried to grope her, she stabbed him in the thigh. He didn't think she was strong enough to fight back because she'd backed down when they were engaged to avoid arguments like that. He underestimated my *tía's* ability to defend herself, and he sorely underestimated my *tío's* retribution for touching his wife. My *tía* came home scared and with bruises on her face and throat. Your father deserved everything that happened to him. He was a fool to hurt a woman and think my family wouldn't respond. He was out of his fucking mind to think he could touch a Diaz woman and survive. Humberto forced Domingo to work for him and believed your father could infiltrate our family because they're cut from the same cloth. Your father was untrustworthy, and so is Humberto. He took my *abuelo* and my *tío* from my family. He sure as fuck isn't taking you from me."

Chapter Five

Pablo

My temper is on the verge of shattering.

A maelstrom of emotions swirls within me, and there are several I recognize but am not used to. I've spent my entire life sharing almost everything I've had with my four cousins. Before my little brother got himself killed because he fucked around and found out Maksim Kutsenko doesn't play when it comes to protecting his wife and children, I shared nearly everything with Juan. Often it was because the shithead took things from me. More often than not, I gave in to keep him from picking a fight where I would've pulverized him.

So, the possessiveness I feel now is utterly foreign and completely unreasonable.

That doesn't stop it from surging through me. That and anger at Florencia's refusal to cooperate, even if I understand why. I can't blame her for not trusting me. I don't trust her even if I want to fuck her into next week. But she needs to come with me, or she may not survive the night. I need to change my approach; otherwise, we'll stay at this stalemate.

"Call your mother and tell her about your conversation with Humberto yesterday. See what she says."

"She'll tell me to be careful and not piss him off."

"And when you tell her he's put a hit on you? When you tell her he's threatened to rape her and kill your *abuelo* and *primos*? What will she say then?"

"Would he really—to my mother? Has he…"

She can't finish her question, and I don't blame her.

"It's rare for women to go to his home, so he hasn't had the opportunity. He knows any of his guards would kill him if he tried. They may work on his estate, but they work for *Tío* Enrique. We have no proof he did before his house arrest, but we can't be sure he didn't commission it before my *tío* banished him to the estate. Do you want to be the reason he figures out how to make it happen?"

She's so quick to stand I barely get out of the way before her head can nail the underside of my chin. Anger shoots flaming arrows from her eyes as she glares at me. They threaten to turn me to ash beneath her feet.

"How dare you?!"

"Did I ask anything you aren't already asking yourself?"

"*If* I told my mother anything, she'd tell me to get as far away from you as I possibly can and to not look back."

"No, she wouldn't."

"Yes, she—"

"As much as your mother hates my family, she knows we have far more honor than Humberto ever has. She knows that despite what we do, we never hurt women."

At least, not intentionally. We've committed our fair share of sins in the last few years, inadvertently making women in the other NYC syndicates collateral damage. It was never the plan to hurt them, but some got caught in the crosshairs. But in an "us versus them," we'll always put our family first. None of the other families are any different.

"She might agree with that, but she would never agree to me going with you. You might not hurt me, but you'll never convince her or me that you won't get me hurt."

"*Chiquita*, you'd be screaming down the house if you believed I'd hurt you. You would've shot me if you believed I was a threat. You didn't. You kissed me instead. You pressed your body against mine, and you enjoyed what you felt. You want me to spank you, and you want me to make you come."

I scoop her over my shoulder again like a barbarian carrying his mate off to his cave. My hand lands across her ass once more. We both understand my double entendre as I turn away from her bed.

"You had your chance to gather your stuff and leave willingly. Staying here any longer makes us both a target. If you make a sound as we leave, I will gag you. I'd die for you, but not today."

Why the fuck do I keep admitting this shit?

Why do I keep oversharing my feelings?

Why am I even having these fucking feelings?

They're massively inconvenient. They'll be my mother-fucking undoing.

"Put me down. I will make a scene."

"No, you will not. If there are more mercenaries waiting for you, you'll make yourself an easy target. I'm not dying today because you believe you're getting back at me."

"Revenge has nothing to do with it. I told you, I don't trust you."

"And I don't trust you either, but I don't want you hurt."

We keep going round in circles, and my frayed patience can't take much more of this. I decide the strong, silent type is my fresh approach. I march out of her place, grabbing the keys and my lock picking kit as I pass through the door. I stop to lock up, and Flora huffs. I offer no comment and keep walking. I can carry all my cousins, *tíos*, and father up and down at least five flights of stairs. I know from practice and necessity, so Flora is like a feather despite her divinely curvy figure. A true hourglass, like a classic pinup model. But I won't risk her fighting me and us both tumbling down the six flights of stairs.

We have to wait for the elevator to arrive. I remain quiet, and so does she. But she wriggles and tries to kick her feet. My arms wrap around her legs to keep her immobilized. When the doors open, she tries to grab one side to keep me from entering. I reach back and grasp both wrists, fearful the doors will close on them or that she'll hurt them when my walking forward pulls them from the metal.

I press the button for the ground floor and put her on her feet. I position myself in front of her as I draw my gun. Unlike her, I have the safety off before the doors reopen. She doesn't give up her attempt to thwart me, but when she moves from side to side, her smaller frame can't get around my larger one. She gives in—for now, because I know she hasn't given up—and waits. She knows I'm shielding her even if she doesn't want my help—doesn't see it as help.

She's back over my shoulder as we leave the elevator. My driver's watching for me, so he pulls forward as soon as he spots us stepping out of the building. As a bodyguard, I would normally sit up front with the driver. But I'm worried Flora might try to bolt from the back seat if she's left alone.

You're also scared someone might get to her if she's out of your reach.

There's that. I want to be close if any threat gets near her. I don't want her out of my sight or my reach.

Normally, my driver would get out and open the door, but

he watches me shake my head. I want him ready to go the second I close the back passenger door. I open it and put Flora on her feet again. I crowd her against the car, catching her between the open door and the car frame.

"Pablo, please, no. Don't do this."

Genuine fear laces her words, and I see it in her eyes. They stare into mine for a second before her gaze sweeps the surrounding area.

"*Chiquita*, if there were another way, I would take it. You aren't safe anywhere in Bogotá. Go willingly. I don't enjoy forcing you."

The hand not holding my gun rests on her waist. It travels up her ribs, then down her back until it reaches her ass. I give it a squeeze then a light tap. A reminder of what I'll do if she doesn't obey but not hard enough to cause any pain. Her gaze locks with mine, and something shifts within her.

"You're really going to protect me, aren't you?"

"Whether you want me to or not."

"Why?"

"Because you're mine, *chiquita*. Now get in the car, please."

She stares at me for another moment before ducking in and sliding across the seat. I follow her and close the door. Once it's shut, I flip the safety back onto the gun. I place it on the seat between Flora and me. She could try to grab it, but she reaches for her seatbelt instead. After having her in my arms, having her on the other side of the seat with a belt between us feels wrong. It's the safest thing for her, but I don't like it.

My driver must have put up the privacy glass when he realized I wouldn't be alone back here. It's usually up by default. I twist and pluck her from her seat, bringing her to sit on my lap. She fights me, surprised and unsure of what I'm doing. I wrap my arms around her, the weight of them heavy, but I'm gentle as I guide her to lean against me. When my hand strokes her hip and over her ass, and I do nothing else, she sags against me. Her head rests against my chest, and I kiss her forehead.

"Pablo, all of this is terrifying. You're scaring me. Where are you taking me?"

"Somewhere safe, *chica*. I know how frightening this must be for you. I'm terrified one of Humberto's hired guns will get you. I'm terrified I won't get you out of town in time."

I'm terrified you hate me for what I'm doing.

"Will you tell me where you're taking me? Who am I going to tell? I left my cell phone in my apartment. I don't have my ID or anything."

"My family's home."

"San Andrés?"

That's the home people know about. It's an island known for the best beaches, and it's a beautiful vacation spot. But I won't take her somewhere people know about.

"We have another home." I tilt her chin to make her look up at me. "I'll protect you because you deserve it as a person sucked into this fucked-up world because of your family's choices before you were born. I'll take care of you because you're you."

I bring my lips to hers, giving her a chance to reject me. She turns her face toward me more, making our lips brush together. A sliver of me worries she's kissing me back long enough to distract me and reach for my gun. But her arm caught between us struggles to move, then fists my shirt at my waist while her other hand cradles my jaw.

The hand that stroked her hip and ass cups it now, and I want to come from the feeling of her pressed against me and how lush her firm yet soft ass is in my palm. My other hand slides up the back of her shirt, and I feel her shiver as my fingertips graze along her spine. I've never felt a more feminine and enticing body, and I've fucked my share of women.

"Do you want me to put you back on your seat, *chica*? Do you want to look out the window?"

She moans in protest when I pull my mouth away from hers. She tightens her hold on me when I suggest letting go of her. She shifts restlessly, twisting to press her tits to my chest.

"What do you want, little one?"

"You."

She freezes at her confession. She pulls away and sits up as she looks at me. Our gazes meet, and neither of us looks away.

"Pablo, I'm kissing you because I want to, but I won't be your Stockholm Syndrome fuck buddy."

I fist her hair like I did earlier, and my hand tightens on her ass.

"You will never be just my fuck buddy. I don't want you to fall for me because you think you're my prisoner, and I brainwashed you. I could've walked away, *chica*. I could've sent men to bring you to me. I came because you matter to me."

"Why?"

"I have no fucking clue."

The words slip out before I can think better of it, but from the way she dives in and kisses me, somehow, they were the right ones. Her kiss is demanding, but I won't give up control of this or anything else. I let go of her ass—which earns me a soft growl of disapproval—so I can slip the gun into a small compartment under the center section of the seat. Then I flip her until she's lying beneath me. She opens her legs so I can settle between them. She tilts her hips up to rub her cunt against my cock. I bring my lips against her ear.

"I will fuck you, Flora. Not as my prisoner. Not as my fuck buddy. You are my *chiquita*. I'll fuck you because I've never wanted a woman more than I do you. I'll fuck you because you're mine to take care of. I'll bring you pleasure because I want to see you come on my fingers, my tongue, and my cock. I will touch every part of you I can reach inside and out. There won't be an inch of you I don't know because you're mine. I won't force you. I'll do all those things, but only when you ask me to."

She's gone still except for the rapid rise and fall of her chest. I want to rip off her shirt and watch her tits.

"I don't know you, yet I want you more than any man I've ever met. I'm not fighting you to get free, yet you're basically kidnapping me. I trust you to do the most intimate things to and with me, yet I don't trust you not to manipulate and use me."

"Flora, I can swear I won't use you or manipulate you, but you won't believe me until I prove otherwise. I don't blame you for feeling that way. I don't fully trust you not to betray me, but getting you away from here is the right thing to do regardless of our attraction. I loathe your family. That won't change, but I don't loathe you. You're stuck in the shitty position your family put you in. We both know they manipulated you into it, and they're using you. It's no wonder you have so little faith in me. Fuck me because you want a distraction or let me fuck you because you want to know what it is to be taken care of. Either way, you know we can stop now, but it won't stop us from eventually fucking. You want to know what I feel like inside you just as much as I do. You want to feel my cum drip from your pussy and stick to your thighs just as much as I want to see it. You want me to suck your tits as much as you want me to suck your clit. You—"

She puts her finger over my lips, and I flick it with the tip of my tongue. She rocks her hips, brushing against my painfully hard cock.

"You want me to suck your dick as much as I want to taste you. You want me to squeeze the cum from your cock as much as I want to feel you come inside me. You want to feel my soft tits pressed against you as much as I want to feel your hard body against mine. We both want you to spank me to prove you're in control of what the fuck is happening, even if it's just between us."

"Is that what you really want? Me to be in control?"

I'm practically holding my breath in anticipation.

"In control not controlling. There's a difference, Pablo. I'll agree to one, but not the other."

"I know, *chiquita*. I'm a man who needs to be in control. It's the only way I stay alive and the only way I can protect the people who matter to me. This situation is beyond your control, so you're looking for someone you can depend on to have it. Deep down, you know you're safe with me. You know I won't hurt you, so you'll give me control of your body because it's your choice."

"How can you understand that about me when we don't know each other?"

"I don't know. I just do."

"If you heard my conversation yesterday, then you heard what he said at the beginning."

"I did."

"Then you know something about me I suspect is true about you too."

"It is."

"Neither of us wants to be fuck buddies. Do you want to be my Dom?"

"Yes." That flew from my mouth.

She watches me for a long moment before she reaches over her head and crosses her wrists as she grasps the end of the seat.

"Then you need to let me have a phone to end things with the man I fucked the other night."

Chapter Six

Flora

I spoke the truth, but I did it to antagonize him. To poke the beast who hovers above me. To get a reaction from him.

"Is his cum still inside you, Flora?"

Anger flashes in his gaze as he lowers his body to press mine fully into the seat. The jealousy and possessiveness I feel radiating from him excite me. They shouldn't. I'm the one manipulating him, and I know it's wrong. But I couldn't stop myself from saying it.

"I'm clean and on birth control, but no man has come bare inside me."

"You didn't object to my telling you my cum will drip from your pretty little cunt. You know what that means. You know I meant it."

"I want your cum inside me because it means you aren't putting it in anyone else."

Where the fuck did that come from? I didn't intend to share that level of my own jealousy and possessiveness.

He pushes my shirt up and pulls down my bra. He scoops my breasts and squeezes until I'm certain he's leaving fingerprints.

"Do you have a sub, Pablo?"

"No, but there are three women I fuck when I go to my club."

It's my turn to feel anger spark within me.

"As in you rotate through them or a *manage à quatre?*"

"Both."

We glare at one another before our lips come together, and we can't get enough of our kiss. His weight pins me in place. I can't even flex my hips or arch my back. His kiss threatens to swallow me whole, and I love it. I moan my submission as I relax into the seat.

His teeth graze my neck as he trails his lips down to my collar bone. He presses his teeth around the bone, but I know he won't leave a mark. He's making a point. He brings his mouth to my ear, and his warm breath makes my pussy ache.

"He's not your Dom twenty-four seven, but I will be."

"I won't share, Pablo."

"Neither will I. They aren't my subs, so there is nothing for me to end officially. I have no interest in fucking anyone but you. You will obey me, Flora. For your safety and for your pleasure."

He pulls away and sits up. I want to reach for him, but I keep my hands over my head as a sign of my submission even when we aren't moments away from fucking. I haven't refused the idea of him as my Dom. I've never had an around-the-clock agreement before, but I know wherever Pablo takes me, that's how it would end up. I'd rather agree than we just fall into it.

"Call him now, Flora. End it. I won't touch you again until you're fully mine."

He wants me to come to him. He could simply take me

away from my current Dom. Wherever we're going is outside Bogotá, so he could force me to end things merely by not letting me see the man again.

"Give me your phone, please."

I sit up and reach out my hand. He pulls it from his back pocket and unlocks it. I pull up the keypad, then look at him.

"*Mamá* drilled it into me never to store any personal numbers in my phone. That's why I can remember his."

Pablo nods as my jaw rests on his palm, and he brushes my lips with a light kiss. But it isn't like before. There's detachment to it. It's what I would get from a Dom who has no romantic attachment to me. Is that what I just agreed to?

No!

"*Chica,* end things with him. Belong to me completely, then I'll kiss you the way we both need me to."

Belong to me completely.

I never felt like I belonged to my current Dom or any other I've had in the past. I didn't feel like that with any past boyfriends. It makes me sound like a possession, but that's not how I feel. A strange part of me wants to strip bare for Pablo before I make this call. Show him I already belong to him.

I enter the phone number and listen to it ring on speakerphone.

"*Hola.*"

"*Hola, Roberto. Soy Florencia.*"

We continue in Spanish.

"I didn't recognize the number."

"I don't enjoy doing this over the phone, but I don't want to wait."

"Florencia."

His tone hardens into the one he uses as my Dom. It used to turn me on and make me want to fuck. Now it grates on my nerves. I watch Pablo, and his jaw clenches. I look around before placing the phone on Pablo's thigh. I slip off the seat to kneel as best I can. I put my hands behind my back and cross my wrists.

Why do I feel like I need to prove myself to Pablo?

How the fuck did things get to this so fast?

What if I'm making the biggest mistake of my life? I'm more likely to get myself killed with Pablo than anything else.

No, you're not.

To your marrow, you know Pablo won't hurt you. You know the man will kill for you. He already has. He might break your heart, but you're safer with him than anyone else alive.

I don't understand how that's true, but it is.

"Florencia?"

"Sorry. Bad reception for a moment. Roberto, I'm ending our contract."

I want Pablo to hear both sides of the conversation. It should be private, but I don't want this to be a secret. It's another submission. Another acknowledgement that he has control even when we aren't fucking.

"Did something happen the other night that I couldn't tell?"

Pablo's hands ball into fists. He stares at me, unblinking.

"No. I met someone the other day. I haven't stopped thinking about him. I—"

"Were you thinking about him when you were with me?"

My cheeks are on fire. Pablo cocks an eyebrow. He wants to know my answer too. I nod.

"Roberto, I enjoyed our time together. You were an excellent Dom, but being with this man is what I need."

"Is it Humberto Diaz?"

"What? Fuck no."

Those words flew from my mouth with such vehemence it shocks me.

"People've seen you going to his house. People've told me about it."

"You didn't bring it up before. If you suspected something, then why not tell me?"

"Because I didn't think you were fucking the piece of shit."

"I'm not. It's not him. I met someone else. Roberto, I'm sorry I'm ending things this way and not in person. But it's better I tell you than just make excuses for not seeing you until you give up."

I'm watching Pablo, and he's pissed to discover people have noticed my connection to Humberto. It scares me. He picks up the phone and pats his leg. I push up on the seat and straddle his lap. He continues to hold the phone while his other arm wraps around my ribs until he can hold my ass. His hand seems to always wind up there.

"You have romantic feelings for this man, don't you?"

I still. I do, but I don't want to admit that in front of Pablo. I'm unconvinced he has those for me. He nudges my chin up as he grips the phone. This kiss is just as brief as the last one, but it's tender. He nods.

"I do."

"Then I wish you *felicidad*." Happiness.

"Thank you."

"Goodbye."

"Bye."

Pablo hangs up and drops the phone beside him. He cups my jaw with both hands as he presses another tender kiss to my lips. I open to him and melt into his kiss. He's so fucking gentle right now that it makes my heart ache. He was all alpha possessiveness not five minutes ago. Now he's still all alpha male, but I feel incredibly precious to him.

We pull apart when we feel the car shift into park. I look out the window and realize we're at the airport. We're on the tarmac near a private plane. My brow furrows. I didn't expect we'd fly wherever we're going since he said it wasn't San Andrés.

"Pablo?"

"It's too far and too dangerous to drive. I don't want anyone to follow us."

He straightens my shirt and adjusts his sleeves beneath his suit coat. I ease off his lap, but he takes my hand as he taps on the window. The door opens, and he steps out. I scoot over and follow him. He lets go of my hand, moving his to the small of my back. He leads me up the stairs and onto the jet.

"*Chiquita*, pick a seat. I'll be there in a moment. I need to speak to the pilot. He knows where we're going because I called while I was on my way to your place. But I want to confirm a couple things with him."

"Yes, sir."

He stares at me for a moment before he nods. It was as though he wasn't sure he liked the sound of me calling him sir. I agreed to twenty-four seven, so I shouldn't have used his name a moment ago.

I walk to a seat and sit down. I have nothing to do and no luggage to store, so I fasten my belt and look out the window. It's only a few minutes before Pablo's sitting beside me and the captain is closing the cockpit door. A guy with a friendly smile approaches us with warm, moist towels and bottles of water. I accept the towel while Pablo opens a bottle of water. He hands it to me before taking his own towel. Once he's done, he opens his own drink.

I can't believe how thirsty I am as I down the entire thing. Pablo's slower, but he finishes his too. He puts his hand out, and I give him the bottle and lid. He screws the top on and gestures for the flight attendant. As we taxi, he lifts the armrests between us and wraps his arm around my shoulders. I lay my head against his shoulder as his free hand rests on my thigh. I twist as much as I can to make it easier for him since he reaches across his lap.

My eyes are drooping closed as we take off. I'm suddenly so exhausted I wonder if he drugged my water. I hear the seatbelt sign ding and watch it turn off. Pablo unfastens my belt and picks me up as easily as he has in the past. He settles me on his lap, and I can't think of a better place to be.

"Let me hold you, Flora."

I burrow against him and inhale his cologne. I haven't realized until now how calming the masculine scent is.

"I didn't know I was so tired."

"A lot's happened in the past hour. I'm tired too."

"Sir?"

"Yes, *chiquita*."

"Thank you for insisting upon protecting me. What happened in the car doesn't make everything perfect between us. It's confusing as fuck, actually. But I feel safer with you than I have since meeting Humberto. I'm too worn out to question things right now. I'm trusting you with more than just my body."

"I know, little one. I'm trusting you too."

I let my eyes droop closed, letting my guard down entirely. As I drift off, I feel Pablo's body relax beneath me as he sighs.

I watch as we fly over a river and plains. I have no idea where we are. I recognize nothing below us. I look up at Pablo, who's watching me. He offers me a soft smile before he gazes out the window. He looks so at ease. The air of danger and darkness that usually surrounds him isn't there anymore. He appears youthful, and it makes me wonder for a moment if he's younger than me. But I know he can't be.

He's older than me by two years. He's nearly thirty-six, and I'm nearly thirty-four. I'm practically an old hag because I've never been married. I'm nearly twenty years older than the Colombian national average for women marrying. I've gotten plenty of comments about that from my *abuelos* and *abuelas*. Both sides of the family. It gets old—just like me.

"Where are we?"

"Arauca."

Holy fuck.

That's one of the most isolated regions of Colombia. It's extremely north—practically Venezuela. There are people here who don't speak Spanish, only indigenous languages. It's bordered by the Ele, Cuiloto, and Lipa rivers. I've definitely never been anywhere near here. I only know about it from grade school geography.

"You really wanted to escape from the city."

"My family descends from the Macaguán before they migrated to Bogotá."

I look back out the window. The term middle of nowhere comes to mind. Never has there been a truer description.

"Your family has a home out here?"

"Yes."

"What do you do if you need something?"

"There's a city not too far from the estate. It's Villa de Santa Bárbara de Arauca, but we have most of the things we need already there."

There's a long stretch of flat land that comes into sight. Close to it, there's a sprawling estate with a wall higher than any I've ever seen around a residence. It has barbed wire around the top. Even Humberto's home doesn't have that. It makes it look like a prison, yet the house—if you can even call it that—is more like a palace.

"We're a large family, Flora. Once upon a time, it was *Tío* Enrique, *Tío* Esteban, *Tío* Matáis, *Tía* Catalina, *Tía* Luciana, *Mamá*, *Papá*, my brother, *Abuela*, my cousins Alejandro, Jorge, Joaquin, Javier, and me. That's fourteen of us. Before my brother, cousins, and I came along, my *abuelo* was still alive and went there too. *Tío* Enrique is married, and my cousin Javier will be soon. That still makes thirteen of us."

His brother Juan.

His *tío* Esteban.

They're both dead, and my family is the reason for one of them no longer being with Pablo's. I tuck my chin and pull my lips in.

"*Chiquita*, you had nothing to do with my *tío's* death. Do you blame me for your father's?"

I shake my head. "It's not the same. You remember your *tío*. I never knew my father."

"That doesn't mean you don't miss him or at least having one. If I blamed you, you wouldn't be sitting on my lap. None of what happened today would have. I'd still have helped you, but I definitely wouldn't want you the way I do. I don't think you'd have agreed to any of this if you blamed me for Domingo's death."

"True."

"When we land, a car will meet us and take us to the house. I know what it looks like from above. It's not to keep anyone inside."

That doesn't reassure me.

"How many people have attacked that your family feels like the estate needs concertina wire to keep people out?"

"None. They know they're not welcome. We have a staff

who'll be there, but they're local. They don't speak Spanish, only Macaguán."

"And you speak that?"

"It comes in handy."

I shift my attention back to Pablo, and I know he means it's a language his family speaks that no one else does. There're probably only a few hundred people who speak it in the entire country. It surprises me his family's passed it down for so many generations.

"How long has your family been Cartel?"

"Since they began in the seventies. They had other— endeavors well before that."

"Did people relearn the language back then, or did your family continue speaking it even after they migrated to the city probably a couple hundred years ago?"

He watches me, hesitant to let me in and to share so much about his family. I look at my lap. I'm prying, asking things his family likely never shares with anyone outside their immediate circle.

"*Chiquita*, I'm not used to telling people things about my family like this, but I don't want to shut you out and make you feel like I'm hiding more from you than I have to. Telling you we speak Macaguán isn't a secret I need to keep."

"Because it's not like I—or anyone else—will suddenly know how to speak the language. It won't compromise your security."

He nods.

He doesn't stop watching me, and I think he fears he's hurt my feelings.

"Sir—"

"Pablo."

"We said twenty-four seven."

"I know, but it's obvious already that we won't have a regular D/s relationship."

It's my turn to watch him before I nod.

"Pablo, I don't think it's just tradition that makes your family keep the language alive. I bet you use it when you're on missions or when you need to speak privately. I've been angry and scared today. I'm still building up to trusting you about more than just my immediate safety and fucking. But I don't wish you harm. If I did, I would've told Humberto or my *abuelo* that you visited me at the pharmacy. I would've screamed my head off when we went outside. I would've fought you harder. I would've shot you."

"I'm glad you didn't."

"Shoot you?"

"Definitely that, but I'm glad you didn't tell anyone, and that you didn't scream. No one outside my family comes here. We don't bring guests."

I sensed this, but hearing him admit that makes the weight of the significance even heavier.

Our conversation's put on pause as we land. We watch the flight attendant open the door and lower the steps. Pablo helps me to my feet and stands. He pulls his gun from his lower back holster. There's an SUV waiting for us. There are metal grates over the front and rear bumpers. The windows are nearly as black as the frame. It pulls so close to the stairs I can practically step straight into it. Pablo's gaze sweeps over our surroundings as I slip inside. He follows me, and a bodyguard closes the door. There are two men in the third row, and the driver's in his seat. The guard climbs into the front passenger seat.

They're all wearing tactical gear with helmets and bullet-proof vests. They carry rifles, and there's a spare for the driver between Pablo and me, leaning against the center console. We ride in silence to the front gate, which slides open. Men patrol the property. It's more secure than any embassy. I look out my window, then turn to look out Pablo's.

He's still completely at ease, which lessens the sudden spike of anxiety I feel. He remains relaxed because he knows he's surrounded by security. It looks over the top, but nothing about him makes me think he's prone to exaggeration or catastrophizing. I doubt anyone else in his family is either. If this gives them peace of mind to spend time together, then I appreciate their preparedness.

"I'll give you a tour of the house, then I need to call *Tío* Enrique."

Chapter Seven

Pablo

I know I have to call my *tío*, but I dread it. It won't thrill him to know I brought an outsider here. This is one of our most guarded secrets. It's why the security is so heightened. We don't believe anyone knows this place exists, but if anyone finds out, we want them dead before they can tell someone else.

It'll also piss him off to hear Humberto put a hit on a woman. He won't welcome knowing I'm protecting an Aguilar, but he'll understand honor and duty dictate I do. I'm not prepared to share more about my relationship with Flora than that. Today's been over the top. Everything about it. The way I barged into her home. The way I commanded her to come with me and gave her no choice, like some marauding *bandito* who takes whatever he sees. The possessiveness and jealousy we've both felt finding out about each other's sexual pasts. The overwhelming desire that shouldn't exist since we barely know each other.

All of that is private.

"Our cook will bring fresh perishables when he arrives. Our housekeeper is his brother, so they'll come together. The rest of the staff will come once we're settled in."

"They're both men?"

"We've a forward-thinking, modern family."

"Or they're trained Cartel members too."

I don't respond. She watches me before she nods.

"There are plenty of nonperishables here, so help yourself to anything you find. Hopefully, there'll be something you like. If there's anything you want, tell me. I'll call our cook and let him know what to pick up."

She sweeps her gaze around the kitchen as I open the pantry door, then the fridge and freezer. There's not much in the fridge, but there's still some frozen meat from Alejandro's last visit down here a couple weeks ago. That makes me pause. He could've just as easily been the one to come down here since he visits Colombia more frequently than anyone else in the family. My position prompted me to come instead. But he could've been the one to meet Flora.

Would she have wanted Alejandro?

He's the hot one in the family. It's not like anyone calls the rest of us unattractive. Just the opposite. But he's the one people fawn over the most.

Would she have responded to him like she has me? Or would she have gone more willingly?

I push those thoughts aside as we walk into the living room. I show her that and the dining room.

"Down the hall is the office. If I'm in there, do *not* go near it. If you call out to me, I'll hear you."

With her in the house, it's likely I'll speak Macaguán. But there's always the chance I may speak Spanish or English. She understands both.

"If you're in there, it's because you're having a conversation I shouldn't hear. I'll respect that privacy, sir."

I told her—blurted out—I want to be her Dom, and I do. But I also admitted I want a romantic relationship with her. Because of that, hearing her call me sir somehow feels wrong. I want her submission and deference, but I also want her to be my equal in nonsexual things. That should be entirely contradictory. It is. It's leaving me conflicted.

We make our way upstairs, and I point out various bedrooms as we walk past them. We come to a guest room, and I open the door. Even though we have no one outside the family come here, it's still ready. It was once my younger brother's.

"This is your room. You'll find towels in the bathroom, and I'll bring you toiletries."

She hesitates before stepping inside. She looks around with an air of detachment.

"It's lovely. Thank you."

She doesn't meet my gaze as she turns back toward the door. We go past Alejandro's room before I open the last door.

"This is my room. It's where you'll sleep."

I step inside, and she follows me. The moment she's through the doorway, I turn and push it closed. I box her against it. I lift her arms over her head as I press my body to hers. She widens her stance as I slide my thigh between hers.

"Ride it, *chiquita*."

Her eyes close as she grinds against my leg. She's not avoiding looking at me because she doesn't want to obey my command. She's concentrating. She moans as my lips nip at her neck. I flick my tongue against her earlobe before tugging it with my teeth. She releases a shuddering breath as her hips move faster. I keep my lips next to her ear, so my breath wafts against it as I whisper.

"Do you want this, Flora?"

"Yes, sir."

"Tell me what 'this' is."

"My obedience. Your control."

"Why?"

"You make me feel safe because you insist on it. You refuse to let anything happen to me. But you can only protect me if I let you, if I obey you."

"What else?"

"Everything about you makes me ache to feel you inside me."

I lift her shirt up, then shift, so she can move away from the door enough for me to pull it over her head.

"Do you know why I want you so badly, *chiquita?*"

"You like to have control, and I'm letting you."

That's a bucket of ice water. She's not wrong, but I hate that she thinks that's the only reason.

"Flora, look at me."

I keep my tone soft, so it's more a request than a command. Her eyes flick open. She's kept her arms over her head, and I love it. But right now, I want her to know what she said isn't entirely accurate. I lower them and put her hands on my shoulders. I want to place them over my heart, but I'm not ready for what that implies.

"*Chica*, you're brave, intelligent, resourceful, stubborn, and challenging. Your assertiveness and willingness to stand up to me is fucking sexy as all get out. Not because I want to be domineering and strip you of those things. Just the opposite. I don't think I can live with a twenty-four seven arrangement once you're out of danger. I'll probably always want to be dominant during sex, and I hope you'll still want to submit. But I want you as my equal when I stop fearing for your life every moment I'm awake."

"You make it sound like this isn't temporary."

"If you agree to it, it's not."

She stares at me, completely uncertain what to say. I've put her on the spot, and I know it. I won't demand she agree or even that she share her thoughts about what I just said. Instead, I grasp her hips and guide her to grind against me again. I unfasten her bra and slide it down her arms. I use the straps to bind her wrists behind her back. I lean forward and lick her right nipple. I lift her tits, enjoying their fullness. I massage them, and she rides my thigh harder.

"Sir, please suck them."

I pinch them rather than give in to her request. She moans and shuts her eyes. I twist until her breath becomes rapid pants.

"How wet are you for me?"

I kiss her lips, not giving her a chance to answer as I unfasten her jeans. I slide a hand down her panties and slip my fingers between her pussy lips. She's drenched. She's as aroused as I am. I push her pants and underwear down. She kicks off her shoes and steps out of her clothes. I turn her away from me, and she presses her left cheek to the door. I spread her ass cheeks, seeing one place I'll fuck her—often.

I press my cock against her. It's pissed that she's naked, and I'm not.

Not yet.

I love squeezing her ass. I have large hands, and I spread my fingers to cover most of it. I press my leg between her thighs again and pull her hips back to me. She rides me without any prompting.

"I'm going to spank you whenever I want. It'll be for punishment and pleasure. I'll fuck your ass because I can. I'll watch it gape, begging for me to slide back inside. I'll make you keep my cum in your tight little asshole until I command you to let me see it drip down to your cunt."

Her bound hands reach down and help spread her wider.

"Please, now."

I didn't expect her to beg for that.

"You want the first place I fuck you to be your ass?"

"If that's what you want."

Fucking tempting.

I drop to my knees and pull her back to my mouth. I lick all of her. I press my thumb against her asshole, but I don't enter her. I flick my tongue inside her over and over until she's shifting her weight with impatience. I turn her toward me.

"Watch me as I feast on your pussy."

"Yes, sir."

I latch onto her clit, biting enough to make her whimper before I suck. I flick it with my tongue before I thrust three fingers into her.

"Pablo! Oh, God!"

Fuck. I love hearing the breathy way she says my name. It's on an exhale. It makes my cock twitch as I picture her saying it that way as I drive it into her cunt.

Her hips jut forward, pressing my mouth to her more. I finger fuck her as I work her clit, sometimes pressing my tongue into her alongside my fingers. My free hand presses against her belly over where my other hand works the front wall of her pussy.

"I need to come. Please may I come?"

I pull my mouth away and pinch her clit as I continue to work my fingers in and out. She stomps her foot in impatience. I slap her clit in response. She screams as her hips thrust forward. I slap it again. She wails her response.

"Oh, God! Please!"

"Who decides?"

"You, sir."

"Why?"

"Because I belong to you."

"Who am I?"

"My Dom."

"What does that make you?"

"Your sub."

"That's right. I'll give you your orgasm when I want. Until then, I'll edge you."

I don't intend it to be a test, but it is. It's a test of her trust in me. She needs to trust I'll take care of her and give her what she ultimately needs. A partner who's promised to take care of her and fulfills that promise. It goes both ways. She's offering her submission, her willingness to put her faith in me. I'm trusting her not to come until I say she can.

"Sir, my mind's telling me not to come. But I don't think my body can stop. I'm sorry. I want to obey."

"I know you do, little one."

I flick her clit with my tongue before I lick. I soothe her, and she releases a shuddering breath.

"Come, *chiquita*."

I suck again, and my fingers rub her G spot. I feel the extra flood of cream before I taste it.

"*Ay, Papí.*"

She moans the phrase. It's one I've heard plenty of times before in many contexts. It's fucking sexy as hell. It might mean "yes, Daddy" in English, but those have very different connotations. As she comes, I realize I wouldn't mind hearing either of those.

I once saw *Tía* Elle mouth "Daddy" to *Tío* Enrique, and I know I heard my childhood friend Madeline say it to my cousin Javier when I walked past the closed door of my parents' half bathroom. There's no doubt he was pleasuring her. It's not a term that's ever been appealing to me before. No woman's called me that, and I've never wanted one to.

Until now.

Flora's legs bend as she presses against the door as though it's all that's keeping her upright. I remove her bra straps from around her wrists before I stand and scoop her into my arms. I carry her to the bed and sit on the edge. Sweat beads along her hairline as she struggles to catch her breath. I kiss her, and she nestles against me more.

"I want to make you come, sir. I want to taste you too."

She tries to pull away, but I hold her tighter.

I chuckle. "You will. But right now, you're going to let me hold you as you come down off that high. You're going to let me watch how beautiful you are with your flushed cheeks and plump lips from my kisses. Sleep if you want, *chica*."

My hand covers her breast and massages like I did earlier, my thumb sweeping over her puckered nipple. Her fingers slide between the top two buttons of my shirt as she nods. Her eyes are closed yet again. She inhales, then sighs before kissing my neck.

"I dozed in the plane. I never take naps. Yeah."

She sounds half asleep as she agrees to my offer. I reach behind me and pull the sheet and comforter down. I'm gentle when I stand, then lay her on the bed. She reaches for me, her hand wrapping around my neck as I kiss her. She lets go and curls up as I straighten.

"I'm going to the office to call my *tío*. Sleep, baby girl. I'll come back when I'm done."

She yawns before she speaks.

"I'm your *chiquita*, *chica*, little one, and now you're baby girl. What are you to me?"

That single word pops back into my head. She'd totally misunderstand what I want if I suggest it. I told her I like all the things that make her independent. If I tell her I want her to call me Daddy, she'll think I want her to be a Little. She knows enough about D/s dynamics that she's bound to know what that is. I don't think she's a Little or even a Middle. But I want her to truly believe what I've told her several times today. I want her to feel safe with me and know I'll protect her and take care of her.

"What do you want to call me?"

"*Papi* when you're fucking me. I don't know what when you aren't."

I won't read into it. It's a common endearment in Latin America. I could call her *Mami* just as easily. In this context, it has nothing to do with parental figures. But I love hearing it.

"If that's what you want, *chica*."

"I'll come up with something else, Pablo. I just don't know what yet."

I kiss her again before I turn away. She's asleep as I walk out the door.

"*Tío*, what was I supposed to do? Risk Humberto successfully killing her? Those men might've been there just to watch her, but I doubt it. I wouldn't take the chance."

Tío Enrique is about as thrilled as I expected that I brought Flora here. Javier took Madeline to another one of our family estates that was supposed to be a secret. That didn't work out so well. Fortunately, the men who compromised their safety can't tell anyone else about that estate's location. I don't blame him for not wanting a repeat of that situation.

"*Sobrino*, I trust you to do the right thing for her. But I've known you since before you were born. You were stubborn and insistent with the way you'd kick in your *mamá's* belly. You were never a disobedient child, but you didn't give in easily. I know I won't convince you otherwise, but I don't think this was a good decision. Are you involved with her yet?"

Yet.

"That's a big assumption, *Tío.*"

"Yeah, well, family history tells me what's happening. Are you sure about this?"

"Yes."

He knows I wouldn't react the way I am and I wouldn't have brought Flora here if I didn't want something permanent with her. I've only known her for a couple days—God, that makes everything that's happened seem so outrageous— but I've had hours to consider what I want and what I'm doing. In my world, hours are like months when you usually decide in seconds. Decisions I can't undo because they could get people killed. Sometimes they do, and that's intentional. But sometimes they do, and I did everything I could to prevent it. I have to get it right because I live with each man's death on my conscience. Getting it wrong only makes it worse.

"You've taken her to the safest place you could get to quickly. But you know Humberto knows where the compound is. He will show up."

"If he makes it off his estate, then I'll kill him just for that. Then I'll punish every guard who allowed it. Even if he were allowed past his gate, I'd kill him for coming near Flora. Even if I didn't want her the way I do, I'd still kill him for targeting a woman."

"But she's your woman."

"Yes."

My *tío* sighs.

I expect him to say something, but he remains quiet. He's waiting for me to confess something, but I won't tell him anything about my feelings for Flora. He certainly doesn't expect me to divulge anything he's guessed has happened between us. He probably thinks I'm already fucking her.

"I'll call you back if anything comes up."

"I want regular reports, Pablo. Don't wait for something to come up. I don't want to invade your privacy with her, but I'll send your *papá* or cousins down there if you make me worry any more than you already are."

"I don't need babysitting."

"I never said you did. I won't risk your life too by sitting back again."

He means Juan. He trusted my younger brother to make better choices than he did. He trusted my brother to accept the consequences of his piss-poor choices. He made me carry out those consequences. He believes he should've intervened and reined in Juan. I doubt there's anything in life he regrets more. He doesn't want another nephew to die.

"I'll update you every few hours. It may just be texts."

"That's fine. You may be an adult—a nearly middle-aged adult—but I still worry about you, *sobrino*."

"If I'm middle-aged, then you're ancient, *Tío*."

I used to tell him that when I was a teenager. He was in his forties when his hair started to gray around the temples. He let it go the first time I said it. The second time, he made me go on a six-mile run and smoked my ass. I'm the second fastest runner in the family. I didn't learn my lesson. The third time I said it, we were boxing. Not only did I wind up flat on my ass, I sported a massive bruise on my kidney for two weeks. My cousins teased me mercilessly. My parents told me I got what I deserved. My other *tío* and my *tías* just gave me "I told you so" looks. I know *Tío* regretted landing the punch so hard, but it taught me to only tease him with love.

"You'll worry me into an early grave. Do you really want to face *Tía* Elle?"

"Definitely not."

My new *tía* is remarkable. There's no better way to describe her. We all adore her, and she fits into the family like she's always been part of it. *She is one of us.*

"Do you want me to tell your *mamá* that you're taking more risks than you need to?"

"Hell, no."

My mother still terrifies me even if she's the only person who can make the world right again when everything goes wrong. Plus, she's still recovering from cancer. She's been in remission for a while, but she's not as strong as she used to be. I don't need to add to her worries or my *papá's.*

"I'll be careful, *Tío.* I'll check in, in a few hours. I need to go. Flora didn't get a chance to pack anything, so she needs some toiletries and clothes. I'm going to ask Daniel's wife to pick up some things before he comes over with groceries. They're about the same size."

"All right. *Te quiero.*" I love you.

"*Yo también te quiero.*" I love you too.

Chapter Eight

Flora

I fell asleep, but not for long. I'm still tired, but it's more emotionally depleted. I lie in bed as I consider everything that's happened in the past couple days.

Humberto and I had a conversation that opened my eyes to family history I didn't know. I also wound up with a bounty on my head for arguing with him.

I went to my club and fucked my *former* Dom and pictured Pablo the entire time. I nearly said his name instead of sir.

Pablo broke into my apartment, kissed me, threatened me, carried me out to his waiting car, kissed me some more, and nearly fucked me before taking me on a private plane to an isolated-as-fuck fortress. He finger fucked and ate me out and made me come harder than I ever have in my life. He held me and gave me aftercare like an experienced Dom. We already agreed at some point to a twenty-four seven D/s relationship when I barely know him. I barely remember when that happened.

It took me months of meeting Roberto at my club and scening with him before I was ready to agree to a monogamous agreement. I was with two other men during that time, but only ones I scened with regularly. I hate knowing Pablo's had *ménages*, but so have I. I don't know how well that'll go over when it eventually comes out. From the way he was talking, he sees there being an "us" after all this fucked-up shit ends—assuming we both survive.

I agreed to submit sexually and even emotionally to a man I've barely known three days.

I'm fucking certifiable.

But something about him makes me feel things I've never felt before.

Maybe it's his aura of self-assuredness. He radiates confidence that he can control any situation he's in, that any and everyone will bend to his will. He exerted that when he hefted me over his shoulder and basically kidnapped me. But he did it because I refused his help. It wasn't because he's using me as a pawn. It wasn't just because he wants to fuck me—though it would be hot if that was part of it. Hot in a fucked-up and warped kind of way.

He's told me several times he'll protect me and take care of me. What makes him different from everyone else who's made that promise is that he's actually proving it. He doesn't say it just to say it—he means it. *Mamá's* taken care of me all my life, and I know she's protected me as best she could. She thought not telling me the truth about my father's past was the right thing to do. But she also did that to protect herself from talking about something that's painful to her. She gave in to my *abuelo* when he demanded I serve as repayment to that old debt. She didn't protect me from him or from Humberto.

Pablo is.

My grandparents on both sides didn't tell me the truth either, making my father sound like nothing short of a superhero. I knew they exaggerated, but clearly, I had no clue just how much. *Abuelo* indentured me to Humberto. I'm certain he knows about the hit, but he wasn't the first to warn me. Maybe he's tried and can't because I don't have my phone. Maybe he sent someone or even went to my apartment and didn't find me. But deep down, I know he didn't. It's not that he wants me dead. At least, I don't think—don't want to believe—he does.

I just don't think he'd do half of what Pablo has. That's a painful realization. One that creates a gaping hole in my heart.

Now that I know Luciana broke the engagement because she fell in love with Esteban on her own and chose him, it paints my father's choices in a far different light. He could've married *Mamá*, but he kept her as his mistress instead. He knew she was pregnant when he died. He could've provided better for her and for me.

He didn't, so my grandparents on both sides stepped in to help. I know I've always been in danger because of him. I just didn't know how grave it was until recently. His decisions have haunted me.

This is a lot of introspection, and it's making me feel worse rather than better. I push back the covers and look around for my clothes. I remake the bed before I slip them back on and open the door. I hear nothing, so I close it behind me. That's how it was before Pablo took me inside. I bet the stars are brilliant out here with no ambient light to hide them.

I wander out to the pool and sweep my gaze around the lawn. There are men patrolling the property, but the ones back here are at the far end of the yard. This place is several acres. It's probably large enough to have half a golf course. The men I can see are little more than dark shapes.

I roll up my pant legs and sit on the edge of the pool. I stick my toes in before putting them all the way in. I'm surprised to find it's heated. I wonder if someone else in the family has been here recently or if it's kept this way in case someone shows up. I saw the solar panels when we arrived. I guess electricity isn't scarce here. It makes sense, so they remain off the grid. I look up, half expecting to see some satellite orbiting the place.

"*Chica?*"

I twist to see Pablo coming through the French doors I passed through.

Fucking hell.

He really is the hottest man I've ever seen.

He took off his suit coat at some point and rolled up his sleeves. His tats peek below his cuffs, and I wonder what I'll find when he takes off his shirt. The material strains across his broad shoulders and chest and—dare I say it—bulging biceps. It's true. They are. Cliché, but honest. His trousers hug his slim waist, and his torso tapers to make his body a perfect triangle. As he walks toward me, I can tell how athletic his legs are, even if I hadn't felt them beneath me—between my legs.

Fuck. That was so damn hot.

I was nearly out of my mind with need earlier. The way he edged me—he clearly knew what he was doing. I was barely clinging to the little control I had. I definitely didn't control the scene, but I maintained enough control over my body to not come until he gave me permission.

Scene.

The idea that it was something performed dampens my feelings.

"What's wrong?"

"Huh? Nothing."

"Yes, there is. Your expression changed. You withdrew."

He comes to stand beside me. When I pull my feet in, he

presses his hand to my shoulder as he toes off his shoes. He lets go to take off his socks and roll up his pants. He sits next to me and sticks his feet in beside mine.

"You thought of something that bothered you, *chica*. I'll never insist you share your thoughts with me, but I hope you will. Something's troubling you, and I'd like to—help."

Did he want to say fix it?

Does he need that much control over everything?

No.

His expression tells me he's worried. But is he worried about what's upsetting me or worried he can't fix whatever it is? Is he worried I won't tell him?

He wraps his arm around my shoulders and draws me against his side. He kisses the top of my head as I lean it against him. He says nothing more. His strong, silent type is comforting now when it was frustrating earlier. I wrap my arm around his waist. I watch him swirl water around his ankles, and it makes me smile. I don't know why. Maybe because it's such a relaxed thing to do. He's truly happy here.

"Pablo, was earlier a scene?"

"No."

He's so quick to answer some questions. It's not that he's shutting me down or shutting me out. He just knows the answer without thinking about it. He's unwavering about it.

"Flora, we'll agree when it's a scene."

"But if our dynamic is nonstop, then doesn't it make every-thing some sort of scene?"

"I don't see it that way. Just the opposite. I think an around-the-clock dynamic means most of it isn't a scene. It's just how two people are when they've agreed to that relationship."

He twists to see me better, so I have no choice but to lift my head. I turn to face him more.

"Little one, I told you I don't see us having this same

dynamic once the imminent danger is over. I told you I want to be your Dom, and I do. That won't change, but when Roberto asked you if you were ending things for a romantic relationship, you looked at me and I nodded. It can be both."

"I know."

He watches me for a moment. "Do you not want both?"

"I don't know."

"I won't press to be your boyfriend or anything more than your Dom if you don't want that."

"Why do you assume I only want you as my Dom?"

"You trust me with your body, but you don't trust me with more."

I shake my head.

"Pablo, you're intelligent, but that's absolutely a stupid assessment of how things are between us. I know what I said earlier, but it turns out I was wrong. I trust you with my life. Not because you forced me to come with you, so I have little choice. I told you I could've put up a far greater fight. I wouldn't have gone with you—at least not without you forcing me—if I didn't want to. I could've shut myself in that guest bedroom and refused to talk to you, refused to come out. You could've forced me to. I'm a willing participant. You may have given me little choice about coming with you, but you gave me some. If I'd really fought you, you would've taken me to my mother or my grandparents on either side. Your idea of taking care of me isn't some twisted Stockholm Syndrome because I don't feel like your captive. If I insisted upon leaving, you'd try to convince me otherwise, but I don't believe you'd imprison me here. You'd take me somewhere else safe. You wouldn't agree with my choice, but you'd respect it. Am I wrong?"

"No, you're not."

He appears uncomfortable now, so he looks away from me. He stares into space for so long I rest my hand on his thigh.

"Pablo?"

"What you said is something easily figured out just by knowing my family's commitment to protect those who can't protect themselves. It's fucked up, but that's why my family's stayed in the Cartel. We know how much worse it could be for people if another family led. We've always made it clear women and children are off limits. It's why, unlike other syndicates, we don't recruit. We don't go near minors to get them to join. Yes, it's a legacy in many families, but *Tío* Enrique accepts no one before they're eighteen."

"You're the one who's withdrawn now. What else aren't you telling me? Is this something you really have to keep secret? I've been around cartels my entire life, Pablo. I know you'll lie to me often. Sometimes it'll be by avoiding telling me anything, and sometimes you'll tell me a bald-faced untruth. I understand why. You're not just protecting yourself. You're protecting your family, the people who work for you, their families. I get that."

"I'll be protecting you too."

He's quiet when he says that. I don't think he likes admitting it, even if I did it for him.

"Is whatever you're thinking so bad you have to protect me from it? Or are you just unaccustomed to sharing your thoughts?"

"I'm unaccustomed to sharing them with anyone outside my family. They can read me so well that most of the time I don't have to say anything. No one else can do that. At least, no one else could. I feel like you can."

I know that confession cost him a lot. He's being vulnerable with me, and I won't take that for granted. I inhale before responding. I might humiliate myself.

"*Papi?*"

He sucks in a breath so deep his stomach caves. He's slow

to look at me. My hand on his thigh presses harder as the arm that was around his waist lets go, so I can cup his face.

"You see way more of me than I've let anyone else see. I don't think I could stop you. You get me."

"Call me that again, *chiquita*."

"*Papi*."

"We understand each other. You don't look at me as a replacement for your father, do you?"

I choke on my laugh as I shake my head.

"Most definitely not. I don't think I have daddy issues either. I don't have a distrust of men because my father failed my mother and me. I don't want a replacement for the father I never had. I don't feel younger than I am and want someone to treat me that way. But you make me feel shielded from everything going wrong. You take care of me in whatever way you think I need. I also think it's sexy as fuck in Spanish. But I think you know I mean it more than just some term people toss around."

"I think it's because you know I call no other woman *chiquita* or *chica*."

"I do, and you didn't have to tell me that. You tried to hide your surprise when you said it the first time. You didn't want me to know you questioned yourself."

We stare at each other as something passes between us. Sometimes it takes months or years to know you're meant to have a deep relationship with someone, whether it's romantic or platonic. Other times, you just know. I just know with Pablo this is more. More than anything from my past.

He helps me stand before he lifts my shirt as I unbutton his. I glance toward the men in the distance.

"We aren't the first couple to come here. We're a large family already. With the way my parents' generation is, I'm surprised we aren't at least four times as large as we are. They know to look away."

"Are you sure? I'm not family. What if they think I might try to kill you?"

He grins.

"Then I'd have to wrestle you to the ground and kiss you until you relent. Then I'd fuck you into wanting me to live rather than die."

He tucks his fingers into the waist of my jeans and tugs me closer. I slide my hands under his shirt and push it off his shoulders as he undoes the last two buttons. I marvel at what I see. He's a canvas of tattoos. They don't cover every inch of him, but there are plenty. I'm sure they each have meaning. His body is fucking chiseled. Like some Roman sculptor from the Renaissance carved him from marble. No. Granite. He's harder than marble.

I trail my fingers over his shoulders, arms, and chest before tucking my fingers beneath his belt and tugging like he did to me. His feet bracket mine as we kiss. I unfasten his belt, then his pants while his hands cup my ass. When I push them down, he lets go of me and unbuttons, then unzips my pants.

"I know what we did earlier, Flora. But if you're more comfortable with your bra and panties on and me with my boxer briefs, then we can stop undressing now."

I skim my gaze over him. He's hard. There's nothing my imagination needs to wonder.

"I thought you said the guards wouldn't watch us."

"They won't."

"Are you worried I won't like what I find?" I waggle my eyebrows at him.

"I've just assumed and pushed you into a lot today."

"Thank you for considering that."

I wrap my arms around his waist and lean against him. He

hugs me back. I slide my hands beneath his boxer briefs and grab his ass.

Definitely granite.

I moan and rub myself against him as I push down the last thing covering him. He unhooks my bra as he steps out of his underwear. He yanks my panties down.

"Don't wear these again. We'll order you new clothes, and you can get anything you want except panties. I suggest you get skirts or dresses, but I won't insist. But I told you, I will fuck you when I want. I will also finger you and taste you whenever the mood strikes. I will not have panties in my way."

This is part of a twenty-four seven I can get used to. Free use hasn't been something I've done because I've only ever met my Doms at my club. It was always a given I wanted to fuck.

"And your boxer briefs?"

"While we're here, if you don't want me to wear them, then I won't. You can take me out whenever you want, but I will still decide how we fuck unless I tell you otherwise."

That dominance makes me so fucking wet and achy.

"While we're here? You make it sound like there will be times when we're together after we leave."

"I want there to be. I'm letting you into my life, Flora, because I want you to be part of it. I know you've been around cartels since you were born, but you haven't been with someone who's part of the ruling family. You haven't been with the heir to the strongest cartel in the world. That brings more danger than you're in now. I wouldn't risk you if I didn't want you to be with me for real."

Fuck.

That's a lot to take in now that he's said it aloud. But it isn't something I hadn't already sensed.

"Pablo, I accepted that already. I think I've known that

since you showed up this morning. I've known it since the first time I saw you and wanted you."

"We'll go as slowly as you need, *chica*. I don't expect you to make decisions as fast as I do. I won't blame you for having doubts."

"I won't blame you for having them either."

He looks at me as though I don't understand something basic. He's not a man who doubts his decisions. Once made, he stands by them. He'll stand by his decision to be with me.

"So, commando for now, *Papí*?"

He practically growls as he dives in to kiss my neck. He finds the spot behind my ear that's so fucking erotic that I shift to grind against his thigh again.

"I'll have to wear boxer briefs when we leave here because there's no way people won't know how hard I get when I'm around you."

I reach between us and wrap my hand around his cock. I stroke him, and he groans.

"You'll wear fucking underwear because I'll kill anyone who eyes your cock. I suspect how big you are is obvious even when you aren't hard."

My vehemence at the first sentence surprises me. That flare of jealousy and possessiveness is back with a vengeance. From the way he kisses me—practically swallows me whole—he likes it. He lifts me, and I wrap my legs around his waist, forcing me to let go of his dick.

He walks around the pool until we get to the wide steps into the shallow end. The water ripples around us as he moves us until we're beside a wall. He presses me against it as one arm supports me beneath my ass. The other hand lifts my right breast for him to suck on. Once my nipple is in his mouth. He kneads the other, his thumb swiping over my tight nipple.

When he looks up, his already deep brown eyes are like pools of onyx.

"Is that right, little one? You won't let anyone near me?"

"Near or far. I told you I won't share."

"And if I'm serious when I tell you I won't let anyone else ogle you?"

"Then you should know I'm just as serious."

We stare at each other before his hands go to my hips. I tilt them forward, and he thrusts into me. He isn't claiming me. I'm not claiming him. We're claiming each other.

Chapter Nine

Pablo

I'm going to come too fast.

Flora's tight and warm and so fucking wet. I thrusted hard, sliding into her with enough friction to feel divine without hurting her or feeling sloppy. Hell, she'd feel incredible no matter what.

I watch her tits floating at the surface of the water as she rides me. Her legs squeeze my waist as her hands press on my shoulders, giving her leverage to rise and fall as I keep surging into her. I slow my pace, but I don't thrust any gentler. I bury myself each time, pushing and pulling her hips to rub her clit. She moans each time I bottom out. With the slower pace, she wraps her hands around my neck before sliding her fingers into my hair. She grazes my scalp, making it tingle.

"Please fill me with your cum."

"Is that what my little girl wants?"

Despite how rough I am, I'm still careful not to hurt her.

I'm so much bigger than her. I'm easily fifty pounds heavier than her, if not more. I'm at least eight inches taller too. I can wrap my arms around her or stand in front of her and make her disappear from anyone's view. I'll never lose complete control because I'd do more than hurt her. I'd harm her. I'd never forgive myself for that.

"So much."

She swoops in for a kiss that I let her lead for now. She's hungry for what I offer, and I want her just as much. Her kiss is fierce and demanding as she sucks on my tongue. She fists my hair and tugs, trying to make us move faster again. I can't spank her beneath the water with any effectiveness, so I pinch her ass.

She yelps.

"You will take all my cum in your tight little cunt when I decide. If I fuck you any faster, it'll be over too soon."

"Then we'll just have to do it again."

"Rest assured, little one, we will. Many times."

I'll never get enough of this. Of how she feels. Of how she makes me feel.

She squeezes her inner muscles every time I plunge into her. She's doing it more than she was before. She's nearly fighting me not to slide up when I lift her hips.

"Flora?"

"Please let me make you come."

My brow furrows at her request. She doesn't want to make this last.

"Am I hurting you? Do you want to finish?"

"What? No. Why would you think that when I just said we need to do this again?"

"You're eager for me to finish."

She offers me a soft smile before she leans in to kiss me. It's not demanding like before, but it's just as hungry. She's trying to communicate something through this kiss I'm struggling to understand. I know insatiable lust. I've felt it before, but never to the degree I am with Flora. I've felt affection for her that's completely foreign to me. But this is something else. I've had subs who were eager to please, but this is more.

"*Papi*, you pleasured me in a way I've never felt before. As much as I wanted to come—needed to—you knew what I really needed was to make it last. To have time to let you control things, so I didn't have to remember reality. You *gave* me that. Please let me do that too."

Our gazes lock, and I realize she wants to take care of me. She doesn't want to take. She wants to give back. It means ceding control to her—even if temporarily—so I don't have to worry about anything, including whether I'm pleasuring her enough to get her off.

"Keep doing what you just were. I won't be able to stop."

Her kiss steals my breath as she tugs my hair with one hand, and the nails on her other graze my scalp. She Kegels with each up-slide and grinds her clit on my pubic bone after each downslide. I buck into her, pounding her as fast as the swirling water around us will let me.

"Fuck, *chiquita*. You're such a good little one."

She shakes her head. "Not right now. I'm your little cum slut you're fucking because you can do whatever you want to me."

Fuck.

I didn't plan to call her anything like that. It didn't appeal to me because I never want her to believe I think less of her by calling her that. It's not like I haven't used the term before, and I'm certain it wouldn't be the first time she was called that. I only wanted praise between us, but she wants dirty talk. She's okay with it.

"That's right. You're going to take my fat cock whenever I want. Your body belongs to me since you're my little cum slut. Beg."

"Please give me your cum. I want to be your whore. I want to be the slut you fuck as hard as you can."

She's pushing me to the edge, and I'm teetering.

"You're going to come for me, my sweet little whore."

"Fuck, Pablo. Keep talking like that. I'm almost there."

"Yeah, you are. You're going to ride my cock because you can't get enough of it. Beg."

"*Please*! Please come inside me."

I rest my hand around her throat, watching for her reaction in case she doesn't like it. She looks at me before she presses her neck forward. I tighten enough to make it difficult for her to breathe, but I won't leave any marks. I lean in to whisper in her ear, feeling her pulse thrum under my fingers.

"Tonight, you will suck me off. I will mark you with my cum. You will lick it off me before you stand in front of the mirror and watch it dry on your tits and face, you little slut. I will edge you again, except I won't let you come. I'll fuck your ass. I'll plug it with my cock. Even when I'm not hard, I'll be so deep in you that you have no choice but to keep my cum in you. You will sleep with my cum in your ass. I will wake you and fuck you however I want because you're my fucking whore."

I lean back and watch her eyes close. I loosen my grip, but her hands fly up to mine, pressing them. Her head tilts back as she goes rigid. I squeeze a little more before I release her. She sucks in a deep breath and moans with pleasure. Her submission combined with how tight she is pushes me over that edge. I blow my load inside her, making me shudder. She remains wrapped around me. I brace myself with my hands on the edge of the pool, worried I'll crush her. I eventually rest on my forearms since my arms shake too much to hold me up.

"*Chiquita?*"

"Fuck, *Papí.*"

She says it with a moan and a sigh.

"Are you all right?"

"So all right."

"Flora, those things I said—"

"Better have been a promise."

I observe her as she assesses me. Her head tilts, and her brow furrows.

"You didn't enjoy the dirty talk."

"I did. I just hadn't planned to call you any of those things."

"You didn't do it to degrade or shame me. You did it because it was exciting. I thought you'd like it, but if you don't..."

She shrugs as she trails off.

"I might have liked it too much."

Her eyebrows shoot straight up. "Are you worried I'll think you mean those things even when we aren't having sex?"

"Yes."

"You said you hadn't planned to say those words. That doesn't mean you don't want to."

My gaze bores into her, and I make sure my tone reflects how serious I am when I respond.

"I will *never* call you any of that outside of sex. Most likely, I'll never say it unless I'm inside you or about to be. Not even as foreplay. I would *never* tolerate anyone speaking to you like that."

"I know. That's why I like it when you do it during sex. Pablo, it makes me feel desirable. It reminds me you're the dominant one, and I want to submit."

"You're perfect." *For me.*

"Hardly. You definitely didn't think that earlier today. I thought you might throttle me and not as breath play."

I feel like I can stand on my own, so I step back from the wall and lower us until our shoulders are beneath the water. She continues to hold on to me as my hands roam over her body and legs.

"We didn't talk about your limits. I did that without asking."

"No, you didn't. You didn't tighten your hold until you knew I wanted it. You didn't ask aloud, but I knew you were waiting for my consent. Nothing too taboo. No blood play or bodily fluids except for what happens during sex. No marks someone else could see."

"What we do is between us. No one will know what we share, Flora. I won't mark you where someone could see and think of you with anything but respect."

She adjusts to pull herself up more, so we're eye level again.

"But you get that means I want you to mark me in other places. I don't mean with just your cum."

"I'll leave fingerprints and love bites, but I won't leave any real bruises. Even if I punish you, I won't do anything beyond leaving your ass hot and red. It might be a few hours before it settles, but you won't see welts or bruises the next day."

"You're genuinely scared of hurting me, aren't you?"

"Harming. We both know we enjoy some level of pain, so things will hurt. But I draw the line at harming you."

She presses a kiss to my lips, her tongue flicking between them. But she pulls away before it becomes something more.

"Pablo, you will always hold back part of you. I know that. It'll suck sometimes because I'll feel shut out and left out. I already know that. But you'll do that to shield me just as much as you'll hold back your physical strength to protect me. I'm not worried about that. I know if we reach my limit, you'll respect that and stop."

"Always. No questions asked, no explanation expected."

"But I will give it to you, so we can understand what we both need and how we can do whatever we're doing without hitting my limit again."

"All right."

Her right hand glides over my shoulder as her left arm wraps around my neck.

"You spanked me earlier today because I was being obstinate. I wouldn't accept your help when you knew how much I needed it."

"I could've explained things far better rather than imposing." I look away, feeling guilty about how I handled things.

"Was there really time to have a lengthy conversation?"

"No."

"Did I endanger us by arguing with you and making us stay as long as we did?"

"If I feared someone else barging in, I would've carried you out much sooner. I wouldn't have given you any chance to argue, and I wouldn't have kissed you. I wouldn't have risked being there that long when the entire point was to protect you. But it was getting urgent."

"Then I deserved that spanking. I probably deserved far more. At least a completely bare ass one. As much as it hurt, I knew—even if I didn't want to admit it—that you were already caring for me. You were protecting me from myself. If I risk my safety again, or worse, yours or someone else's, then punish me properly."

"What does that mean to you? Time in a corner with a bare ass?"

That doesn't appeal to me in the least. Thankfully, she laughs and shakes her head.

"You don't have to look so nervous. We know I'm not a Little or a Middle. I don't need to stand in a corner, lose privileges, or anything like that. But I would like firmer punishments that would mark me longer, so I remember the choice I made was the wrong one."

"I need to think about that. I don't know that I can do that. Is it something you need?"

"I don't need it. I'm happy to submit in other ways. Does it remind you too much of—work?"

My eyes widen.

"No. At least, I don't think so. I just don't want to be that kind of man."

"It wouldn't be abuse."

"I know you consent, but the only reason I could do that is because I have the strength to. I may call you little girl because you're smaller than me, but I don't want to use my size to have my way."

She nods as she considers what I said.

"Can we discuss it when the time comes?"

"Of course. Always. I don't think I'm going to punish you that often."

"I definitely won't look for trouble."

"I know. But I will punish you if you put yourself or anyone else at risk because you were thoughtless. It might be a mistake, but if it's something you could've avoided by thinking about things more, then I will punish you. If you're in a situation where you don't know better or couldn't make a different choice, then I won't."

"Will you reserve spankings only for punishment?"

She doesn't sound like she likes that idea. I step back until I'm in the shallowest part of the pool. I lift her over my shoulder like I did earlier today and swat her ass. I know it stings as I do it five more times. I pull her back into the water and against my lengthening cock. She hooks her legs around me like she did before, and I slide into her again. I carry her out of the pool and grab two towels as I walk past the cupboard. I fling one over a chair before reclining on it. She leans forward, and my hand lands across her ass once more before I shake out the second towel and drape it over her. It rests across her mid-back, leaving enough room for my hand to spank her while the material covers her.

"You have an incredible ass, little one."

"Thank you. I like yours too."

"The things I plan to do to yours."

"I know. You told me."

"Does that excite you, *chica?*"

"So much."

"Sit up. Let me watch you ride me."

She follows my command, adjusting the towel, so it doesn't slip off her. It hides her ass from anyone who might draw close enough to see. It won't hide what we're doing, but my men have the sense to not come near us if they have even a sneaking suspicion we're having sex.

I watch her tits bounce, and I'm starving. I sit up with ease and suck one then the other. Flora continues to bounce on my cock, rocking sometimes. I love running my hands over her ribs, back, and belly. Her hips flare, begging for me to hold on to them. I love watching the muscles flex as she moves with me, but she's soft in all the places I love to squeeze. It's intoxicating.

This position is emotionally intimate. Everything we've done together has been intimate, something for only us to know about and share. But this brings our bodies together in a way that leaves no space between us. No end and no beginning. Just one. As we watch each other, I think we both know there's something poignant about it. Something deeply moving.

It's erotic and scary at the same time. I feel bare and vulnerable like earlier. Her expression tells me she feels the same way, almost tentative about everything except how she moves on my cock. I brush her hair back from her shoulder, and she leans in to kiss my neck. I do the same until our lips meet.

"Make me come, my sweet *chiquita*."

"*Sí, Papi*."

That's obedience, not just the common Latin American phrase that can be playful or serious. The difference in context between two synonyms. *Ay* and *sí*. Maybe she'll say it in English one day too. I crave hearing both.

"You feel amazing, Flora. I want to stay buried in you. I don't want to stop. I want to claim you. You're the only one who's ever gotten my cum."

She stares at me, missing a beat before riding me again.

"You've never gone bare before, either?"

"No. Too many risks."

"But you'll take them with me?"

"Aren't you doing the same thing?"

"Yes."

We both know there are the health risks, but since we both belong to clubs, we know we test regularly. I could get her pregnant. Then our lives would be irrevocably bound no matter what would happen to a baby. We'd never be able to undo creating a life together.

Maybe one day we will, but for now, it's a push and pull. A give and take from both of us. I don't know what tomorrow will bring, but for now, I couldn't ask for better.

"Pablo, come in me, please. It'll get me off."

I rub her clit with my thumb as I pinch her nipple.

"Getting you off will make me come, *mi pequeña flor*." My little flower.

She rides me, throwing her head back. I watch the flush rise along her neck. Her body tightens, and I pin her hips in place as I come again. I didn't think I could come as hard as the first time I was inside her. I thought it was the novelty of it being the first time, but this one is just as strong.

The sound of a helicopter approaching makes us freeze. I look toward it before we scramble off the lounger. We grab our clothes and run toward the house. I know Flora's worried about someone seeing us in a compromising position. I'm worried because I know who it is.

Chapter Ten

Flora

Pablo and I bolt inside. He stands near the French doors as he dresses. I move farther inside, hoping no one caught a clear view of what we were doing. I doubt it would be difficult for anyone to guess, considering we're both naked, and I was clearly straddling his lap. He swore this place was a secret, so I wonder who this is.

"Pablo, are you expecting family?"

"Not this family member."

"Humberto?"

Fear spikes through me as Pablo nods. He dresses faster than I do. I'm stunned into inaction for a moment, but as I watch him move to a coffee table and reach beneath it, I already know what he's going to pull out. It spurs me back to getting dressed as fast as I can.

"Flora, I'm going to take you down to our panic room and seal you in. No matter what, you do not leave there. I don't care if you think it's me. If it's safe for you to come out, I'll let myself in."

He takes my hand and guides me into the basement. He presses a button and moves aside a set of shelves like something out of a movie or *Scooby-Doo* cartoon. With biometrics, he unlocks a door that could fit a bank vault. I've never seen one so thick in real life.

Lights with motion sensors flicker on as we step inside. It's an entire apartment down here. He moves around, switching on what must be a generator. There's a bathroom with a shower off to the right, and on the other side of the living room is a small but full kitchen. I notice two doors are open, and they reveal bedrooms with two sets of bunk beds in each. He leads me into a pantry that's well stocked.

"If someone breaches that door, there's a tunnel that will get you out to the river. It's a mile long and has motion-sensor lights too. There's a small rubber motorboat with an outboard engine. Have you ever driven one before?"

"I've only driven one once, but it's been years. Is it a pull cord to start?"

"Yes. You'll have to push it off the bank to begin with before you lower it into the water. There's a lever on the right side of the engine. Once you're deep enough, you can do that and start the engine. All you have to do is cross to the other side. It's wide and fast moving, but manageable. We own the land on that side too. There'll be guards who can take you to Bogotá. If anything feels even remotely out of my control, I'll trigger my tracker. It sends an alert to *Papá*, my *tíos*, and my cousins. They'll turn on the feed for here and see what's happening. If there's the opportunity, I'll get inside and activate the alarm system."

Alarm system. That's the only reassuring thing Pablo's said so far.

"It makes this an impenetrable fortress. Metal barriers will slide down the windows and across all doorways. No one can get in until someone inside turns it off. They need biometrics to do that. Let me program you into this door."

I offer my hand, and he places it on the screen, adding my fingerprints then my retinal scan to the system. He wraps his arms around me and gives me a brief kiss before guiding me back to the living room. He points to screens on the wall before he turns them on. They look like multiple TVs in a sports bar, but they're linked to security cameras around the property. We watch the helicopter land.

"I have to go, *chiquita*. Stay here. I'll be back as soon as I can."

"I know, Daddy."

The word stuns us both for a heartbeat.

Then he's kissing me deeply, but it's over far too fast. I watch him leave, and the door seals with a whoosh behind him. I turn my attention to the screens as Humberto approaches the wall. Unlike when we arrived, there's no one there to greet him warmly. It forces him to walk around to the front of the estate. I see Pablo dash out of the front door with a rifle slung across his chest and a pistol in his hand.

I wonder if I'll be able to hear what happens. That curiosity is satisfied only a moment later as the pedestrian gate opens rather than the one for vehicles. Pablo shoots, hitting the wall beside Humberto as he passes by. I hear the bullet ricochet off the wall.

"You're not welcome here."

"This should have been my home, not your *pedazo de mierda tío's.*"

"You believe you're entitled to everything when you deserve nothing. You were never the elder son. Everything passed to my *abuelo* the way it was supposed to then to my *tío.*

No one ever intended the inheritance go to you. God and fate ensured you fucked yourself over by changing the path this family took. You had your own brother killed, thinking you would take power from him and from *Tío* Enrique. All you did ensured we became the most powerful men in all the Western and Southern hemispheres. Thank you for that."

I can see Pablo's smirk. If I were Humberto, it would make me want to slap it off his face. It's the most patronizing expression I've ever seen. I wonder how much practice it took for him to do it so well. Or does it come naturally when you're second-in-command of the Diaz Cartel?

"You and your *tío* believe you've kept me locked away for decades. All you did was remove distractions. I've had plenty of time to plan this. I've bought the people I need, and they are loyal to me."

Pablo laughs as Humberto takes another step forward. The guards he didn't arrive with surround him. There are others on the outside of the wall who must have traveled with him. I watch as each of those men outside the wall collapse. I scan the screens, trying to find the sniper. I realize he's crouched on a platform to the left of the gate, allowing him to see over the wall.

It was shoot now, don't bother asking questions later.

The men who surround Humberto press him to move forward. Pablo doesn't lower his gun. He continues to aim directly at Humberto. The guards position themselves, so there's an easy line of sight for Pablo, but not enough room for Humberto to break free. It's not like he could. He's not in horrible shape for a man in his mid-eighties. He looks better than most men his age, but he's certainly no match for the men in their twenties and early thirties who surround him. He may act like the king of his castle, but he looks like nothing more than a peon here.

"What do you want, Humberto?"

"Florencia."

"And you came all the way here?"

"Don't bullshit me, Pablo. I know she's with you."

"And what makes you think that?"

"Because you didn't kill all the men watching her place. I know you carried her out and took her to the airfield. Now you're here."

"Do you see her with me?"

"You've got her hidden somewhere inside."

"Who says?"

"I saw you fucking the bitch on the lawn chair."

Mortified doesn't even begin to describe how I feel. Not only did he see us, it means all the men who were on the helicopter saw us too. They may be dead, but the guards here had it confirmed. If anyone doubted it or hadn't heard, they know now.

That pisses me off, but there's nothing I can do. Pablo shoots the ground between Humberto's feet, making him jump back. The guards behind him move enough so that he falls, landing hard on his ass and back.

Pablo strolls forward as though he has all the time in the world to continue their conversation. He says something far too quiet for the microphones on the security cameras to pick up. He kicks Humberto in the belly before he gestures for men to help the old man onto his feet. As Humberto stands, he's bent over. Pablo's fist shoots out and lands an uppercut that snaps Humberto's head back. It looks like he would've fallen over if not for the guards already holding him up.

Pablo spins on his heels and gestures over his shoulder for them to come. Blood covers Humberto's face. I suspect Pablo recalls I can see everything and perhaps there'll be a recording of all of this. He doesn't need Humberto's assassination caught on film to be used against him later. He heads toward what I believe are the guards' barracks. They go inside, disappearing from the cameras for a moment.

Then I see them move past rooms that have two beds in each. There's a kitchen similar to the one here in the panic room. Then there's a doorway that opens to a basement. Once the door closes behind all the men, there's little left for me to observe except for the other men patrolling the property. I watch men gather the bodies of the executed guards who betrayed the Diaz family.

I don't want to know what will become of them. My guess is they're destined for an incinerator, most likely. I'm sure any ash will soon be silt on a riverbed, but I don't need that confirmed. I'm left with nothing to do but wait as I look around.

My stomach growls. The sun's already setting, and I don't remember the last time I ate. I open cupboards and find various canned and packaged goods. There's a wide variety, all of which look surprisingly good. I settle for a cup of instant soup. It's hardly a delicacy, but it's quick and only requires water.

As it heats, I wonder what kind of person it makes me that I will happily have a meal while I know a man's being tortured near me. I have no qualms with what Pablo's likely doing, despite how I've always felt knowing my *abuelo* has done the same things. It's always revolted me to know he's a man who depends upon violence to get his way.

I have spent a lifetime feeling morally superior to him, even though I've known I could and would kill if I needed to. But I choose not to. I get my *abuelo* does these things to survive and to provide for the family. But there was the opportunity to leave the cartel life when he arranged for my father to marry Luciana. Yes, obviously that didn't work out, but I know *los Diaz* gave him another opportunity to get out. I suspect I wasn't told the full truth about why he didn't.

My family always told me *los Diaz* threatened our family with extinction if *Abuelo* submitted to them—which never made sense to me. He always fought to keep that from happening. He always made it sound like my father's family were rivals to *los Diaz*. I think it was machismo that refused to allow him to give in and made him decide to continue with a vendetta rather than make peace.

I don't know.

The microwave dings for the hot water, and it pulls me out of my musings. I pour it over the soup concentrate and stir before wandering to a rocker recliner. They set this place up for comfort, not just necessity.

How long do they expect someone to remain down here? Days? Weeks?

That's both terrifying and reassuring at the same time. It makes my stomach cramp.

I don't have my phone, so there's no doom scrolling the news or social media. There are books on the shelves, but I don't believe I can concentrate. I spy the remote for a TV mounted on a different wall from the security screens. If this room's powered by a generator, then perhaps they have satellite reception down here too.

Success!

I flip through the channels, having to choose between *telenovelas*, game shows, and football—soccer. I don't need the fabricated angst that goes along with the *novelas* when I feel enough in real life. If I watch a game show, the noise, flashing lights, and fake excitement will wear on my nerves. I settle for the football match. This I can handle.

Argentina versus Brazil. The Cain and Abel of the football world, except they've taken turns winning and losing for decades. It's the OG sibling—neighbor—rivalry in international sports.

I don't pay attention to the time as the first quarter moves into the first half, which ends with halftime. Then it's the third quarter, and the fourth quarter winds up pushing the second half into overtime. The final score is zero-zero. A perfect match.

I'll never understand sports in the States where someone can score two, or three, or even seven points, and games can wind up with scores over a hundred. One touchdown or one basket, one point. Either the ball crosses the line or goes in the basket one at a time, or it doesn't. Real football doesn't need to give extra points just because the shot comes from a distance. Though male football players are little bitches. They cry if someone taps their ankle. They'd never survive playing with their period.

My mind wanders now the game is over, and there's no sign of Pablo. I know Humberto's no threat and never really was. I know Pablo is the master of this domain. But I'm still worried that somehow something went wrong, and I can't see it. It makes me anxious as I switch to a game show I don't need to listen to, to know what's happening as the letters turn. It's less noisy than the other choices, but I still mute it. Trying to solve the puzzle keeps me occupied until the episode's done.

Movement on the security screens catches my attention. Pablo emerges from the basement alone. I doubt he wants me to see him as he is now, but I can't look away. There's blood splattered across him. It's on his hands, forearms, and chest. It soaks his shirt. It sprayed across his pants. He appears to be sweating as he ducks into a bathroom. A guy knocks and hands a stack of clothes to Pablo through the partially opened door.

When Pablo returns to the screen, he appears refreshed. Just as put together as he always does. He's in a suit now, and I assume the man who brought his clothes found it in a bedroom here in the house. From what I've heard, the men are all roughly the same size—huge. I never looked in Pablo's closet, but I bet the men in the family leave clothes here for this reason. He hands a bag to a different guard, and I'm certain it's his original clothes that'll get burned to leave no evidence.

I watch his movements across the yard and into the house shift across each screen until he's outside the door to the panic room. I hear it unseal. Then he's there. He walks in and opens his arms. I don't hesitate to rise and rush to him.

Chapter Eleven

Pablo

I hate leaving Flora alone in a place called a panic room. She appeared fine, and it's a comfortable space, but I worry about her getting bored. I worry about her wondering why we need such a well-stocked and furnished place. I worry she'll see something on the monitors I can't shield her from. However, she needs to know what's happening on the estate in case Humberto's arrival masked some genuine attack waiting to happen.

All the guards are on high alert without me saying anything. They all knew Humberto was aware of this location. He grew up coming here. However, he hasn't visited since before I was born, so nearly forty years ago. It's the first time he's been outside his walls in thirty-six years. It was supposed to be a life sentence.

But here we are.

I'm leading Humberto and a group of guards through the barracks down to our version of Madame Tussaud's Chamber of Horrors. It looks straight up medieval down here. Some of the shit down here dates back to when my *abuelo* was a child. Since it's rarely used, it's still in good shape. We've added other things over the decades to keep the place more modern than it looks.

"*Ponlo en el potro.*" Put him on the rack.

Medieval *and* effective.

I watch the men hoist a struggling old man onto the table then strap him on. It takes little effort on their part, but he's panting and sweating—more than he was as the men basically dragged him down here. I wouldn't have batted an eyelash if he'd tumbled down the fucking stairs since he flailed his arms and kept trying to yank free.

Dumbass.

Once he's attached to the table, I signal the men to leave. I retrieve a knife that's magnetically attached to the wall. I exaggerate my examination of the blade. I whirl around and slice across his belly. It's deep but not deadly. He howls as blood splatters my shirt and pants.

"You've been nothing but a shit stain for this family since you were born. Your father couldn't kill you even though you were worthless from the start. Your brother took pity on you. My *abuelo* gave you chances to prove yourself worthy of the family name. You proved you were always worthless. He looked out for you while you were both growing up. He protected you from my *tatarabuelo*." Great-grandfather.

I slash his left thigh.

From the stories I heard, my *abuelo* used to take the blame for shit Humberto did when they were growing up because he was always small for his age. He felt duty-bound to protect Humberto from their father's wrath because he wasn't a benevolent man. Perhaps it spoiled Humberto because he thought it entitled him to whatever he could get his hands on.

He tried to get his hands on my *chiquita.*

For that, I stab just below his right ribs. His blood sprays across my face. Disgusting but not unprecedented. I notice, but I don't bat an eye at it. Not the first nor the last time I've worn someone else's blood.

He wheezes as he continues to talk, not unaccustomed to pain and being forced to account for himself, even when he's bleeding.

"My brother was weak. Maybe he should have taken after our father more."

Benevolence is lost on me.

That's not the man life raised me to be. I was a lot like *Abuelo* was when I was younger. I took the blame for crap Juan did despite him treating me like shit. There was a year when we were the same height. He had a massive growth spurt early, so despite me being two years older than him, he caught up to me. Then I hit fifteen and filled out to nearly the size I am now. I knew I could never outright beat the shit out of him because my parents wouldn't forgive me, but I made sure I was the one who trained him to fight. He took a lot of punches he didn't need. I broke his nose once. Oops.

My strength and detachment didn't go unnoticed by *Tío* Enrique, *Tío* Matáis—Alejandro's father—or *Papá.* Alejandro's bigger than me now, but he's a couple years younger, so it wasn't until he turned seventeen that his shoulders broadened wider than mine. For years, I was the biggest of my generation. My size and ability to compartmentalize led me down the path to being our top enforcer. I've seen and done shit I could never have fathomed as a kid. But I do my duty.

I pick up a hammer and circle it through the air like a baseball player warming up. Then I toss it up and let it spin clockwise before catching it. I tap his left shin once as I walk toward his head.

"Weak like this?"

I bring the hammer down on his left kneecap. He howls.

"Or weak like this?"

I swing the hammer sideways and slam it into his pisiform —one of the two most fragile parts of the hand. It's the bone on the outside of the hand that's above the knobbly one at the bottom corner before the wrist starts. I ignore his wailing as I turn the tool around in my hand and bring the claw down on the flesh between the thumb and index finger. The other most sensitive part of the hand.

"Tell me what I want to know, and I'll kill you before I pour the acid on you and set you ablaze. Make me work for the information, and I'll inflict more pain than you imagined the human body could withstand."

He stares at me, and he knows nothing I say is exaggerated. He's heard of my reputation. So have I. It's understated if anything.

"*Bien.*" Fine.

"How did Domingo Aguilar wind up indebted to you?"

"I knew he liked to gamble. Usually, it was racing his cars, but he played some cards. He was in Monte Carlo when I was, and we chatted at a baccarat table."

"How very James Bond of you."

I loved playing as a kid because it was a simple game with two cards a player. Each one tries to get close to nine without going over. If the value is in the double digits, then you only count the second number. If it's sixteen, then only the six counts. My cousins and I would bet M&Ms. Our parents taught us various card games because we own casinos and run underground gambling rings. We visit places like Monte Carlo, where wealth and skill make you powerful.

"He was a talker when he drank too much. It took me hours to get him liquored up enough to share how badly his father needed him to marry my *sobrina*. His father picked a fight with Josue he couldn't win. He thought he could edge my brother out and take over Bogotá and eventually run Colombia. Fucking delusional." Niece.

"You conned him into thinking you could help his father get the information he needed to overthrow my *abuelo*. You were going to mutiny against your brother anyway. You never would've helped Ernesto Augilar."

He nods as best he can with a leather strap across his forehead. "I planned to do that, but the *cabrón* didn't trust me once he realized what he revealed. He left the card table and the casino to sober up."

"Jump to the part where he sells his soul to you." I'm getting restless.

"It was May, so we were both there for the Circuit de Monaco. People placed plenty of hefty bets on the Formula One race. Domingo and I championed different drivers. Once I knew that, I paid a member of the pit crew to deflate a tire during the last stop Domingo's favorite took. It blew only seconds before the finish line. We'd placed a massive wager between us because his driver was favored to win. He was certain he'd make a fortune. Instead, he lost it."

"You knew he couldn't pay."

"I knew neither he nor his father could pay. If he'd won, it would've been enough money to buy off half the officials in Bogotá and given Ernesto the power to oust Josue."

"You had the money, but you didn't want to dirty your hands by outwardly leading a coup against your brother. You also didn't want the power to go outside the family."

"Right. I went to Ernesto and said Domingo works for me or I kill him. He knew I took after my father more than Josue did."

That means I'm like Humberto. That makes me want to vomit. From his smirk, he knows what I'm thinking.

"I'd never betray the family, Humberto. We couldn't be more different."

It's the only consolation I have because thinking I'm anything like Humberto will fuck with my head.

"And fucking an Aguilar isn't a betrayal?"

"She's not her father or grandfather. You forced Domingo to spy for you because Ernesto arranged the marriage to *Tía* Luciana. It was supposed to give *los Aguilar* a senior position with my family while forcing them to bend the knee because Domingo had to work for *Abuelo*."

"It was working until Esteban Cardenas betrayed me."

"Betrayed you? Your eyes are brown because you're full of shit. He worked for *Abuelo* and was *Tío* Enrique's best friend after *Papá*. He infiltrated your network."

"Shit load of good it did any of you. Josue is dead. Esteban is dead."

"And you're the only one being tortured before you're dead. Why did Domingo's death matter enough to you to put a hit on *Tío* Esteban?"

"I told you, he betrayed me. He found me when I returned to—"

"Fled to."

"—New York City. He gave my whereabouts to Enrique, who had the feds pick me up. My lawyer couldn't keep them from extraditing me back to Colombia."

My *tío* and *Papá* had already torn through Colombia on their revenge tour. It took months to get Humberto back to Bogotá. In the meantime, *Tío* Esteban and *Tío* Matáis helped *Tío* Enrique and *Papá* run things down here when they had to be in New York. My *tíos* who still lived here arranged for the *Fiscalía General de la Nación* to hand Humberto over to *Tío*

Enrique. In English, it's the General Prosecutorial Office of the Nation or Attorney General.

Once Humberto was in Bogotá, he got "lost" in the system for a while—*Tío* Enrique sentenced him to house arrest for the rest of his life. The government was happy to see the end of a civil war within the ruling Cartel family—ours has always been *the Cartel*, and that's why people think to challenge us.

"You're lucky *Papá* and *Tío* Enrique are benevolent because you've been breathing for thirty-six years longer than you should've. Domingo's dead because he refused to take defeat as graciously as you did."

By graciously, I mean Humberto begged like a little bitch to live and cowered with his tail between his legs. He was decent at running the low-level street hustles and overseeing our local business. After *Tío* Matáis, *Tía* Catalina, and Alejandro moved to Queens, it was *Tío* Esteban who ensured Humberto followed orders. He still lived in Bogotá with *Tía* Luciana and *Tres J's*.

"Domingo's dead because he broke his promise. He wasn't the one who gave the information that allowed me to trap Josue and watch him die."

"You didn't even do that yourself. You didn't have the *huevos*, so you hired someone else."

Humberto shrugs but otherwise ignores my interjection. "Because he wasn't the one to give me what I needed, his debt remained unpaid. Domingo figured if Esteban hadn't wooed Luciana away, he would've gotten what he needed first. He was also pissed he couldn't fuck Luciana anymore. I guess she was a good lay."

"That's your *sobrina* you're talking about, you sick fuck."

I switch to a metal pipe and bring it down on his sternum. He wheezes for a moment before grunting.

"Domingo shot at Luciana while she was in the car, leaving the party where she chose Esteban over him. It was a bullet-proof vehicle, so Esteban didn't kill him. He drained his bank accounts instead. However, when he cornered Luciana one day and tried to force himself on her, he signed his death warrant. Esteban killed him. His debt to me was still there."

I consider what he hasn't told me as he rehashes history I already know. I let him speak since he loves to hear his own voice. Given the chance, he'll tell me what I want to know simply because he'll come up with more to say to keep the conversation going. He thinks it's buying him time to strategize an escape. No prisoner comes down here and leaves as anything besides ash.

"Ernesto paying you monthly wasn't enough recompense, was it?"

"Not once I discovered his granddaughter trained as a chemist in the States. She came back here because her mother had cancer a few years ago."

That's *not* something I wanted to have common with Flora.

"She trained to be a pharmacist instead because it gave her a less stressful job with more flexible hours to help her mother."

"You decided the debt wasn't about the money but the control. You forced Domingo to work for you, but you didn't get what you wanted out of that. Rather than continue to extort Ernesto, you insisted Florencia work for you. It was still trading information."

"You were always the smart one of your generation."

There isn't a man among my cousins and me who didn't attend an Ivy League or Top Tier university on merit. All the members of the Four Families earned their spots at the most competitive and rigorous universities in the States. No parents bribed their kids' way in with a massive donation or by being a legacy. We all understand the value of education and networking, so we made sure we had the best of the best.

"Except you'd made sure *los Aguilar* never paid off the

debt. You'd keep demanding more if you could. Ernesto decided to keep his money and sell his granddaughter to you."

"It was working out well."

"Was it, though? You didn't have the finished product. Florencia hadn't even brought you a big enough sample to offer a buyer. You don't know where the lab is, so you'd still need her if you wanted the product you paid her to create. The biggest problem you have now is that you'll be dead before dawn. Everything you smuggled and invested in trying to deal behind *Tío* Enrique's back was for nothing."

He remains quiet because he knows I'm right. We found out what he was doing, so *Tío* Enrique ran out of patience. My job was to come down here, find the labs, get the product and recipe, then kill Humberto. No one in my family will force Flora to reveal the location or formula because we won't intimidate her. I hope she volunteers it, but I won't manipulate her to get it.

"You never got over the idea that *Tío* Esteban betrayed you and that killing Domingo took your bloodhound from you. Why'd you wait so long to have *Tío* murdered?"

"The fucker was too hard to kill. I tried over and over, but he kept finding out my plans. Ernesto wanted revenge even more than me. He happily took my money and passed it along to the men who finally got your *tío*. As usual, my hands were clean if anything went wrong since I didn't hire anyone myself. I realized the only way I could get him was while *Tres J's* were nearby. The mercenaries knew not to hurt them because no women and children, but the threat was enough to make Esteban expose himself to protect his sons. He died thinking he was protecting them."

"If no women and children, then why'd you let men go after *Tía* Luciana and try to force her into remarrying? Try to assault her? Why let the street gangs you could've controlled attack *Tres J's?*"

"Nothing happened to them."

I flick open the knife I carry in my pocket while walking around to the other side of the table. I stab him in the shoulder.

"You sick fuck. You forced my cousins to kill to protect each other and themselves before they were even out of elementary school. You forced them to kill to protect their mother."

"I needed to know whether they'd make excellent soldiers one day. They do."

"They were never going to work for you!"

My temper is getting the better of me. But I know what my cousins endured living down here without a father. They have personas they developed once they moved to the States. They thought they needed them to protect themselves like they would've needed them down here. The other three families say they're psychopaths and other shit like that. We're *all* something like a sociopath since we commit crimes and do heinous shit without remorse, knowing we'll keep doing them.

But Javier is an introvert; Joaquin is shy; and Jorge has social anxiety. They'd all rather stay home than do anything else. That's what Humberto's plan did to them.

"They would've if Luciana married a man I chose. She would've had no choice but to let them if she wanted a peaceful home life with a man who treated her properly."

"You really are stupid as fuck. The moment any man tried to hurt her around her children or targeted her children, she would've killed him. She killed men to protect them. That's why they moved to New York. Besides, there's no chance in hell she'll ever remarry. She'll never move on from *Tío* Esteban. He was her soulmate. She'd never force a man to live with her husband's ghost in their marriage, and she'll never give another man room in her heart."

There's one more thing I want to know.

"You put a bounty on Florencia's head. Make your last words to the outside word a command to call it off."

"It's far too late for that. There's no way I can reach everyone who's heard about it. It's on the dark web. Any mercenary who knows how to access shit like that has seen it by now. There's nowhere you can take her that's safe. She'll spend the rest of her life looking over her shoulder. You can't protect her. You'll fail like your father and *tío* did protecting my brother. You'll fail like your father and *tío* did protecting Esteban. When you have to live with that, you'll know that in the end—even when I'm dead—I still won."

"All you've done is shut yourself out of the most powerful family in Latin America. You've spent *decades* in near solitary confinement rather than enjoying the freedom the rest of us have had. You ate the food my *tío* allowed. You slept in the bed my *tío* allowed. You breathed the air my *tío* allowed. Now you will die by the hand my *tío* allowed. You went after my woman."

"*Your* family and your soulmates." His voice drips with disgust.

"They are *my* family. You're not part of it."

I slice his throat from ear to ear, severing his jugular and carotid arteries. It geysers, splattering me. As it gurgles from his mouth and dribbles down his chin, his eyes dim. I lean in close, so the very last sound he hears—besides his own spluttering—is my voice.

"That's why I feel no guilt killing you. You stopped being a Diaz the day you plotted my *abuelo's* death."

"Is it done?"

"Not yet, *chiquita*."

Not the response Flora wanted.

She burrows against my chest, and my arms tighten around her. I rub her back as I kiss the top of her head. I practically scrubbed myself raw in the barracks' shower. I craved feeling my *chica* in my arms, but I wouldn't go near her without being sure nothing lingered to remind her of what I did. If she was watching the security screens, then I'm certain she saw how I came out of the basement. Seeing it on a monitor is far different from seeing someone else's blood on a person you want to touch. As secure as this home is, I don't need to leave any trace evidence either.

"Are we still safe here?"

"Yes, because no one else can find this place. I spoke to the head of security at Humberto's estate. Apparently, he bribed some state official to use his private helicopter. The men who accompanied him weren't our guards, but men on loan. It's why we didn't question them."

Before we killed them.

"But he still left the estate. Did he tell anyone where he was going?"

"Our team leader said the helicopter arrived unexpectedly, tore up half the garden, and barely touched down before Humberto ran out. The guard had never seen Humberto move that fast, and the guard started working for *Tío* Enrique when he was in his twenties and is now in his fifties. As far as we've determined, no one on the inside helped him. It's an ongoing investigation."

In other words, we haven't finished interrogating every guy who works on the estate. If we find anyone helped Humberto, the guy will pay for his crimes just like the others did. Whoever the official was is now on the short list for a death march.

"Could he have told the man he borrowed the helicopter from where he was going?"

"Possibly. The only way they found the compound was from Humberto telling the pilot where to go. We run signal and radar jammers around the clock. The property doesn't exist as far as any local or national records show. But there's the slim chance, so we need to leave."

"New York?"

"Definitely not. Humberto ran many things down here for us, so he has connections around the world. He ran New York while my *tío* and father were in boarding school, then university. Since his banishment, *Tío* Enrique's given him specific tasks to oversee several parts of our day-to-day business. It was the condition of his house arrest. He knew if he didn't remain useful, there was no reason to keep him around. He told your *abuelo* he'd forgive the debt in exchange for you. He believed you working for him would give him a leg up over us by undercutting our sales. If he could do that, he thought he could outmaneuver us. He realized this last stunt—especially involving you—made him redundant now."

Redundancy. The excuse corporations use to lay off people.

Here, it meant Humberto's death regardless of the hit. That just confirmed there was no way for him to escape the inevitable. Flora's probably wondering what information I got from Humberto before he died. I made a couple calls before I left the barracks and learned more than what Humberto confessed. I can't tell her it was more than just about her family. I consider sharing the full extent of her *abuelo's* involvement.

"Pablo, please tell me what you learned about my family."

Chapter Twelve

Flora

That's been a lot of shit to take in. I haven't forgotten the part where Pablo said we need to leave but didn't say where we're going. But my burning need to understand my family history feels more dire. I trust Pablo to know where to take me and when to leave.

He guides me to the sofa and eases me onto his lap. I kick off my shoes and curl against him.

"I hate how you feel you need to shrink into a ball to feel safe, *chiquita*."

"No. I just like feeling you wrapped around me."

"Because you're scared and need a shield."

"Not a shield, *Papí*. You."

He nudges my chin up, and our gazes lock. I want to believe there's something between us that'll last beyond this emergency. That the feelings we have aren't adrenaline and cortisol pumping through us from fear. It's not like we've been in a state of fight or flight all day. We enjoyed each other's company by the pool. We thought we'd have time to get to know each other here. But this is certainly an extraordinary situation where our emotions are running high. I'm insanely attracted to him and have been since the moment I saw him. But, normally, I wouldn't have had sex with him so soon.

It's not like I fucked him because I seized the opportunity, fearing there'd never be another chance. I didn't do it as a distraction, either. I did it because it felt right because I trust him about most things. Even that's a result, though, of this extreme situation. I don't trust easily. I certainly wouldn't trust any other man from a cartel—especially not from *the Cartel*—so easily. But Pablo's a loadstone. I'm drawn to him, and I can't—won't—fight it. He's my compass through all of this, and I'm depending on him for that. But necessity didn't guarantee I'd like him or be attracted to him. That's entirely separate.

"Little one, I'll be your shield whenever you need me."

He says he wants something long-term. That he could've stayed detached, helping me out of honor and duty. I recognize he could manipulate me, spewing lies to build my trust. He could've taken advantage of me and gotten me to fuck him because he had nothing better to do. But down to my very core, I know he isn't that man. Despite everything I've heard about *los Diaz*, I sense honor, loyalty, and duty drive his every decision.

"I wish I could offer you the same, Pablo."

"You don't see it, but you do."

I sit up and twist to look at him more easily. "How?"

"When you challenge me, you spark excitement in me. Very rarely do I feel that anymore. It's usually dread. When we're together like this, even though the world around us is trying to fuck us over, you bring me peace. It feels like I never get to relax anymore. Even when I'm away from work, I'm thinking about some obligation or duty I have. Some meeting coming up or email I need to send. Someone I have to visit, or some deal I need to create. Our situation is ever-present, so it's not like I forget why we're here. But when you're touching me, I'm calmer as I plan. So, you shield me from the outside world in your own way."

His expression and tone are so earnest, and he's letting himself be vulnerable around me. He knows I could manipulate him or at least try. But he's opening up to me. It's not calculated. He wants me to trust him by showing he trusts me. I think he senses the same things I do.

My left hand rests against his jaw by his ear, my thumb sweeping over his cheekbone then his stubble. It wouldn't surprise me if he could grow a full beard in like two days. He's not hairy all over, but he has a definite five o'clock shadow when he was clean shaven earlier today. It's rugged and manly. I love it.

I lean forward, but I don't bring my lips to his. I offer the kiss, but I'll let him lead. I want him to. He may have commanded what happened in that basement, but he couldn't control Humberto showing up. He can't dictate what could happen next in this fucked-up situation. I can let him control what we're doing.

"Do you want me to kiss you, *chiquita?*"

His whispered words brush across my lips. He must have had a mint on the way to me. The scent fills my nose, and I can practically taste it.

"*Sí, Papi.*"

I haven't forgotten what I called him before he left. We speak Spanish together, but we're both fluent English speakers. With no father to speak Spanish or English to, I've never used that word before in my life.

"Who does your body belong to now?"

I blink for a moment longer than usual as I brace myself.

"You, Daddy."

I grasp his shoulders and cling to him as he lurches upward enough to flip us. I'm on my back as his weight presses against me. His lips crash onto mine, and his kiss threatens to inhale me. He's hard as fucking stone beneath his trousers. He thrusts against me, and I want nothing more than to strip while he does the same. I want him inside me again. It's been nearly two hours since he pumped me full of his cum. I want more.

"That's right, *chiquita*. I'm going to make your body ache for my cock. Fucking you is the only relief that'll satisfy you."

"I already ache."

My pussy feels painfully empty after having Pablo inside me. I'm so aroused I can barely keep from writhing beneath him, trying to get more pressure from his cock against my clit and opening. I want him to fill me again.

"And if I want an appetizer before my main course?"

"You wouldn't be that greedy, Daddy. Not unless you'd let me have an appetizer too."

I cock an eyebrow and reach between us to rub my hand over his dick. I open my mouth before running my tongue over my top lip.

"Make an offer like that again, and I'll fuck your mouth and come down your throat."

"And if I want to suck you off instead?"

"I thought you wanted to give me control. That doesn't sound like an offer, but a challenge." He sits back on his knees before standing. "Strip."

I watch him for an instant before I rise and follow his command. Once I'm naked, he catches my wrist and pulls me around the side of the couch, positioning himself behind me. His hand between my shoulder blades pushes me to bend over. He's still holding my wrist, so he lifts my bent arm to rest against my lower back. He positions the other arm the same way, holding both wrists in one hand. He shifts, and his hand comes down on my ass. Hard.

"Fuck!"

"Subs don't give orders. They follow them. My little sub says, 'Yes, Daddy' or '*Sí, Papí*.' She doesn't tell me what she's going to do instead, even if she poses it as a question."

He spanked me throughout that, but he punctuates it with a particularly hard one across my horizontal crack. I stomp my feet, but I don't fight him. I relish what he's doing. I haven't forgotten about needing to leave or about wanting to know more about my family. This is calming me because it distracts me from my fears.

"I want you to fuck my mouth, Daddy. I want your hands in my hair as you shove your cock down my throat."

I'm not convinced I can take all of him, but I'll sure as shit try.

"Your cunt is glistening, *chiquita*. It was when you bent over, but now you're nearly dripping. You're enjoying this punishment too much."

"It hurts! That's not en—"

"Don't finish that sentence. We both know you're enjoying receiving this as much as I'm enjoying giving it."

We're both getting more and more aroused because this isn't a proper punishment. My suggestion was a challenge on purpose. I wanted to provoke a response, and I'm happy with the one I got. I love the feel of his hand on my ass.

"Keep your hands where they are."

I hear him unbuckle his belt and unzip his pants. The head of his cock nudges my pussy before his hands grip my hips. He surges into me until he's balls deep. He slides in and out, but he's not thrusting like I want. When he pulls out with a grunt, and then spreads my ass cheeks, I realize he's using my cream as lube.

"What's your safe word, Flora?"

I've just used colors in the past. I don't want to do that with Pablo. I want something different. Something specific to us.

"*Rios*." Rivers.

Pablo was nudging my asshole with the tip of his cock, but he pauses. He leans over me and kisses my shoulder.

"Because of where we are?"

"Yes, Daddy."

He nips at my shoulder, his teeth grazing my skin.

"Lean farther forward."

I'm unprepared to feel his lips on my ass cheek as he sucks. It's the first time he's marking me. He thrusts into my pussy, coating himself again. Then he's easing into my ass.

"Safe word if it's too painful, Flora. Don't take more than you can."

I exhale a whistling breath, then I feel him withdrawing. I reach around before clutching his wrist.

"Don't stop. That was nothing more than me breathing. I was focusing on relaxing to make it easier for you to enter me more. I want this, Pablo."

I use his name, knowing what I risk since we're in our D/s dynamic right now. But I want him to know how serious I am. He squeezes the unmarked ass cheek hard enough to leave fingerprints and to make me dance onto my toes. It allows him to slide in farther. He could be rougher, pressing forward harder and faster. Instead, he's slow and gentle. He's sworn not to harm me, and he means it. He could fully dominate me by pleasuring just himself and using my tight ass to get himself off, leaving my clit ignored.

"*Chica*, you're so fucking tight. *Fuck!*"

He reaches around and rubs my clit. I didn't expect to get off. I widen my feet and turn them inward, making it easier for him to bottom out inside me. He wraps his other arm around my waist. I reach down and place my hand on his forearm while my other hand on the sofa cushions braces me. He slides his arm back, so I can lace my fingers with his over my belly. I might take it in the ass, but there's something poignant about what's happening.

We move in silence as we both race to get off. We move together as though we've been fucking each other for years. We're in sync in a way I haven't been so soon after starting a relationship with past partners. I don't know if it's the same for him, but he's definitely the best I've ever been with.

"*Chica.*"

"*Sí, Papí?*"

He kisses my shoulder. I don't think he has more to say. He just wanted to hear the name he calls me. I love that. It feels special. He wanted to hear a name I call him.

"Fuck, Daddy. May I come?" My orgasm's about to seize me, and I may not be able to stop it.

"Yes, baby girl. I'm close too."

My back arches as I tense. My ass clenches without my thinking about it. Pablo holds me against his body as I shudder. The moment I relax, he withdraws and spins me around. He jerks himself off until his cum sprays across my belly. I lean back, pushing my tits up and out. A few jets of cum land on them while the rest sprays my middle. We both stare where he marked me like he promised earlier.

He wraps his arm around me again, bringing my body flush to his. Our kiss is slow and tender despite how we just had sex.

"You're mine, Flora."

I gaze into his eyes, and I don't know if I should read more into that.

"You've claimed my body."

"Now I'll claim your heart."

His declaration surprises me, but it warms me from the

inside out. My hands rested on his upper arms as he hugged me. Now I slide them up and wrap my arms around his neck. I observe him for a moment.

"Do I get more than your dick?"

"All that I can give you."

It's a veiled reminder that the Cartel will always get a part of him. More of him than I will.

He holds me in place as his thumb and forefinger lock around my chin.

"You will get more of me than the Cartel if you want it, Flora."

"Are you a mind reader?"

He stares at me. I won't get an answer aloud. The silent one tells me he's learned to read people because of his work. That's a part that belongs to the Cartel.

"You know the man I am, little one. It was never my choice. I do what I must. That won't change, and I don't want it to. I serve my family and the people who depend on us. But that's not all of me anymore. Not now that I know you."

"But I can't compete with the Cartel."

"You don't have to. The part of me that belongs to the Cartel is the monster in me. It's a part I never want near you. It's the part I'll never want to share with you."

I nod as best I can. He'd say that to any woman he was with. It's not because it's me.

"*Chica*, there's never been another woman. I've dated in the past—you're likely to meet an ex-girlfriend because she married into the bratva. But I knew from the start it would never become something serious. I was in a fucked-up love quadrangle with an O'Rourke when we were in college. We dated the same women for the same reason they dated us. It was a power move. I had no emotional connection to either of them any more than they had to me or the O'Rourke jackass. I've never offered these parts of myself to someone else."

"Do you know what I'm thinking because you were trained to read people?"

I guess I'm not leaving that alone after all.

"I can read you because it's the same thing I'd wonder if I were in your shoes. It's what I want to share. I don't know how you'll feel about me when this shitshow is over. Maybe this is Stockholm Syndrome for you. But I know what I feel for you is entirely different from anything in my past."

He kidnapped me, but I went mostly willingly. He's distracted me with sex, and I've given him control of more than just my body. It's kept me from panicking. And I've enjoyed the fuck out of it. I trust him now, and I'll pick him over just about anyone and anything.

Fucking hell.

It might be the fastest case of Stockholm Syndrome ever.

But I don't think so. I think it's far more than that. I think it's fate. Sometimes you get lucky, and you just know you've met the right person. It could just be a close friendship in the making. Or it could be your soulmate. I won't go so far as to believe Pablo is mine, but maybe he is. I want to find out.

"I don't recognize these feelings either, Daddy. I've dated in the past. I've had some serious relationships, and I lived with a guy once. It lasted five years after college. But something held me back. When he proposed, 'No' flew out of my mouth before I gave it any thought. It just wasn't right. Maybe it was because he wasn't you."

He grimaced when I said I lived with another guy and that he proposed. It tells him I've been in love before. His confessions tell me he's never felt that for someone else. I think I loved the idea of being in love and of being loved more than I actually did my ex-boyfriend.

Maybe I had Daddy issues back then. But that's not what I feel now. I haven't been lonely like I was back then. I haven't felt like I was missing out by not being in a relationship. Thinking about not being with Pablo feels like a gaping hole will open and consume my heart.

I draw my hand down his chest and slide my fingers under his shirt. They surround the button like a *Star Trek* greeting. I rest my cheek against his chest; my bare chest pressed to his covered one.

"Daddy, it's not Stockholm Syndrome."

I won't say it's love because we don't know each other well enough. But maybe it could be.

"*Chiquita*, before you decide anything, I need to tell you what's going to happen to your *abuelo*."

Chapter Thirteen

Pablo

"Part of me knew Humberto would follow us. It's not that I wanted to jeopardize our safety. But it lured him from Bogotá and prevented any allies from helping him. I knew he'd be selective about who he brought with him because as much as he wanted to find us, he wouldn't want to violate the sanctuary of this place. Since he intended to take it over, he'd want to maintain the privacy here so no one could find him any more easily than someone besides him found us."

She steps back so she can see me as we talk. "You banked on the fact he wouldn't bring an army with him."

"*Chiquita*, he had no army. If he ever had, he wouldn't have spent thirty-six years under house arrest. He would've mutinied if he could. This was a small-scale attack."

"But he had to know if he killed you, then your family would retaliate. He knew he'd never see his power without killing your uncle and everyone else first."

"We both know that, but he's never been a reasonable man

of sound mind. He proved that when he thought he could kill his brother and both his nephews, or that he could subjugate *Papá* and *Tío* Enrique into working for him. *Papá* and *Tío* Enrique were born before my *abuelo* took control. He and my *abuela* married while they were in college. *Tío* Enrique came along the year after my *abuela* and *abuelito* married. They'd graduated a month earlier. Two years after that *Papá* was born. *Tío* Enrique was six, and *Papá* was four when my *abuelo* took control."

It makes me think about how I came to be heir. *Tío* was married before *Tía* Elle. He married for the first time when I was entering college. It was political and a disaster. We all heaved a massive sigh of relief when he divorced the lying, cheating bitch. We assumed he wouldn't remarry, which meant he wouldn't have children. But that's not part of the story Flora needs right now, so I continue with what I was saying.

"*Abuelo* had an heir before he assumed his role as *jefe de jefes*. *Tío* Enrique may have only been in kindergarten, but his future was set. *Papá* was a preschooler, so no direct threat to Humberto at the time, but he still existed. It pushed Humberto down to third in line when *Abuelo* assumed his position. Humberto knew *Abuelo* was far too powerful from the beginning. It's why it took him twenty years to succeed. He had to amass a small fortune to pay all the people involved in my *abuelo's* murder."

"And you don't think he's done that again? That he hasn't been saving money to attack you and your family now?"

I shake my head. I'm prepared to share some of my family history since she'll learn it anyway if she becomes part of it. However, I'm still cautious about what I say since she's not officially one of us yet.

"When Humberto encouraged your father to make his first move against *Abuelo*, he failed. *Tía* Luciana left a party with

Tío Esteban. She chose him, and it infuriated your father to watch them drive away. Domingo shot at the car, knowing the bullet wouldn't penetrate, but he did it to make a point. *Tío* Esteban obeyed *Tío* Enrique's order not to kill him. He still served a purpose. However, *Tía* Luciana wasn't safe. *Tío* Esteban couldn't ignore that, so he drained Domingo's accounts and would've hospitalized him for two months if *Tío* Enrique had allowed Domingo to go to one. Instead, he had doctors who visited and nurses who worked around the clock since he was in a coma for half that time. When Domingo refused to take the hint and targeted *Tía* Luciana again, *Tío* Enrique sanctioned *Tío* Esteban's revenge."

"That's when my father died."

"Yes."

I feel no remorse admitting that to her, but it's still unpleasant.

"Pablo, he tried to rape a woman. He's lucky all Esteban did was kill him."

Our gazes lock, and her mouth drops open.

"Oh."

She exhales the word.

"My *tío* did far more than just kill Domingo. He made sure the *pedazo de mierda* knew why he was dying. He made sure Domingo understood exactly how it would feel to do what he intended to *Tía* Luciana."

She flinches, but she doesn't turn away in disgust or anger.

"Pablo, I understand the men in our world live a violent life and usually die a violent death. Very few make it to old age."

As she watches me, she licks her top lip before she continues. In another situation, that would be sexy as hell, but I know her mouth has gotten dry from this uncomfortable conversation.

"My *abuelo* is older than most, but he won't live to a ripe old age and die of natural causes, will he?"

"That's still to be determined. *Chica*, I spoke to *Tío* Enrique before I came out of the barracks. It was while I was getting dressed."

"So, in the bathroom where the security cameras couldn't record you."

"Yes."

"What did Enrique say?"

"For now, your grandfather lives, but it's only by *Tío* Enrique's grace that he does. Ernesto could've done far more to protect you, little one, but he didn't. He could've sent you away the moment Humberto came sniffing around, but he didn't. He could've had guards at your place to ensure you got home safely every night. His guards would've prevented mercenaries from staking out your building. I wouldn't have gotten in so easily."

"But you would have anyway."

I nod. She knows nothing would've stopped me since I was on a mission. But it might not have felt so urgent if she'd had guards.

"You said you went to the lab alone. Your *abuelo* allowed that. He didn't send guards with you and didn't insist Humberto did either."

"Humberto wanted to keep that location secure."

"That just proves neither Humberto nor Ernesto had men they entirely trust. They both knew the risk to sending any other men because those men might've revealed their secrets. They might've gone to *Tío* Enrique or sold that information to someone else. That Humberto didn't have that kind of loyalty is unsurprising, but your grandfather should've."

Flora's taking in everything I'm saying, and she knows it's the truth.

"Deep down, Ernesto knows he's not as powerful as he

projects. He could've negotiated terms with Humberto that limited your time. We've said he indentured you to Humberto, but that's not true. Indenture has a fixed time period or an amount that the person must earn to be released. Your service was indefinite."

I certainly won't say Humberto enslaved her, but her grandfather sold her to Humberto in no uncertain terms.

"*Chiquita*, I know you didn't trust my family. It makes sense considering no one gave you the full story of your father's role in harming mine. Yours told you a warped version of the truth. However, Ernesto knew he could've gone to *Tío* Enrique. He could've scheduled a meeting with *Papá* or Alejandro one of the many times they've been down here. It meant humbling himself, but he knew *Tío* Enrique would've helped you. Not to thwart Humberto, but because women and children aren't supposed to be caught in the middle of this. Ernesto didn't care about you enough to do that."

She listens to everything I say. She's crushed by the realization of how neglectful her *abuelo* has been. It was intentional neglect—dereliction of duty in my mind.

"*Chiquita*, I'm certain by now your grandfather knows you're with me, even if he doesn't know where we are."

"Wait, would Humberto have told my *abuelo* where we went?"

"No, definitely not. Your *abuelo* is the last person Humberto wanted to know about this secret compound. *Chiquita*, your *abuelo* hasn't called *Tío* Enrique. Not to demand where I brought you or to ask for help."

"Maybe he doesn't trust Enrique to help him. Maybe he's searching for me on his own."

I can't help the sadness I feel as I shake my head again. I don't want to say—and she doesn't want to hear me admit—her *abuelo's* done nothing to find her. Instead, I draw her back into my arms and hold her tighter.

"Your *abuelo* will live as long as he serves as a vassal to *Tío* Enrique. If he's uncooperative or refuses to pledge his fealty, then he's outlived his purpose."

"Fuck, Pablo, that sounds so goddamn medieval."

If only she knew what lurked beneath the barracks. If she understood the true nature of a cartel, she'd know it's a fiefdom where *Tío* Enrique is the king. My cousins and I are the princes below him, and those who serve us do so at our will. They pledge their loyalty to *Tío* Enrique as vassals. They have men beneath them, but they all ultimately owe their lives to *Tío* Enrique.

"*Chica*, you may not know all the inner workings of how cartels operate, but your *abuelo* certainly does. The reason your family became tied to mine was because your *abuelo* thought he could oust mine. He started a war he could never win. The ceasefire came when our *abuelos* agreed to marry their children to each other. It was never a truce because neither of our *abuelos* trusted each other to maintain peace."

"Once your *abuelo* died, why didn't mine try to take over during the transition?"

"Because *Tío* Enrique and *Papá* arrived here and wreaked havoc for two months straight. There are buildings that're still in rubble because my family owns that land now. They're a reminder to anyone who thinks of rising against us. They practically wiped out every other cartel. Not only in Colombia, but Brazil, Bolivia, and Paraguay."

"The countries that supply you. The ones who could stand in the *jefe de jefes'* way."

"That's right. The boss of bosses isn't just the leader of the strongest cartel in a single country. He is the ultimate boss of every cartel in Latin America. It doesn't matter what country it is. Every other *jefe* knows they answer to him if they step out of line. He can call upon any of them and expect them to answer."

It's that medieval fiefdom at work.

"My *abuelo* didn't want to submit to your *abuelo*. I'm the collateral damage three and a half decades later."

"I don't enjoy agreeing with you, *chica*, but that's right."

She remains quiet as she digests all I've shared.

I decided I'm taking her to Switzerland. We have a mountain property even more isolated than this one. It may be summer in South America, but it's the middle of winter in the Northern Hemisphere. It will be an arduous journey to the property. More than just a plane ride. *Tío* Enrique assured me the weather has been severe enough to keep most people away. She'll discover just what wealth and power can buy us.

"I'll call Daniel to bring over a meal. You must be starving, little one."

We're standing together in the kitchen. Each of us has a soda we discovered we enjoy more than any other. It's sugar-free, so I don't feel guilty about extra carbs. Not that I ever do, considering I work out twice a day most days of the week. I can consume nearly thirty-five hundred to four thousand calories a day. I'd wither away if I didn't eat that much.

"His wife is a similar size to you, so I'll ask her to bring some clothes for you."

"No, Pablo, I won't take from a villager here."

I know what she assumes, since this is a lower socioeconomic area in Colombia because of its remoteness. But it is an agricultural area, so people are comfortable. However, that's not Daniel and his wife's situation.

"They're distantly related to *Papá's* side of the family.

Daniel's worked for us since he was eighteen. *Tío* Enrique put him through culinary school in France. This man is trilingual. He was *Tío's* personal chef for years in the States. However, he and his wife, Esmeralda, prefer the quiet here, so they asked to be reassigned. It's not that he wanted to work less. He and Esme never had children because she couldn't carry a pregnancy all the way through. They prefer to be on their own more than to have watched my ever-expanding family. It's been thirty-two years since a baby was born into my family. However, our size was a constant reminder to them. They're financially far more than just comfortable. Same thing for his brother who's our housekeeper. They're the only family they have except for their wives. They wanted to live in the same town, so David and his wife moved here too."

Her expression shows she no longer feels guilty. She nods and even smiles.

"Where are we going next?"

I want to tell her, but something makes me hesitate. It's not a lack of trust in her, but the flash of hurt across her face tells me that's what she thinks.

"*Chiquita*, it's not like I believe you're going to run off and call your *abuelo* somehow or send a message by carrier pigeon or Morse code. It's more about your safety and ensuring there's no way this could leak."

"Do you believe this house isn't secure? Like someone could hear us talking?"

"No, but the less you know, the less you can share if something goes wrong."

That makes her shiver. I know she doesn't want to think of us being attacked on our way to our next destination, but I won't rule out the possibility.

"It'll be a long flight. That's as much as I'll tell you."

We move into the living room and turn on a movie while

we wait for Daniel to arrive. Neither of us is truly paying attention, but it's a distraction as she sits curled next to me with my arm around her. She strokes my chest as I stroke her hair. It's soothing to both of us. It takes only an hour before someone knocks on the door. I rise and check the security camera, already knowing it must be Daniel. The guards wouldn't allow anyone else on the property without asking me first.

He comes in, and I introduce him to Flora. She didn't expect him to be a man in his late fifties. Too much time outside in the Colombian sun has weathered his kind face. He's a man who would've made an excellent father or *abuelo* to a passel of kids, but that's not what life planned for him. However, he sets Flora at ease, and they chat about the region. He fills her in more on the biodiversity of the area. I suppose it speaks to the scientist in her and why she appears to like this area as much as I do. When she sat by the pool earlier, I could tell she enjoyed the landscape.

It doesn't take us long to finish the meal, and now that she has fresh clothes, we take a shower together. It could've been much faster, but we got distracted. I could get used to this kind of distraction.

"*Chiquita*, we'll leave in the morning. Everything will be arranged for us. The best thing we can do is get a good night's sleep before we travel. Tomorrow's going to be a long day."

I fold back the covers on my bed. I offered her a separate room earlier today, but I never expected her to use it. It was a courtesy more than anything else. She and I both know that now. We curl up together much like we did on the sofa. I lie on my back, and she's on her side, her head resting on my shoulder, her arm draped across my waist, hand pressed against my ribs as though to keep me close.

My arm drapes across her back while the other hand strokes her hip. It's not long before she's breathing deeper, and I feel her twitch twice before she's asleep. I don't let myself drift off because I'm waiting for a call. It's nearly midnight before it comes. I ease my arm out from beneath her and slip out of the bedroom. I head down to the office.

I'm certain if she wakes, she'll know that's where I've gone. If I were headed anywhere else, I would've woken her to tell her. I trust she won't come near the room since I warned her against it.

Chapter Fourteen

Pablo

"*Papá?*" I keep my voice low as I walk down the stairs to the first floor.

"*Sí, mijo.* How're you doing?" Yes, my son.

"I'm all right. Better than what's left of Humberto."

A couple of armed men incinerated him, and the ash has joined the silt on the bed of the Le River.

"Alejandro and I are in Bogotá. We took off as soon as we found out you left."

My cousin makes so many trips between Colombia and the States that he has his own private jet. It's his second since that motherfucker, Carmine Mancinelli, fucked around with Alejandro's first one. Alejandro's not the only one who enjoys expensive toys. Carmine lost six race cars he owns, two NASCAR and four Formula One. Too bad, so sad for his teams that went without vehicles until he could replace them.

I used our family jet to get down here and to fly Flora to this estate. *Papá* traveled with Alejandro.

"Do you know where you'll start?"

I'm certain *Papá* and Alejandro already have a plan. They're calling to share it with me rather than to ask whether I want their help. They know the answer to that without asking.

Of course, I do. I'll take any help that means I can keep Flora safer.

"Alejandro will investigate who conspired with Humberto. He'll find out who in the government thought they had more power than your *tío*."

Find out who had the death wish. My cousin will not only find out who it was, he'll dispose of them as well. If more than one person was involved, Alejandro won't disclose the secret of why he punished those men. But he'll make an example of them, so others don't make the same mistake they did.

"What about you, *Papá*?"

"I will check into *la alcantarilla*." The sewer.

He names the worst penitentiary in Colombia. It houses the most violent criminals. Ones who are there for life without any possibility of parole. My father comes and goes from these prisons like he's racking up points at a Hilton or Marriott. There are plenty of prison wardens and guards who could retire any time now and live a comfortable life, never working another day.

It's a dangerous role, but he's had it since he was in his twenties. It's how he earned the name *el Espíritu Santo*. He slips in anywhere and delivers *Tío* Enrique's message as though it were being handed down from above. Most men know if he seeks them out, they will "shuffle off this mortal coil"—Shakespeare had such a turn of phrase. They're just more likely to go down than up.

He'll find out which mercenaries were a part of this. The men who lead the street gangs will know what's going on since some of them will have been foolish enough to send members after Flora. It wouldn't be any gang member who succeeded, but rather some professional mercenary. Men will try if they think the money is right, and they're desperate enough either for a cash payout or to improve their reputation as merciless killers.

"When will you take off?" *Papá's* voice draws me back to the present and away from my wandering ruminations.

"I'll let her sleep for another couple of hours, but we'll leave well before dawn. I don't want there to be any possibility someone sees us take off or recognizes our plane."

"Is the jet fueled?"

"Yes. I made sure it was as soon as we arrived in case we needed to turn around and leave abruptly."

"Good. Stay in touch, Pablo. Don't make your *mamá* and me worry."

"I know, *Papá*."

We rarely talk about Juan anymore. It still causes my parents deep-seated pain to think about him or hear his name. They accept his fate and know I took no pleasure in my role. Neither of them blames *Tío* Enrique either. Juan lived by the sword and died by the sword. He made his choices. I did what I could to get him away from New York when *Tío* banished him, but it left him vulnerable to make more shitty decisions.

Once he came back to NYC on his own, he put himself back on Maksim Kutsenko's radar. If he'd just stayed away and accepted the support *Tío* Enrique and I offered him, then perhaps he would've remained exiled rather than dead. But ever since that disaster, *Mamá* and *Papá* worry about me even more than they did before. Not because they believe I'll fuck up. They don't want to lose another son.

None of what happened was a secret kept from *Mamá*. She came from a cartel family, just like Domingo's. They thought they could rival *los Diaz*. They discovered how wrong they were. *Papá's* and *Mamá's* fathers arranged their marriage. I know my *abuelo* and *abuela* learned as much about *Mamá* as they could before they even introduced my parents.

Their situation differed from *Tía* Luciana and Domingo's. It's unfortunate they couldn't pick *Tía* Luciana's soulmate from the beginning like they did for *Papá*. But *Tía* Luciana wound up with the man destiny meant for her.

Papá and *Mamá* fell in love almost immediately. It took them a while to get to know each other, but much like Flora and I share an instant mutual attraction, the same was true for them. Except they were already married when they discovered how much they wanted their futures to blend.

I hope Flora and I can be soulmates like my parents are and that we can have a future like the one my parents have built. We just need to survive.

"*Papá*, I'll check in with you when we get to the house."

"Check in mid-flight, Pablo."

"*Sí, Papá.*"

It's not like I have to call every couple of hours to let my family know I'm okay. But it's a courtesy that we always check in when we're traveling, especially in a situation like this where there's more danger than usual.

"*Papá*, I need to go. I don't want Flora to wake up and wonder where I am."

I wince as I realize what I just admitted. It's not like my parents believe I'm a virgin. It wouldn't surprise me if they knew I belong to a BDSM club. They probably know all my cousins and I do. Even my brother did.

However, that's different from basically confessing to your parents that you're sleeping with a woman. If we were good Catholics, it would be even more uncomfortable since Flora and I aren't married. But that's the least of my concerns.

"Take care of her, *mijo*. It sounds like she's someone special."

"*Papá*, she is."

Silence rests between us for a moment, and I know he understands. I believe Flora's the one. I don't have to say it. He already figured it out since I'm going to such extremes to protect her. It's not like I would've washed my hands of her if I weren't attracted to her and thought she might be my future. But he knows my various tones, so he understands what I'm not saying.

"*Te quiero, mijo.*" I love you, son.

"*Te quiero, Papá.*" I love you, Papa.

We hang up, and I make my way back up to the bedroom. I slip into bed beside Flora after I set my alarm for two hours from now. It goes off entirely too soon.

"*Chiquita.*" I kiss her cheek and give her a gentle shake. "*Chica.*"

"Daddy?"

Her sleepy voice shoots lust straight to my cock. When her eyes flutter open, her groggy look is the most beautiful thing I've ever seen. I watch her come alert enough to realize what's going on. We sit up together, and she looks toward the window before looking back at me in fear. I shake my head and tuck hair behind her ear.

"It's all right, *chica*. Nothing's happening, but we need to leave."

"Now? In the middle of the night?"

"Yes, it's safer for us than when the sun's up."

"Will you please tell me where we're going?"

"Switzerland."

It's not against my better judgment to tell her like I thought it would be earlier. It's not that my fear that something could go wrong is gone, but I understand how out of control she feels about this entire situation. She's placed her trust in me, and that's invaluable. However, it doesn't mean she doesn't want to have some semblance of control of her life. She'll let me lead, and I love that she's willing to follow. But it doesn't mean we're always in a D/s arrangement.

I realize that would never work because I want her as my equal outside of sex. I want to get her opinion on things, and I don't want her to ever feel like she doesn't have a voice, or that her thoughts and feelings don't matter to me outside of sex.

"Switzerland? Like to a chalet?" The left side of her mouth twitches into a hint of a smile.

"Something like that, little one. But there's no resort nearby."

"Good."

Her answer is swift and emphatic.

It's my turn for my lips to twitch. "Are you hoping for a sex hideout? Somewhere where I can keep you naked all day with no distractions?"

"I wouldn't say no to that, Daddy."

"Neither would I, *chiquita*."

I push back the covers and get out of bed. She notices the suitcases I brought up earlier. Daniel's wife provided her with nearly an entire wardrobe. It surprised us both how much he brought.

I already told her we'd leave the unopened packages of panties behind. She nearly flipped out on me, refusing to leave any hint to anybody that she's agreed to go commando under her clothes. I don't know how Esme managed it, but most of the clothes still have tags on them, and the bras and panties are brand new. I just know we owe her a tremendous debt of gratitude.

We pack in near silence, since there's not much more for us to discuss. She knows there's little more I can share, so she doesn't ask questions I can't or won't answer. She doesn't want to put me in that position, and she doesn't want my blank stare or my lies. We both know it's unfortunate, but it's better that way.

Once we have everything ready, I carry our suitcases downstairs, and she follows behind. I lead her into the garage where men stand outside of our armored SUVs. One man takes our luggage and puts it in the trunk as she and I climb in. Just like when we arrived, there are guys in the third row, and each of the guards has a rifle. It's not until we shut all the doors that the driver turns on the engine and opens the garage door.

We ride in silence as we follow the driveway to the gate we passed through, and it's only two minutes later that we're boarding the plane. Within five minutes, everything is secure, and we're taxiing down the runway. We hold hands as we both look out the window. There's little to see but the bright stars. One of these days, perhaps Flora and I can come back here and lie beside each other at the pool and look up at the constellations. But for now, the plane continues to climb.

When the seatbelt sign goes off and the flight attendant offers us drinks, we both shake our heads. I reach across and unfasten her seatbelt, scooping her into my arms as I rise. There's a private cabin in the aft, so I take her back there. As we undress, I grow concerned about the dark shadows that have formed underneath her eyes.

"Are you still exhausted, little one?"

"Yeah, but not so exhausted I can't enjoy the privacy of this cabin. I'm not a member of the mile-high club, but I'd like to be."

"Same, little one, but only because it's you."

I won't share with her that I took a couple quick trips with my last girlfriend, who's now married to the bratva's accountant. We were together long enough that we could've, but someone in my family was always with us as an extra bodyguard. Neither she nor I were comfortable fucking knowing my cousins could hear us.

As I trail my fingers over Flora's tits, I realize I want her so much that I don't have those same reservations. It's not that I respect her less than I did my ex-girlfriend. It's that I know my cousins would respect our privacy and sit as far from the cabin door as they could. I don't want to turn down any opportunities for intimacy with Flora. It's not just about fucking and getting off. It's about sharing something with her I share with no one else.

"Daddy, I think you'd be more comfortable sitting right now, don't you?" The teasing glint in her eyes makes me wonder what she has in mind.

"I think you're right, little one."

I lower myself to the mattress and spread my legs open, offering both my hands to her, thinking she might straddle me. Instead, she sinks to her knees and crosses her wrists behind her back.

"Daddy, I think one of these days we're going to need something other than my bra straps to make it easier for me to keep my hands in place."

I cup her chin and tilt her head back. She raises her eyes to gaze into mine.

"Would you like a set of handcuffs that are just for you?

"*Sí, Papi.* We might need more than one, depending on what positions you want me in."

"Tied naked in our bed is the position I want you in most."

She doesn't miss the pronoun that shows my plan for us to share a room in the future.

"Daddy, I think you told me earlier you intend to plug my ass with your cock so I can fall asleep with your cum inside me. We can't stay like that when we go out. I think you'll have to find something else to make sure my ass is always ready for you."

"Would you like a jeweled plug?

"*Sí, Papí.*"

"What else would my *chiquita preciosa* like?" Beautiful little girl.

"There're so many things that'll be on my list for my Santa Daddy."

Her smile is pure seduction. I fist my cock and stroke as she licks her lips, swiping her tongue all the way around, making her lips glisten. She opens her mouth, resting her tongue flat in invitation. The hand that cupped her chin slides into her hair. I apply light pressure as I nudge her to lean forward. I guide my cock into her mouth.

She does nothing until I'm as deep as she can take it without having to swallow. I let go, and she licks me from stem to stern. Swirling her tongue around the tip, she flicks the head and sucks lightly before moving down to the thick vein on the underside. She flicks that too, making my cock jump. She does it a few more times before sliding her mouth back down my length.

Even though my hand is still in her hair, I allow her to lead. I could fuck her face like I said I would earlier, but I'm letting her suck me off instead. She works my cock, and I watch as her cheeks hollow each time she sucks. It's the most magnificent sight I've seen besides when I'm licking her pussy or taking her ass from behind.

I've seen four of the Seven Wonders of the World. Eating

her out, getting sucked off, fucking her cunt, and fucking her ass. The fifth will be watching her as I titty fuck her. The sixth is watching when she jacks me off. And the seventh will be when I fuck her tight little pussy, then her ass in missionary position, so I get the best of both worlds while seeing her face.

Thinking of those various positions pushes me to my climax far too fast. She senses it as her mouth lifts from my shaft. She takes a couple deep breaths as her hand takes her mouth's place. Then she's back again, stroking what she can't swallow with one hand while the other plays with my balls, then rubs my taint.

"Fuck, *chica*. I'm gonna come."

She lets go of me and sits back. "Daddy, I really think it would be more comfortable for you if you stood. That way I can swallow you, don't you think?"

Again, she poses her suggestion as a question, as though I control what we do.

"That sounds like a wise idea."

I rise and both of my hands go into her hair as she returns both hands behind her back. I press my cock into her mouth as my hands press her head closer to me. I rock my hips. I'm not as forceful as I could be. I don't need to be. I'm not truly trying to dominate her. Instead, it's more the guise of me leading and her following.

She can't move her head anywhere I don't want, but I'm also not trying to make her gag or choke her. She breathes through her nose, and I feel her throat relax until she's swallowing me. She gags but forces herself to swallow again. The pressure is more than I can bear. I explode, making her choke. Her hands fly out to grasp my ass as I pull back. I don't move except to tilt my head back. I barely contain my roar as my dick keeps pulsing in her mouth.

When I stop coming and she pulls away, I lean forward and

wrap my hands around her ribs. I hoist her from the floor and practically toss her onto the bed. I crawl on and am ready to position my head between her legs when she puts her hand between us, her palm on my forehead.

"Daddy, just snuggle with me."

Immediately, concern surges through me nearly as forcefully as my orgasm. I push myself up until I'm hovering over her.

"What's wrong, *chica?*"

Her eyes widen when she realizes I'm worried about her. "Nothing. I just want nothing in return. I want this to just be about me blowing you and getting you off."

Her arms encircle my back, and I lower myself until our chests brush. I nuzzle her neck as her calves wrap over mine. She pulls, wanting more of my weight.

"*Papí, por favor.*" Daddy, please.

I watch to ensure I don't crush her, but the more weight I settle onto her, the tighter she holds me. My cock's ready for a siesta until it brushes against her wet pussy. It feels too good to ignore. She moans and rocks her hips to match my motion. Our mouths find each other. Our kiss makes her wetter, which only makes my cock swell all over again. When I know I'm hard enough, I thrust into her. Her fingers press my ass, making me sink deeper into her cunt. She tilts her hips, so I bottom out.

"Let me warm your cock. Just stay inside me."

Chapter Fifteen

Flora

Aside from Pablo dealing with Humberto, the last nine hours have been a sex fest. You can't put the genie back in the bottle. We've started, and we can't seem to stop. But Pablo's been so attentive to me, giving me the best orgasms of my life. He's so attuned to what I need. I don't want this to be one-sided. I don't want to just take. I've tried to explain that, but now I want to show him.

I kiss along his shoulder and neck as my left hand burrows into his hair, and my right hand holds onto his ass. Our kisses are purely affection, and I love them as much as I do the lust-driven ones.

"Fuck, Flora. Every moment of being inside you is fucking heaven."

"Daddy, fall asleep inside me. Let me hold you."

He observes me for a moment before he rests his head on the pillow beside mine. I know he's still holding some of his weight off me, but I love the feeling of him pressing me into the mattress. I love how much broader his frame is than mine. I love how he's hard where I'm soft. His left hand trails along my thigh, along the side then the back. He groans, telling me how much he enjoys touching me.

I run my fingers through his hair, my nails scratching his scalp. He sighs as his eyes drift closed. I know he isn't asleep because his hand's still moving on my leg, but he's relaxed. It's as soothing to me as it is to him. I don't know when he falls asleep, but it's only moments before I do. I've never been so emotionally connected to a person before, and feeling him inside me as I drift off fulfills one of my oldest fantasies.

"*Chiquita*, wake up."

This is the second time he's woken me in bed, but this time there's sun brightening the room we're in. I realize we're in the private jet's cabin, and we're still in the sky. From how bright it is, I know it must be early afternoon as we fly toward the sun.

"We're going to land in twenty minutes."

Shit!

I slept way longer than I thought. It's over a twelve-hour flight from Bogotá to Zurich. I don't know which city we're going to, but where we left from had to have added at least an hour.

"Have you been awake long?"

"No. It was the flight attendant knocking that woke me."

I dart my gaze to the door and then down to where the sheet drapes over me. I heard nothing before Pablo woke me.

"Flora, I would never let another man see you naked if you didn't want that."

He moves to get off the bed, but I grab his wrist.

"What the hell does that mean?"

"I'll always protect your privacy."

"No, not that part. I already know that about you. What the hell do you mean if I don't want it? Why do you think I want another man to see me? Do you plan to share me?"

His expression darkens as he looks at me.

"No, I do *not* want to share you. But we're both part of a lifestyle that isn't foreign to *ménage*. I saw your reaction when I mentioned my past. I know you've done it too. If it's something you want, then—then I'll learn to live with it."

I laugh. I shouldn't, but I do.

"The fuck you will. You look like you're going to be ill, Pablo. Just suggesting it makes you miserable. I appreciate you offering it if you think it's something I need. You wouldn't do that if you thought it was just a want. But I absolutely refuse to have another man touch me now that I'm with you. Do you still want m—"

His mouth on mine keeps me from finishing my question. Is his insistent kiss because the idea excites him so much? Or doesn't he want me to finish that thought?

His hand encircles my throat and squeezes just enough to be tight without keeping me from breathing. He kisses along my jaw until he can whisper in my ear.

"You are the only woman I'll ever fuck again. You know I've never fucked without a condom. Not only have we had sex several times without one, but I've come in you every time I've fucked your tight little pussy."

His hand slides from my throat to cup my jaw on the opposite side from his mouth. His fingers tangle with my hair as his thumb rests near my ear. It's so fucking arousing to sit like this, naked beneath a sheet when he's already dressed.

"I will give you whatever you need, Flora, in and out of bed. If sharing you is part of your sexual needs, I'll figure out how to live with that. But—"

It's my turn to shut him up with a kiss. I turn my head and nip at his lip, tugging a little before I press mine fully against his. I thrust my tongue into his mouth, coaxing his into mine. I pull away when I'm breathless.

"The only thing I need is you. Pablo, I can't share you. I—"

I shake my head as tears suddenly prick the back of my eyelids, and a lump rises in my throat.

"*Chiquita?*"

"I—I—I don't know why I'm being so emotional all of a sudden. I just really don't like the idea of anyone else joining us. It's visceral how much I dislike thinking about that."

"Shh, little one. I didn't mean to upset you."

"I know you didn't. You were trying to be generous. I don't enjoy seeing how much the idea of another man touching me hurts you. I'll lose my ever-loving shit if I have to see another woman near you. I can't do it. I'm not used to feeling so fucking territorial, but I want to claw the eyes out of women who don't even exist. It's fucking primal how possessive I feel right now. I shouldn't feel this way." *Not yet at least.*

"Flora, I feel the same. But I'll do anything you need, and I'll try to do most of what you want."

Until Cartel life gets in the way.

I know what he isn't admitting aloud. I don't want to hear about the Cartel right now, but neither of us can escape it as part of our lives.

"I know you don't need anyone else with us, Pablo. But what *do* you need? Do you enjoy being watched? Do you have a particular kink?"

"I don't mind being watched, but I'm not an exhibitionist or a voyeur by nature."

"Same."

"If we go to a club, *chica*, then I'll only get fully undressed if we're alone in a room. My tats are too recognizable. It's why I always wear a mask."

"I've always worn a mask too. I prefer it for my privacy, but I also never wanted it to get back to my family that I'm into BDSM—'cause gross. I don't need them to know that about my sexual preferences."

His lips tuck between his teeth.

"What?"

"I know my cousins share the same proclivities as I do. I'm pretty fucking sure all our parents know we belong to and are silent owners in several of New York's most exclusive BDSM clubs. It wouldn't surprise me if all of their generation were into it too. I don't want to think about it, but I'm pretty sure they are."

He pretends to shiver, and it lightens what just got intense. But these conversations are important. They're ones most couples don't have within the first twenty-four hours of hooking up.

No. That's not right.

Pablo and I aren't just hooking up. I'm not even sure we can call it dating. We just are, as in we're together, and I don't know how to define it. Frankly, I don't want to.

It's just intense to have shared so much, been so intimate, and determined so many boundaries for our relationship in a matter of just hours.

"I need to get dressed, don't I?"

"Yes. Put on layers. You'll need the coat Daniel brought too."

I can't believe all the things he delivered. His wife assembled an entire wardrobe for me. There were clothes for all seasons. I can wear them as separates or layer them and be comfortable just about anywhere. She also brought me a thick coat. I don't know where she got it since it's summer in South America, and it doesn't get that cold in the plains regions.

I climb out of bed and rummage through the case until I have what I need. I look out the window and see the snow-capped mountains below us. If we're landing soon, we should be over one of Switzerland's cities. It's not a large country, so there aren't that many. I shift my gaze, but I see nothing that resembles a city or even a town.

"Where are we?"

"There's a private airfield where we'll land near Lugano. We have to transfer to a helicopter that'll take us near Graubünden. From there, we have another ride."

I don't know where these places are, and I don't know what he means by "another ride." If he wanted to give me more details, he would. I think the less I know the better right now.

We return to our seats and fasten our belts for landing. I don't know what to expect when the flight attendant opens the door and lowers the steps. The icy blast of air isn't surprising, but the armed guards are. Do *los Diaz* have private security firms on speed dial around the world? Or do they have their own security details awaiting them wherever they go?

"*Chica*, these men got here a little before us. *Papá* sent them from Bogotá. They took my cousin Alejandro's plane."

He points to a jet similar to the one we're disembarking. I look over my shoulder.

"Is this jet yours?"

"No, it's the family one. Alejandro travels the most, so he bought one for convenience. He doesn't have to wait for the family one to return if someone else is traveling when he needs to. It doesn't keep the rest of us from traveling when we need to."

Both sides of my family are affluent, but they aren't multiple-private-jets kind of rich. I sweep my gaze over the tiny airport and see two helicopters waiting with a woman standing beside each.

"Those aren't ours, but the pilots are."

We walk toward them with the armed guards surrounding us. The flight attendant trails behind us with our luggage. It's apparently a team effort to transfer us from one mode of transportation to the other. I could've wheeled my case.

From the way Pablo wrapped his arm around my shoulders, pressing my head down, I can tell he wants me to rush. He doesn't want me encumbered by anything. He has his handgun resting against his right thigh as we hurry.

The pilot of the helicopter we approach flashes a thumbs up before climbing inside. Pablo helps me and then follows me. Three guards join us as Pablo hands me headphones and then fastens my belt. He secures his own while I watch the rest of the men take seats in the other helicopter. I don't know where our luggage wound up since it disappeared. I hear Pablo's voice through the headphones.

"We have about an hour before we arrive at our next stop. We can have something to eat after the last leg of the trip."

I nod. I'm starving, but I didn't want to complain. I watch as we take off, but my attention shifts when Pablo takes my hand. He laces our fingers together. I look up at him and smile. He pecks my lips, and it shocks me. I didn't expect the public display of affection in such close quarters to his men. He squeezes my hand and brings it to rest on his thigh. He looks past me to see what shrinks beneath us as we take off. His thumb strokes over mine absentmindedly.

If it weren't for the armed guards and the ever-present danger, we'd be a normal couple on a romantic getaway. It's a shame there are people trying to kill me. It dampens the mood.

When I glance up at Pablo again, his gaze meets mine, and I know he feels the same way. There's nothing either of us wants to talk about since the others aboard will hear us through the radio. We both enjoy the view until we're landing again. The time flew for lack of a better pun.

I don't know what to make of our newest destination. I don't know that we can even call what we landed on a helipad. It's so small that the second helicopter can't land until the one we're in takes off again. We're basically perched on a ledge on a mountainside. We hurry to get off, and Pablo pulls my hood up since the wind is ferocious when we get out. He shuffles me to the edge of the concrete slab closest to the mountain. He waves to our pilot who offers us another thumbs up. She never spoke.

I observe the second helicopter doing the same thing: touch down, people climb out and rush away while carrying our luggage and things I can't make out, then take off again. I sweep my gaze over our surroundings. There's no road and no vehicles waiting for us.

Are we rappelling down the mountain?

"Hold my hand, Flora. It's icy."

I follow his lead as we appear to be walking to another part of the mountainside, but I realize there's something like a white industrial garage door. As we approach, it opens.

What in the James Bond–evil-villain's-lair kind of shit is this?

I don't know what the fuck kind of vehicle I'm looking at, but it's somewhere among a train, tank, and an SUV. I can see what looks like train tracks leading into the mountain. It's not like one of those old-fashioned Western cartoons with the two miners on a wooden platform pushing a seesaw-looking thing up and down. But that's what comes to mind. It must be the altitude.

I follow Pablo as he follows two guards. There are three men behind me and two standing watch on the helipad. The vehicle has tires like a tank, but they're on the railway tracks.

The body looks more like an SUV with four doors and comfortable seats. We climb in, and Pablo helps me with my belt because the light is so dim. He takes my hand like he did in the helicopter, and we all ride in silence.

It's eerie as fuck.

Lights turn on as we move forward and turn off once we're past them. We're headed deeper into the mountain, and I'm questioning what I got myself into.

Salir de Guatemala para entrar en Guatepeor.

It's a play on words meaning from Guate-bad to Guate-worse. It's a common phrase that changes *mala*—bad—to *peor*—worse. It loses something in translation, but it's a common phrase in Colombia.

Basically, have I jumped out of the frying pan and into the fire?

Is my trust in Pablo utterly misplaced?

Where the fuck is he taking me?

He must sense my anxiousness because he lifts our hands and brings the back of mine to his lips. He kisses my temple as he brings our hands to rest on his thigh.

Is this some Hansel and Gretel shit where his kindness is the gumdrops and candy he uses to lure me into his magical house that'll trap me?

How high up are we? The altitude is making me delusional.

It's not long before we arrive in a garage. I see four snowmobiles and a sled. The latter looks like something Pablo, his brother, and his cousins probably played with when they were kids. A door closes behind our vehicle, but only the front passenger gets out. He walks to a box on the wall that looks like an alarm system control. I watch him tap it, and the screen comes to life. He swipes a few times before looking over at us and nodding. I reach for my belt, but Pablo covers my hand.

The five guys who were in the second helicopter get out,

and the six men go inside. They're sweeping the place even though nothing concerning appeared on screen. My emotions tumble around inside me, and I'm not sure if the vigilance reassures me or terrifies me. Pablo gives my hand a squeeze and leans over to whisper in English.

"No one's been here in a while. We keep our security systems on, so we would know if there's ever a breach. But the men know no Diaz would allow family into one of our foreign properties without guards checking it first."

He's the only Diaz here, so there's no one who's family with us.

"You, little one. You're the family I'm talking about."

"Mind reader."

Him thinking of me as family so soon after we got together should freak me all the way out. However, it's the only reassuring thing that's happened since we landed.

He helps me with my belt again, and the driver opens my door. I climb out and walk around the front of the vehicle to meet Pablo. His arm slips around my waist as we enter the house. I don't know what to expect, but it's definitely not what I find. It's clear the house is huge—he has a massive family after all. But it's cozy like a cabin. The furniture's inviting, and there's a fireplace one of the men lights. I can see into the kitchen, and it's definitely gourmet.

But what's most impressive are the floor-to-ceiling windows. I can tell they slide open to give the feeling of being on a deck with nothing protruding. I walk toward them, and Pablo follows. I peer out of one, and I realize the house is truly built into the mountain face. There's nothing overhanging that a blizzard or avalanche could snap off. We're hundreds of feet above ground, so snow couldn't accumulate high enough to barricade us in. It's also high enough that no one is climbing up or rappelling down easily.

I see what looks like it could be a trail down the mountainside, but I wouldn't take it without an experienced or knowledgeable guide. I'm certain the untrained eye wouldn't see it. The snowmobiles must be for this path in case they need another route to escape. It makes me wonder where Pablo and his relatives used the sled.

He takes me on a tour of the house, and I discover there's a plateau of sorts on the far end. There's a concrete wall along the wide ledge's length. This is where Pablo played as a kid. There's also what appears to be an ice plunge pool with a lid on it.

Yeah, no, I'm not a Viking. This Latin American *chica* only does warm water.

Besides, Daniel's wife didn't include a bathing suit in the assortment of clothes she brought me. I have nothing to wear in it. I turn away, but Pablo wraps his arms around me.

"It's heated, *chiquita*. None of us are polar bears. It's nice in summer, but we don't need to use it in winter unless we want to."

"Why would anyone do that?"

"If you can handle the cold as you get in and out, it's pretty magical to watch the steam rise as you stare at the stars."

He gives me a quick kiss before we finish the tour. He shows me our bedroom before showing me the office. We head down a set of stairs, and a flash of fear surges through me. He wouldn't take me down to see a torture chamber, would he?

He flicks a switch that illuminates an enormous marble room. It's like being in a Roman bathhouse. There's a pool long enough to do laps that has a bench running along both lengths. You could swim or sit. The front wall is windows, like the main floor. It's absolutely spectacular. I spot a hot tub and sauna in the back.

"The windows are avalanche proof and bullet proof, *chica*.

This is our most secure property, but that's more about protecting it from Mother Nature than attack."

"But your family built into the side of a mountain as a fallout shelter or something."

"That's a fortunate outcome. *Papá* built it for *Mamá* as a wedding gift after they honeymooned in Geneva, among other places. She fell in love with the Alps. She took up skiing and has always enjoyed hiking. *Papá* wanted to give her the most breathtaking view in Switzerland."

It's breathtaking all right when you realize how high up you are. I'm looking more closely out the window.

"*Mamá's* in remission now, but when she was in between chemo treatments and well enough to travel, *Papá* brought her here. We're all convinced it helped her. My entire family comes here on vacation sometimes. We came a lot more when I was younger, but it's *Mamá* and *Papá's* special place when they want to escape the world."

"They don't mind you bringing me?"

"I'm certain they both knew this is the only place I'd suggest."

"It's incredible."

Pablo slips his arms around me, and I lean against his chest as we look out the window. My fears slip away, and I pray we can come here again one day under better circumstances.

"*Chiquita*, you must be starving. Let's make something to eat. My stomach doesn't know what meal it's expecting. It just wants something."

"I am, and mine too."

We head upstairs again and into the kitchen. Much like the house in Colombia, there are plenty of nonperishable items stocked in the kitchen.

"*El patrón?*"

"*Sí.*"

"*¿Podemos traer las compras?*" May we bring the groceries in?

"*Sí.*"

Three guys enter the house from the garage with our luggage and bags of food. I expected the luggage but not the food. It's what I couldn't identify earlier. Maybe they loaded these provisions before the jet landed since they were at the waiting helicopters before us.

They didn't enter the house without Pablo's permission. It makes me wonder where they sleep when they're here. I help unpack, and it surprises me the variety of fruits, vegetables, and meat I discover. We'll certainly eat well while we're here.

The men disappear, and it leaves Pablo and me to move around the kitchen. We work well together, and it's not long before we have steak and three side dishes ready. We share stories about our childhood, and he learns more about my time in America and why I moved back. He admitted he'd heard about my mom's cancer. We share silent sadness as we both reflect upon our mothers' illnesses.

We do the dishes and tidy up the kitchen together before making a bowl of popcorn. I don't expect him to practically soak it in butter, but he can tell I'm not objecting. He confesses it's a secret indulgence.

It's not long before we're curled up on the comfiest couch I've ever been on. The fireplace crackles beneath the television mounted on the wall. It shouldn't surprise me that the Wi-Fi signal is so strong. We watch three movies on a streaming service Pablo projects from his phone before we head to bed. I love every minute of our evening together. It was like one a normal couple has, and that makes me nervous.

Chapter Sixteen

Pablo

I rarely sleep in because I have far too much on my mind between the businesses I own and Cartel responsibilities. There's just not much time to sleep beyond sunrise if I also want to work out twice a day. Before spending time with Flora, working out and hanging out with family were my only ways to relax. I've always been someone who needs physical activity to remain focused.

I used to drive my parents nuts because I was constantly on the go. I can remember *Mamá* hearing other parents who had daughters watch my brother and me play. We were what people would call "all boy all the time."

The parents of girls would smirk at my parents and say things like, "Don't they keep you on your toes?" while my parents were going in different directions after us. It's not like Juan and I were disobedient children. Just the opposite. We had a healthy fear of disobeying our parents, but we were just active.

Me in particular.

My parents would grin and bear the comments. But I remember when I became a tween, I overheard *Mamá* once talking to my *tías*, who also only had sons. It was when the other parents' daughters moved into puberty and hormones. She said Juan and I might have been exhausting for the first ten years of our lives, but the other parents had the rest of their lives to deal with their daughters.

The sun is barely peeking over the horizon, and the house faces west, so the room has only a hint of soft light. It's enough to allow me to see Flora sleeping beside me. I continue my silent musings while enjoying observing the gorgeous woman beside me.

There are my companies I own separately from the Cartel. I have a biotech company based in California. An oil refinery off the coast of Colombia. The region where our family's home is produces nearly a third of all the oil drilled in Colombia. I have three international car dealerships. One in Monte Carlo, one in Dubai, and one in Tokyo. I also own an all-inclusive resort in the Caymans. Those are just my foreign enterprises.

I think about my duties that fall to my cousins now that I'm mostly incommunicado. At home, I oversee our legal Cartel enterprises. That's all our bodegas, cash-checking stores, and strip clubs. They're heavily cash-based businesses that allow us to pass money through them that comes out squeaky clean. I've left all these responsibilities to the other guys, but I'm certain they understand.

None of us has been into strip clubs since we were barely legal to drink. Since my cousins and I have either had subs or arrangements at BDSM clubs, we don't need to watch women slide up and down poles at our strip clubs if we want to get hard. Besides, we absolutely allow no touching at our clubs, so it's not like we went to any of them to get off.

Javier's with Madeline now, so I know he won't take over their management. I'll pass them on to either Joaquin or Jorge since I have even less than zero interest in going now that I'm with Flora. Besides, I don't want to put her in that position. Not because I fear her being insecure, but more out of respect. Alejandro's far too busy with his travel to even consider.

As I continue to gaze at Flora, the temptation is far too great. I slip the sheet down to her waist as she sleeps on her back. Full round tits are like a homing beacon to me because it's clear she spends plenty of time outside in a bathing suit. Her bikini tops leave half of her breasts paler than the rest of her chest, shoulders, and arms. They're like a lighthouse in my raging storm of lust.

I lean forward and suck on one, loving how the nipple hardens against my tongue. I watch her face as she moans but does nothing else. I switch to her other one, massaging the breast I just left, my thumb rolling over the nipple to keep it hard. When her tits have matching puckered darts, I stroke my cock twice. I slip my fingers between her legs, rubbing her clit. In her sleep, she opens her legs to me. I inch my fingers inside, finding she's still wet from the cum I left in her before we both passed out hard last night.

Her pussy's ready for me.

I push the sheet down all the way, loving the sight of her round thighs that will soon hug my hips as I fuck her. I align my cock with her pussy; the tip glides up and down as I stroke. If I keep doing that, I'll come before I'm even inside her.

I thrust into her, and she moans with pleasure, not pain. Her hips tilt to me, inviting me in again and again, deeper and deeper. Her eyes flutter open as her legs tighten around me.

"Daddy."

"That's right, *chiquita*. Daddy's fucking you."

She moans twice, and I move faster.

She confessed last night that, along with having a man fall asleep inside her, one of her other strongest fantasies is waking up to a man fucking her. I know she wants to feel so desired the man she's with just has to take. It's no problem fulfilling that wish.

As she wakes all the way, that sleepy expression she has—the one I discovered on the plane yesterday—makes my heart feel like it'll beat out of my chest. Other men may have experienced it in the past, but I'm the only one who'll ever experience it in the present and the future.

I roll over, bringing her on top of me, and she leans forward, her hands gripping the pillow beside my forehead. She bounces on my dick, her tits swinging in my face. As she braces herself on one hand, she presses her left breast to my mouth. I latch on, and she puts her hand back on the pillow. I squeeze and suck on both of them, going side to side like a starving man.

"Fuck, Daddy. Harder."

I've never been a tits or ass man. I'm equal opportunity, and since Flora's got both in spades, I'm in fucking heaven. My right hand squeezes her breast and pinches and twists her nipple. My other hand grabs her ass. Marks I made the day before yesterday are already fading.

I need to fix that.

I draw back my hand and slap her ass, the sound ringing in the room, spurring her on to ride me faster. She rocks back and forth, pushing her ass into my hand as it lands across her flesh, pulling away as my hand draws back.

"¡Ay, Papi!"

"*Mi chiquita sexy.*" My sexy little girl.

Some words work in both languages.

"*Cógeme profundo.*" Fuck me deeper.

This is the longest we've lasted. I pinch and twist her nipples over and over, progressively spanking every part of her ass. I alternate hands to make sure I cover her entire ass. She begs to come. Each time she does, I lift her off my cock. She whimpers and pleads with me, both of us enjoying our self-inflicted torture. Neither of us wants this to end. We'll definitely fuck a few more times today, but in this moment, we can't get enough of our bodies working together for our mutual pleasure.

When I know she's on the verge of frustration and I can't handle much more self-denial, I move my hand to the back of her neck and pull her down to me. I kiss her as I pin her against me, thrusting harder and faster as she rocks her ass on me, barely able to keep up.

"Come for me, *chiquita*. Coat my cock with your cream as I fill you with my cum."

"Daddy, I'm gonna be a sloppy mess for you. I'm getting too wet."

"You feel perfect, little one. You're still so tight, but it's easy for me to slide in and out of you. Easy for me to pound your little cunt."

I pant each word, punctuating them as I jackhammer her pussy.

"Daddy, I'm coming."

"Me too, baby girl."

We cling to each other as we come down off our high. She slides off me because we're too warm. She inches closer, and I slip my arm beneath her neck as she cuddles along my side. Holding her in my arms fulfills another part of me that yearns for her as much as I do during sex. I experience an emotional and physical release when I come, and the afterglow perfectly complements it.

"How're you doing, *chiquita*?"

"Feeling blissful? You?"

"Never better."

I look forward to being home where we can explore more kinks. I plan to order every toy, implement, and tool we can conceive of so we can deepen this bond.

The sun finally fills the room by the time we both have rumbling stomachs.

"I can't have you starving all the time while we're traveling."

That's better than saying hiding.

"I can think of something I could have for breakfast."

She looks down at my cock and waggles her eyebrows.

"Maybe for lunch, *chica*."

"Humph."

I offer her a robe that hangs in my closet and stays here permanently. I pull a pair of pajama pants from the dresser, another item that's here whenever I arrive. When I get home, I almost immediately change out of whatever clothes I wore that day. It's a leftover rule from when I was growing up. *Mamá* insisted Juan and I get out of our school clothes before we sat on any of the furniture. She said it helped protect it and didn't leave germs on it where we'd later put our faces.

Maybe *Mamá* was onto something because my brother and I weren't sick nearly as often as other kids in our classes. The habit allows me to leave work behind and feel like my home is a sanctuary.

As she slips the rope on, she frowns.

"What's the matter?"

"I don't feel comfortable going out in just a bathrobe if your men will see me. This is huge, and it covers me completely, but I don't like them thinking I might be naked under here."

"None of the men come in without an invitation. You heard the guy knock yesterday and wait for permission."

"Yeah, but they must sleep somewhere. You didn't show me

their rooms, but I know there are a few parts left of the house we didn't see on the tour."

"Those were linen closets and snow gear. Stuff like skis and snowshoes. The men have barracks you get to from the garage. There's a side tunnel that leads to it. It comes out to a building on the far side of the patio. They have windows that face out, but not toward that area. There are security cameras out there, but none point toward the hot tub. It allows the family privacy."

"You said your *papá* built this for your *mamá*."

I nod. Her cheeks pinken. I nod again. I don't want to think about how my brother and I came to be. I'd rather think we were the product of immaculate conception.

"But yes, the cameras angle away so my parents can do whatever it is they want to do out there. Same with my *tías* and *tíos* who have visited here. When the heat wasn't on, and it was an ice plunge, my cousins and I used to dare each other to jump in naked."

It's not like our men haven't seen us from time to time when we've had to strip out of contaminated clothing that needs burning. But generally, we don't parade ourselves around in front of our guards and soldiers.

I still need to know what she wants to eat. "What are you in the mood for this morning, baby girl?"

She smiles at me, loving each little term of endearment I have for her. I've enjoyed coming up with each of them.

"I can make eggs while you make waffles, *Papí*."

As we put away the groceries last night, I showed her around the kitchen. This morning, we work together in companionable silence. Once we're seated in the breakfast nook, we continue to chat about our childhoods. We get into the things we enjoyed during high school, the sports I played, and the clubs we belonged to. She wasn't a competitive athlete but loved to cycle. That worries me as I picture her riding her bike in parts of Bogotá that aren't safe for a woman on her own. I wouldn't suggest a man without the training I have go alone either.

She reaches across the table. "Daddy, I never went alone. I had guards with me when I cycled. Both of my *abuelos* insisted upon it. *Mamá* grounded me for two weeks the one time I tried to go out on my own. I didn't even make it."

She smirks as her gaze slides over me. I wonder if she's picturing me in tight cycling shorts.

"I have a home gym, little one, and I have a spin cycle in it. So, while I don't ride on the street often, I do cycle at home. I also enjoy trail riding and mountain biking."

Her eyebrows shoot straight up.

"So that's something we can do together?"

"Yes, *chica*, I'd love that. We could even cycle through Central Park if you wanted."

She curls her nose at that. "Isn't that too crowded for you?"

"We'd have our mini peloton along with us only because I'd want you protected. I cycle with Alejandro when he's around, but not that often anymore. I take a guard with me rather than go alone. If you don't want to do Central Park, there're plenty of trails outside the city where we can go."

We finish breakfast and move to the living room where we watch a movie.

"I can't believe how similar our tastes are."

She comments on it because we keep pointing out the same movies at the same time. It's something small, but it confirms we're compatible. It's another confirmation she's the right woman for me.

Since there are only cameras in the hallway outside the indoor swimming pool, I convince her to go skinny dipping with me. It's a repeat of the last time we swam together. I know eventually the novelty and newness of being able to fuck whenever we want will wear off, but for now we're insatiable. When we finish swimming, I think about what else we can do after lunch. I'll suggest board games since she noticed several she liked on a shelf beneath the TV.

I know it's much easier to pass the time and enjoy this house with a large family since there's always something to do and someone to hang out with. But we both enjoy the solitude. We have nothing we must do after the games, so we nap. I know mine is a lifetime of accumulated exhaustion since I never ever nap.

The constant stress and adrenaline of the past two days are probably affecting Flora. Even when we've been relaxed, there's the ever-present knowledge there could be a credible threat at any moment. That's exhausting. Plus, we're not sleeping much at night considering we wake each other at least twice for sex.

The day isn't creeping by, but we have a couple hours of daylight left before dinner. I ask her whether she wants to go outside for a while. We bundle up, and I take her out on the snowmobiles.

"We can't go too far from the house, little one. But we can enjoy the fresh air and sunshine."

"That would be nice after being inside all day."

"There's a second garage door that leads to a path that can be our escape route if we need it."

"I spotted it from the window yesterday. It's steep."

"It is, but I've ridden snowmobiles along it for years."

We head down the mountainside. Flora's riding behind me since she's never been on one before. They're like jet skis, which she's been on plenty of times apparently, but they're not exactly the same. I'll give her lessons another day. For now, she laughs and squeezes my waist, enjoying the speed. I don't go as fast as my father and *tíos* trained me to since this isn't an emergency escape.

It's just a joyride. Our cheeks are red from the wind and excitement by the time we get back inside. We shower together, but surprisingly, no sex, just plenty of kisses and long embraces. Then we cook together again. It's a good thing we both enjoy this since it's more time we can spend together. All this togetherness could be stifling.

I know we'll wind up wanting to do things apart even while we're here. It wouldn't be healthy for us to spend every single minute together no matter how much we enjoy each other's company. But for now, we want to do most things as a couple.

I wake up to an empty bed, but I can see the light shining underneath the bathroom door. I roll over, but I'm only dozing since I'm waiting for Flora to get back in bed with me. As the minutes tick away and I don't hear the shower, the faucet, or the toilet, I get nervous. I knock on the door.

"Flora, you all right?"

She opens the door, her face pale, and tears brimming in her eyes.

"What happened? What's wrong? Do you not feel well?"

I have a lifetime of training and practice controlling any hint of panic. It all goes out the window.

"I'm all right." She's speaking and shaking her head at the same time. That's hardly reassuring.

"Baby girl, what's the matter?"

She looks over at the counter where our toothbrushes and toothpaste stand.

"Pablo, I don't know how I could've forgotten, but I don't have my birth control pills with me. I've taken them every day for fifteen years. Somehow, I completely forgot over the past three days."

A tear tumbles down her cheek as I pull her into my arms.

"I know I should probably be okay, but that's certainly no guarantee."

"Flora, nothing but abstinence is one hundred percent guaranteed. I've told you before that I've never come inside another woman. That hinted at the risk I know we're both taking. If I didn't see a future with you that could include kids, I would never have done that."

"Yeah, but you thought I was on birth control. I told you I was."

"I know, but I also knew there was always a chance."

"Pablo, what if I am pregnant?" She pulls away from me, wanting to look me in the eye.

"Then we talk about it and plan together. But I'll always respect your wishes, Flora. You have more say in this than I do. I won't trap you into a relationship you don't want. But I also don't want children out of wedlock."

"Is that because you need an heir or because you're Catholic?"

"No, I'm not worried about an heir. *Tío* Enrique proves the *jefe* doesn't have to have a son to inherit. I have four cousins who may have sons at some point. There's bound to be another Diaz in line to be *jefe* after I'm gone. But yes, as lapsed a Catholic as I am, I admit that's part of why. I've also watched Carmine Mancinelli grow up with a dysfunctional set of parents who are better off now that they're separated. However, his life was hard enough because his mom got pregnant at nineteen. Her father, the old don, and her father-in-law forced her and Carmine's father to marry. I can guess how much worse his life would've been if they hadn't married at all."

She leans back against me and sighs. I feel her head nod against my chin as I continue.

"Not everyone in our branch is as forward-thinking as my family is. No one in my family would hold it against us if we didn't marry but had children. However, I don't want to make life hard for my kids. Even if any sons stayed out of the Cartel, they'd still be around it. I don't want daughters with that stigma any more than I would sons. What about you?"

"I feel the same way. My children'll inherit nothing substantial from my father's side of the family despite their influence. My mother's side has money but no power. However, there're plenty of people on both sides of my family who are still old-fashioned. It definitely wasn't easy growing up with a mother who never married my father. Even though he was dead, it was rough. She didn't have the respect of being a widow. There were things said to her and to me over the years that confirmed I want to be married if and when I have children."

"What do you want to do? I can pull out, or we can abstain."

It's my turn to lean back so I can see her. She looks about as thrilled at those solutions as I feel. I brush my lips against hers.

"*Chiquita*, do you want me to pull out?"

Her expression shows how conflicted she feels. I'm certain her emotions mirror mine until we both shake our heads. I may have asked her, but I'm wondering whether I want to.

"Pablo, I'm thirty-four. I'm not getting any younger. I know plenty of women these days have babies well into their forties, but it still doesn't change the risks associated with advanced maternal age. You're a trained biologist, just like me. You know what I know, even if neither of us are geneticists. We've talked about a future together, even if it hasn't been specific. We know there's something between us that won't go away."

"You're right, Flora, and I don't believe this is just the result of being trapped in houses together. Or because we're relying on each other."

"I don't know that you rely on me that much, Pablo, but I'm definitely relying on you."

"I told you yesterday how you make me feel. I've definitely come to rely on you, little one."

"Then, do we take our chances? I have no idea how fertile I might be, if at all."

"I don't know either. I could shoot blanks for all I know."

I flash her a smile, and she relaxes. We both know she could get pregnant. We accept that, but neither of us has said we love each other. It's odd to think of marriage and a family without having said that. I'm positive neither of us is there yet, but it's inevitable. We just need to stay alive long enough to have time.

Chapter Seventeen

Flora

We've been here two weeks.

Pablo and I are getting a bit stir crazy, but we aren't bickering or anything. We sense when the other needs some space, so we find things to do on our own. I enjoy curling up on the sofa and reading. Apparently, his mom and I have similar tastes in books: psychological thrillers. His new *tía* is an amazing author, so I've devoured all her books. Turns out Margherita's been reading them for years. Long before Enrique met her.

While I read, if he isn't pouring over some scientific journal on his phone, he gets a deck of cards to play solitaire and a couple other solo card games. They're all patience and logic games. I noticed he often sets a timer or stopwatch. I sense these were games his father or *tíos* taught him to train him to think fast and make decisive choices.

He's admitted he's highly competitive but mostly with himself. With so many other guys around his age in his family, there was always a potential rival. But they worked as a team more often than they competed against each other. Apparently, they saved rivalries for the other syndicate families. They played peewee through high school sports with and against the other major syndicate kids. Sometimes they were teammates, and sometimes they were opponents. Fucked-up world he grew up in where you can be friends with someone until you're twelve and get your first weapon—a pocketknife. Then you become enemies who try to kill each other.

I've been catching up on some shows I love that are a couple seasons behind in Colombia. He'll go to the expansive full gym in the other half of the basement. It's nearly as large as the pool area. It has everything from free weights to machines along with cardio equipment. He works out at least once a day, if not twice.

The pool is wide enough for both of us to swim, so we head down there every day at least once.

He's magnificent.

All rippling muscles.

There isn't a stroke he hasn't mastered. Apparently, he was an open-water lifeguard on the Jersey Shore when he was a teenager and during his college summers. I bet plenty of people on those beaches who saw him had the same dirty thoughts I have. I'm a strong swimmer too, and he calls *mi reina sirena.* My mermaid queen.

We enjoy our workout and then frolic in the water. Not a bad way to start our morning before we even have breakfast. He'll head out to the pool on the patio. We haven't turned on the heat yet, so he takes an ice plunge while I have my first cup of coffee. I watch him but run away when he's headed back inside. He caught me unprepared the first time. He slid my robe off and hugged me. It was like having an iceberg pressed against me. No, thank you!

We plan to heat the water for tonight because there's a new moon, so the stars should be extra bright.

"The switch is to the right of the barbecue."

Pablo's drying off as I look around the covered grill. I spot it and flip it on. It's not long before I see steam rising, but it'll probably take a few hours for the water to be completely warm. We head inside, but his phone rings before we can start breakfast.

He glances at it before looking at me and showing me the screen.

Tío E

That doesn't make me nervous or anything. Fucking hell.

"*Hola, tío.*"

"*Hola, sobrino.*"

"*Flora está conmigo. ¿Debería ir a la oficina?*" Flora is with me. Should I go in the office?

"*No, ella también debería escuchar esto.*" No, she should hear this too.

I make out what Enrique says since I'm standing so close to Pablo. That makes my heart rate spike. I figure it shouldn't since Enrique wouldn't allow me to hear anything that's too bad, right? If it were Cartel business, he'd tell Pablo to take the call alone.

Pablo puts the call on speaker.

"*Hola, jefe.*"

Pablo takes my hand and leads me into the living room as the conversation continues in Spanish.

"Enrique, please."

"All right. Thank you." What else do I say?

Pablo senses my nervousness, so he tugs my hand as he sits. He pulls me onto his lap, and I curl up. He hands me the phone as his left arm wraps around my back, and his right hand slips under my robe to stroke my ass. I rest my head on his shoulder and put the phone on my thigh as I brace myself.

"*Tío*, have you heard from *Papá* or Alejandro?"

"Yes. They both checked in tonight."

We're six hours ahead of New York, so it's two in the morning. Did Enrique wait until it was a reasonable time to call us, or is he a night owl?

"What did they have to say?"

"Alejandro discovered who helped Humberto. It was Néstor Guzman."

"The Minister of Finance and Public Credit? He's—he's— Does my mother know?"

I pull away from Pablo. I'm furious. I ball my hands into fists and clench my jaw.

Maldito pedazo de mierda. Motherfucking piece of shit.

"*Chiquita?*"

Pablo whispers the word, but my gaze jumps to the phone. I don't want Enrique to hear him call me that. Pablo pats my ass as he mouths his words this time.

"He knows."

I don't want to know how. I can't think about that right now.

"He's my mother's boyfriend. They've been together for years. She has a habit of picking men who won't marry her. He says he can't have any public ties to a cartel family."

Technically, neither side of my family is officially in a cartel. They definitely aren't in *the Cartel* since Enrique wouldn't have them after the disaster between my father, and Luciana and Esteban. But my father's family's rivalry with *los Diaz* and my *abuelo's* ongoing business with them as Enrique's underling keeps them connected.

It's Enrique who speaks up. "She found out, but I'm confident she didn't know beforehand."

"How can you be certain?"

"Because Néstor had four knife wounds when Alejandro found him. They were deep but not anywhere fatal. It was punishment. He admitted he was at your mother's house when I called him. I wanted to hear his excuses before I sent Alejandro to visit him."

To visit.

That's diplomatic.

"She overheard the conversation. Apparently, she waited until after I hung up to strike. She kicked him out of the house. As he staggered onto the street, she got in her car. She nearly ran him over, but he got outside the gate and stayed on the sidewalk where she couldn't hit him. His driver took him home. Alejandro paid a house call."

"*Tío*, why did he help Humberto?"

"Humberto swore he had far more money than he did. He claimed he had enough to buy legislative members and influence taxation laws to levy higher ones on industries we don't dominate. He told Néstor he could bankroll his bid for president."

Pablo scoffs. He rolls his eyes and shakes his head. I guess Humberto really was as delusional as Pablo claimed the other day. Apparently, Néstor was in the same boat. He was always an ambitious guy who loved having my beautiful mother on his arm for events but wouldn't commit in case someone better came along. Someone who wasn't a single mother with a former lover who was a failed, murdered narco-trafficker. Someone younger. Someone with more money. Someone who could give him perfect children for posters and junkets. I definitely wasn't the right person to go on those publicly funded political tours.

"What happened to Néstor?"

There's dead air on both ends of the call. Enrique says nothing, and Pablo just looks at me.

"Okay. So, he's dead. Good."

"Good?" Pablo didn't expect my response.

"I never liked the creepy *cabrón* around my mother. He made my skin crawl whenever he cornered me."

"Cornered you?"

If I didn't know Pablo wasn't directing his silent rage at me, it would scare the shit out of me. It's like watching a wall drop in his eyes. His gaze doesn't appear distant, but it's like he's void of all emotion. I only sense his anger because of that change. I'm looking at the man ready to kill for me. The man who has killed for me. I'm looking at the man who did unspeakable things in that basement. The one who has done it before and will do it countless times again.

Is this who I want to have children with? The person I want to make a life with?

As I stare at him, those questions roll around in my mind. The longer I assess him, the more remote his gaze becomes. He must know what I'm considering. It's like he's challenging me. He's daring me to walk away.

I don't like this coldness. It hurts. It's pushing me away.

It's also giving me a choice. Pablo wants me to know what I'm getting myself into. He can't admit these things aloud, so he's letting me see it. I don't believe this is who I'll come home to. I don't believe this is how he'll be with me. I think he'd rather keep me far from this. But I need to know. Make an informed decision.

I nod once before I rest against him again. I wrap my arm around his waist, and he relaxes. He'd tensed as he waited for my decision.

I remember he expected an answer to whether Néstor cornered me.

"Yeah."

"*Tío?*"

"I'm sorry, but Alejandro already spoke to him."

Enrique's apologizing because Pablo doesn't get to kill him on my behalf. Doesn't get to defend *his woman*. That's archaic, but fuck if I don't find the idea of being Pablo's woman arousing as fuck.

"What about *Papá?*"

"Luis's visit was successful too. He learned what he needed from the *Nuevos Reyes.*"

The New Kings—one of the deadliest street gangs in all of Colombia. Their *capitán* is serving like ten life sentences with no possibility of parole. He planned and led a raid on a house owned by *el capitán de Toros Callejeros*—the Street Bulls' leader. They massacred them. Like slaughtered them.

If Luis visits that man in prison and directly holds influence over him, then I wonder who the true mastermind was. Hell, if he can get visitation with anyone at *la alcantarilla*—the sewer, the nickname for the worst of the worst prisons—then he really has divine powers. *El Espíritu Santo* at work.

"What did *Papá* hear?"

"He knows who posted the bounty on the dark web on Humberto's behalf. Alejandro chatted with him this morning."

Another dead man.

"Does the hit still stand, *Tío?*"

"Your *papá* took care of that after meeting with Alejandro."

"Enrique, how much did that cost your family? How much was my life worth?"

"Florencia, your life is priceless. Money is no object when it comes to family."

I sit up and look at Pablo before leaning to whisper in his ear.

"Did he just give us his blessing?"

I sit up again, and he nods. He brushes hair back from my ear and brings his lips to it.

"I'm glad he gave it, but we don't need it."

"Enrique, that's kind of you to say. But I want to know what it took to cancel a quarter-million-dollar bounty."

There's a pause before Enrique answers. "Two and a half."

Holy fucking shit!

Two point five million to keep me alive!

"Florencia, your *abuelo's* looking for you. Ernesto found out about the order. He wants you to go to him."

"No."

The answer flies out of my mouth before I realize I'm going to speak.

Pablo squeezes my ass gently. "Flora, we can protect you when you and I go back to Bogotá."

"I don't want to see him. Not now and not for a long time. Maybe never. I wouldn't have had mercenaries from who knows what corner of the world after me if it weren't for him. Does he really want to be sure I'm safe? Or does he want me away from your family? Does he want to make sure I can't tell anyone what happened?"

I'm watching Pablo and waiting for Enrique to answer. When neither of them responds, I wonder if those are questions they won't answer or if they expect the other to speak. Pablo's hand was resting on my ass, but he strokes it again.

"Probably yes to all of those, *chiquita.*"

So much for that being private between us.

"It's safe for you both to leave the cabin. I'd like you to come home."

Cabin?

If this is a cabin to Enrique Diaz, what the ever-loving hell is a house? The palace in Colombia?

Home?

Does that mean Bogotá? I just said I don't want to go there.

"Flora, we can go to your apartment and get whatever you want before heading to New York until we can finish this."

My brow furrows. That's a lot to take in from one sentence.

Home is New York? The way Enrique said it, it sounded like that's not just where Pablo lives but me too.

"Finish? Humberto's dead. Néstor's dead. The hit's been called off. Do you think someone will still try to carry out the hit? Who for?"

I had a moment's reprieve from my fear, but Enrique's response isn't what I want to hear.

"Florencia, the hit is definitely done. You don't have to worry about that. But someone put Humberto up to this. Someone filled his head with the idea he'd have the money to buy Néstor. He probably thought the money from your formula would do it, but when that went away, he believed he had the money from somewhere else to pay for the hit and to pay Néstor. Someone promised him funds to replace that missed opportunity. Someone wanted Humberto to give them an in with the government. They wanted to buy the next president."

"None of that involves me. Why do I need to go to the States?"

"Florencia, I guarantee Humberto told someone you were his newest *pozolero*. He will have bragged to someone. Most likely, it's whoever promised him the money. They figured they'd get more out of him than they'd have to invest. Until we know who that is, you're not safe in Colombia. Someone's probably looking for you, but they'll want you alive."

Wonder-fucking-ful.

Enrique's explanation does nothing to reassure me. Pablo's arms tighten around me. I close my eyes and exhale.

"And what about my *abuelo*? You said he's looking for me.

Did he play a bigger role in all of this than forcing me to work for Humberto?"

"I'm sorry, Florencia."

"That's a yes that you don't want to say out loud, Enrique."

Chapter Eighteen

Pablo

My rage roils inside me like a hurricane ready to make landfall, destroying everything in its path. I didn't mean for Flora to see my anger—see the man devoid of all emotion except rage—but she did. Rather than soften my expression and push my hatred aside for her sake, I let her see inside that monster. She needed to know who I can become. She needed to decide whether she can live with that.

I wasn't always like this. *Mamá* used to call me a sensitive soul. Maybe I was once upon a time. But I'm also the best at compartmentalizing my emotions. I had to do it with Juan. He'd antagonize me until I wanted to beat the shit out of him. But I never could. I loved him because he was my little brother, but I rarely liked him. I almost never respected him. I would push those feelings aside until I could go for a long run. I could've run a marathon by the time I finished middle school because he'd push me to where he had to be out of my sight for a couple hours, and I needed to burn off steam.

It taught me to look at situations objectively and respond accordingly. *Tío* Enrique and *Papá* realized that meant I was the one most suited to be an enforcer. *Tres J's* reputation makes them ideal for stirring the pot and fucking up shit for anyone who looks sideways at my *tío*. Anyone who doesn't learn from that warning comes to see me. I can put aside the man's family and friends. I can put aside the man's insistent apologies, pleas for forgiveness, and prayers for absolution.

What soul I might have left is far from sensitive.

"*Tío*, can you tell Flora more?"

I don't like my *tío's* pause. He's always one step ahead in a conversation. A pause doesn't mean he's considering his answer. It means he's preparing me for it. I stroke Flora's entire ass as I pepper her forehead with kisses.

"Shhh, *chiquita*. It'll be all right. I'll make sure it is."

I whisper my reassurances to her, and I pray I'm not blowing smoke up her delectable ass. I never wanted to make something better for another person more than I do right now. The arm wrapped around her tightens to press her fully against me. She shifts to pull the robe open, so we're chest to chest, skin to skin.

"Florencia, Ernesto didn't admit to Humberto you're a chemist because Humberto brought it up. He approached Humberto. He was going to get thirty percent of the revenue. He told Humberto he would use his portion to help pay down your student loan debt."

"He could've paid it all off if he wanted to. He could've kept me from having any debt and paid for my entire education. I never asked because I knew he'd never do it."

"I know. He's been planning to kill *Tres J's*. He's not done with his grudge either. It wasn't enough to have played a part in my brother-in-law's death. He wants my *sobrinos* dead too."

Flora trembles in my arms, overwhelmed by the magnitude

of this situation. It doesn't surprise me, but I know she's not prepared for these manipulations and machinations. It's all too much for a sane person to handle. There's a bit of a sociopath drilled into everyone in a syndicate. It doesn't faze me anymore.

"Was he going to use the same mercenaries Humberto sent after me?"

"Possibly, but I doubt it. It would be a suicide mission, and most mercenaries know that. Most know the stories about after *Papá*'s death. Some were alive for it. Many know what happened after Esteban's death. It's a deterrent."

It was *Tía* Luciana who made sure people understood what a grieving widow's capable of. Usually, we leave no trace. We dispose of bodies, so people just disappear. One day they're there. Another they're gone. Poof.

Not my *tía*.

She took a page from the Mexican cartels' book. She wanted people to know it wasn't her brothers who avenged *Tío* Esteban's death. She made heads roll.

Like literally.

She'd sent *Tres J's* to stay with us in New Jersey before she got to work. She had a dozen men who worked for Ernesto kidnapped and beheaded. Back then, the intersection of Avenida Boyacá and Calle 80 up in the northwest part of Bogotá was the most dangerous spot in the city. She had the heads dropped into traffic, so cars swerved to avoid them, ran over them, or pushed them along the road.

That wasn't enough.

She had the bodies hanged from the neck over the side of Puente Calle 92, one of the busiest bridges in all of Bogotá. She sent a hand or foot to every major street gang or minor cartel leader. She sent one of Ernesto's *huevos* to his wife because she wouldn't let Estrella have a real man if *Tía* Luciana couldn't have hers. She sent Ernesto's second-in-command's entrails to him wrapped up like a Christmas present. She included a handwritten note that said, "Watch over your shoulder while you can. Come after my family again, and I will pluck out your eyes. Then you'll never see me coming."

I should let *Tía* Luciana handle Ernesto for good, but he's still Flora's *abuelo* as much as I despised him before and as much as I want him dead now.

"Will you do the same thing as Luciana?"

I guess she knows more than I thought.

"No, he's your family, Florencia."

"Thank heaven for small mercies."

She mutters her response. I don't know if *tío* heard her.

"Flora, do you want to go to Bogotá before going to New York? I'll take you to see your mother and to get anything you want from your apartment. I won't allow Ernesto near you."

I made the offer earlier, but that's before we learned everything we know now.

"I need to see *Mamá*, but I don't want to risk your life or mine if there are people searching for me."

"Florencia, my brother and nephew are still in Bogotá. I have a small army of men down there with little to do now."

That Humberto's dead.

"We can protect you."

I feel her uncertainty as she tenses, relaxes, and tenses again. She leans away from me so she can see my face.

"What do you think, Pablo?"

She's deferring to me even though my *tío* is *jefe de jefes*.

"We have the house on San Andrés. She can say she wants to get out of the city for a while because of everything that's happened. You can meet her on the island. You said nothing about your apartment. Does that mean you don't want to go there?"

"I don't care about anything in there. It's not worth the risk."

She's unconvinced we can protect her. It makes me feel like a failure. I'm not giving her the reassurance she needs. I put the phone on the armrest of the sofa and guide her to straddle my lap. I push down the pajama pants, and her eyes widen as though they might fall out. I guide her onto my cock, then press her to lean chest to chest again. Both of my hands grasp her ass. She releases a shuddering breath before she picks up the phone.

"*Tio*, can we call you back when we decide?"

"*Sí, sobrino.*"

"*Te quiero, Tio.* Talk to you soon."

"*Te quiero también.* Bye."

Flora hangs up and puts the phone back on the armrest. She burrows against my chest as I feel tears drip onto it.

"*Papi*, I don't know what to do. You decide, please."

"Right now, you're going to stay right where you are. You can cry. You can sleep. You can just let me hold you. You're safe."

"I don't know what to do. Can I stay like this forever? I feel safest when we're like this. You're a part of me, and I feel like I have the strongest, most powerful shield around me."

"You know I'll move heaven and earth for you, *chiquita*. You belong to me now. You're a part of me. You're mine."

My possessive comments make her sigh with each one. She's relaxing now.

"I know you're completely drained from that conversation. You're going to let me decide. You're going to nap with my cock buried in your cunt. When you wake, you're going to be my good girl and let me fuck you hard. I'm going to fill your tight little pussy with my cum because you can't get enough. You're going to beg for it. Do you know why?"

"Because I belong to you. You get to decide, Daddy. You're in control."

"That's right, *chiquita*. I decide."

She nods. I look down, and her eyes are closed.

There are things as her Dom and as her boyfriend I will never do. I will never slap her face. I will never fishhook her mouth. I'll never spit in it. That's just not how I want to treat her. Real degradation and shame aren't our kink. But if dirty talk while I'm buried in her reminds her she's given me control so she doesn't have to worry, then I'll say the most perverted things I can come up with.

It's been two days since Flora and I spoke to *Tío* Enrique. I've had three conversations with him since then, but Flora wasn't part of them. Each one included my father as well. One of them had Alejandro on the line too. There were things I needed to discuss that she couldn't hear. Some of it was regular Cartel business to keep me caught up on what's happening and what I'll need to do when I get home.

Tío Enrique's been very understanding and isn't rushing me to get back to work once I arrive. He knows Flora will need me. However, I still feel guilty that my cousins are carrying the burden of work I normally do on top of their own responsibilities.

I mentioned that while Alejandro was on with us because I apologized. He threatened to break my jaw the next time we boxed if I insisted upon babbling shit nobody wanted to hear. That made me feel a little better, but it still doesn't assuage all my guilt entirely.

One day I will inherit from *Tío* Enrique, and I want to be as good a leader as he is. He works harder than anyone else. He never expects people to do more than he's willing to do.

"*Chiquita*, you ready?" I offer Flora my hand as she stands from the seat in our family's private jet.

"I guess I'm as ready as I'll ever be."

"We'll meet *Papá* and Alejandro outside."

"I know. You've gone over it, and I understand the plan."

"I know you do, but you look terrified."

She grimaces before plastering a smile that only includes her mouth. Her eyes tell me how nervous she remains.

"*Chiquita*, I know you trust *Papá* and Alejandro about as much as you did me when we met, but—"

"No, Pablo, that's not it at all. I trust them. I just don't know how they can possibly trust me. If you believe they're okay with me, then they must be. You wouldn't lie to me about that because you wouldn't put me in that kind of position, but I'm still an Aguilar. My family has caused nothing but trouble and pain for yours."

"*Chiquita*, if you trust me not to put you in a position where you'd be around people you don't trust, then you need to know my family feels the same way about it. They trust I won't endanger them by bringing someone untrustworthy around them. I swear it'll be okay. I get how intimidating this is."

Just like I had several conversations with my family about what to do next, I had the same with Flora. She woke from her nap feeling much better about what she heard while we spoke to *Tío* Enrique. I did exactly what I promised. I reassured her I'm still in this for keeps despite all the trouble that surrounds her. She knows I don't believe any of it is her fault.

I admire her courage. It took a brave woman to work for the Cartel. It takes a brave woman to place her trust in me when she knows I'm the most dangerous man she's ever met. She's brave to trust my family can and will protect her while we're here in Bogotá. And she's brave to have agreed to start a new life in New York where she only really knows me.

The time we've spent together has been brief, but I feel like she knows me better than anyone. She knows me in ways no one else does. Not just because she's the only woman I've come in without a condom, but I've let her see parts of me no one else does. Not even other members of my family.

I've shared things with her about growing up with Juan and what that was like. My cousins know because of what they saw, which were things my parents' generation never did. But Flora is the only one I've spoken these things to aloud. She's offered insights I didn't expect, especially since she's an only child. She's helped me come to terms with a lot of shit from that part of my past. It's certainly helped build my faith in her and us.

"Daddy?"

"Sorry, *chica*, lost in thought."

"Is everything okay?"

"Yes. I didn't mean to scare you. Just making sure I remember everything."

She cocks an eyebrow at me. It tells me she knows I'm lying. She reaches for her bag, but I take both of her hands.

"Flora, I'm used to keeping so much to myself. Mostly to protect others but also to protect myself. Not just my physical safety. I don't want to lie to you when I don't have to. I'll never ever lie about how I feel about you. But some habits will take a while for me to break. I was thinking about how much you mean to me. That I admire and respect the choices you've made, and how you've made the best of situations you never asked to be put in. That isn't something I should've kept to myself. I'm sorry I tried to."

Now her smile reaches her eyes as she goes on her toes to give me a kiss. What begins as a peck goes much further when I wrap my arms around her and deepen it.

"Daddy, we have to get going. The door is open. Your father and cousin will wonder if something went wrong if we don't hurry."

I shoot her a guilty look as I shake my head. Her eyes widen.

"Oh, God, Pablo! They'll think we're having sex, and that's why it's taking us so long to get off the plane. We have to go."

The shock, embarrassment, and urgency in her voice make me chuckle.

"We're going to be around people for the next few hours. I intend to make the most of our last few minutes of privacy."

"You make it sound like it'll be days even though you admit it'll only be hours."

"Yeah, well, it'll feel like years. I'm spoiled after days of being able to touch you whenever I want."

"Well, you'll just have to survive. If you do, maybe I'll give you a reward."

My hands slip down to her ass. My right one squeezes as my left one spanks. She knows this is purely for our enjoyment. I help her with her bag. I hold her hand as we go down the steps together. The attendant follows us with our luggage.

There are five SUVs waiting for us on the tarmac.

"Daddy!"

She hisses the word as her hand clutches mine. She didn't notice them as we landed. There's one for each side of us, and our SUV will be in the middle. It's more than just *Papá* and Alejandro waiting for us, so I know she's worried all the men will believe we were fucking.

"Did Enrique or Luis believe this much security is necessary?"

"No, but I do."

"Is this an overabundance of caution, or do you think they aren't taking the threat seriously enough?"

"It's me being insanely controlling and a pain in the ass to everyone, but I don't feel an ounce of remorse if it protects you."

Alejandro and *Papá* step out of the SUV, and Alejandro goes around the trunk. He nods as we take the last step, and they walk toward us. Flora hangs back a moment, unsure what her role should be now. I hug my father as she offers Alejandro a tentative greeting. He's as unsure what to do as she is. They settle on a handshake. When I let go of *Papá*, I move to hug Alejandro.

We aren't a family who shies away from affection even in public. It's no secret to anyone that we're a super close family who're dedicated to each other. We see no weakness in showing that. It reminds people you never get just one Diaz; you get the entire family. It also reassures families who work for us. They know they can depend on us and that we're reliable. There are no internal squabbles that could distract us from our responsibilities. I glance at Flora as *Papá* steps forward.

"*Hola, Señor Diaz.*"

"*Hola, Señorita Aguilar.* It's Luis."

"Florencia."

There's another moment's hesitation as my father considers what to do. I know he doesn't want to overstep, but he wants Flora to understand he's not there out of obligation to me. He opens his arms, and she takes a wary step forward as he hugs her. I watch her eyes close, and her body relax. My father tightens his hold, and she wraps her arms around him.

I'm certain she's getting the hug she's always wished she'd had a father for. It's a reassurance I can't give her even though she calls me Daddy. I'm not a paternal figure to her. I hope she lets *Papá* be one. They step apart, and an understanding passes between them as *Papá* gives her a warm smile. She's tentative but returns it. I didn't realize how anxious this made me until I see their silent agreement, and I relax.

Alejandro watched me as much as he watched my father and girlfriend. He smirks at me and leans forward to whisper. It makes me want to elbow him in the throat.

"Should I make an appointment at the same jeweler the other families use?"

"Shhh, *cabrón*."

He means the Kutsenkos, the O'Rourkes, and Mancinellis. The men have entrusted the same jeweler to create engagement and wedding rings for every couple. I already know I will go to the man, but I'm not ready to discuss that with anyone. *Papá* saves Alejandro from my elbow in his gut when he speaks.

"Florencia, we can head to your apartment now unless you want to see your *mamá* instead."

"No, let's do that first, please. I still want to get all of that out of the way. I don't want to have that lurking in the back of my mind while I'm with *Mamá*. I don't want to worry about whether I'm taking too long with her."

"Flora, you can have as much time with your mother as you want. There's no rush."

I know she wants to believe me, but she's more than just apprehensive about being back here. She's terrified. It's a sign of trust that she came at all since she suggested we just go to New York instead.

We all climb into the SUVs and set off from the airport. We chat in the car about how cold it was in Switzerland, and how Latin Americans just aren't cut out for that sort of thing. We share how Flora spent a lot of time reading while I played my usual card games. And how we swam, and I still worked out. We name some movies we watched.

Alejandro's in the third row behind me and next to *Papá*.

He's discreet, but he flicks my ear enough to sting when we mention swimming. He knows precisely what Flora and I got up to that we would never dare mention.

I ignore him just like I have since we were kids, and I tried to hide something I did wrong from my parents. Even though I'm a few years older than him, we've always been super close. *Tres J*'s have each other. I never liked my brother, and he always preferred to hang out with our neighbor, Laura Doyle, who's now Laura Kutsenko. Alejandro's an only child, so we gravitated to each other. We're a lot alike and have wound up with similar jobs as enforcers.

It means we've worked together and received the same training. *Tres J's* knows the same things we do. However, since I'm the head enforcer and Alejandro often works alone here in Colombia, our family forced us to practice some things more than *Tres J's* has.

It's not long before we reach Flora's apartment. Her hand grips my thigh just above my knee.

"Pablo, we're not exactly inconspicuous. Are they surrounding the building?"

She obviously knows what to look for and realizes we have guards along this street besides the five veritable tanks we arrive in.

"Of course."

She stares at me and nods before waiting for me to get out first. She slides over to my spot once the driver and front passenger stand beside me. We let her out. The four of us move forward, enough for Alejandro and *Papá* to get out too. The five of us surround her as we head inside the building. She cranes her neck to see into the mailroom and the steps to the basement.

She spots guards there. There's one positioned in front of

the elevator. We ride up to her floor, and we find another guard outside the elevator. There are three guards next to her door.

"Pablo, tell me these are the only men here. That there are no others."

I give her an unrepentant stare.

"Oh, God. Pablo, are they in the stairwell and on each floor by the elevator?"

"Of course."

Papá, *Tío* Enrique, and my cousins all said this was excessive. I know Flora believes it is too. I told the men that it makes a point.

Stay the fuck away from my woman.

I might not have sworn when I was talking to *Papá* and *Tío* Enrique, but I did when I spoke to my four cousins together and separately.

Her shoulders droop, and she sighs with resignation. "Let me guess, they've already been inside and swept the place."

"No. I told you I'd be over-the-top controlling, but I haven't violated your privacy. Please let Alejandro and Paco go in ahead of us."

I nod toward one man guarding the door. She pulls her keys from her pocket and hands them to me. I unlock it, but not until *Papá* gently takes her arm and backs her away from the door. He stands behind her as the other two guards step in front of them. If anything happens, I'll be the first target, and the other men can protect her.

When nothing happens, Alejandro and Paco go inside. I move to stand beside Flora, slipping my arm around her waist. I don't have to draw her against me. She leans instead. It's a few minutes before we get the all-clear to go inside. She'd already spotted the packing supplies outside the door.

We move through the living room and dining room together

as she tells the men what she wants to bring with her. She believes we'll put it all in storage either here or in New York. I haven't told her I'd like to go through everything and combine our households. I don't want to overwhelm her entirely with all these major changes.

Chapter Nineteen

Flora

Pablo and I head into my bedroom with packing supplies, and I appreciate the privacy. I don't want any of those men seeing me pack my panties or vibrator. I twist to look back into the living room as Luis holds a box shut, and Alejandro tapes it.

"Your father and cousin don't need to do this. This is so far beneath them."

"Helping you will never be beneath them."

"Moving—packing boxes. It's menial labor. They're in suits."

As though they can hear me despite how I whisper, both men remove their suit coats and pull off their ties. They toss the coats on the sofa and stick their ties in their pockets. They roll up their sleeves. It's impossible not to notice the shoulder holsters they wear or how they both have a gun under each arm.

"*Chiquita,* they'll never be too good to help family."

His gaze bores into me, practically daring me to disagree that I'm now part of his family. I don't have his last name. I'm not wearing a ring. We haven't even said "I love you," but he speaks as though I'm already a Diaz. I love it, even if it's intimidating and makes my head swim.

I don't want to argue, so I take the box Pablo assembled while we talked. I open my dresser and start to clear it out.

"What do you think you're doing, *chiquita?*"

Pablo's warm breath tickles my ear. I think he's reaching around me to wrap his arms around my middle. Instead, he plucks the panties from my hand. He steps back and grabs the scissors from the top of the dresser.

"Pablo!"

I glance out to the living room, worried I said his name too loudly. I try to snatch my underwear from him, but he holds them above my head while he cuts a pair into shreds.

"Stop. Daddy, I can't go without panties."

My hushed voice is urgent as I try again—unsuccessfully—to get my underwear back. He slices a thong this time, destroying it with two cuts.

"Did you wear panties in Switzerland?"

"No, but that was different. It was just us."

"Consider it my solution to panty lines under your clothes that might draw unwelcome attention."

"And I suppose you decide what constitutes unwelcome."

"Anyone other than me looking at your ass."

"I cannot be around your family without panties on. Let me have a couple pairs."

"You are now."

I bite my lower lip and shake my head. His hand slips down the front of my jeans and tugs me until our shoes meet. He puts the scissors down and unfastens my pants. I grab his wrists since anyone could walk in here. He pulls the top of the waistband apart just enough to see the cotton top inch. He leans in and growls in my ear.

"When we're alone tonight, I will punish you. I made my expectations clear, *chiquita*. I forbid panties. I will *not* have an unnecessary layer between your cunt and me. It is my secret to share with only you. That you have nothing on beneath your clothes, and I can have that pussy whenever I want. When we get to the condo tonight, you will go directly to our bedroom. You will strip and lie on the bed on your belly. I will punish you for disobeying me."

I can't help the way I shiver. A small part of me was too embarrassed to meet his family while feeling partially naked. But most of me did it to get a rise out of him. I cup his hard cock and stroke it through his suit trousers. He grabs my wrist and pulls it away.

"I edge you, *chica*, not the other way around. I will never embarrass you in public. That's the only reason you aren't naked now with my cock in your ass. You're lucky I don't take you in the bathroom and fuck you, taking the chance everyone will figure out what we're doing."

I don't want to be embarrassed, but the risk of someone catching us excites me. Pablo can tell. He slips his fingers down my panties and between my legs. I widen my stance, so he can inch his fingers into me. They're in just long enough to coat them. He pulls his hand away and licks his fingers.

"*Deliciosa*."

He kisses my neck, moving up to behind my ear. He knows how erotic I find that spot. How it makes me want to beg or do anything he commands.

"Think about how I could be finger-fucking you right now if you had a skirt on and no panties."

"Your family would still be here."

"There's not a man out there who'll come near this bedroom while I'm alone with you in here."

"Do they think we'd fuck with the door open?" I'm aghast at the thought.

"They know I respect you too much to do that. They just won't intrude upon a couple. We could be discussing something private, or you could have something private out while you pack."

"Like my now-shredded panties?"

"Or that." He points to my vibrator.

"That I can leave behind. My panties? No."

He plays with my nipples through my shirt and bra. He pinches and twists and then tugs. He kisses me to swallow my whimpers. He rolls them between his fingers and thumb.

"Bring them, little one, but don't be surprised when you get home, and they're gone."

"And my vibrator?"

The grin he gives me...

I might come just from the promise it holds.

"You're definitely bringing that. It'll tide us over until we can order any and everything we want—any and everything we're curious about. I already know what's on my list."

He steps back, letting go of me. He wants me to ask, so I do. I'm happy to oblige and play along as I drop all my panties in the box. I put my bras and socks in after, then I move onto the other clothes in my dresser.

"What's that, Daddy?"

"A jeweled butt plug like we talked about. Nipple and clit clamps, obviously."

"Obviously."

I parrot him as I roll my eyes. He chuckles as he takes a box and moves to the closet. He keeps his voice low, so only I can hear him.

"A spreader. The handcuffs you mentioned. Some Ben Wa balls. A bullet vibrator."

Oh, fuck. He intends for me to wear that when I'm not at home. They have apps now to control them. He could insist I insert it, then he could turn it up while he's not even around. He'd know he was tormenting me, even if he's not there to see it.

"A flogger, a couple paddles, a whip, and an around-the-thighs vaginal spreader, maybe some labia weights."

He's given this some thought. Is this what he's had with his previous subs? Are these things he knows he already enjoys? I shouldn't feel this intense wave of jealousy since I was with someone the night he and I met. I ended things with him to be with Pablo. But I haven't hinted at anything I've done in the past.

He notices I just nod. He comes over to stand beside me, putting his hand on my wrist as I reach to take another shirt from a drawer.

"*Chiquita,* I don't sleep as much as you do, not that you sleep nearly enough. I know how stalkerish this sounds, but I love to watch you. You're so at peace. You sleep naked next to me, so I can see and touch every part of you."

"I know. You wake me at least once to have sex every night."

"You do the same thing. I've lost track of how many fantasies I've had about all the ways I want to share my dominance with you."

"How many ways you want me to submit."

"Yes."

"And if I told you I could've read all those books twice as fast as I did?"

He slips his arm around me and pulls me against him. "Why didn't you?"

"Because I have my own fantasies that distracted me. I want you to tie me to a Saint Andrew's Cross or an A-frame rack. I want you to bend me over a spanking bench and fuck my ass while you spank me. I want you to DP me with your cock and one of those fucking machines."

I've never used one of those dildo machines that thrust and retreat. I want to try it with Pablo.

"What else?"

His voice rasps, and I know he's imagining everything I said. I cup his cock, and it's like a metal pipe in his trousers.

"I'll come if you do that, *chiquita*."

"I want you to command me to strip and then get on my knees while you're fully dressed. You just let your cock out through your zipper. You push my face to it and make me suck while anyone at a club who wants to watch can. I want you to mark me with your cum."

"Flora, we need to hurry and finish your apartment."

That bursts the bubble we were in. I pull away, but he cups my jaw, his thumb on the left, and his fingers on the right.

"We need to finish your apartment, then we'll see your mother. We'll take as long as you want there, but I'm not spending longer than we need here. I want you in our room, bent over the bed, as I fuck you until you scream."

I look toward the en suite bathroom and tilt my head. We rush in there, both of us pushing our pants down by the time the door closes. I grip the edge of the sink as I tilt my hips back. He thrusts into me, pounding my pussy until it hurts. I take all of it, reveling in how big he is and how he stretches me. My clit rubs against the lip of the basin each time he surges into me. It only takes two minutes before I'm coming. He's right there with me.

We're pulling up our clothes as I wiggle my hips, snapping the elastic waistband of my panties against my skin.

"This'll trap all the cum in my pussy. They're not so bad after all."

"I'll keep you tied to our bed with your legs in the air when I really want my cum to stay in you. I want your thighs sticky with it."

"Yes, Daddy."

All of that sounds fantastic. It's certainly an incentive to hurry. We return to my room and finish before the other men have done my living room and kitchen.

"Pablo, if my mother doesn't want to hold on to all my stuff, then I need to find a storage place. I'm assuming she will. She has space in the garage for my furniture since I don't park in it anymore. But if she won't, do you know anywhere safe?"

He hesitates before darting his gaze to Luis, who studiously ignores us as he and Alejandro hoist my queen-size box spring. It wouldn't surprise me if, despite its awkward length and width, either of them could carry it on their own. A moving van showed up twenty minutes ago, so I really have to plan for what I'm going to do with everything that's now packed.

"*Chica*, you labeled all the boxes clearly, so it'll be easy to tell what's what. We can ship the things you want in New York, and we can store or get rid of the rest."

I stare at him for what feels like forever.

"Am I really moving to New York?"

"I know this is a huge decision, but I hope that's what you want."

"I want to be with you, and you're based in New York. I know you have to be. It's just a lot for me to wrap my head around. Not only would I be moving to another country, I'd also be moving there for a guy."

Before *Mamá* got sick, I thought I'd stay in the States. I thought I'd be living there right now, but I'm not. I changed my plans for the sake of my family. Knowing I could go back to what I wanted all along should reassure me. However, it's still intimidating, especially when I add a romantic relationship into the mix.

"Are you afraid we won't work out?"

I hear a hitch in his voice. He hates the idea of my leaving him. I know he's committed to me. He wouldn't do all of this—ask me to be part of his world—if he didn't want me to be at his side permanently. I fully understand that now.

"That's one thing I absolutely do *not* fear. It's a lot to think about, though. Moving to a new country, setting up a new place."

Hurt flashes in his eyes before he nods.

"What did I just say that bothers you?"

His eyebrows shoot straight up. He didn't realize he let me see his emotions. Or maybe I can read them when most people can't.

"Until we're sure the threats are entirely gone, I'd like you to stay with me, please."

He's hedging.

"And after that?"

He watches me. I'm waiting for an answer, but he's not giving one. That's when I realize what I said a moment ago.

"Daddy, I don't want to assume we're going to live together from the get-go. You might not want someone in your home this quickly."

"*Chica*, why would I say, 'our bed,' 'our room,' 'at home,' if I didn't want you there for good?"

"I didn't want to read too much into it."

"You need to read a hell of a lot more into it. Flora, I want you to live with me."

The men are still moving around my kitchen and living room, but a guy knocks and asks if we're ready for them to take the boxes in my room down to the truck. We step into the bathroom again, but we keep the door open.

"Pablo, that's a massive step. Are we there yet? Maybe I can put my stuff in storage in New York and get somewhere furnished for a while."

He observes me again before he nods his head. It's just weird to think I might live with a man I don't love. It seems premature, or at least out of order. To live together, then maybe —eventually—say I love you.

"Daddy, I'm not saying never. Let's just get to New York in one piece, then we'll decide."

The way he looks at me makes me think there's more he wants to say, but he's holding back. He's following my lead in this, and I appreciate it. But I also don't think I like it as much as I tell myself I should.

"*Chiquita*, I know you're giving up your job and your family to come to the States. You're giving up your home and your friends. You're giving up the plans you had."

"I'm giving up time with *Mamá*. I'm not excited about going long stretches without seeing her, but I don't always see her weekly. It can be two or three weeks, even though we live in the same city. It's just not months anymore like it was in college and grad school. I'll miss *Mamá's* parents, but I won't miss my father's."

I want to vomit thinking about my *abuelo*. I'm sure there's still a shit ton I don't know—a shit ton I don't want to know.

"Once you're settled, maybe your mother would like to move up to New York."

I consider what he's saying. I said I don't want to move in with him yet, but I want to eventually.

"Where would *Mamá* fit into that?"

"Would you want her to live with you?"

"No. And when we live together, she's definitely not going to be there either."

Relief eases the strain around his eyes when he hears me acknowledge we'll live together at some point.

"I never thought she would. But she could live near—us."

He tests out "us," and I nod. His body relaxes, even though I don't think his stance changes. I can just tell. I don't want to stress him out on top of how he's worrying about my safety, but I want to look before I leap.

"That would be nice if she wants to move to New York, but I don't think she ever will. She'll visit, but I don't think she'd give up her life here."

"You have a career here."

"No. I have a job. I always wanted to work in a lab. I became a pharmacist because it was somewhat parallel to what I planned, and the hours were convenient for when *Mamá* was sick. I thought about going back to the States to work, but *Mamá* asked me not to. I'll miss friends, but it's not like I hang out with them every night. I live in an apartment, which I like, and it's home, but it's not something I'm overly attached to. I was saving for a house before I moved back here. The more I think about it, the more I feel like my life is getting back on track by moving to New York."

"*Tía* Luciana and *Tía* Catalina are in the real estate industry. They can help you with anything you need."

"Thank you."

The men carry down the last of my stuff before I lock my door. Then we're on our way to my mother's.

Chapter Twenty

Flora

"*Mamá?*"

"*Hola, niña. Estoy en la sala. Ya voy.*" Hi, little girl. I'm in the living room. I'll be right there.

Mamá's always called me that. Her greeting has nowhere near the same connotation as when Pablo calls me little girl. Thinking that makes my toes curl in my shoes.

My mom has a basket of folded laundry in her arms. Her smile drops the moment she sees Pablo with me. She marches forward, putting the basket on the entryway table. I reach to give her a hug, but when I move, it allows her to see the line of black SUVs outside the gate. There's one in the driveway. I barely convinced the guard to let it in. Apparently, the Diaz men are very recognizable.

"What are they doing here? How could you bring these men to my home?"

"*Mamá*, can we sit down? There's a lot to tell you."

"No. No Diaz man is welcome here. I want them gone."

"*Mamá—*"

Luis interrupts me. "Magdalena, Alejandro and I will wait in the car, but you need to speak to my son. It's the only way to ensure your daughter is safe."

It's weird to hear Luis call my mother by her first name. It shouldn't surprise me they know each other, but it does. I don't know how they do, but I guess once upon a time, they floated in similar social circles. That or he knew my father cheated on his sister with my mother.

"Why would I ever trust a Diaz with my daughter's safety?"

"Because no one means more to my son than Florencia."

Mamá's eyes widen before she scowls at me. Her gaze darts to Pablo, and I step in front of him as though I could protect him. Perhaps from *Mamá* I can, but he's a shield at my back for everything else.

"No, I refuse to hear any of this. Florencia, come inside. Tell them to leave."

"*Mamá*, I won't do that. Luis is right. You need to hear what Pablo and I have to say. It's not safe for me here, but I couldn't leave without seeing you."

"You couldn't leave?" She crosses her arms and cants her head to the side.

"Yes, I can't leave without seeing you."

"But you already did. You left Bogotá and went somewhere without telling me where. Your grandfather had to tell me you'd run away with a Diaz, and now you show up with his family on my front doorstep. How could you betray our family like that?"

"*Mamá*, please let us come inside and have this conversation in private. Your guards don't need to hear all of this."

"They need to hear me when I tell them to kick out Luis Diaz."

"Magdalena, always a pleasure to see you."

I watch Luis nudge Alejandro as I glance back over my shoulder. The men turn around and walk down the steps. No one speaks until they're in the SUV. The vehicle doesn't go anywhere, but now, with the windows so tinted, Luis and Alejandro are out of sight. I step farther into the entryway. *Mamá* tries to stand her ground, but I shift to the right and make room for Pablo to come inside. He reaches for the door and shuts it softly.

"No, I didn't say he's welcome here, Florencia. Whatever is going on ends right now. Send him away."

"*Mamá*, the only person who's kept me alive for the past two and a half weeks is Pablo. He's the only one who's risked his life to make sure I'm okay. It certainly wasn't *Abuelo*. He's the reason I needed Pablo's help in the first place."

"He's just manipulating you, *niña*. That's what his family does."

"While ours murders."

The words fly from my lips before I realize what I'm going to say. My mother's expression darkens, and her laugh crackles in the air, so shrill and brittle.

"*Los Diaz* have murdered more people than you and I could ever imagine. That's how they maintain control. They kill anybody who looks in their direction."

"They defend their own. Why did Enrique and Luis come down here all those years ago? It was because their uncle murdered their father. They were reacting. Why did my father die? Because he tried to hurt Luciana. Esteban was only reacting. Why did Luciana do what she did after Esteban's death? Because she was reacting to his murder. Why did Pablo take me away from the city? Because Humberto put a hit on me, and *Abuelo* did nothing to stop it. He was just reacting. It's easy to blame *los Diaz* for everything because they have so much power. But *Mamá*, you and I both know our family isn't inno-cent in this. That our family instigated everything. You and I are lucky we even have family left after the way ours has hurt Pablo's. That my grandparents are alive is nothing short of a miracle, perhaps an act of God."

"Yes, because that's how Enrique Diaz sees himself. He is God, and everyone else must bow to him."

"*Mamá*, I'd be dead right now if Enrique Diaz said Pablo couldn't help me."

I glance over at Pablo, and I know without a doubt, Pablo would've defied his uncle—would've defied anybody in his family—to help me. But that's not the point I want to make right now. I want *Mamá* to see Pablo's family is on my side.

"You ran away when your *Abuelo* could've helped you. He could've protected you."

I fist my hands as I control my temper. I don't want to blurt anything else out.

"*Mamá*, it was *Abuelo* who brought me to Humberto's attention. He's the one who suggested I work for Humberto. He claimed he'd use shares of the profit from the drugs my formula makes to pay down my student loans. You and I both know he'd never do that. He could've prevented my having that burden, but he didn't. And that's fine because I never wanted to accept money from him, and I sure as hell don't want it now. But he wasn't really going to spend that money on me. He wanted to put a hit out on Pablo's *primos*. Killing their father didn't satisfy him. Now he wants to go after more *los Diaz*."

"That's your *Abuelo's* decision. It has nothing to do with us."

She's pushing me to the edge with her obstinance. I guess I know where I get it from. I want to shake her.

"It has everything to do with us because we're caught in the middle. I think you knew *Abuelo* was the one who suggested me to Humberto. I think you knew it wasn't the other way around."

"So what if it was? There was nothing either of us could've done to stop your *abuelo* or Humberto. It was better for you not to know."

"How can you think that?"

"Because I knew you would've held it against your *abuelo*, and you would've been uncooperative. It would've angered Humberto and risked your life."

"Even if I pissed Humberto off, it was *Abuelo's* responsibility to protect me."

I stretch my fingers out, realizing my nails had dug into my palms. When I slide my hand into Pablo's, I think my mother's head might explode. Right now, I need to feel his solid presence. I know the only way to get that is for us to be touching.

His arm around me would be more than *Mamá* could stand. She's having a hard enough time accepting our clasped hands. I'm tired of standing in the foyer, so I lead Pablo into the living room. *Mamá* can come if she wants. I know she will because there's still more she wants to say. I'm certain of that. There's nothing I want to hear, but walking away now won't make peace between us.

"*Mamá*, I know how you feel about *los Diaz*. I felt the same way too when I first met Pablo. I didn't trust him. I didn't want to be anywhere near him." I glance over at him. "I told him to fuck off twice, but despite my rudeness, when he found out I was in danger, he came to help me. He could've turned his back. He could've ignored discovering there was a hit put on me. Instead, he risked his life to intervene."

"He just wants you to work for his family instead."

I ignore that comment. I won't share that it crossed my mind, but only for a hot second.

"It cost his family a fortune to get the hit called off. It

wasn't *Abuelo* who took care of it. He didn't want to, and he didn't have the means to."

"You exaggerate. Men followed you home. You didn't give your *abuelo* a chance to help."

"*Mamá*, it wasn't just some men. There was a quarter million-dollar bounty on my head. It cost *los Díaz* two and a half million dollars to end that."

Mamá scoffs, but her expression changes when her gaze meets Pablo's. I look up at him. He's steadfast in his attention to me. His expression is relaxed, yet it's intense. It's loving.

"Two and a half million?"

"Yes, *Mamá*."

"Why were they willing to spend all that money?"

That question hurts. I know she isn't asking in general why anyone would spend that much. I know she's asking specifically about Pablo's family. But that's how it feels.

"Because your daughter is my future."

I didn't expect Pablo to admit that. At least not so early in the conversation. Actually, it feels like *Mamá* and I have been going around in circles for hours, but it's the first time he's spoken up. I sit back from where I perched on the edge of the sofa. I lean against him, and his arm comes around my shoulders.

"And how do I know you're not manipulating Florencia any more than Humberto or Ernesto?"

"Because what do I have to gain? There's nothing Ernesto has that I want, and Humberto's no longer a problem. Neither is Néstor."

I suck in a breath when Pablo mentions *Mamá's* ex-boyfriend. I know she attacked him the last time she saw him, but they were together for nearly fifteen years.

"Thank heaven for small mercies."

Sarcasm drips from her words while she glowers at Pablo. I

want to snap at her for being ungrateful. But she's hated Pablo's family far longer than she hasn't. Three and a half decades of hate won't disappear in half an hour.

"How much do I owe you for that favor?"

"Nothing. I did it for Florencia's sake."

My elbow pokes into his ribs. I don't enjoy hearing my full name from him. It feels so distant even though I get he's trying not to antagonize my mother even more than he already has.

"*Mamá*, there's so much *Abuelo* could've done, and he did none of it. Hating Pablo and his family doesn't change what our family didn't do to protect me. Doesn't change how *Abuelo* started this whole mess. He did it for himself. He didn't care about me and the dangers it put me in. He didn't care about you and how it would've hurt you if something happened to me. He did it all for himself. We've never been part of his family. Not really. He never really accepted me because he wouldn't do this to my *primos*."

"He wouldn't do it to your *primos* because they're useless. They have no skills that benefit him. They're *idiotas*."

"And I'm supposed to be proud that I'm well educated enough for him to risk my life? To sell me like a sack of potatoes to a man who had no conscience? A man who had his own brother killed. A man who could do that would've just as easily murdered me."

"He wouldn't have gotten his hands dirty." Pablo mutters his comment, but *Mamá* and I both hear him.

"What Pablo said is true. That's why Humberto put a bounty on me. It wasn't dead or alive. I'm certain he only would've paid if I were dead."

Mamá just won't relent. "You're distracted by his good looks and charm. Those will wear off, and then where will you be? Probably in the same position I am."

"I am not Domingo. No man in my family is anything like him. I would never abandon Flora."

"Flora, is it? How long did it take before you slept together? An hour? Two hours?"

"*Mamá!*"

My cheeks are radiating heat. This isn't something she and I have ever talked about. I can't believe she's bringing up something so private with Pablo here. I can't believe she's talking about my sex life at all. We've never ever done that.

Pablo's thumb rubs against the base of my neck. It soothes me.

"I care about your daughter more than I do anyone else in the world. I understand you don't believe me. Perhaps with time I can show you. But whether you believe me doesn't change the fact that I'll protect Flora from any threat. It doesn't matter if they're her family. Anyone who threatens Flora will discover just how protective *los Diaz* is about family—by blood or by choice."

"Oh, so now she's part of your family. She's my daughter."

"And that will never change, *Señora* Bautista. But she will be my wife."

I force myself not to react. It's been a foregone conclusion, but it's still a lot to take in to hear him say that. It's one thing to think it—even imagine it—but it's altogether different when it's said aloud, especially with the conviction *Mamá* and I hear in Pablo's voice. My hesitation is slipping away.

It's not just hearing that; it's his reassuring presence. He was silently supporting me by being beside me, but now he's ready to declare himself. It feels like he and his family are the only ones on my side. Despite how much *Mamá* loathes *los Diaz*, she should at least acknowledge how they've protected me so far. I understand she doesn't want me to have a future with them, but she should acknowledge they're part of my present and not as a threat.

"*Mamá*, if you won't believe me about *Abuelo* and you won't accept that Pablo's the one who's been protecting me, then there's really nothing more to say. I wish it weren't this way, but I can't reason with you if you insist upon denying the truth."

"The truth is *los Diaz* are manipulating you. Blood is thicker than water, *mija*." My daughter.

"Not in this case, *Mamá*. I know there're limits to what you can do, but you're still my mother. Even if you couldn't have stopped *Abuelo*, you could've warned me. You didn't."

My voice cracks as I repeat the refrain that's run through my head on a loop every time I think about what's going on. I want to think I can get over that—that I can reason it away—that I can forgive her—but I don't know that I can. It feels like such a betrayal.

The only way I can stomach thinking about it is knowing how little power *Mamá* has. I don't doubt she did what she thought was best for me. However, she couldn't have been more wrong.

Chapter Twenty-One

Pablo

My heart breaks for Flora as I listen to her argue with her mother. Empathy isn't a quality I've been accused of. I can feel it for those within my family, but I'm never interested in feeling it for others. In my line of work, you reap what you sow, so there's always been a reason for my actions.

But I'm trying to be understanding for Magdalena's sake since I hope she's my future mother-in-law. It worries me that if this forces Flora into a contentious relationship with her mother, she'll pick Magdalena over me. I can't blame her, and to be honest, it's the one thing that could drive us apart. I don't want to put a wedge between her mother and her. Even if Flora accepts it for now, eventually it will corrode our relationship too.

"Pablo, leave now. I don't want a *hijo de puta* in my house corrupting my daughter, spinning untrue stories that prove my daughter's gullible." Son of a bitch.

"*Mamá*, don't call him that!"

Flora jumps out of her seat, her face flushed red. If it were some other situation, the sparks flying from her eyes would be arousing as fuck. However, this is hardly a moment I want to revel in. My cock's ready to shrivel, and my balls want to tuck up inside me. That's how far from excited this conversation makes me.

I rise and slide my arm around Flora's waist.

"Flora, your mother loves you more than anything. For better or for worse, she has dedicated her life to you. You can't blame her for being protective after the lies she's heard. She's reacting the way she should."

"I don't need your help with my daughter. I told you to get out. You're nothing more than a monster."

I take that in stride since I've been called that too many times to count. It's hardly the first and hardly the last time. I see how it's hurting Flora, though. I won't leave without her, but I can try to diffuse things a little.

"*Señora* Bautista, I will go outside, but the door remains open, and I remain on the steps."

"You believe the world revolves around you. That's not how it works. This is my home, and you are intruding. Get off my land and take your shitty family with you."

"*Mamá*, if he leaves, I leave too."

"Flora, you need to resolve this with your mother. I can give you privacy to do that. But like I said, the door remains open, and I stand on the steps. I won't go where I can't see or hear you."

"See? He's controlling you already." She turns her fiery gaze on me. "What? Do you believe I'd hurt my daughter?"

"I think you already are with the way you're upsetting her. I also won't relent when it comes to her safety. I've promised to protect her, and that's what I'll do. I can't if I'm unable to see and hear her. My promise to Flora comes before anything else."

"I give it five minutes when the Cartel comes calling for you to break those promises."

"*Mamá*, I understand what it means to be involved with a man in the Cartel. I know what Pablo means with each promise he makes. I understand their limitations, and I accept them for what they are. But he's not lying to me. He's endangered his own life to protect me over and over. I'm sorry it's come to this, but I'm leaving, and I won't be back."

"You're picking this *hijo de puta* over me?"

"I'm picking being safe over likely dying young. I'm picking the person who stands up for me. I'm picking the person who makes me happy."

We've been speaking Spanish so far, but as far as I know her mother doesn't speak English, unless she's been hiding that from Flora. That's what my *chiquita* told me in Switzerland. I switch languages. I know it's rude, and it'll antagonize Magdalena more, but it's the only way to have some semblance of a private conversation.

"Little one, you need to resolve this with your mother. I don't want you leaving here resentful. There's nothing more important to me than family, and you know I consider you part of mine. Things are testing your loyalty right now, but family's important to you too. You'll regret not coming to peace with your mother. You know I won't rescind my protection, but I won't be what causes you to end the longest relationship you've ever had. I won't break up your family."

Tears fill her eyes. "You're the only one trying to keep my family together, Pablo. I admire you for that, but it's not your decision whether my mom and I can reconcile. The ball is in her court. I'll tell her as much. I don't want to destroy things with her, but even if you weren't in the picture, she still hurt me."

Flora takes a breath as she watches me. I hope my expression shows I'm on her side no matter what she decides.

"I know, little one, but I believe she did the best she could. It was a poor set of choices, and I believe some of them were selfish, but I don't believe she set out to hurt you. I know she's spent a lifetime trusting the wrong men, but it's all she's known since before she was your age. *Los Aguilar* sank their talons in and haven't let go. Look at it as if they brainwashed her."

I watch Flora inhale deeply before she turns back toward her mother, and the conversation switches back to Spanish.

"*Mamá*, please don't do this. Don't make me choose between you and Pablo. He'll walk away before he comes between us, but you need to understand I'll follow him."

"He's willing to give up that easily, or is it he'll manipulate you into chasing him?"

"*Mamá*, you insist upon seeing things that aren't there. *Papá* betrayed you by forcing you to be his mistress rather than marrying you once Luciana made her choice. He could've made a happy home with us, but he chose revenge over us. What kind of man does that? He might've claimed he did it for his family, but it proves he never considered you and me a part of that. You keep siding with a man who lied to you your entire relationship. You're choosing to support *Abuelo* when he risked your only child's life. *Abuelito* and *Abuelita* have warned you about *Abuelo* over and over. They've seen what he's like, but you won't believe your own parents. Why does *Abuelo* have such a hold on you?"

"He's all I have left that connects me to Domingo. You never knew your father. Ernesto looks and sounds so much like Domingo. It's as though every time I'm with Ernesto, I'm with Domingo again."

Holy fuck!

Does Flora get the implications of what her mother said?

From the way she jerks away and bumps into me, I'd say she understands completely. She shakes her head so vigorously her hair whips around her face.

"*Mamá*, how could you?"

"It was the price of his supporting us in the beginning. Then it was my chance to keep a part of your father with me."

"Did Néstor know?"

"Of course. Who do you think introduced me to Néstor? Who do you think suggested I'd be a good match for him?"

"Is that why you didn't marry Néstor? Because you were sleeping with my *abuelo*?"

I'm as horrified as Flora. This is *not* the direction I expected this conversation to go.

Holy hell.

"No. I didn't love Néstor, but I loved the lifestyle I lived with him. He felt the same way."

"Do you love *Abuelo*?"

"No, and he doesn't love me either. I told you he's a way for me to remain connected to the man I've always loved."

What kind of twisted mind does Magdalena have? I can't imagine Domingo would ever be all right with that from how possessive he was with my *tía*. Not because he loved her, but because the idea of another man having what he claimed was his drove him to his death. Sharing his mistress with his father is something he never would've accepted. From what I heard, much of what drove his jealousy and possessiveness was trying to prove he was better than his father. I heard he claimed Ernesto was too old to lead the family, and that Domingo was ready to step into his shoes.

"So, you picked *Abuelo* over me. You could've sacrificed for me, but you didn't. I gave up my chance for a career in the States and rushed home to you the moment I heard you were sick. Once you were better, I could've gone back, but you asked me not to. It was never about wanting my company or needing me because of your health. You did it so I was available to *Abuelo*. I can't believe how you've betrayed me, *Mamá*."

"I admit I've done plenty of selfish things in my life. But I had few career options. I got involved with your father when I was nineteen. He promised I'd never have to work a day in my life. When I discovered he accepted a marriage contract with Luciana, I tried to break it off with him. I even got a job. But he was so apologetic and kind to me. I know Ernesto and Josue forced him. He valued family too."

I barely keep from snorting when I hear that bullshit. But I remain quiet since we might actually get somewhere with Magdalena's confession.

"He was willing to set aside his happiness with me for his duties to his family and to the cartel."

"*Papá* was never really cartel. I know the entire story now, *Mamá*. Even the parts everyone's always left out. *Los Aguilar* tried to overthrow *los Diaz*. It didn't work. That was the whole reason for the marriage contract. *Papá* would've worked for Josue. It meant he would've been an underling to the *jefe de jefes*. In exchange, *los Diaz* agreed not to obliterate *Papá's* family. It wasn't some great sacrifice on *Papá's* part to be the price of peace. It was to keep himself alive. Yet he still pursued his revenge. Look where it got him. Dead."

Magdalena knows what happened better than Flora or me. She nods along with what Flora says, but it's as though she's waiting for her daughter to finish, so she can carry on with her side of the story.

"Once I had you, I was a single mother without a job. I relied on *los Aguilar* and my parents, so I wouldn't have to get a nanny for you. I wanted to be the one who raised you. That was more important than being independent and struggling to put a roof over our heads. By the time you were old enough not to need me as much, it felt like I was too old to learn anything new. And everyone knew my connection to *los Aguilar*. That's when things began with Ernesto."

"He provided for us, but at what cost, *Mamá*? My life. That's what it would have come down to."

"He told me you'd work in a lab. I had no idea it would be in the jungle. He told me he was getting you a professional position. But it wasn't until the second time you went to the lab that I truly discovered what he was doing. Believe me or not, but I argued with him. He threatened both of us. That's when I learned you'd met with Humberto directly. Things were beyond my control, *mija*. I didn't want to fill your head with ideas that you could disagree with Humberto or your *abuelo* because I knew they wouldn't forgive you for that. Ernesto lied to me about you not having protection. He swore up and down you had guards going with you. That's why I thought they were just men at your place watching out for you. After all these years—even as duplicitous and calculating as your *abuelo* has always been—it's hard to accept he'd risk your life. I knew deep down he would, but it's far easier to blame *los Diaz*."

She shifts her focus to me. She observes how I hold Flora close. I believe she sees the genuine affection I feel for Flora. How I really am dedicated to her daughter. However, unlike the other men in their lives, I am not lying when I pledge to make Flora my priority.

Her shoulders droop as she sighs. Resignation makes her look older than she did a moment ago. She's a beautiful woman who didn't look her age until now.

"*Mamá*, can you accept Pablo?"

Her gaze bores into me.

"I can't promise more than I'll try. I need to see him with you longer."

"We aren't staying in Bogotá, *Mamá*. We're going to New York."

"Why? If Humberto's dead and so is Néstor, the threat is gone."

It's time for me to interject with more truth that'll only hurt her. But secrets at Flora's and Magdalena's expense got us in this mess.

"No, *Señora*, it's not. Humberto didn't have the money to pay such an expensive hit. Neither did Néstor. Someone bankrolled that. We still need to find out who. They may not kill Flora. But if they let her live, it's because they want her knowledge and the formula. We have more resources at our disposal when we're in New York."

"But in New York, you have more syndicates than just the Cartel."

"That's true. But like I said, we have more resources there than we do here. Flora's also not as recognizable there as she is here. She can blend in far better."

Magdalena assesses me, and I know she's finally accepting what we've said is true and that Flora hasn't exaggerated. I don't believe she's a fickle woman who's simply thrown up her hands in annoyance and given in. I think we've cracked the shell she's kept around herself for decades, that she knows the things we're saying resonate because of how the men have been in her life. I don't know that she'll ever fully believe in my innocence and Ernesto's culpability, but it's a start.

"*Mamá*, Pablo and I need to get going. We've already packed up my apartment. I didn't want to leave again without saying goodbye. I don't know when I'll make it back down here, but I hope you'll consider coming up to the States."

Flora hedges her bets and doesn't suggest Magdalena move there but at least come for a visit. I squeeze Flora's waist.

"Once I'm certain you're not in danger, I'll bring you back down here to visit whenever you want."

I'm careful not to say "if." I leave it open to Flora saying never. I don't believe it'll come to that, but my guess is it'll be a long time before she's comfortable here again. Perhaps not until after Ernesto's death. As much as I'd like to hurry that along, he's still Flora's *abuelo*. If most of our troubles stem from betrayal, killing her grandfather would hardly redeem me or prove my loyalty.

Magdalena nods. I know she regrets now that she spent this entire visit arguing with her daughter, but Flora wants to get away from here. I don't blame her. If it weren't for Flora, I would've bolted ages ago. I don't want her to feel rushed and squeeze her waist again as she looks up at me. I hope she understands we can stay longer if she wants. Her gaze tells me she wants out of here fast, so I won't push the issue.

"*Señora* Bautista, I wish we'd met under better circumstances, but I hope to see you again in New York whenever you're available to visit."

I'm just as careful not to say "us" as I was about "if." Let her draw her own conclusions about Flora and me living together. I don't need to add insult to injury. I let go of Flora's waist to offer Magdalena my hand. She glances at it before extending hers. While she squeezes hard to make a point, I'm careful not to crush hers.

Flora hesitates when I let go of Magdalena's hand, then she hugs her mother. I watch as a couple of tears drip from her eyes. I want nothing more than to be the one hugging her now, but that'll have to wait.

"*Te quiero, mija.* I'm sorry for all my mistakes. I hope one day you'll believe I did what I thought was best. I know many of my decisions were selfish, but I never made them to hurt you."

"I know, *Mamá*, and I don't want you to think my relationship with Pablo is to spite you or *Abuelo*. It's because he's the only man who's right for me."

"I hate admitting it, but even a blind man can see that. I can fight you on this, but I'll only lose you. I can tell Pablo would encourage you to pick me, but you wouldn't forgive me for putting you in that position. I don't want to. Pablo, please take care of my *niña*. I've always loved her more than anything, even if it doesn't seem like it."

"I believe that, *Señora* Bautista. We all make tough decisions in life, but when you live ones like ours, the ripples reach farther than for most people. I swear I'll always do everything I can to make Flora happy."

"I know you will, Pablo. When a man in your family commits to a woman, it's forever. The only person whose marriage failed was Enrique, and that was his first one. He married out of duty to your family. But it was obvious from the start that woman was never destined to be his soulmate."

"My *tío's* met the right woman, and he's with her now. You're right that my family waits for the one person they've always been meant to be with. We're blessed with that. Flora is my one person."

"Pablo is mine, *Mamá*."

If we were alone, I'd admit my feelings to her, but I won't tell anyone else before her. When you know, you know.

Flora gives her mother another hug. "Bye, *Mamá. Te quiero.*"

"Bye, *niña*. Let me know you arrived safely, please."

"I will."

Magdalena walks us to the door and watches as we climb into the SUV. I wish Flora and I were alone after all that. I'd pull her onto my lap and hold her, but that's not an option. So instead, I draw her to sit in the middle seat so she's close to me.

I wrap my arm around her shoulders, and she leans her head against my chest. My other hand takes hers, and she wraps both of hers around mine.

Her breathing is steady and deep, but I know she's fighting the tears that threaten to come back. Alejandro and *Papá* remain quiet, as do our driver and the bodyguard in the front passenger seat. We pull through the gate and take our place in the motorcade. You'd think we were some type of international delegation. This is how the *jefe de jefes'* family rolls when we need to make a point.

Flora agreed to lie down in the plane's cabin. She was exhausted by the time we made it onto the jet. Once it was safe to move about, I suggested she go back there. If my father and Alejandro weren't with us, I would've stayed. Even if we didn't have sex, I would've lain in bed with her and held her while she slept. Instead, I made sure she knew where everything was, then offered her a kiss before walking out. I looked back over my shoulder as she climbed into bed.

Now I'm sitting with *Papá* and my cousin as we discuss Flora's and my conversation with Magdalena. Alejandro scowls throughout, but *Papá* reasons with me about Magdalena's choices. He doesn't agree with them any more than I do, but he's a parent, and I'm not. He tries to get me to see that.

"*Papá*, I'm sure you're right, but it still wasn't easy to witness that conversation. Putting aside the things she called me, it upset Flora, and there was nothing I could do about that."

"And that's part of being in a relationship. It's accepting the things you can't fix as much as you want to. I know you would've done just about anything to shield Florencia from the pain that went along with talking to her mother, but it was a necessary evil."

"I know—"

My phone vibrates in my pocket. I pull it out and show my father and cousin the screen. We recognize the phone number, even though there's no name associated with it.

"*Hola Marcos. ¿Cómo estás?*" Hello, Marcos. How's it going?

"*Hola, El Tigre.*"

The Tiger.

It's one of several titles I hold as second-in-command. It's what generals are called in cartels. I'm a four-star. I'm a *jefe* in my own right since I technically oversee our New York operations. Nobody calls me that. Many call me *el capitán*. Some even believe I'm *el secretario*—the *jefe's* right-hand person—because I'm inline to inherit *Tío* Enrique's position. But that's really more my father, since he has been *Tío's* right-hand man longer than I have been alive. I respond to all of them.

"You probably won't like this, *El Tigre*, but Ernesto's already on his way to New York. He didn't know you'd come back to Colombia, so he took off to the States, assuming that's where you went rather than to the estate or wherever else you traveled. He plans to bring *Señorita* Aguilar back to Colombia."

In reality, Flora's last name is Aguilar Bautista since the mother's last name comes last in Spanish-speaking cultures. However, her connection to the Aguilar family will always stand out among our men. I'm certain those who know she and I are together doubt my decisions. They know the open hostility between them and us. With time, I'm also certain they'll realize Flora is nothing like her father's side of the family.

"Do you know when he will land?"

"In an hour or two. He left a little before you."

"You're certain he doesn't know we came back to Bogotá to pack up the *señorita's* apartment?"

"No, *El Tigre*, I'm positive he would've stormed over there if he'd known. Instead, he purchased a one-way first-class ticket to JFK."

It's not like my family never flies commercial. We do sometimes, but it's hardly our only option with two private planes at our disposal. Ernesto has no private plane. And while it could sound snooty of me to think it, it just shows he isn't playing in the same league as my family. Though very few are. The only true rivals to our wealth are the Kutsenkos, Mancinellis, and O'Rourkes.

That last set of fuckers wish they had as much as the rest of us. They trail behind. Sure, some of them have finally made it to billionaire status, but not all six of the men in that ruling family are there. They're barely more than knuckle-draggers. The Kutsenkos are vodka-swilling meatheads. They're the biggest of all of us, but not by much. And the Mancinellis spend far too much time eating pasta than hitting the gym. They believe their history as Italian Mafia still holds sway in New York City. They wouldn't have to strike the other families so often and so hard if they truly mattered.

It's my family that has a dynasty running an entire hemisphere. Nothing happens in the Western one without our knowing about it. That's how we're aware Ernesto's on his way.

"Marcos, keep me informed about what's going on. I want to know when he lands and where he goes, who he sees, and what he talks about. Please contact *Tío* Enrique and let him know what's happening."

"*El Tigre*, I already called *el jefe*. I know this is about you, but I still figured I should go to him first."

"You made the right choice. Keep us posted."

I hang up with one of our senior leaders and look at *Papá*

and Alejandro. I had the call on speaker, so they heard the same thing I did. I shift my focus to the closed door, where Flora sleeps on the other side.

"I don't know whether I should tell her yet. I don't want to keep unnecessary secrets from her. I know she'd believe me if I said I kept it from her because it's Cartel business as much as it's about her, but she wouldn't appreciate it. *Papá*, what do you think? Is it even safe for her to know?"

"I think it's safe, but what will it gain you if you can't answer all the questions she'll have?"

Alejandro shakes his head. "It'll piss her off if you tell her later you knew all along that Ernesto got to New York ahead of us."

"It probably will, but will that upset her more than me not having answers to her questions? I'd rather her angry at me than scared about him."

I look between my father and cousin, and they both shrug and nod. Our family traits are so deeply ingrained into our DNA that it's almost eerie. The Diaz blood most certainly pumps through all of us. *Papá* and I are mirror images of each other. Our looks and our mannerisms. Alejandro looks the most like *Tío* Enrique, who looks so much like *Papá*. Despite that, Alejandro sounds just like his father. He has many of *Tío* Matáis's mannerisms too.

"I think I'll wait to say anything until I know who he's going to for help. If I need to tell her before that, I will, but I don't want to make her any more anxious than she already is."

Papá looks skeptical, and Alejandro appears resigned. I don't think I'll win for trying on this one.

Chapter Twenty-Two

Flora

I slept harder than I expected while on the plane. It's a lot to take in when I arrive and find Enrique waiting for us on the tarmac. As though Luis and Alejandro weren't intimidating enough, now *el jefe's* greeting me.

Luis has been nothing but kind to me. However, he's still my boyfriend's father and *el Espíritu Santo*. Alejandro's reserved and kind of gruff, but not unkind. It's his size that's overwhelming. As huge as Pablo is, Alejandro's even broader. He's built like a mighty oak tree.

It amazes me how much Pablo and Luis look alike. It's a mirror into the past and window into the future. It's easy to see what Luis must have looked like twenty-something years ago and what Pablo will look like as he ages.

Alejandro is practically a mirror of Enrique. However, Pablo explained that when I meet Alejandro's father, Matáis, I'll realize Alejandro is simply a younger version of his father.

As a biologist, genetics fascinates me. That Alejandro can look so much like a man on one side of his family yet have the personality of a man on the other side intrigues me. It makes me wonder how much of the latter is nature versus nurture.

Enrique greets me with a smile. The man is pure silver fox. He has laugh lines around his eyes and mouth. There's gray at his temples and a little shot through his hair. He's charming, and it puts me at ease until I realize that's probably how he is with men right before he kills them. That makes my stomach twist into a knot that sits heavily in my lower abdomen.

"*Señorita*, welcome."

His accent is so familiar. I suppose I expected him to sound more like Pablo, even though Luis has the same accent as his brother. It's obvious Enrique and Luis grew up in Colombia, whereas Pablo and Alejandro have that distinct New York Spanish accent. I know Pablo grew up in New Jersey, though. I'm familiar with the area because I did my undergrad at Rutgers.

"Thank you, *jefe*."

"Please call me Enrique."

"*Tío*, it's good to see you. Thank you for coming out."

I appreciate Pablo taking the attention off me.

"Of course."

The men embrace as though it's been years since they've seen each other, even though it's only been a few days since Alejandro and Luis left here. I've never seen men on either side of my family be so demonstrative. If I didn't know it was affection, it would appear like mighty titans clashing.

All four men look like they could be Atlas with the weight of the world resting upon their shoulders. I'm certain on many days they feel more like Sisyphus with a boulder that keeps rolling back downhill and a lifetime sentence of pushing it back up.

It's not long before we're in SUVs. I take a moment to realize why Enrique and Luis are in one vehicle, and Pablo, Alejandro, and I are in another. The *jefe* and his heir don't ride together. If that isn't enough to make the fear tempt me to vomit, then I don't know what is. It's not like I didn't think there'd be dangers here in New York, but I've only been on the ground for fifteen minutes, and I'm reminded someone could blow up either or both men. I'm right here alongside Pablo.

"Flora."

I look up at Pablo, and I know he senses what I'm thinking. It's unnerving to both of us how we can already read each other. He tested me when we were in Switzerland to see whether I'm prepared for the man this life makes him, but he's worried now as I realize what reality means here. I offer him a reassuring smile and a kiss on the cheek.

"We can get something to eat along the way if you're hungry, or I can cook when we get home."

He still refers to his place as home rather than his condo or apartment. It could feel like he's putting pressure on me to move in, but it just feels reassuring. It's as though I already belong here.

"We can cook together if you want."

We already know we work well together in the kitchen. It's so ordinary, and that's what I love most about it. It feels like we're just a normal couple who enjoy their daily routine.

"That would be nice. I know my cousins brought fresh groceries over."

And I'm right back to feeling like I might vomit. He doesn't mean Alejandro. He's referring to *Tres J's*. That sucks the wind out of my sails since I know I'll inevitably meet Luciana, Joaquin, Javier, and Jorge. That's the thing I'm least eager to do, but I'll have to get it over with eventually. It doesn't take long to get from the private airfield in New Jersey to Pablo's condo in

Manhattan. As much as I'd like to be alone with him as I get to know his place, I understand that's impossible.

Pablo has a couple of spare bedrooms. One's his office, another's a gym, and the third is a guest bedroom. He made it clear that's not where I'll sleep. We brought several boxes with us in the airplane's hold while others will be shipped here rather than stored in Colombia. He instructs his men to put the boxes in the guest room. There are some things I want to get out, so I head in there while the men talk in the living room. It tempts me to eavesdrop, but I don't dare.

I'm certain I don't want to hear whatever they discuss, and Pablo wouldn't trust me anymore if I did. I spend the next half hour going through things, repacking some boxes now that I've had more time to consider how to organize my belongings. I nearly jump out of my skin when I hear Pablo's voice. I didn't hear him open the door.

"*Chiquita*, can you come and join us? We need to discuss a few things."

Pablo warned me about the conversation to come. I just didn't think it would be this soon. He slides his hand into mine and laces our fingers together.

"It's okay, *chiquita*. I'll stay beside you. I won't leave you to deal with this alone."

"Thank you, *Papí*."

Just calling him that calms me more than I realized. Before we step into the hallway, he gives me a searing kiss. I'd rather he stripped me naked and fucked me among all these boxes than have to speak to his uncle, father, and cousin.

"Later, *chiquita*."

His free hand cups my jaw. I love it when he does that. It's so damn sexy. He pulls away all too soon, and we join the men in the living room. They all stand as I enter. Enrique takes the lead. Hardly surprising.

"Thank you for coming out here."

Do I really have a choice?

I can't ask that question aloud, but my face must say it for me because Enrique's expression becomes far more sympathetic. He's not the cruel narco-trafficker who eats his enemies for breakfast, like I was told as a child. It surprises me how fast I lowered my guard with Pablo, considering my childhood indoctrination.

It speaks to Pablo's character and the man I know he is that I never tried to run or kill him. My faith that he'd never put me in a situation where someone could harm me is the original reason I didn't panic when I realized Enrique and the others were coming upstairs with us. Now I see nothing but a man who's welcoming his enemy's daughter into his world without malice.

I can't imagine anyone on my father's side of the family welcoming Pablo like this. I take a seat on the sofa next to Pablo. It puts me between Luis and him. Alejandro and Enrique have the two armchairs.

Pablo has an enormous sectional that can probably hold all the men in his family. But it would be odd if we spread out around it as though we needed a distance or had factions. Instead, Luis sitting beside me reassures no one will ostracize me. Enrique jumps straight in, and I'm glad there are no prevarications or small talk.

"We ended the open contract, but I'm unconvinced you're out of danger for a couple reasons. As you know, we suspect someone here funded Humberto, but we don't know who yet. However, my bigger concern is Ernesto. You know he's an unforgiving man, and you chose our family over his. Ernesto is likely to come after you and expect you not only to go back to Colombia but to beg forgiveness."

Just like when Pablo says "our," and I know it includes me,

I feel the same way when Enrique says it. It doesn't leave me feeling lost in the middle since I've never fully felt like an Aguilar, and I definitely don't feel like one now.

Pablo squeezes my hand, and I shift my attention to him.

"Flora, I found out on the plane that Ernesto was already on his way here. He landed a couple hours before us."

"My *abuelo's* already here in New York?"

Panic makes my chest tighten. Maybe in a little while Pablo not telling me this as soon as he found out will piss me off. But right now, fear is the stronger emotion.

"Flora, I said nothing to you because I wanted more information. I wanted to explain things to you rather than leave you with more unanswered questions than there has to be."

He means things I'll ask that he'll never tell me. The things I don't want to know, and the things the U.S. or Colombian governments could ask me about. The less I know, the less I can say.

I remind myself Pablo has my best interests at heart. He's not manipulating me like my family has. I might not agree with his idea of what's best for me, but I trust that each of his decisions takes that into consideration.

"Do you know where he is?"

"Yes, he's staying at the Waldorf Astoria."

I huff and shake my head. "He certainly isn't going for inconspicuous."

I haven't stayed there, but I've seen photos. They say the interior is lavish. I think it's gaudy and ostentatious. In other words, perfect for my *abuelo*.

"He's been there since he got into the city. He went directly to his room from JFK."

"I'm certain *Abuelo's* in a foul mood flying commercial, but he doesn't have any richer friends right now to fly him where he wants to go. With Néstor dead, his connections to the government and their resources are gone. He'll want to shower and change since he feels flying commercial is so pedestrian. Yet he does it anyway."

I scan my gaze around the men with me and find them grinning. Clearly, they agree with my assessment.

"Florencia, we have men who work at the hotel and others staked out around it. I made sure our guys are also in the rooms next to his and across the hall."

I don't want to know how Enrique made that happen since I'm sure at least one of those three already had occupants. Probably some type of maintenance issue that made those guests move. I'm certain Enrique will know his comings and goings.

"He can't come near you, Florencia, unless Pablo allows it."

I like that even though Enrique leads the family, he's deferring to Pablo on this. It reassures me, and I feel more confident than I did a minute ago. Pablo squeezes my hand, and I relax.

"Flora, if you decide you want to see Ernesto, I'll make it happen. But if you don't, then he won't breathe within a ten-mile radius of you."

I nod and squeeze his hand in return. I shift my focus back to Enrique as he speaks.

"Pablo and I have discussed your role several times. Both of us agree you don't have to tell us anything you don't want to. Neither of us will ask. Share what you want or keep it to yourself. I don't want you to fear I'm going to demand information at any moment."

I observe Enrique and wonder if this is the manipulation my mother warned me about. Is he trying to put me at ease so I lower my guard and confide in him? Maybe, but I don't believe that about Pablo. He hasn't asked me anything about the lab or the recipe I came up with. That sounds like such a benign term compared to formula. It's as though I were baking a cake rather than baking cocaine.

Part of me wants to tell Enrique where the lab is and share the formula purely out of spite because I hated every moment of working for Humberto. I'd rather not think about it anymore, especially since the man is dead. I never have to see him again or work for him. However, part of me is saving that information for a rainy day. I want to say my faith is blind with Pablo, but all of this is still so new. I feel like the formula is my life vest that I can take out in case of emergency.

I nod and remain quiet. Luis finally speaks up, so I twist to look at him.

"Florencia, I know the things you've been told about our family, and not just from your own. We know the reputation we've cultivated. It's been on purpose. Maybe you haven't heard much about what we're like together as a family, only what we do to other people as a family. You are the woman Pablo chose. He has an opportunity I didn't."

My brow furrows. I know little about Pablo's family's private lives except for what he shared in Switzerland. We talked about our pasts with our families, but we shared nothing overly private.

"My parents and my wife's parents arranged my marriage to Margherita, but my *mamá* and *papá* knew we'd be a perfect fit. I count my blessings our family's in a position to let the younger generation choose who they want to be with. Pablo chose you. I know he's meant to be with you because I trust my son's decisions. That makes you family to all of us. Our loyalty is to you. We understand why you might not be ready to give us yours entirely. But no matter what, nothing I do will ever be to hurt my son intentionally, which is what would happen if we betrayed you. Whether you believe us because we're making this promise for your sake, or it's because you know we also make it for Pablo's, we're on your side no matter what."

I'm not sure what to make of it when my possibly—maybe—probably future father-in-law pretty much says you're his son's soulmate.

We've been in New York for a week, and I've slept a large part of that. Apparently, the stress of the past few months slammed into me now that I feel completely safe, and I've become a narcoleptic. Pablo's bed is comfier than any other I've ever slept in, but I suspect that's because of him and not the mattress. I'm certainly spoiled getting to curl up next to him every night and waking up in his arms every morning. Hell, at least twice in the middle of every night. I know eventually the novelty will wear off, and we won't wake each other to fuck. But for now, I certainly won't complain.

He's left the apartment a few times to deal with work stuff. He ends up coming back stressed out. He swears nothing is wrong, but clearly something bothers him. I think some of it is leaving me here without him. I know there're adequate guards because I see the men outside his door whenever he leaves. When we go for walks, they blend into the surrounding crowd, but I know they're there.

He's the only unit on the penthouse floor. There's more to his top-floor Manhattan apartment than just the breathtaking view. It's so nobody can get to him easily. By the time anyone who comes to attack him gets to the second floor, he'll know about it. Nobody's coming down from the roof because the angle of the slanted tiles is too steep. It would be like something out of *Mission Impossible*.

Lavish doesn't even begin to describe this place. His decor

isn't over the top. It's actually really homey, but he certainly has the best of the best. He even has a pool up here. Plenty of buildings have rooftop pools, but this is for his private use. It reminds me of Switzerland. Who would've thought I could be nostalgic over something like a mountainside lair where I hid from mercenaries for two weeks, but it certainly felt safer than the wilds of New York City.

"*Chiquita*, are you ready?"

"Yeah, I'm coming."

If only I were saying that during sex. Instead, we're about to meet his entire family at a restaurant. It'll be my formal introduction to people I've only heard about. People who absolutely despise everything about my family. I can't help but be nervous that they'll only be polite for Pablo's sake, but they'll hate me behind my back. Worst-case scenario, they'll reject me to my face. However, I don't believe they'd do that, and that's purely because of Pablo. They wouldn't hurt him like that, but that doesn't mean they'll welcome me or accept me any more than the bare minimum.

"*Chiquita*, you look beautiful."

He kisses me behind my ear, and I get a waft of his cologne that's so incredibly familiar to me I even dream about it. Lavender used to be my favorite. It has always been so calming, but getting a whiff of Pablo's cologne tells me he's nearby. Not only does that calm me, it reassures me.

"You look pretty good too, Daddy."

"Just pretty good?"

"Pretty gorgeous. Is that better?"

"Much. Little one, I want to make sure I look the part for being the man on your arm."

"Oh, you're the arm candy. I could get used to that."

"Only for you, *chica*."

"Damn right, Daddy."

He offers me a searing kiss that has me grasping the front of his shirt as he pulls away. I slide two fingers between the buttons and kiss him back with full force. His hand rains down on my ass, and it stings. He does it four more times before he backs away. It's the distraction I need to get me out the door.

The restaurant is an unprecedentedly quick ride into Queens—at least that's how it feels. He fucks me hard enough I fear the driver and bodyguard on the other side of the town car's privacy glass will know what we're up to. It should embarrass me to meet his mother with his cum on the inside of my thighs, but he understands how comforting that is to me. It's a little part of him with me when I know he'll have to step away to talk to other people. I can't be glued to his side during the entire dinner. I don't want to appear that needy and childish, but it's certainly tempting.

"*Chiquita*, I wouldn't bring you around people who have ill intentions for you. I understand you're scared, but I swear it'll be all right."

I nod once, the trepidation clogging my throat.

"Flora, if you don't feel comfortable or anything happens, we leave immediately. No questions asked. I won't be upset with you. I won't have you somewhere you feel unwelcome or unsafe."

"Thank you, Daddy."

I appreciate his saying that now, but I know he'd resent it if I made him leave his family dinner because I'm having a tantrum. I can't do that to him, so I'm going to have to suck it up. It may not be easy, but I've dealt with far worse. I can deal with this too.

When we are presentable, he raps on the car window, and the driver opens the door. Pablo slides out and offers me his hand as he buttons his suit coat. I think it's so fucking sexy watching him do that whenever he stands and watching him unbutton it when he sits.

The way he can do it with just one hand is some suave *James Bond*–level shit. Sean Connery *James Bond*. None of those other wannabe guys. Though, I'll take Daniel Craig in a pinch. My mind's wandering to distract myself from how apprehensive I feel right now. This is straight up a thousand times scarier than meeting Humberto for the first time. It's even scarier than when Humberto arrived at the Colombian estate, and I didn't know if we faced a full-blown attack.

I don't realize how tightly I'm clinging to Pablo's hand until he stretches his fingers. I ease my hold on them, and he smiles down at me.

"It's all right, little one, I promise."

He kisses my temple just before we step inside and walk to the private dining room. A sea of faces greets me. So many of them are practically mirror images. I keep thinking that phrase over and over because I don't know a better way to describe how dominant the Diaz genes are. It takes only a moment for me to realize which woman is Luciana.

Two men stand beside her who could practically be twins. I scan the crowd and spot another man who could be a triplet to the first two. He's got a blonde woman on his lap in the back corner. That must be the third member of *Tres J's*. I heard he's involved with a woman who was Pablo's childhood next-door neighbor. I wonder why they're so far away from the rest of the crowd.

Does he need to be at the opposite end of the dining room from me?

I look back at Luciana, and she's clearly assessing me. Pablo's arm wraps around me, and his hand sits heavily on my waist. It's only when my body brushes against his that I realize I'm trembling. My gaze locks with one of the three brothers. I don't know who he is, but his stare is so fucking penetrating it feels like he sees right into my soul. I don't intend to, but I burst into tears.

"I'm so, so sorry. So sorry."

Pablo pulls me fully against him and kisses my forehead. I'm so embarrassed right now. Mortified would be a better word. I want to sink into the floor. I can't believe all that fortitude I believed I had just evaporated. I look like a weak ass bitch in front of his entire family. He's going to be *jefe de jefes* one day. He's been talking about me being his wife, yet the first time I encounter something hard, I burst into tears. Talk about humiliation.

It unnerves me when Luciana steps forward and places her hand on my left forearm. Her fingers tug a little and embolden me to step away from Pablo. She engulfs me in a hug, and her hand presses gently against the back of my head encouraging me to rest it on her shoulder.

"Florencia, none of this was ever your fault. If we could choose the family we were born into, none of us would want to have anything to do with a cartel. None of us would pick a life of loss and pain. But that's what we've been given. I don't blame you for your father's actions. Whether or not you ever knew him, he was a man who did what he wanted, and that had nothing to do with you. None of us blame you for any of this."

"Thank you, but I know I look a lot like my father. I hate that I'm a reminder to you."

Luciana squeezes the outside of my shoulders and presses me back so our gazes lock.

"Florencia, I do *not* see Domingo when I look at you. I see the woman my nephew chose. I see the woman who chose him. I trust Pablo. I've known him his entire life. I've watched him since he was a baby. He's always been a natural leader, and not just because he's the oldest of his generation. He doesn't make choices lightly. He's always considered how his decisions affect other people. He trusts you. That tells me more than enough. It might be hard in the beginning, but we'll all figure it out eventually."

I shift my gaze over her shoulder to two of her sons. My attention switches to the man in the back of the room who's now standing with the woman tucked against his side. I'm not convinced they're as accepting as their mother.

Maybe one day, but not today.

Luciana looks over her shoulders at her sons, gesturing them forward. "Florencia, this is Joaquin and Jorge."

She points to the man on the left first. I see the third guy approach.

"This is my middle son, Javier, and his fiancée, Madeline."

All four of them watch me with varying levels of suspicion before Madeline steps forward and offers me her hand. I force myself not to hesitate and take it. She comes closer and offers me a light embrace as she whispers in my ear.

"Don't mind them. It's not only women who can have resting bitch face. They don't realize how much they scowl. It's not you. I get those looks sometimes. Luciana's forever reminding them not to look that way at family."

I hear the humor in her voice, and it helps ease much of my apprehension. Maybe, just maybe, I'll survive.

At least that's what I thought until I'm introduced to Margherita. Pablo looks nothing like her at all except for their eyes. He shares the same brown and gold hazel his mother does. It's only now that I realize he doesn't have the same purely brown eyes Luis does. But besides that, the woman seems to have had no say in her son's appearance. She's a bit thinner than I expected. But I know she's still pretty fresh off cancer treatments. I remember what *Mamá* was like back then.

"Florencia, welcome. I'm so glad to finally meet you. Luis

has told me how highly Pablo speaks of you, and you impressed my husband and nephew on the trip here."

"Thank you, *Señora* Diaz."

"Please, it's Margherita. If you call me *Señora* Diaz, you'll have far too many people answering."

"Thank you." I sound like an idiot repeating myself.

In non-Spanish-speaking cultures, it would be far easier to keep track. However, with the way a mother's maiden names comes at the end, someone could have like six last names. That's how I'm Florencia Aguilar Bautista. I know in the States they don't do that as much.

Traditionally, in Colombia, if a woman changed her name after marriage, she would add *de* and adopt their husband's first name as their second last name. Not so much these days. Some now use *de* and their husband's surname. But if an unmarried woman only uses one of her last names, it's her father's. I can't get away from being an Aguilar.

Since Margherita also grew up in Colombia, she may have kept her father's surname and mother's surname. I doubt that's what she did. I think she conformed to what plenty of women do in the States. She took her husband's name and simply goes by Diaz.

Luciana and Catalina still have Diaz somewhere in there, but I don't know what Catalina's husband's surname is. All five younger men are Diaz. Pablo because of his father's name and the other four because of their mothers' maiden name. But for the sake of family unity, I know they all default to Diaz.

Another woman steps beside Margherita and looks similar to Luciana, Enrique, and Luis. Pablo makes the introductions.

"Flora, this is my other *tía* and her husband. *Tía* Catalina and *Tío* Matáis."

"*Hola.*"

I shake hands with the other couple. They appear the most

easygoing of everyone in the room. I know they're Alejandro's parents. It's hard to imagine Alejandro having the same personality as his father, despite what I've heard about their similarities. It's when Matáis smiles and Alejandro steps between his parents that I realize the truth in that. Alejandro smiles genuinely for the first time since I met him. He's the one I'm sure most people consider the hottest in the family. But it's almost too good to be true. I much prefer Pablo's brooding sense of authority. It does things to me.

"Florencia."

I turn toward Enrique as he walks over with an attractive woman who's clearly not a Diaz by birth.

"I'd like you to meet my wife, Elodie."

If I thought *Tres J's* could see all the way into my soul, it's as though Elodie can read my mind. I don't know what it is about her that's both disarming and nerve-wracking. It's as though she can will you into trusting her right before she takes you out at the knees. She is the perfect woman for her position. I feel as though she knows more about me than she should. Not just what Enrique may have told her, but some type of first-hand knowledge or something. It's monumentally disconcerting.

"Florencia, it's wonderful to meet you. Please call me Elle. If there's anything you need while you settle in, please let me know. I work from home, so I have plenty of time to help you sort out anything you need."

"I appreciate that. I went to college in New Jersey, so I've been to New York plenty of times, but I've never lived here, so it's new to me."

"Perhaps we could go out to lunch sometime."

"I'd like that a lot. Thank you."

There I go again. I am thankful, but I feel like a parrot repeating the same phrase over and over.

She's doing her best to put me at ease, but I still have this feeling she knows far more than she's letting on. It makes the skeptic in me wonder if she might try to whittle information out of me she can pass on to Enrique. I shouldn't assume the worst. However, I've learned to always remain on guard since people often wanted to get close to me to get to my *abuelo*.

Pablo's been quiet during all the introductions, but he speaks up now. "Be careful with *Tía* Elle. She looks innocent, but she's likely to get you in the most trouble. She has a wicked sense of humor and loves to play practical jokes on people. I never imagined that when I first met her, but I've been on the receiving end several times. I much prefer it when she's going after my *tíos* and cousins than me."

"Calm down, Pablo. You just need a thicker skin than that. Your cousins don't complain." She grins at me as she teases my boyfriend.

"Perhaps because they're terrified of what you'll do next."

"As they should be."

Enrique chimes in before giving his wife a smacking kiss on the lips. Again, how demonstrative this family is surprises me. I'm unprepared for how incredibly normal they are. I can only nod along as I try to keep up with everything when I feel like I'm drowning. Luciana's observed me the entire time and takes pity on me.

"Why don't we all find our seats? I'm starving, and I know it's been at least ten minutes since my *niños* have eaten, so they'll be getting cranky soon. Madeline will deal with Javier, but I'll be stuck with these two whining about needing a snack if this is going to take much longer."

I chuckle, but I feel entirely out of my element right now as this petite woman makes fun of her three sons who tower over her as though she's a pea on a mountain. They turn their resting bitch face to her, and I now understand what Madeline meant.

I suspect a lifetime of projecting menace has made them unaware of how they might come across to other people. It's not that they intend to be this way; it's just what happens. I follow Pablo's lead and take a seat at the table between him and Luciana.

I wonder if she is being a bit over the top in her welcome to make a point that she accepts me. It's not until we strike up a conversation with her asking me about what I like to do for pastimes that I feel she genuinely has an interest in what I'm saying. She's attentive during the entire conversation, and it puts me more at ease than I imagined.

It's not long before I hesitantly join in with other conversations swirling around the table. By the end of the first course, I realize I haven't gone up in smoke like I feared. However, as I observe the couples, I pay surreptitious attention to Javier and Madeline since they're the newest couple in the family. I wonder if Pablo and I look as at ease with each other as they do.

I hope so.

It's a family-style dinner, and it surprises me when I realize Pablo and I already know so much about each other's preferences that we can serve each other. I know that doesn't go unnoticed by anyone at the table, but they all take it in stride. I noticed because all the couples do that for each other. Then I see Luciana offering her sons Joaquin and Jorge food, and they do the same for her. It jackhammers home that she's the only woman at the table who doesn't have a partner. And that makes me feel like shit all over again because it's my family's fault she's on her own.

"*Chiquita?*"

Pablo's voice is soft beside my ear. His hand rests on my thigh as I look up at him. I nod, too choked up to say anything. He simply nods to me, and I know he understands. I'm not ready to talk about how I feel.

By dessert, some of my discomfort eases, but it's not gone entirely before Pablo and I climb back into the town car. For the second time tonight, I burst into tears.

What is wrong with me?

For a moment, I think the answer to my unspoken question is that I might be pregnant, but it's far too soon to tell. I discovered during the meal that Madeline and Margherita are both midwives. It made me wonder if they could tell something about me I couldn't. I don't believe I'm pregnant, but Pablo and I know there's always the possibility.

Pablo lifts me onto his lap and wraps his arms around me. I sag against him.

"You did so well tonight, little one. I know it must've been incredibly frightening for you to face so many new people. With our families' history, it only made it harder. But I hope you know the welcome you received was genuine."

"It was hard, and I appreciate everyone's effort to include me. It was realizing Luciana's the only one there without her partner that upset me. All the other couples were joking around and just serving each other without giving it a second thought. Instead of having her husband do that, she had her sons. It was super sweet, but it reminded me yet again of all your family's lost because of mine."

Pablo strokes my hair as he kisses my temple.

"*Chiquita*, I'm grateful you're aware of these things and that it moves you. However, the only person feeling any blame right now is you. I know my family as well as they know me. There's nothing we can hide from each other. We've spent our entire lives relying on each other. We can read each other's thoughts in silence because we're often in situations where we can't openly discuss things. If I believed anybody begrudged your being there—being with me—I would've found an excuse for us to leave early."

"I know all of that, Pablo. I hope you don't feel you have to keep reassuring me of these things. My guilt isn't as easily assuaged as I'd like it to be. Hopefully, it will go away with time. It's just with so much unresolved and more problems for your family to deal with than usual, it's hard not to remember I'm still an outsider."

Pablo merely tightens his embrace. I know he doesn't want to argue with me or invalidate my feelings. I'm glad he remains quiet because I don't want him to feel like he must offer me platitudes. We're quiet for ten minutes. The companionable silence is a reprieve after all the noise from dinner.

"*Chiquita*, I have to go to Atlantic City tomorrow for a meeting with some developers. It'll take all day because I have to go around the resort site. We've recently purchased a property, and we're completely renovating it. We're practically taking it down to the studs."

What he's not saying is that it'll be the longest we've been apart since leaving my apartment the first time.

"Is there anything you want to do tomorrow? I don't want you to feel imprisoned at the condo. I can arrange for guards to accompany you anywhere you want to go."

It tempts me to remain holed up in the condo, but I don't want to spend my life waiting for Pablo to come home.

"I'd like to—"

I release a sigh because I know what I should do, but it no longer feels as appealing as it did when I thought of it. I try again with some false bravado.

"I think I should start looking at apartment listings."

It's only for a second, but Pablo's entire body tenses. I know he hoped I'd changed my mind about that and that I would make the condo my permanent home.

"Do you want *Tía* Luciana or *Tía* Catalina's help? *Tía* Luciana is in commercial real estate, but *Tía* Catalina is in residential. Between the two of them and their connections, they're bound to help you find a place you'll like."

"That would be really sweet."

I hope he sees it's a sign of good faith and that his *tías* will see it the same way. We are quiet the rest of the way back to the condo, and I fear I've ruined the entire evening, not because I cried twice, but because I want to move out.

Chapter Twenty-Three

Pablo

I know tonight was like walking into battle for Flora. If you didn't know my family's rightfully earned reputation, they would seem like a jolly group that eats and laughs a lot. But if you know who we are, it probably feels like your last meal before an execution. I can't blame Flora for her wavering emotions. No one faults her for her tears. She's left behind her life to join me here.

Yeah, most of it's because of the ongoing silent threat. In the past week, we've discovered nothing. It's driving me up the wall. But she also left for me. If she'd refused, I would've set things up to protect her in Bogotá. We could've set her up anywhere in the world if she'd wanted to be anywhere else.

Her suggestion that she look at apartments hurts, but it's what we talked about. I suspect she feels like it's what she's supposed to do. I won't push her to stay with me, but I'll show her what life can be like if this is our shared home.

"*Chiquita*, it looks like there're some boxes for you on the table."

Her brow furrows. "I didn't order anything."

"Are you sure they're not yours? Take a look."

All packages get X-rayed before they come up here. If anything appears questionable, the boxes get opened. I told my men in the security room downstairs that if they had any concerns, they were to set the boxes aside and let me investigate. Under no circumstances were they to open the boxes without me. It's not like they don't know what's in there after the imaging, but I didn't want to reseal anything or embarrass Flora by having the boxes already opened. I thought about unpacking it all for her, but I want to see her surprise. I'm practically ready to clap and bounce on my toes like a five-year-old going on a pony ride. I'm afraid I'd look more like Dr. Evil from *Austin Powers* instead.

Flora watches me as she walks into the kitchen and grabs a knife. She's still watching me as she heads to the dining room table. She examines the boxes and notices her name is the addressee. She slices open the first one with care, unsure what might be inside and not wanting to damage anything. I observe, and my excitement builds. I want to rush over and rip it open for her like Juan used to try on Christmas.

"*¡Papí, qué es esto!*" Daddy, what's this?!

"*Divertido para nosotros.*" Fun for us.

"I'll say."

She lifts out the packaging with the thigh harness vaginal spreader. She puts that on the table and lifts out a small velvet bag, which she opens and finds a box within. When she lifts the lid, there's a set of onyx Ben Wa balls. She rolls her finger over the top of one. She hesitates and then sets it aside. She slaps the paddle against her palm before twisting to push her ass toward me. With her mouth open in a perfect circle, she spanks herself.

"Keep your mouth like that much longer, *chiquita*, and you'll unpack that box with my cock down your throat."

She opens her mouth wider and shakes her ass.

I cross my arms and nudge my chin toward the box. She rolls her eyes and goes back to the contents, lifting them out one by one until there's nothing left.

"You did a lot of shopping, Daddy."

"I had some time on my way to a meeting yesterday."

"Did you buy out an entire store?"

"It's not that much."

She moves on to the second box where she discovers a swing. Her smile explodes as she rips open the package. However, she stops pulling it out midway.

"This doesn't come with a stand. It's meant to be suspended from a hook in a load-bearing beam. We can't use it yet."

"Gather what you want to use tonight and go in our bedroom."

Her brow furrows as I take the swing from her and place it back in the larger shipping box. She scoops up everything she can like she's in the old game show where people sweep through the supermarket and knock as much stuff off the shelf and into their cart as they can. When she nearly drops half of it, she gives up and tosses things back into the original box. She hoists that and hurries toward our room, looking back over her shoulder. I'm on her heels as I laugh at her excitement.

After the stress this evening put on both of us, it's nice to see how relaxed she is. I know it's because we're alone—and the prospect of kinky ass sex—but at least she isn't crying. My heart ached for her when she burst into tears the first time. I couldn't fault her for it. It frustrated me the second time. Not at her but at myself. I can't fix this and make it right for her as fast as I want.

I'm a man who eats, sleeps, and breathes control. I feel useless and adrift when I don't have it. It usually means shit's about to go sideways. It's one thing when it's a business deal. That'll piss me off. But when it's my girlfriend's life—I'm ready to go positively apeshit.

We both need some time to explore and play together. We set the boxes on the bed, and I point up near the floor-to-ceiling window. Her mouth drops open, and once again, my mind conjures dirty, dirty things I want to do to that pretty little mouth.

"Keep looking at me like that, and you'll swallow my cock rather than play with our new toys."

She licks her lips, and I pounce. I hope she doesn't like her shirt that much. I grab it where the buttons run down the center and yank it apart. She squeaks as I pull it down her arms. I'm quick to unhook her bra, then I spin her around. I grab a set of handcuffs from the box and snap them on her wrists.

"Face me."

"Yes, Daddy."

I fish around and find a set of nipple clamps and a light labia weight. I practically shred the packaging in my haste.

"Squeeze your tits together."

She obeys, pushing them up in offering. I lick her right nipple, then roll it between my thumb and index finger. When it's nice and hard, I clip the metal prongs around it. These aren't the ones with the rubber pads. I repeat my actions on the left side.

"Tell me when to stop tightening, *chiquita.*"

"Yes, Daddy."

I'm slow as I turn the little dial on each. I assess her expression and how her body reacts to the increasing pain. When she flinches, I stop. It's just as she speaks.

"That's enough, *Papí*."

"Good girl."

I unzip the skirt she's wearing and push it to the floor. I reach behind me and pull out the crop she stood up in the box. She watches me with curiosity and then a smidge of trepidation. She widens her feet as I run the leather flapper up the inside of her thighs. I flick my wrist to I swat the flesh on both sides. She sucks in a breath, but it whooshes from her when I slap her clit.

"I was going to hang the swing for us, *chiquita*. But you distracted me with that generous offer. On your knees."

She obeys as I let the crop trail up her body as she lowers herself. I attach the weight to the chain between her tits. She whimpers.

"*Chiquita*, what's your safe word?"

"*Rios, Papí*."

"Say it if you need it."

"I will. I promise. You haven't done anything I don't like. That was an 'I want more,' not an 'I want less,' sound."

I lean forward and brush a kiss on her lips before straightening and unfastening my pants. I kick off my shoes as I push my pants and boxer briefs down enough to free my cock. I love that Flora's only in her high heels and that I'm still dressed. I stroke myself and graze her lips with the tip of my cock. I tap her bottom lip, and she opens for me. She curls her tongue as though it's an invitation for my dick to rest in the valley.

It would be rude to decline.

I slide into her mouth, but before she can wrap her lips around me and suck, I fist her hair and tug back. I'm careful not to make it feel like I'll scalp her, but it makes her immobile if she doesn't want to hurt herself.

"Lick."

She obeys immediately. It's like watching her eat an ice-cream cone. She's thorough, moving around it, not letting any part go too long without her attention.

"Suck."

Holy fucking heaven. I think I just saw an angel.

I ease my hold on her hair as her head bobs. She closes her eyes and focuses on what she's doing. She takes me deep, but not enough to gag. She's silent as she works me, which I appreciate. I find intentional slurping sounds annoying and distracting.

"Can you take more, baby girl?"

She hums her answer. I'm not fucking her face, so I let her decide the pace and how deep my dick goes.

Our relationship is symbiotic.

She ultimately has control and can stop or start our dynamic.

With that control, she cedes decision-making to me, so I control our sexual interludes.

Because I have control of our sexual interludes, I can give her some control of how I want us to fuck.

It's full circle and works for us. It's not unlike other D/s relationships we've each had, but I know—for me at least—the emotions I feel for Flora far exceed any I've had with past partners.

"*Chiquita*, it's time for you to know how good this feels."

I sit back on the bed and inch toward the pillows before holding out my arms to her. I help her balance since hers are still cuffed behind her back. The trust in her eyes and eagerness to continue our roleplaying has depth I haven't seen in past partners. I want to believe her feelings for me are deeper and more complex than she's had with men in her past.

I lie down after I grasp her hips. She's quick to kick off her shoes as I lift her toward me. She straddles my hips, but I pull her closer.

"You're going to sit on my face while I stick my tongue in your pussy. You're going to ride it like you're fucking my cock. You will not come until I say you can."

"Daddy, you make it impossible to control my orgasms."

Symbiosis.

She'll control what happens because she can safe-word, and everything ends without a question. But I control whether she gets an orgasm.

She inches forward until her knees are beside my ears. She lowers herself, and I lick her pussy. I press her down, so I can thrust my tongue inside her.

"*¡Ay, Papi!*"

"Fuck that's hot, Flora."

I pull my mouth away to mutter that one sentence, then I dive back in. My fingers grip her ass as I move her at the pace I want. I watch as her hips roll, bringing her clit closer to my nose and then retreat. The movement makes her look like a belly dancer, and it's erotic as fuck. Our gazes meet, and I know she's observing me to see what I want and what I like. What I want is to torment her until she begs to get off.

She moans as I suck her clit while pulling her ass cheeks apart. My chin stubble rubs against her cunt and between her cheeks. She shifts as though she wants more. I press down on her hips, holding her in place as I open and close my mouth around her clit, flicking it with my tongue.

"Fuck, Daddy."

She tries to move faster, but I don't let her. Just the opposite. I stop altogether.

"*Daddy!*"

She's not a fan of being edged right now. I wait her out until she stops squirming. Then I stick my tongue as deep into her pussy as I can. I slap her ass, pushing her forward to ride my face. I do it over and over as she moans. It makes my cock leak. I haven't come, and I feel like I'm about to explode, but I'm not ready to end this.

"Daddy, please...Please...Please, Daddy."

The sound of her begging has me reaching past her to fist my dick. I'm ready to jerk off because my balls are so fucking tight, but I'm not wasting my cum on myself. I either want to mark Flora with it or sink it deep inside her pussy.

I've done everything I can to make sure I never got a woman pregnant. I've practically double bagged it, and I always withdrew even with a condom. I only ever came in women's asses, and that was with a condom. I've fucked Flora bare every way I can. I thought discovering she'd forgotten her birth control would freak me out once its implications settled in.

It didn't.

Just the opposite.

I want to fuck her full of my cum until she's carrying our child. The kinky bastard in me wants to know she'd belong to me in a way that's permanent and in a way no other man can ever claim. I want to know a part of me is inside her and that we made a new life together.

The tender part of me that never existed before her wants to be a dad like the one I have. I've never once doubted my father loves me—and loved Juan—more than his own life. Even when I've fucked up and feared disappointing him, I never questioned his unconditional love. I didn't imagine I had the capacity for that before meeting Flora. Now I believe I can because I'm falling in love with her.

I nip at her clit until she screams. I rake my teeth over it before I suck.

"Daddy, I'm going to come. *Fuuuuck!*"

She throws her head back as her ass clenches. She grinds her pubic bone against my upper lip, her ass pushing at my chin. The moment I know she's done, I lift her off and guide her to kneel with her shoulders on the mattress. I grab a paddle and bring it down on her ass.

"*OWIE!* Fuck, Daddy!"

She wails the first word and barely hisses the second two. I spank her again and again.

"Did I give you permission to come, *chiquita?*"

"No. But you made it impossible for me not to."

"Excuses, baby girl."

I spank her again, and I'm so fucking tempted to thrust my dick into her and come. But that's not what she wanted when we came in here.

"Stay where you are. You can sit up if the position hurts your neck."

I climb off the bed and finish stripping since I still have all my clothes on. When I'm naked, I stroke myself twice. Some of it is to relieve the ache, but some of it is to tease her. I chuckle at her scowl before grabbing the swing. I leave the packaging on the bed as I grab the stepladder from beside the dresser. I told my guy to leave it there for me. I'm tall, but I'm not a fucking giant.

She sits up to see more easily. "That hook wasn't there when we left for dinner."

"I know. I had it installed."

"Pablo, one of your men knows we're into kinky shit if he had to install a hook in the ceiling."

"Maybe he thinks we're into hanging plants."

"With a hook that size? Hardly. Please tell me you didn't say what it was for."

I connect the swing's links to the hook before I climb down. I walk over to the bed and perch on the edge. I gesture for Flora to sit on my lap. I brush hair back from her face.

"*Chiquita*, what happens between us is private. Maybe the

guy figured it out. Maybe he didn't. But I certainly didn't tell him why. If I'd had the tools handy, I would've done it myself. I should've planned ahead, knowing the delivery was coming today, but I didn't. The packages had to be X-rayed before they came up here, so a security guard knows what I ordered. But neither man will discuss what they know or think. They understand why that wouldn't be a good idea. If we go to a club, and you want to scene where others can watch, then we can explore that. That's the only way anyone else will know what we do together."

"Thank you for reassuring me. I already figured out the boxes went through security, but that felt way different than someone being in our—room to put in a hook."

She tries to cover how she stumbled over "our." I don't point it out, even though I want to insist she quit thinking about another place since she already considers at least part of this condo as hers. But I won't pick a fight. Instead, I give her a quick kiss before helping her off the bed.

Chapter Twenty-Four

Flora

Orgasms with Pablo are undeniably the best I've ever had. It's not just how our bodies move together. That's certainly part of it, but it's also how we feel about each other. I know from my studies in human biology that falling in love complexly combines physical and emotional reactions to stimuli. I know men often admit to falling in love sooner than women—the difference of at least thirty days in some studies—but I don't doubt my feelings.

"Come with me, *chiquita*."

When I accept Pablo's help to get off the bed, I feel it in the electric current that flows up my arm from his gentleness. I've just had my cunt grinding his face in one of the most intimate acts, but how he treats me in moments like this make me feel treasured. I have a sudden urge to show him affection. I rise onto my toes and press a kiss to his lips.

"*Gracias, Papí.*"

His expression softens as he kisses me back. It's not a

passionate one. It's just a soft brushing of our lips before he leads me to the swing. Before he positions us, he slides his left arm around my waist. He pulls me close, and my body happily touches his. It's his turn to offer me a kiss. It's a series of pecks before one longer closed-mouth kiss.

He grabbed the handcuffs' key as he helped me to my feet. He unfastens them and lets them drop to the floor. He moves my arms around, his fingers trailing over my skin in the most tantalizing way. He's helping me get the circulation flowing again and keeping me from getting stiff. But he's also seducing me—not that he needs to try.

"Come to me, little one."

He steps backward until his thighs nudge the swing. He sits and positions the straps for me. I slide my knees into loops near his. My hands find purchase just above his shoulders. I wonder how acrobatic we can get with this. I examine the straps for a moment before glancing down at Pablo who's observing me.

"What're you thinking, little one?"

"Maybe we can do the things we just did but on here."

"Creative."

When he nods, I climb off and wait while he adjusts straps into what we both think will support me. It takes a couple tries and a few laughs, but eventually, my knees rest in slings while my forearms rest through loops. Pablo leans back, adjusting the straps again, so he's in a position where my mouth can lower onto his cock while he laps at my pussy. The gentle sway of the swing pushes and pulls us apart as we work each other into a frenzy.

"Fuck, Flora. You're killing me. Your ass in my face makes me want to fuck it."

"If that's what you want, Daddy."

There's a bottle of hypoallergenic, lavender scented lube in the box. He knows that was my favorite scent until I discovered his cologne. He eases me out of the swing, and I fetch the lube.

"Bring the plug and the wand too."

I kneel between his legs as I apply the lube. I tease him until he slaps my nipples which still have the clamps on them. When I rise, he removes the clamps, sucking each of my nipples as the blood and sensation floods back into them. I moan from the exquisite pain. I climb back into the original position I was in, and he guides me onto his cock. He's pushing off with one foot, the motion easing him into my ass.

"*Te sientes increíble, chiquita. Estás tan apretada. Estoy justo donde debo estar. Enterrada en el culo más suave y ardiente que he visto. Eres tan hermosa, Flora. Por dentro y por fuera.*" You feel amazing, little girl. You're so fucking tight. I'm right where I belong. Buried in the softest, hottest ass I've ever seen. You're so damn beautiful, Flora. Inside and out.

"*Gracias, Papí.*"

We've spoken mostly English since my return to the U.S., so I can get into the flow more easily, but it's natural for us to lapse back into Spanish. As much as his possessive dirty talk turns me on, I love the praise too. He gets I need that tonight.

I use the straps to rise and fall on his dick. He takes the foam head vibrator and turns it on. He watches me as it rubs against my clit. I think my eyes roll back in my head from all the sensations bombarding my pussy and ass. I feel full and yet empty. I feel antsy yet content. He's bringing me to the edge, and I debate whether to tell him.

Is it better to ask forgiveness than permission?

"You're about to come, aren't you, *chica?*"

"*Sí, Papí.*"

My body's practically humming as I feel my core tighten. I can't think in English anymore. I pant as my clit warns me I'm about to orgasm. I don't know how to move anymore because I'm impatient to find my release.

"*Por favor!*"

"What do you need, baby girl?"

"*¡Tú!*"

"You have me."

"*Ay, Papí.*"

I tense as my orgasm starts. My ass squeezes around Pablo's cock, making him groan.

"*Joder, Flora. Sácame toda la leche. Llénate el culo. Eres mía. Toda mía para follar como quiera. Dormirás con mi leche dentro de ti, chiquita.*" Fuck, Flora. Squeeze the cum from me. Fill your ass with it. You're mine. All fucking mine to fuck how I want. You're going to sleep with my cum inside you, little girl.

I guess Pablo can't think in English anymore either. The way his voice is so gravelly and sexy does me in. I've listened to men speak Spanish my entire life, and I get why people all around the world think it's hot. But it's Pablo's deep voice along with the Spanish that fucking detonates me.

"*¡Papí!*"

I can't help but scream as I come. I ride his dick, bouncing on it as he keeps the wand on my clit. I tremble with how hard I'm coming. He tosses the vibrator aside and forces me to stop moving as he comes in my ass. He spanks it twice, the swing and the pressure driving him as deep as he can go. When he's done coming, his arms wrap around me. He presses my head to his shoulder, and I gasp for air. I rest a hand over his heart, and I feel how it pounds beneath my palm.

That was so fucking intense.

He leans to get the plug from where I left it when I kneeled down. I cling to him even though I know he'll never drop me. He turns his head to snag a kiss before he stands. He takes his time, so I can slip out of the slings. I'm holding onto him like a koala on a bamboo tree. He carries me to the bed. He watches me for a moment before kissing me. I'm happy to let him lead because I'm spent.

"*Cariño*, you mean everything to me." Sweetheart.

"*Príncipe Azul,* you say all the right things. You mean the world to me." Prince Charming.

I rub my nose against his. With a quick kiss, he turns toward the bed. He eases me onto my hands and knees and plugs my ass. He slips into the bathroom to clean up, then we're curled into bed together.

Fuck. If I don't love him, then I don't know what love is.

It's been three weeks since I met the entire family at the restaurant. I've been poring over listings online. Pablo knows what I've been up to; however, we don't talk about it. I sense how much it bothers him I'm still considering moving out, but it feels like the right thing to do. It hasn't changed our commitment for a future together. That said, I want to make sure I can stand on my own feet and not be entirely reliant on him or his family. It has nothing to do with the Diaz name, but that I have the wherewithal to survive New York on my own if one day I'll be the *jefe's* wife.

I want no one to believe Pablo chose a weak woman who must hide behind him. I also need to fill my days, so I've been looking for jobs too. I know he takes no issue with that. It's purely my moving out.

I didn't fully believe Pablo when he said Luciana and Catalina would help me look at apartments. I thought he was just being generous with the offer, but that neither woman would have time nor the inclination to go anywhere with just me. It turns out they haven't had free time since the family dinner. It's why I haven't been to see any yet.

"*Buenos dias, señoras.*"

"You really don't have to call us that. Please, I'm Ana, and she's Cat."

Luciana gives me a hug that doesn't feel perfunctory at all. Catalina's is just as warm as her sister's. It feels like the hugs I get from my own *tías* back home in Colombia.

I remind myself that's not home anymore. I need to revert to thinking about the States the way I once did. That Colombia is where I'm from, but the States is home now.

"I have six properties we can look at today."

Catalina hands me her tablet, and I check out the first one. I've spoken to them both since dinner. I told them I see no way for me to afford Manhattan. They completely understood.

When I said the Bronx would probably be the most cost efficient for me, their responding texts came in half a second apart. They were adamant Pablo would never agree to my living there. When I asked him why, he explained that not every part of the Bronx was rough. However, even though there were some nice neighborhoods, I don't know my way around well enough to not get lost somewhere unsafe. I argued I'd learn my way around easily enough. That I survived going to school at Rutgers, which is in New Brunswick—not the best city in New Jersey—and I'd lived in Newark—an even worse city— when I worked there.

He pointed out that while I was in undergrad, I lived in a dorm for the first two years. After that, I had two roommates. He didn't love discovering they were both guys, and one of them was my boyfriend.

We were out to dinner a couple nights ago and ran into a couple. Pasha, apparently, is the bratva's syndicate accountant, and his wife, Sumiko, handles their legal books. Turns out she and Pablo dated for a few months. He tried to talk Sumiko out of a relationship with Pasha. He admitted it was never because he wanted her for himself. He never let her see sides of him he's shown me, but he genuinely worried for her safety. And he wished to piss Pasha off.

It was uncomfortable coming face to face with the beautiful Japanese Brazilian woman. She has curves for days. It made me wonder if, even with my hourglass figure, Pablo preferred women with more generous proportions. He sensed my moment of insecurity, and we talked about it like grown-ass adults. He didn't make me feel crazy or petty or anything like that for my emotions. It was refreshing to share my thoughts with him without hesitation.

He made sure I understood that night just how much he enjoys my body. He even anticipated a thought that flashed through my head. No, he wasn't picturing her.

I'm lost in thought as I scroll through listings on the tablet, not fully paying attention to what I'm seeing. I almost jump when Catalina speaks.

"We can start with this place in Brooklyn. It's a gentrified neighborhood, but it's still affordable. Then we can go to the two others in Brooklyn, the one on Long Island, the one on Staten Island, and finish with the one in Queens."

"I feel bad making you go all over New York."

"It's all right. We don't mind since we do this all the time anyway."

"Thank you."

I feel as though I'm forever expressing gratitude, but *los Diaz* have been far more generous than I could have ever imagined. They're nothing like I expected. Though I realized before I arrived in the States, they aren't the monsters my family indoctrinated me into believing they were. They're still so normal compared to any other cartel family I've met.

Mamá shielded me as best she could, and I really only spent time with *los Aguilar*. It was unavoidable that there were times I met other families at events my *abuelo* and *abuela* hosted. There were other men my mother dated besides Néstor who were cartel-adjacent as well.

The three of us set off, and Catalina and Luciana fill me in about the first neighborhood as we head over there in an SUV. There's another one that accompanies us, full of guards. We have a guard and a driver with us now. It's easy to forget the second vehicle is with us. But having the armed driver and bodyguard is a constant reminder things aren't entirely different in New York from Bogotá.

When we arrive at the first apartment, I already suspect it'll be out of my means pretty damn fast if I don't find a job like tomorrow. It's lovely, and once upon a time with the career I had after grad school, it wouldn't have been a struggle to afford it. I wouldn't have even thought twice before signing the contract. I had a great job, but I was looking to move onto something else after a few years. I had several offers on the table when *Mamá* got sick, and I abruptly uprooted my life to go back to take care of her. A couple even offered to wait three months for me to return. Eventually, I had to decline both.

"This walk-in closet could double as any additional storage you might need since it's practically a second bedroom."

"It's enormous. I wonder how many clothes the previous owner had to need something with this many shelves and racks."

It's not quite as big as you'd see in some reality TV shows about the rich and famous, but it sure feels close considering the relative size of the rest of the place.

"What do you think?" Catalina's question is casual but direct.

"I like it, but I'm not sold on it. You know what I have in

savings is enough for a down payment, but I'm unconvinced I could manage whatever the mortgage would be. I haven't used any credit in the States in years."

"You don't need to worry about that."

Luciana gives me an encouraging smile. I suppose they work with a few lenders, and at least one of them would give me a favorable interest rate. We take off to the next place, and it's much the same as the first one. I like it, but I'm unconvinced I can afford it without being certain I'll have a stable job soon.

I feel foolish having the women come out here and waste their time once we've seen the fourth place. Even with the third and fourth places being rentals rather than for sale, I'm not confident it's wise to get any of the ones we've seen. I assume the last two will be the same as the apartments we've visited. I finally speak up since this is turning into a pointless endeavor.

"I don't think checking out the last two places will be a good use of time. Everything's more expensive than it was a few years ago. I expected that. I just didn't anticipate by how much. My savings won't go as far as they would've a few years ago."

When I consider how long I was back in Colombia, I realize it was far more than just a few years. I've told myself that's all it was, but it's been closer to eight years. I was back there longer than I worked full-time in the U.S.

Catalina comes to stand beside me. "I know you're worried, and I get why. I won't suggest you rely on Pablo even though he has the means to get you any place you want. I get your need for independence right now, but if you need help, Luciana and I are here. We can guarantee a zero percent interest mortgage."

"How is that even possible? Is there such a thing?"

"Usually not, but we know the right people."

People.

My eyebrows shoot straight up as I look between the two women. It's Luciana's turn to explain things to me.

"No, neither of us is going to buy the place for you and then make you feel indebted to us. We know legitimate financiers at reputable banks who owe us favors because of how much business we've brought them over the years. It's easy enough to call in one of those favors."

"I'll think about it."

We head back to the SUV and agree to a late lunch instead of the other two apartments. Both women live in Queens. They're actually in the same neighborhood as most of the other top syndicate families. I learned a wife in another syndicate named them the Four Families. The Kutsenkos, Mancinellis, O'Rourkes, and *los Diaz* dominate the East Coast and have influence in the entire world.

We choose a restaurant near their neighborhood. It's a silent hint of where Pablo and I might one day live. It seems like the only neutral territory in any New York borough.

"It's been a while since I've written a cover letter for a job application. Are they still the same as they ever were?"

We're at the restaurant, and Catalina sits to my left. I look at her as she answers.

"Sort of. These days, you want to focus on interpersonal skills along with your scientific ones. Like you work well in diverse teams, that you believe in inclusion in the workplace, and that you're—"

"Wait. Isn't all of that a given? I mean, I know Colombia isn't the most diverse country in the world, but we have many ethnic backgrounds and varying social classes. That's not so different from the States. Do I need to say that because I'm from a foreign country?"

Both women shake their heads. They don't offer more explanation than that, so I'll take their word for it.

"How do I explain the years spent as a pharmacist rather than a lab chemist?"

"You can be honest and say you had a shift in career path when you returned to Colombia to help an ailing parent. Now you've returned and are ready to resume your original plans."

I nod.

"What makes you still apprehensive?"

Luciana reads me too well. When I glance at Catalina, I know she sees my trepidation despite how hard I try to mask it.

"I fear they'll think I've been out of the labs too long and that I only merit an entry-level position. That certainly won't be enough to pay for a place on my own. It's not like I can tell them the type of lab I've worked in for nearly the past year. I explained to Pablo while we were in Switzerland that Humberto made me prove my skills by working for him for several months before setting up the lab. He made me study and replicate formulas from existing samples. It pissed Pablo off to realize my involvement stretched back further than he thought. Unfortunately, there was nothing he could do from Switzerland, but I'm certain he'll take it out on my *abuelo* at some point."

We know he's still in New York. He's contacted Pablo. My boyfriend, along with Alejandro and *Tres J's*, met with *Abuelo*. Pablo made it clear, in no uncertain terms, that I do *not* wish to see *Abuelo* and that he needs to stop trying because I wouldn't change my mind. And if he insisted upon pushing the issue, Pablo would put him on a commercial flight—in Economy— back to Bogotá. Then Pablo would put him under house arrest just like Humberto was.

It's kept *Abuelo* away from me, but he hasn't given in and gone back yet. Pablo assures me he's being watched. *Los Diaz* are tapping all of his phones and email. He can't conspire to do anything without Pablo knowing about it.

"Keep trusting Pablo like you do, and everything will work

out." Luciana covers my hand and squeezes it as our food arrives.

"I've never trusted anyone more. I've just known since the beginning that even if he was my enemy, I could still trust him. I'm glad we're on the same side."

"He makes you happy, doesn't he?" Catalina offers me such a maternal smile that my heart aches.

"Very."

"Our *sobrino* is like the other men in our family. He can talk a lot, but he doesn't always communicate well. When he messes up—which he inevitably will—find patience. You might not agree with him—and that's fine—but he'll consider your wellbeing with the same seriousness and dedication as he does everyone else's he's responsible for."

"I know, Ana. I admire him for all that he does for others. I've seen hints of it since we got here. I don't know everything about his work, but I know he's dedicated to the people who rely on him."

"He's been that way since he was a kid. He always looked out for the other *niños*. He kept them out of trouble as much as he got them into it. My *niño* is damn Houdini reincarnated. Alejandro can disappear from right in front of you, I swear. It used to give Matáis and me heart attacks when he was little. It's why we stopped at one. Pablo would always come, take my hand, and say, '*Tía* Catalina, I'll help you. He's not hiding. He's hungry.' He used to make me laugh because half the time he was right. Even when he knew Alejandro wasn't anywhere near food, he understood it made me panic a little less. He always knew where his *primo* was."

I think about the little boy Catalina describes. He sounds adorable and sweet. I can almost picture him with his soulful eyes. I know many people describe them as soulless, but I've seen depths of emotion in his gaze I know he reserves for me. I've also witnessed how he can completely shut someone out. It's like being shoved out into a blizzard. It saddens me to think why he's become the man he is, but in the next breath, it comforts me to know he can be like that. It's what's kept me safe.

Catalina, Luciana, and I continue chatting as we eat. We discuss my résumé and cover letters a little more. They assure me *los Diaz* know people in various industries who would want a trained chemist. They don't promise me a job, but they promise to get my name in front of people who could offer me one.

"That was a wonderful lunch. Thank you, Cat."

"It's been lovely spending the day with you, Florencia. We hope we can do it again soon." Luciana gives me a quick hug and squeeze as she finishes speaking.

The sisters are going home, so they head to the SUV we were in earlier. Another one pulls up to take me back to Pablo's place in Manhattan. I wave to the two women as I approach the vehicle. I have a guard on each side of me, so I think nothing of the three guys who approach from the front, left, and right. Catalina and Luciana's SUV pulls away moments before two men pull out Tasers.

The man coming straight toward me has a gun pointed at my chest. I reach inside my purse for mine. I might not have a license for it yet in New York, but I still carry it. Old habits die hard. Pablo gave me a weapon the day after we arrived. He took me to a private shooting gallery, and I showed him I'm properly trained.

I don't have a chance to draw it before searing pain lances my back. It's near my kidneys, and my knees buckle. I can do nothing but fall to the ground and watch as men kick my guards in the head. Then I'm scooped up as Pablo's men run toward us from the Diaz SUV. They're too far away. I writhe in pain as I'm tossed in the back of a van.

Chapter Twenty-Five

Pablo

"Speak up, Ernesto. Can't hear you."

I had men pick up Ernesto a week after we arrived. I've been holding him at the bodega—corner store—we have on Long Island. Each family has "a place" where they conduct business no one else can ever know about.

We own several small businesses in Jackson Heights. The other three families believe we hold our inquisitions in the basement of a Queens bodega we use for our underground gambling rings. They think there's another in Queens that's our torture chamber. We let them believe whatever the fuck they want if it lets me work in peace here on Long Island.

Ernesto's been hanging from his wrists for a day and a half. We had him tied to a chair for a couple days. He's been in and out of a meat fridge. We've kept him guessing for weeks. I've already worked him over a little each day. Enough to keep him in constant pain, but not enough to kill him. I'd love to do more, but he needs to be conscious.

"I know nothing else, Pablo. I came here looking for my granddaughter, and that's it."

"*Huevonada.* You're such a horrible liar, Ernesto, and you're being stubborn. You can end all of this if you just talk." Bullshit.

"I can't tell you anything I don't know."

I drive my fist into his gut.

"If you insist upon being useless, then I may as well just kill you. I enjoyed torturing you at first, but now it's boring. I'd rather just get this over with."

I watched him meet with some American businessman, but it was no one who surprised us. I had surveillance running in his room and the area surrounding the Waldorf Astoria. The guy is an insurance CEO who has some shady dealings with a biotech company Ernesto invested in years ago. The conversation was as boring as watching Ernesto swing from a meat hook.

"I know you must be starving and thirsty and in pain. End it for yourself, if not for Florencia. Just tell me what I want to know. Who paid Humberto? It wasn't just Néstor. Who did you get money from besides Humberto?"

"No one. There's nothing left for me to tell."

"Really? Because we intercepted a courier with a briefcase of cash. How cliché, by the way. We followed him back to the dispatch office."

The courier was Asian with no accent besides one from Brooklyn. He was no use and a waste of time.

"How would I know who that was from if I never even received the package? I can't answer questions I know nothing about. Maybe if you'd allowed that delivery to go through, I would have something I could tell you."

"You really think I would let you get more money in your grubby little hands? Money that could pay for you to head back to Colombia? Money that could pay you off to stay quiet when somebody else goes after Florencia?"

"I had no idea about those fucking hitmen! That wasn't anything I agreed to. Humberto did that on his own. Why do you think I came here searching for her?"

I try not to laugh in his face. His righteous indignation is a fucking joke.

"I think you came because she's inconvenient. I think you would've told those mercenaries exactly where she was."

"You *chuchamadre*! I'd never do that to my granddaughter." The cunt of your mother.

I let the insult about *Mamá* slide. Not the hill to die on right now. But another one...

"Really? Because you're the one who put her in front of Humberto. You knew exactly what kind of man he was. And you knew the risk that went along with it. That at any time she could've stepped wrong, and he would've put the hit on her. You were fine with that risk."

"Until she met you, she was such an easygoing girl. She always obeyed instructions. She never talked back, and she never caused a fuss. If it hadn't been for you, then she wouldn't have ever stepped out of line."

This fucker doesn't know Flora for shit.

"That's where you're wrong. Flora has a backbone of steel. She decided before I went to see her that she wanted to end things with Humberto. It was hearing her conversation with that *pedazo de mierda* that made me realize how much danger she was in. I rescued her before Humberto could get his hands on her."

"Rescued? Tell yourself that. You did nothing more than kidnap her. You won't convince me she's any less your hostage than I am if I don't get to speak to her."

"Ernesto, she's made it painfully clear she has no wish to

see you ever again. I definitely won't force her to speak to you if she doesn't want to."

"Such convenient lies you tell me to justify keeping me away from her. You probably have her holed up in some equally dingy and disgusting warehouse."

"That's where you couldn't be more wrong. Flora chose me. She could've insisted upon going to you. She could've refused my help. I could've helped her start a new life anywhere, but she chose here with me."

"I don't believe you, you lying *puta de madre*."

We have so many ways to swear in Spanish. People say the Colombian Spanish accent is pretty neutral. They also say we're pretty profane.

I pull my phone out and open my photo gallery. I take very few pictures and store even less in my phone. But I have one of Flora from last night when we went out to the movies. It's a selfie of us together with our hands in our shared popcorn. I'm giving her a kiss on the cheek as she laughs. I hold my phone out to Ernesto.

"Does this look like a woman being held captive?"

"You've fucking brainwashed her. She's some Stockholm Syndrome victim."

"Don't confuse you for me. I don't need to indoctrinate her with anything. I've never lied about who and what my family is. All I've done is tell Flora the truth from our side. She decided about the things your family told her. She also spoke to Magdalena before we came to New York. Her mother confirmed what I told Flora is the truth. We also learned a few other interesting facts about who you spend your spare time with. How long did it take for you to forget about Domingo when you climbed into Magdalena's bed?"

"You think I ever bothered to fuck that whore in a bed?

Bent over my desk or up against a wall is as good as she ever got."

"I wonder what Estrella would think about that. Your desk means it was in your house. Does your wife know you brought your mistress home with you? And not for a minute do I believe you and Magdalena didn't fuck in a bed. You're getting too old to stand up for that long."

"Leave my wife out of this. She has nothing to do with any of it."

"Of course, she does. She surely spun as many lies about my family and about Domingo as you did. You knew your son's shortcomings. But Estrella still thinks the sun shines out of your son's dead ass, even though she knows exactly what he did that led to his death."

I sneer at him as I walk around his naked body. I flick his ear just because he wasn't expecting it. My knife glides diagonally between his shoulder blades. It leaves a thin trail of blood. Nothing deep enough to bleed excessively, but just enough to hurt. It matches countless other cuts my cousins and I gave him during the time he's been with us.

"You've spent more than thirty years being spiteful to a ghost. You wanted what your son had, so you've been fucking his mistress for decades. Your son's dead. He can never know about your pathetic habit of fucking the woman he supposedly loved. You are trying to make up for a past that never happened. You should've fucked her while your son was alive and made sure he knew about it. You just enjoyed being with Magdalena."

I take what Flora's mother confessed and toss it back in Ernesto's face. I don't enjoy trashing Flora's mother, but what Flora can't hear won't hurt her.

"How many times did she call you Domingo? How many times did she moan his name? You settled for knowing the woman you had an affair with was always thinking about another man—your son—just to get revenge on someone who'll never know it happened."

I kick the back of his left knee and send him swinging as I walk back around to face him.

"I'm giving you one more opportunity to tell me what I want to know before this situation grows dire. I can't let you live now that you've been here, but that doesn't mean I can't punish your grandson for your choices."

"Leave him the fuck alone! He has nothing to do with this! He's only a kid!"

Ernesto's voice is already hoarse from not having enough to drink over the past ten days. His voice cracks throughout his plea. I laugh.

"He's not a kid at eighteen. You've recruited younger men than that to try to fuck over my family. You can't have it both ways. You can't say other guys your grandson's age are men and old enough to work for you, then claim he's too young to be involved."

"He's only eighteen!"

"Which makes him an adult, so all's fair."

I close out the photo of Flora and me after flashing it toward him one more time. Then I pull up a Colombian phone number.

"One call, that's all it takes."

I'm growing more and more frustrated by the moment. I'd really hoped the courier might give us a clue who's involved. Between no information from the delivery guy and no information when we inquired at the courier's office, we've gotten nowhere. Not even with the heavy incentives we offered the courier and the dispatcher. Perhaps this is the negotiating card we needed.

Ernesto sees it's a Colombian phone number, and even

though it doesn't have a name attached to the contact, he can guess what this means. He knows I don't issue threats I won't follow through on. He tries to spit on me, but his mouth is so dry he produces next to no spittle. I step aside in time, and Alejandro swings a baseball bat that strikes Ernesto's kidneys. The man howls in pain and twirls on the hook. He must have forgotten my cousin was behind him. Joaquin has his own bat that he jams into Ernesto's lower abdomen.

"It'll be your *huevo* next time."

He only has one nut left after what *Tía* Luciana had done to him. Joaquin taps the baseball bat against his open palm. Cliché threatening move, but effective, nonetheless. I tap my phone screen and make it a video call. Immediately, it's answered with the camera facing toward the front steps of a high school. It's only a couple minutes before kids pour out of the front door.

I recognize Flora's cousin since he's a near replica of Ernesto. It also means he looks a lot like Flora. The guy's hanging out with friends, but eventually he's one of the last left. He's looking around, waiting for his chauffeur to show up. He'd be waiting forever if that's how he was leaving.

"Leave him!"

Ernesto jerks forward as though he can actually get me to obey as he yells. His fingers open and close uselessly with his arms strung up over his head.

"Then answer me."

"I can't."

I tsk and shake my head. "Won't is more like it. Take him."

Men rush out of the van where the video is being shot. I force Ernesto to watch his grandson being kidnapped. They scoop up Pedro and toss him into the back. We hear the doors slam as the man holding the phone turns the camera toward Pedro. It only takes a few moments before my guys strip the young man down to his tighty-whities. Definitely not a good look if he ever wants to get laid.

"Tell me now, Ernesto."

"I can't."

"Still the wrong answer."

I speak to the guy on the phone and give the order. Only seconds later, we're watching arms and hands move through the air with socks filled with bars of soap or coins. They're wailing down on Pedro, who's crying like a little bitch begging for my men to stop. Wouldn't surprise me if he cries for his *mamá*.

"Wait, wait. Maybe I know something."

"Maybe?"

Sarcasm drips from that one word as I put up my hand in front of the camera. A voice barks an order, and the beating stops.

"I didn't ask Humberto questions, but there was definitely someone from New York involved. I met another Latino man at a restaurant. He gave me a deposit to convince me to get Florencia to work for Humberto. I didn't ask who he was or who sent him."

"Was there any hint of an accent or a dialect?"

There're tons of dialects throughout Latin America. People estimate there are somewhere between six and fifteen varieties of Spanish spoken in Colombia alone. If it were someone other than Ernesto, they might have a difficult time telling me whether it was a fellow Colombian. But he'd know if it were a homegrown rival. Ernesto shakes his head.

"Maybe Guatemalan or Mexican, even Costa Rican."

At least that rules out Cubans. We had some problems with them a few years ago. They got involved in a sex trafficking ring, and one of their leaders set his sights on Maria Mancinelli. Fucking idiot he was. He went after the most untouchable woman in the underworld. She's a don's niece, a *consigliere's* daughter, an underboss and *capo dei capi's* sister, and wife to one of the seniormost *capos* in the world.

It wasn't just the Mancinelli family. This same ring of traffickers also scooped up a woman who became Misha Andreyev's sister-in-law. Misha is Maksim Kutsenko's cousin. Maksim is the bratva's *pakhan*. Their equivalent to a *jefe*.

It was one of the rare times any of the other three families saw a more humane side of us. *Tres J's* took care of the Cuban and made sure Maria could see a doctor when she needed it.

Shitty trip down memory lane. I force my mind back to the present as I continue interrogating Ernesto.

"That money we intercepted here in New York. Do you have any new thoughts on who it could be from?"

"Probably the same person who sent the nameless man I met in the restaurant."

"That's not enough to go off of."

I look down at my phone and dip my chin. The beating recommences, and Ernesto watches in horror as one of my guys uses pliers to pull out two of his grandson's teeth. Blood streams from the young man's mouth as he whimpers. A wet puddle forms on the front of Pedro's underwear.

"I know nothing more. Please stop! Stop! Don't hurt him anymore. It's not his fault. He has nothing to do with this."

I don't give any orders, so my men continue to work Pedro over. Ernesto witnesses one of my men stick bamboo shoots under his grandson's fingernails. Then, using the same pliers that took out a couple of teeth, the guy inches off a fingernail, making it as excruciating as he possibly can.

"I think it's the O'Rourkes."

Ernesto's outburst surprises me, but I refuse to allow my expression to show it. I wonder if this is payback for our involvement in the demise of a mob leader in Albany. Javier's fiancée—my childhood neighbor Madeline—lived in Upstate for years and wound up involved with the mob leader.

I know the O'Rourkes feel no loyalty to the O'Sheehans, but they do feel some obligation since the O'Sheehans are the O'Rourkes' vassals. It could be retribution and retaliation for that, or it could be something entirely different.

"All right, let him go. Keep an eye on him, though."

The camera spins to show the two back doors of the van opening, and two of my men push Pedro onto the street before the van moves. The doors close as they drive away. I spit in Ernesto's face to prove I can.

"You should've cared about Flora as much as you did Pedro."

I drive my fist into his mouth. As much as I'd love to throat punch him, I'm unconvinced I won't have more to ask him later. Instead, I have another call to make.

Chapter Twenty-Six

Flora

I'm not hurt, but I'm fucking pissed off. These *puta de madres.*

I force myself to inhale yet another deep breath to keep from losing my shit. I'm still terrified of what might happen next. But so far—besides the whole motherfucking taser—they've only manhandled me. I remember writhing on the ground in pain. My head spinning and my body aching like nothing I've ever experienced before. Two guys scooped me up and hauled me away like out of some shitty TV show, with one guy carrying my legs and the other one with his arms wrapped underneath mine. A different man pulled the little electrode-dart-fucker-thingies out of me in the van they tossed me into.

All I know so far is that these fuckers are also Latino. I heard them speaking Spanish to me even though I was in a daze when they shoved me in the vehicle. But now we're at some house in a place called Yonkers. I was out of it for most of the car ride, but I saw road signs out the window. They're utterly inept kidnappers or they're pretty fucking confident I won't get away, so it didn't matter if I saw road signs and street names.

From listening to them, I'm pretty positive they're Mexican, but I can't be entirely sure since they could be trying to confuse me. However, some things they've said make me believe they must be. They use terms other Latin American countries rarely do. Two guys are arguing right now about where they were going to sit while they babysit me.

"*Vete a la chingada.*" Go fuck yourself.

Colombians don't use *chingar* to mean fuck.

"*Pinche pendejo.*" Fucking asshole.

Pinche means the cook's assistant or scullery maid, but in Mexican Spanish it means fucking. That's one of those words they usually don't translate right on subtitles. It means more than just damn.

"*No mames.*" Don't suck.

It basically means, come on. The first guy's refusing to get up, so pissy pants storms off. Besides this measuring *huevos*, they've switched mostly to English. I assume they believe I don't understand what they're saying. Perhaps they believe that since I'm newly arrived from Colombia, I must not speak that much English.

Shitty stereotype if ever there was one.

Many families with means—not rich but with some money—send their kids to private school. I learned English before I ever left Colombia. The situation isn't entirely different in Mexico. I guess they don't know that much about me because they seem to assume I'm not well-traveled or well educated.

I pay close attention to what they're saying.

"The boss won't be happy that you fucking tased her. You didn't need to do that once you got her guards on the ground."

I've been observing the men trying to figure out their dynamic. The one who just spoke seems to be the leader of this operation, even though he mentions some guy who outranks them all.

"Yeah, well, I had to make sure the bitch came with us without screaming her fucking head off."

"Yeah, well, hurting her wasn't part of the deal." The first two words are a sarcastic mimic.

"She's fine, isn't she?" The asshole who tased me walks over and grabs my hair. "*Estás bien, ¿verdad?*" You're all right, aren't you?

I refuse to respond. I hit my tracker when I finally felt like I had enough control over my fingers to press the button. It's on the underside of the clasp on the bracelet Pablo gifted me right after we arrived here. He gave it to me in case something like this should ever happen. I wondered when he did it if he was tempting fate.

Now, I don't think that's the case. I think he was smart and cares about me and wanted to be sure he could do everything to protect me. Hopefully, it's transmitting, and he got the alert. He explained everyone in his family wears a tracker. They don't watch each other's daily comings and goings, but in case something like this should happen, then they're prepared.

The alert not only goes to Pablo, but to Enrique, Luis, Alejandro, and *Tres J's.* So, if it's not Pablo who leads the charge, then it'll be one of them. I just need to hang on long enough for them to get here.

I listen to the men continuing to bicker amongst themselves in English about why I refuse to speak and how they should handle that. It dawns on me that they have a Boston accent. It's not quite as bad as "pahk the car in Hahvahd Yahd," but it's pretty damn close when they speak English.

The guy in charge—*Cabrón Uno*—comes to stand before where I'm seated on a sofa. There are too many of them for me to make any type of run for it. I'm outnumbered six to one, so they haven't bothered to restrain me. I count my blessings as he speaks to me in Spanish.

"This can all be over, and you can go back to your boyfriend's place if you just tell us what you know."

I stare at him blankly as if I have no clue what he's talking about.

"Give us the formula, and then we'll send you on your way."

I cock an eyebrow but remain quiet. Like hell they'll just let me go now that I've seen all their faces. If Pablo or another Diaz doesn't show up before they give up on me, then I'm dead. I don't believe they're holding me for ransom, but maybe they are. Nobody's said anything about that.

"Make her talk. We don't have all day. The boss wants the formula."

The guy who's been giving me a hard time since the beginning, the one who yanked my hair a moment ago—*Cabrón Dos* —leans forward and gets in my face.

"You really want to make this harder on yourself? We have ways of making you talk."

What type of corny-ass shit is that? I merely stare at him, unflinching. I know he's the type who wants to see me cower, but I refuse to give in to that. When his hand lands across my face, I force myself not to flinch. I tensed as I saw his hand move through the air, but I was prepared. It hurts like a mother-fucker, but I don't react. Instead, it's *Cabrón Uno* who does.

I barely contain my reaction when that man grabs the shitbag who slapped me. He drags him over to the dining room table and pulls a knife from his belt that's practically a fucking machete. Before I can anticipate what'll happen next, it's slicing through the air. Then it's slicing through the man's hand, taking off everything from the knuckles forward. It's just a stump with a thumb attached to the man's wrist.

Blood geysers everywhere. I watch as the amputee struggles to stay on his feet as he howls in pain. A third guy rushes forward, but he hesitates before helping my tormentor. *Cabrón Uno* nods, and the new guy wraps a shirt around the stump, trying to staunch the blood.

He's going to need to see a doctor.

I've been told I have a dry sense of humor.

Cabrón Uno comes back and sits on the coffee table in front of me. "We have orders not to manhandle you. Sorry about that. But just because we're not allowed to touch you now that you're here doesn't mean the silent treatment will keep you out of trouble. We have other ways of making this miserable for you. So, you decide. If you want anything to drink, then you're going to have to earn it. A sip for every ingredient."

I thin my lips when I press them together, jutting out my chin. Pablo claimed I was stubborn when we met. He doesn't know the half of it. These men are about to discover just how obstinate an only child can be when she doesn't get her way.

What I want is to leave. I've been with these men for more than an hour now, and I can't help but wonder when Pablo will get here. I don't know where he was today since he left before I was awake. There were fresh pastries in the kitchen with a sweet love note doodled next to it saying he hoped I enjoyed my day with his *tías*. It also said he can't wait to have me on his lap while I tell him how it went.

When I think back about that note, it makes me wonder if his *tías* got away safely. I believe they did, but I can't be sure. I'm alone here with these men, but perhaps there were others who took Catalina and Luciana to a different location.

Perhaps they saw what happened and contacted Pablo or even Enrique. But if that were the case, then they'd know to check for my tracker. Perhaps there's some kind of signal jammer here at this house, and my tracker isn't pinging for them.

I don't want to believe Pablo's family could be involved in this, but the part of me that's battling my fear wants to plant that seed in my mind. It also wants to plant the seed that perhaps this was my family who did this.

Could it be my abuelo?

"*Señorita* Aguilar, you don't have that many choices. If you want to keep the people you love alive, you'll cooperate. If we tell our boss you're being a pain in the ass, then he'll go after Pablo. Do you want to know you caused his death? My boss isn't a forgiving man. He'll drag out Pablo's death to punish you. Every minute you make us wait for the information we want is a minute he'll spend torturing Pablo. If you refuse to tell us what we want to know, then my boss will just move on to your mother. We have contacts in Colombia. It won't be hard to snatch Magdalena. I hear she's a beautiful woman who loves to host parties. I wonder how she'll entertain the men who visit her."

I grit my teeth. I don't underestimate the men in front of me or whoever they work for. I believe they could try to kidnap Pablo and try to torture him. But he has the skills and wherewithal to avoid capture or to survive whatever they might do to him until his family can rescue him.

My mother's an entirely different story. She's not equipped to handle the things Pablo can. I'm not equipped for it, and my mother's not as physically or mentally sturdy as I am.

"Oh, you don't like the idea of us going after your *mamacita*. Maybe we'll string your *abuelo* up right next to her."

I grin at that. I finally decide to speak.

"You can do whatever the hell you want to that *viejo pendajo*. Hell, I'll even watch." Old idiot.

"Oh, what do you know? You even speak some real Spanish."

"That's what you call Mexican Spanish? Real Spanish? I didn't expect you to string three words together when I saw you approaching me."

I practically bite my tongue to keep from saying more. *Cabrón Uno's* the only one on my side right now. I don't need to antagonize him.

"You really have a death wish, don't you, *señorita?* I could easily turn you over to somebody who won't have the restraint I do. I could walk out of this room and let these men do whatever the fuck they want with you."

I don't shift my gaze from him, but I've already been observing all the men in here. I've done my best to memorize their tattoos and scars. I've looked at their faces to memorize their eye color and any distinguishable features. These are men who aren't new to cartel life.

I don't know which ones may have grown up in the U.S. and which might have grown up in Mexico, but none of these men are that young. I put them all in their early thirties to early forties. They're seasoned veterans in this world.

I'm hoping against hope I'm wrong, and they are holding me for ransom. Nobody's said anything to me about what will happen after this. They aren't trying hard to get information out of me. Even though they're rude, they're still asking rather than torturing me. Since I don't want to answer any of their questions, I'll ask some of my own.

"How much am I worth? The last hit on me cost a quarter million. I'll be insulted if it isn't at least that much."

"This isn't a hit."

Good to know I might live.

"All right, then what's your boss asking for in ransom?"

"It's not a ransom either. We want information only you have."

"We know that already, but how much is your boss paying all of you to grab me and hold on to me? Again, if it's not at least a quarter million, I'll be insulted."

"Don't worry about what we're getting paid."

"Ah. That means it's nowhere near how much the original hit was. Isn't that rather insulting that one man was supposed to get all that money for killing me and not even that much is being divided among the six of you?" I gesture at each of them as I speak.

"*Señorita*, you've gone from being silent to talking far too much. If you don't shut the fuck up or give us the information we want, I'll gag you."

I open my mouth and say, "Ah," just like you would at the dentist. The man sitting in front of me lurches to his feet and with his hand open. I think he's about to break his own rule and wrap it around my throat when I hear his pocket ring. He pulls a phone out and answers it in English. He puts it on speaker so the rest of his men can hear it as well.

Whoever this guy is on the other side of the phone has no accent. Not one that hints at a foreign language, or even one that tells me a region in the U.S. As I listen to the two men go back and forth, I'm positive now this group of cartel men is from Boston.

"*Señorita* Aguilar."

"*Sí, señor.*"

"You have a choice to make. I know you've understood everything you've heard so far."

That declaration surprises the men who realize they've talked, and I've understood everything.

"You have information many men want right now, probably

even several women. It's dangerous for you to be in New York. You can't rely on the Diaz family to protect you."

"Why is that?"

"Because they're using you."

"And you're not?" I barely keep myself from snorting since his claim is so fucking ridiculous.

"Oh, I am, but at least I'm honest about it. I won't play you for a fool like Pablo is."

"And just who are you keeping me safe from? Is it only the Diaz family or someone else?"

"It's everybody else, *señorita*. You have people on every continent but Antarctica interested in your knowledge."

"And yet, you won't pay these men you hired as much as a single mercenary would've made if they'd killed me."

"You don't need to worry your pretty little head about who's getting paid how much. My men know this job is worth it."

I ignore how he tries to antagonize me. It won't get me anywhere if I let my irritation fog my mind.

"If you want me to believe all this shit you're shoveling, then let me speak to Pablo."

"I already talked to him. He knows I have you, and he knows I'm keeping you safe."

"If that's the case, why didn't your men tell me that from the beginning instead of trying to coerce information out of me?"

"Because if they have to keep you company, you may as well have something to talk about."

"You know I don't believe a word you're saying about Pablo, but I don't doubt there are people after me. You've made that obvious, but I know I'm safest with the Diaz family, so I can be patient."

"You're smart not to trust me, but it doesn't change who you are in this scenario and who you're with. Your choice, *señorita*. Tell my men what they want to know, and we keep you safe, or we'll turn you over to the wolves."

Chapter Twenty-Seven

Pablo

"Why?"

I'm surrounded by the O'Rourkes at their shitty strip club 4Play. None of us are interested in the women in next to nothing—or entirely nothing—since they're all married, and I have Flora. What the fuck do I need to look at another woman for when I have my *chiquita?*

"You're going to have to be more specific, Pablo. Why the feck are you such a fucknut? Why the feck are you such a shit-stain? Why the feck are you bothering us?"

I called Dillan, the mob boss, and demanded a meeting. This isn't about swapping pleasantries. Hell, it could devolve into something far more violent. The strip club is the closest place to anonymity since it's dark, and the fuckers here aren't interested in anything but the women and their hard-ons. It's also still public enough to remind us we shouldn't shoot each other's brains out.

I ignore Dillan's questions or how he uses "feck" to irritate me. It sounds ridiculous to begin with, then it sounds utterly stupid when he uses fuck in a common phrase but feck for everything else. Instead, I sweep my gaze around his cousins. Fucking red hair and green eyes. Fucking leprechauns. All six of them share the same features.

Dillan's cousins—Seamus and Cormac—are built like fucking oxen and are standing on each side of Dillan. I'd like to say they're as dumb as beasts of burden, but they're both lawyers. Finn, the second-in-command, and his twin brothers —Sean and Shane—stand to the right of their other three cousins. My family is freshly from Colombia, so no wonder we still all have Spanish names. But the O'Rourkes have been here for like four generations. A fucking stereotype based on truth.

"I can tell you're cursing our names, Pablo. We've heard it all before. I want to be home with my wife. Get on with it."

"Patience is a virtue, Finn. Shut the fuck up and keep looking pretty."

He's the most handsome one in the family. Kinda like Alejandro, but my cousin actually looks like a man, not a Ken doll.

Dillan's patience is wearing thin to match mine and Finn's. "I'd also like to be home with my wife and baby, Pablo. Keeva has an ear infection and is miserable. If I have to be miserable too, I'd rather be holding my little one."

She's an adorable baby. Even I can appreciate that, especially since she takes after her mother. At least they didn't fuck that kid by spelling her name the Irish way—Caoimhe. I've seen the original spelling of his wife's name since she was born in Northern Ireland. Most Americans wouldn't get it.

"Poor baby."

Javier chimes in from where he stands behind me. We all know he isn't referring to the infant. My cousins are here in force just like Dillan's. We look like rival football teams about to face off.

"I get you're obligated to defend the O'Sheehans, and that's why you're doing this."

"What the ever-loving feck are you going on about?"

"You're targeting my girlfriend to get back at my family for Drew."

Dillan takes a menacing step forward. Of course, that results in his cousins following him. I can't ignore it, so I take my own step forward, which brings my cousins with me.

"We don't target women."

"Anymore."

"You can wipe that sneer off your motherfecking face."

"Could you just pick feck or fuck, for fuck's sake? You're impossible to take seriously. It won't distract me. You've been expanding into Eastern Europe for the past couple years. You've pissed off Maks. Now you're pushing into Latin America. We let all of you have your little labs as the price of peace. But you went way too far getting Humberto involved."

"That old fart? He's dead, and you killed him. We can't do business with a dead man."

It doesn't surprise me news already left Colombia and reached New York. Annoying, but not surprising.

"Before I took care of him. You still want something from us, and you're using my girlfriend to get it."

"Look, Pablo, we—"

All at once, my cousins' and my phone go off. We keep them on silent except for two things. The emergency group text and the tracker alerts. I glance back at my family as I pull out my phone.

"What the fuck did you do?!"

I'm ready to lunge at Dillan, but I restrain myself at the last second. It's Flora's tracker that's going off.

"What are you talking about? Whose tracker is that?"

All members of the Four Families wear one. The women have them in bracelets and necklaces. The men have them on watches or belt buckles. Just like in my family, the only time the other men's phones make noise is for the family emergency text or their trackers.

"It's Flora's. I swear to God, Dillan. I swear to mother-fucking God."

His eyes widen as he realizes just how close to the brink I am. I'm one of the few who nearly never takes the Lord's name in vain. My mother would kill me if she just heard me.

"Pablo."

I look back at Joaquin, our chief intel gatherer. He hands me his phone, and I read a message from one of our men saying an attack happened as a car arrived to pick up Flora. She was leaving her lunch with *Tía* Catalina and *Tía* Luciana.

"I'll call *Mamá*."

Javier and Alejandro speak, and I know they're calling my *tías*. It'll be to check on their mothers and to see if either of them knows what happened. Maybe they saw something.

"Pablo—"

"What?!"

Dillan holds up his hands and takes a step back. "This isn't us. We won't defend the O'Sheehans. They know that. Whoever went after your woman wasn't connected to my family."

I narrow my eyes at him, but I see his cousins on their phones. I watch Sean in particular. He's their family's intel chief. The man can find a country's nuclear secrets if he wanted. I hate admitting anyone from another family is better than mine. But his grad degree in national security trained him to find shit buried as far back as when his family were probably Druids.

"Pablo, I'll do what I can. I swear, but I can't make any promises. Whatever the feck goes on between us has nothing to do with our women." Sean knew I was watching him.

Joaquin is nearly as good. Sergei and Anton claim they are since *everyone* knows they went to an Ivy—UPenn isn't even the best one. It takes two of them, but chiefly Sergei. Lorenzo and Carmine are the guys in the Mancinelli family. Carmine's always been a nosy little shit, and Lorenzo dabbles in computer science. Since Flora went to Rutgers, I won't be able to insult Lorenzo about that anymore.

"We need to go."

I spin around and nudge my chin toward the door. I don't give a shit about this meeting anymore. If Dillan's lying, then I'll annihilate his family. I'll leave the women to grieve, but the men are dead to me already.

"Yonkers." Joaquin keeps his voice low as we walk outside.

"What the hell is there?" Alejandro wonders the same thing I do.

"I don't know what's there now, but it'll be us soon enough. Are they already there?"

Joaquin's enlarging something on his phone as he speaks. "No, that's my best guess for right now. Assuming Florencia's tracker transmitted to us the moment it went off, they'll be in Yonkers in ten minutes."

I glance at my phone's clock. It's already been ten minutes since the alert went off. Without too much traffic, it's about twenty minutes from Manhattan to Yonkers. We're in Queens right now. It'll take us at least thirty minutes to get there.

We came in two SUVs with bodyguards in each of them. I hold out my hand, and my regular driver, Arturo, tosses me the keys. I jerk my head toward the second SUV. The guards will go in that one. My cousins and I will go in the lead vehicle. We rarely all ride together, but I want any conversation we have to be for my family's ears only. I hand the keys to Jorge. My youngest cousin drives like every trip is the Indy 500.

Joaquin and Javier climb in the back. Alejandro's in the front passenger seat. I sit in the middle as I prep Jorge's and Alejandro's gear. They'll need it once we arrive. My other cousins and I slip off our suit coats before putting on our bulletproof vests and strapping on thigh holsters. We fasten belts around our waists that carry extra ammunition and at least one knife. It's not ideal that we're in suits rather than tactical clothes, but we've done this before. We have Kevlar helmets if we need them. Javier passes rifles forward to me. I hand two to Alejandro. He keeps one by his left knee for Jorge. He holds the other.

My right knee bounces. It surprises me when I feel my body shaking, so I take a moment to realize it's my leg doing it. I never allow my nervousness to show. Just the opposite. I'm always the most stoic one.

You won't do Flora any good if you don't get yourself under control.

I can't let the woman I love be the one who ruins me. If I do, then I'll risk her life. She needs me to be the monster I hide from her. She needs me to be so much worse than the hint I gave her.

You love her.

I love her.

That realization's been nipping at me the last few days. I knew it was coming. It's why I abandoned the idea of a twenty-four seven D/s relationship. I need her by my side. If she were here, I'd ask her what she would do in my position. I've never wanted to rely on someone outside my family before—let alone actually do so. It's disconcerting as fuck, but it makes me even more committed to bringing her home.

"Jorge, why are you driving like a *vieja abuelita?*" An old granny.

"Do you want to die on the way to rescuing your woman? Unless I plow through these cars, there's nothing I can do. This vehicle isn't exactly known for its agility."

That's not entirely true. These SUVs are surprisingly light on their feet—tires. They handle extremely well and take some tight-ass corners. We weave through traffic when we need to, but never excessively. We don't need someone calling the police on us.

I inhale so deeply my chest expands. It pushes my shoulders back, and I force myself to relax them. I'm so tense I'm a rubber band about to snap.

"I just finished texting *Tío* Enrique. He's tracking me and sending *los toro* to meet us."

The bulls—official soldiers in a Colombian cartel who're overseen by a *matador*.

"Thanks, Alejandro."

I watched his fingers moving on his phone and figured he was messaging our *tío*, but I couldn't be sure. Since neither of my cousins said anything about their mothers, I'm assuming they're fine but had no news. We'd be going in separate directions if *Tía* Luciana or *Tía* Catalina were targets too. I don't think Alejandro could take anything else happening to his mother after her abduction while *Tío* Enrique and *Tía* Elle were dating.

I force myself to look out the window rather than watching the vehicle's GPS. We keep our location services off on our phones. After all, we have the trackers if anyone really needs to find us. We always turn our phones off entirely when we're at least five miles from the Long Island bodega because protecting that place's secrecy is paramount to carrying out our most unsavory duties. But we keep our vehicle GPS on because we don't know every nook and cranny of the tri-state area. We can turn it off if we need to.

Since we aren't headed to the bodega—yet—our phones remain on.

"Finally."

I mutter to myself, but in the quiet SUV, everyone hears me. We just passed the sign welcoming us to Yonkers. I allow myself to look at the map now, then I stare at my phone app that's tracking Flora. She's been in one place for a while. Traffic hasn't been on our side, so she's been with her kidnappers for an hour. When I figure that out, my knee bounces again. I press my palm against it to soothe my sympathetic nervous system that's in fight, not flight. I need my parasympathetic nervous system to kick in and put me at rest.

In times of stress, I force myself to examine situations like a scientist. I do my best to remove emotion from the equation and study the situation objectively. That includes how I handle my body's reaction to stressors. I don't think it's a dissociative disorder, but maybe it is. It's the compartmentalizing I've been good at since I was a child. It's the part of me that feels no remorse until after my job is done. It's the part that convinces me not to punish myself for what I do in service to my family.

Joaquin taps me on the shoulder. "*Los toros* are five minutes behind us. They were already in the Bronx."

It's a Thursday, so pay day for businesses and families who made shitty decisions and now belong to us. Some pay us protection money against the other syndicates. Some have debts they'll never repay, but they can try. Some just looked the wrong way when we were around and pissed one of us off. Our guys were collecting what people owe us.

"It's up there on the left."

I point between Jorge and Alejandro's shoulders. Joaquin and Javier lean forward to see over mine, and Alejandro turns around in his seat. The four of them watch the flashing dot on my phone screen. Jorge takes my word for it.

"Do you want me to pull over here? None of us have seen a lookout, so we should be good to wait for the others."

"Yeah."

We have four guards in the SUV that followed us, and there will be ten *los toros* between two other SUVs. With those of us in this vehicle, that makes nineteen. I don't know if that'll make things easier or not. I know, regardless of how many men we face, the odds are in our favor. The men who have Flora are in this for the money. I'm certain it isn't personal to them.

My cousins know my feelings for Flora without me saying anything. They'll do everything they can to help me. Javier wants to get home to Madeline, and we'll protect him to make sure he does. The other men want to survive us, so they won't fuck up. They know they'll face me if they don't put Flora ahead of their own lives. Some have families of their own, but they know what they pledged when they promised their loyalty to *Tío* Enrique.

It means the Cartel comes before everything else. It means they support *Tío* Enrique—and by extension his family—above all else. We've all made that pledge. For other men, being in the Cartel isn't automatically hereditary. It pretty much is, but not always. The men make their choice to be in. Now they'll prove it.

"They're here."

Javier announces the other men's arrival. We climb out of the vehicle, but we leave the rifles inside for now. It's broad daylight, so we don't need anyone freaking out about men with automatic weapons prowling down their street. The other guys put their vests on, and we all put our suit coats over them. It makes us slightly less conspicuous while we discuss what's going to happen.

"*Señorita* Aguilar is in the third house on the left in the next block. We don't know who's in there with her. We don't know how many there are. We're going in blind. We take as many as we can to the bodega, but anyone who does anything to endanger the *señorita* dies."

"*Sí, El Tigre.*"

Right now, it's clear I'm leading the mission, so I go by the moniker that means general. The men will address Alejandro and *Tres J's* as *capitán* or *capo*.

"I want you four—" I point to the men I mean. "—to circle around the back. Check for any exit routes for them. Go now and report back."

They nod as we all slip our earpieces into place. There's a frequency for us collectively. But my family's radios have another frequency that is just for us. It's locked, so no one else can join it.

"You two check how we enter."

I nod to the two men directly in front of me. The six guards reach into their SUVs and grab their rifles. They carry them held tightly against their chests, their suit coats somewhat disguising them. As long as they appear casual as they walk down the sidewalk, they should be fine. Old Cartel members train recruits to blend in when they're in crowds and when they're in open spaces. I know these men can spy without being spotted.

Now we wait.

I turn toward my cousins, and the other men step away, surveying our surroundings. The five of us form the same tight huddle we've been making since we were little and driving our parents crazy. We were a group of five—back then six—energetic boys who loved exploring and climbing, as long as we didn't get seriously hurt and obeyed our parents. I take comfort in Alejandro and *Tres J's* being with me. We don't need our *tíos* or *papás* here, even though we wouldn't turn down *Tío* Enrique's help nor my dad's or Alejandro's.

Tío Matáis doesn't go on many missions these days because he works as a financier in Manhattan. He handles the legal money that goes through the Diaz conglomerate. It keeps him busy and very public, so he doesn't have time. But he will in a second if we need him.

"*Gracias, primos.*"

"Don't get sappy, *primo*. Flora expects your *huevos* to be where she left them not sucked up inside your *culo*." Ass.

"*¡Cállate, carajo!*" Shut the fuck up.

I shove Javier's chest playfully as I swear at him and he teases me. I need the momentary distraction.

"We're happy to help. We know you appreciate it."

Joaquin's the shyest of us, and the natural peacemaker. Javier just dislikes most people—a total misanthrope and utter introvert. Jorge hates crowds and has social anxiety, so he's like his brothers and is a homebody. Alejandro lets everything roll off his back like water off a duck.

I'm the worrier.

That's amplified to the extreme since this involves Flora. Like exponentially worse.

"There they are." Alejandro shifts to look in the direction of our returning men.

"*El Tigre*, the house backs onto a lot that's under construction. There's a foundation poured, but nothing else."

"*Gracias.* What about you?" I look at one guy who went to surveil the house.

"There's a kitchen door and the front door. There's no direct access to the basement except for a couple small windows. *Señorita* Aguilar would fit through them, but none of us would."

Unless I insist the men address Flora as *Señorita* Aguilar Bautista, the custom is to use her father's surname as hers. Maybe the men talk about her connection to Domingo, but no one in my family's heard about anyone talking shit about her. They all really seem to like her because she's polite and smiles at every guard or employee she's met. She's kind and makes small talk with them, asking about their families in a general sense. She keeps a professional boundary, and she knows it makes Cartel men antsy when someone seems nosey.

"Can we get to the front door?"

"Yeah. There's no screen door or metal security door. There's no gate either. We saw no hint of who's inside. No one —not even a shadow—in the windows. None are patrolling the yard either."

Javier's distrusting nature comes out. "They're probably hiding but have cameras somewhere."

"We looked, *capitán*. We saw none. Not even one of those doorbell cameras."

"Any windows open? Did you hear anything?" My cousin still isn't convinced.

"One in the living room is open but not all the way. We barely heard a man and a woman's voice. The woman sounded disgusted but not hurt. *El Tigre*, they were speaking Spanish."

I glance at my cousins. Obviously, whoever this is, is a rival. But could it be a Latin American family or cartel? Are they Latinos working for one of the other three families?

My guard didn't mention it was Castilian, so I can assume it's no one from Spain. He would've pointed that out. This guy calls it "*colonizador español*"—colonizer Spanish. He had a nasty break up with a girl he met in Ibiza ten years ago. Never got over it. Bitter bastard.

Can I rule out the O'Rourkes?

I've known those fuckers my entire life. I grew up in New Jersey, so I never went to school with them, but Alejandro and *Tres J's* did. I played peewee and little league sports with them. We read each other nearly as well as our own families do.

I'm leaning toward believing they're innocent from their reaction to the news. It wasn't their denial, but their offer to help without hesitation. Their family caused the breakdown of the cardinal rule: no women and children. It wasn't any of their faults, and the men who did it are now dead. They've been working to redeem their family for the past six years. They might have actually done that.

My mind jumps from one thought to another like a flea in a dog pound. I'm taking everything in and evaluating all the information at warp speed. We need to move, so I don't have the luxury of contemplating the meaning of life. I have to consider the implications and decide.

"Jorge, you come through the front door with me. Alejandro, lead six men to the back door. Enter that way. *Dos J's* take the open window. The rest of you spread out around the block in case any of them turn rabbit. No one shoots unless you're a second away from death. You protect *Señorita* Aguilar before me."

I won't tell the men to sacrifice my cousins, but I will tell them to prioritize Flora over me.

"*No seas un pollon.*" Don't be a dick.

Javier huffs at me before he looks at the men. He doesn't agree with my altruism. It's his way of saying Flora's family. All he has to do is cock an eyebrow, and the men know they're to protect Flora before my cousins and me.

Once *Tres J's* got over the initial shock of me being with Flora and all the fucked-up baggage that goes with that, they've been nothing but gracious to her. That doesn't mean I haven't had doubts about whether they've meant their warm welcome. Now I know they do.

We move into position as we fan out. Alejandro and his men split into two groups and cut through yards. We're all praying the people who live in those houses aren't home.

Joaquin and Javier go ahead of Jorge and me. They've always seemed to line up by age since we were all little. That would mean Joaquin breaking off to the left first, then Javier to the right, leaving Jorge in the center. Neither Joaquin nor Javier approves of the idea their little brother be the most obvious target. The only thing they fight over is who gets the worst spot in the team. They all want that one.

With Jorge alongside me, Joaquin and Javier know where to go. I walk ahead of Jorge as we reach the path up to the house. I'll be the first one inside. I always would be, not just because we're going after my girlfriend. I won't send any man where I'm not willing to go first. Jorge follows to protect my back and to take over if I go down.

I sweep my gaze around the area. The men I can see are in position. I test the doorknob, but it doesn't turn. I nod, and we all count to three silently. My foot thrusts into the door, sending it flying open.

Chapter Twenty-Eight

Flora

I barely swallow my scream as there's a loud splintering sound. Then the front door swings open and nails the wall before it bounces back. I dive for the floor and cover my head. I don't look around, instead, trying to get my bearing from what I hear. It only takes a moment for me to realize it's Pablo. I've never had a greater sense of relief in my life than knowing he's here.

I almost don't care what else happens now that I'm certain he's here to protect me. But I need to remain alert and vigilant because this is just starting.

"Where's my woman?" The only way to describe Pablo's question is a snarl.

I keep my arms over my head, but I rise enough to peer over the sofa.

"Pablo."

His attention jerks toward me, and our gazes lock. Once he's seen I'm all right, I duck back down. Pablo doesn't hesitate to shoot two men. I don't witness it, but I see the result. They collapse to the floor each with a bullet between the eyes. He's making a point. I twist so I can observe him now rather than see the outcome of his rage.

The window shatters, drawing my attention away. I watch a man fall and then see Javier on the other side of the window frame. Joaquin comes through the front door only a moment later, and I'm left wondering where Alejandro is. Jorge was directly behind Pablo when I first looked up.

I follow Pablo's gaze and realize he's noticed *Cabrón Dos*. He glances at Joaquin then shifts his focus to Stumpy—his new name. Joaquin follows the silent instruction and grabs the injured man by the front of his shirt and hauls him out of the chair at the dining room table. Joaquin shoves the man toward Pablo who puts the barrel of his handgun to the man's forehead.

There's silence in the room for a moment, then another crash as the back door bursts open. I can't help my curiosity, so I sit up. I feel more confident about exposing myself, so I look around. Alejandro storms in with men in front of him who tried to flee. He has Colombians with him. It's easy to tell the difference among men I don't know since all the Colombians are in suits, and the Mexicans are in jeans and t-shirts or hoodies.

There's an unofficial hierarchy in Latin America that's antiquated and colonial, but it flashes in my mind. Right now, I have no problem with my snobbery considering where I find myself. Let's just say Colombia and Mexico aren't on the same line when the countries are listed from best to worst, most desirable to be from to least desirable. At least neither country is at the bottom.

The men Alejandro and his guards stopped are shuffled into the living room and forced to kneel with their hands behind their heads. I've been in that position with Pablo before, but it had an entirely different outcome. I sweep my gaze around the room as Jorge comes to crouch beside me.

"*Señorita*, are you—"

I ignore him when I suspect he's asking if I'm okay. I scramble for the pistol on the coffee table in front of me. I grab it, click off the safety, and fire a round. It grabs everyone's attention as the bullet goes through *Cabrón Uno's* kneecap. He was trying to fade into the hallway I assume leads to the bedrooms.

Pablo walks around the sofa to me and sticks out his hand. I don't hesitate to take it, and he pulls me to my feet. His arm wraps around me, and he kisses me. It's over far too fast, but at least we both know the other is okay. He leaves me with Jorge and Javier, who's joined his brother and me by the sofa.

"What did this *hijo de puta* do to wind up with half his hand chopped off?"

No one answers. I'm not sure that I should speak up and get involved, which is an odd thought to have after shooting a man in the leg. I guess I'm already pretty fucking involved.

Pablo waves his pistol, so the man with the half-amputated hand moves to follow Pablo's silent directions. It puts him with his back against a wall. There's nowhere for him to go. He's Pablo's singular target.

"What did you do to get half your hand chopped off? Did you touch my woman?"

Whatever word means something worse than menace is what I hear in Pablo's voice. I don't know what that is in English or in Spanish. I don't even know if there is a word that means something worse. There should be. It sends chills through me as I watch the man I love become the man I'm certain he wishes I never saw, but I can't fault him for it.

This is the man who rescued me. This is the man who'll end all of what's happened since I met Humberto. Hell, even before I met the dead pig.

"You really should tell me the truth yourself because if I hear it from someone else, especially my woman, it'll go way worse for you. If *Señorita* Aguilar has to relive whatever you did while telling me, any punishment you imagine I could dole out will only be a sliver of what actually happens. What did you do?"

Pablo's asked three times now, and it's obvious that he won't ask again.

"I slapped the *señorita* because she was being defiant."

It's like a collective silent gasp in the room. Everyone takes a metaphorical step backward. The entire atmosphere shifts. It wasn't when the man admitted to touching me. It's when he called me defiant. He added insult to injury.

Now Pablo's ready to rain down hellfire. He grabs the man's hair, spins him, jerks him away from the wall. The barrel of his gun goes to the side of the man's throat as he pushes him to face the wall. It's a horrible sight as Stumpy's face smashes into the brick that surrounds the fireplace. Joaquin heads over to Pablo and Stumpy. He yanks the makeshift bandage that's barely hanging on around the guy's hand. I wince when I see the damage done to his amputated fingers.

"Tell me everything, or you will enter a living hell from which there'll be no escape until I'm done with you."

Jorge moves to block my line of sight. I lean to see around him, but Alejandro walks up behind him. They're a wall that's impenetrable. I go onto my toes for a moment and can barely see between Jorge and Alejandro's shoulders, but I watch as Pablo slaps the man over and over. There's blood gushing from the stumps again. It's pooling on the floor.

Alejandro peers back over his shoulder, then issues orders for men to go through the entire house and others to guard from the outside.

"Turn on the grill and make it look like you're hanging out in the backyard."

I suspect the gas grill will eventually accidentally catch fire and burn down the entire house. We seem in limbo while the men obey Alejandro. It only takes a few minutes before they give the all-clear. Pablo walks back over to me. His gun is still in his right hand when he wraps his arm around my waist and pulls me against him. Our foreheads rest together.

"Did they hurt you any other way, *chiquita?*" He keeps his voice low, so it's barely more than a murmur.

"No, *Papí.*"

I'm certain only he hears me. We lean back and look at each other. There's a depth of emotion I feel that would scare me if I felt it toward someone or something else, but it's love for Pablo, and it's giving me strength. His hand slides up my back and over my shoulder to cup my cheek. His thumb brushes over my cheekbone. This isn't where we'll make any declarations.

It's the wrong time and the wrong place, but we're silently communicating what's built between us over the past month and a half. We press our foreheads together one more time before our lips brush. Then he backs away.

"Jorge, take the *señorita* to a bedroom. Stay there while I finish."

Joaquin holds up Stumpy's hand as Pablo pulls the knife from his pocket and flips it open.

"Pablo, no, please don't make me go. I want to know..."

His expression changes, and the words die on my lips. It's not quite as harsh as the one he gave me in Switzerland while we were on the phone with Enrique, but it's a hint of that. I know now isn't the time to argue with him, not in front of his men and not when he needs to finish this. Jorge guides me to the room, but I refuse to enter. I keep my voice low, so it doesn't carry out to the living room and dining room where the rest of the men are.

"I am *not* going in that bedroom. I have the right to know what happens. I'm the one they took. I'm the one they held hostage. It's my life they were going to trade."

"Florencia, Pablo doesn't want you to see what's next. It's why he sent you back here. He sent me, not as your jailer, but because he trusts me to keep you safe. That includes not letting you see what's going to happen."

"It's still my right to know."

"No, it's not."

We stare at one another, neither of us wanting to back down. I'm furious, but I know he's right. My having a tantrum won't solve anything, and it's selfish of me to demand my curiosity come ahead of my safety and Pablo's wishes for how to handle this situation. I know he wants what's best for me, and now isn't the time for me to second guess that.

I relent and dip my chin, but rather than go into the bedroom, I merely agree not to force my way back into the living room. Jorge concedes that. However, he's so much larger than me—like Pablo—that I can't see past him with how he angles me inside the doorway. There's no need for Alejandro to be the second peak of their mountain range.

The living room isn't visible, but Jorge cocks an eyebrow as if to ask if this is really what I want to do. I can't observe, but I can still listen to what's going on. The injured man howls in pain. Part of me wants to slam the bedroom door shut and go curl in the farthest corner, but I refuse to cower. I know I'm safe where I am, and I want to know what happens to these men.

I nod.

"No, no, *El Tigre*. No more. I can't take any more."

"You *carechimba*. That was only one finger I stuck my knife in. You still have three more to go. I'll dig out every vein and piece of flesh I can before cutting off the skin. I'll leave just bones sticking out your stumpy little hand unless you answer my questions. Who the fuck ordered this?" Face of a vagina.

"I don't know. Only Manuel knows the details. The rest of us just follow his orders."

"If you're that low on the ladder, what made you think you could touch *Señorita* Aguilar?"

"I—OW!"

He howls again. The screams of pain I hear are unlike anything else. I know this isn't about getting information from the man. This is purely about punishment. Clearly, he didn't answer fast enough. He should've expected Pablo's question.

"*El Tigre*, please. *Por favor*. I can't take any more."

"You'll take as much as I fucking give you. You'll do it with a goddamn fucking smile if I tell you to."

I know Pablo rarely takes the Lord's name in vain, so he must really be on the edge right now, even if his voice doesn't waver at all.

"I have a temper, *El Tigre*, and I didn't control it. I let it get the better of me, and I took it out on the *señorita*."

The man bellows again. I can only assume Pablo jabbed the knife into another finger. The tormented bellows continue, and I hear a hand hitting flesh over and over. It won't be long before the man bleeds to death. Pablo's making sure Stumpy knows just how I felt when he struck me. It goes quiet, and I assume Stumpy is unconscious, if not dead.

"Who sent you, Manuel?"

That must be *Cabrón Uno's* name. There's no sound but Pablo's voice now. The silence fills the house for a moment before I hear Manuel's response.

"My *jefe*."

"You'll have to be more specific than that."

"A *jefe* in Boston."

I watch for Jorge's response. A muscle in his jaw ticks. He must know exactly who this man refers to.

"So, it was Felipe Iglesias."

There's a gagging sound for a moment then Manuel's voice drifts to me.

"I don't know why *el jefe* wants *Señorita* Aguilar. I'm not high enough in the organization to ask those types of questions. I say '*Sí, jefe*' and do what I'm told."

"Get your phone out. Unlock it. Call Felipe on speakerphone. Tell him the job is done."

There was a lull for a moment while I assume Manuel dialed. Now I hear the phone ringing.

"*¡¿Qué tal, pendejo?!*" What's up, asshole?

I know, given the context, *pendejo* can be an insult or a casual term between friends. Seems it's the latter. Manuel being on such friendly terms with Felipe won't be good for his health.

"*Jefe*, the job is done. We have *Señorita* Aguilar, and she's spoken to *el hombre*. He told her he's keeping her safe, that Pablo knows no harm will come to her."

The man. I guess Manuel doesn't even know the name of the guy I spoke to.

"Did the *puta* believe you?" Bitch.

I cringe. This man in Boston won't be alive much longer. Adding profanity to his list of crimes against me won't endear him to Pablo.

"Yeah, she hasn't put up any arguments. She asked to speak to *El Tigre*, but no one's allowed her near a phone except for that one call."

"*Bueno*, you're to meet *el hombre* at the warehouse. You remember the address, right?"

"*Sí, lo sé.*" Yes, I know.

"Then hand her off to him and collect the money. Come straight back to Boston."

"*Sí, jefe.* I'll call you again when we're on our way."

"*Bueno.*"

It gets quiet again until I hear Pablo's voice, so the call must have ended.

"End them. I'm taking *Señorita* Aguilar home."

The muted gunshots still ring in my ears. They sound so loud within the house, but there've been no sirens approaching, so the silencers clearly work. The neighbors haven't called the cops.

Jorge ushers me out of the bedroom and toward the front door. *Tres J's* encircle me, keeping me from seeing what happened. As we head outside, I hear Pablo giving orders to pull SUVs into the garage and to take the bodies, that his men know where to dispose of them.

It's not until I'm in his arms again in the SUV that my heart stops pounding. We finally have a proper kiss, and it's like he breathes life back into me. The other men are in the vehicle with us, so we keep it pretty tame. Pablo's gaze runs over me, and I place my hand on his heart.

"I'm okay, I swear. Other than the one slap and pulling my hair, really nothing else happened to me."

"How can you say that when I know you got tased?"

"I did, but other than my body still aching, I don't think anything adverse happened from that."

I feel like utter shit and have the entire time, but allowing myself to consider that wouldn't make my situation any better. While I was alone with those men, I needed to be as attentive as I could be. Now that Pablo's here, I feel like the weight of the world has lifted from my shoulders, that his are broad enough to handle everything. I rest my head against his chest, and he wraps his arms around me.

I know if we were in a town car alone with the privacy glass up, I'd be sitting on his lap. Hell, I'd be sitting on his dick right now. His hands run up and down my back and over my arm as he continues to hold me. He keeps his voice down, but I'm certain Javier and Joaquin can probably hear him since they're sitting behind us.

"*Chiquita*, I'm taking you to my parents' house. Then I have to leave."

Chapter Twenty-Nine

Pablo

I hate leaving Flora immediately after arriving at my parents' house, but there's little choice. I need to make it to the rendezvous the Boston Mexicans were going to have with this nameless man. I'm certain she's safe with *Mamá*. The woman lives and breathes protectiveness for her children—even when she couldn't protect them from themselves. She always has, and I know she considers Flora her daughter already. She hasn't said as much to my girlfriend, but she's told me.

I want this meeting over as fast as possible. We barely arrive in time since we had to take Flora all the way to Jersey before turning around and coming back to Yonkers. My cousins didn't even hint at sending Flora with any of them or our men. They knew there wasn't a chance in hell I'd let anyone else oversee her movements until we got to my parents' house. They don't live in a gated property or community like my *tíos* and *tías*. My father's reputation is enough to keep most people away.

Also, the fact they're in Jersey while all the other syndicate families live in parts of New York City helps too. Some would say the remoteness of their home and *Tío* Enrique and *Tía* Elle's would make them easier targets, but it hasn't.

"Alejandro, you follow me in but hang back. *Tres J's*, take men and go around the back. See if you can find a way in."

I hate arriving somewhere without time to scout, but it's tight. We noticed an SUV similar to ours at the house we raided, so whoever's waiting for the Iglesias men won't question the black SUV pulling up in front. Alejandro and I drop *Tres J's* off half a block away. Alejandro takes over driving, so my attention's fully on the building we approach. We don't have our guns drawn as we walk inside, but they're ever at the ready. He and I have a knife in each hand ready for us to flick open the moment we need them.

"*Puta de madre.*"

I mutter it at the same time Alejandro does. We recognize the man standing in the center of the warehouse. Light shines in from the bay door that's open behind him. There are men hanging out back there. The guy waiting for the Iglesias men is a mercenary my family's used many times. After Robert Simms died a few years ago, Mason Harrison filled the void.

Simms had been the world's top mercenary for decades. He ran an intricate network of men and women who hired themselves out. Like Simms, this man has loyalty only to himself. One day he's your ally. The next day he's your enemy. It all depends on who's paying him.

That's what I need to find out.

"Mason, you weren't expecting me, were you?"

"No, you're certainly taller than the person I'm supposed to meet."

"Who ordered you to take *Señorita* Bautista?"

"Oh, Bautista is it now? I could've sworn she was only going by her father's name while she was in Colombia."

"No, that may be what people called her, but her name has always been Bautista. Who hired you?"

I refuse to get into an argument over semantics—especially since I was guilty of thinking of her as only an Aguilar. I want everyone to understand her ties to her father's family are over. If Mason survives this—that's a *huge* if—then he can tell everyone else that Ernesto no longer controls her and doesn't dictate shit about her life. Until she becomes a Diaz, she can be just a Bautista.

"If you were going to kill me, Pablo, I'd already be dead, so what do you want?"

"Your death is yet to be determined. I can make that happen if you're asking."

"You won't kill me until you know who hired me."

"Then you can decide between receiving an even larger payment or your death. Which do you want it to be?"

"There's no way you're carrying enough money in your pockets to pay me more than the person who hired me. If I have to, I'll take my secrets to the grave."

"Dead men don't earn money. I know that's the most important thing to you. You always wanted to prove you were better than Simms by earning more. You're not a man with integrity, so why pretend?"

I watch his reaction for a moment, but how he's positioned also allows me to see outside to the back loading dock without shifting my gaze. *Tres J's* creep forward and take out one mercenary after another. The silencers on their weapons do the job they're supposed to. In an enclosed space, the silencers muffle the sound, but don't eradicate it. However, with little for the sound waves to reverberate off when you're outside, they truly are irreplaceable in our line of work.

Alejandro pulls his gun at the same time *Tres J's* enters the warehouse. I don't reach for mine. Instead, I'm in a standoff with Mason. He barely flinches as my cousins kill the men here who work for him and might have even been his guards against the Mexicans. It only takes a couple minutes, then it's the five of us surrounding him.

"Decide now. Speak or you can die by firing squad."

"After you torture me, of course."

"You decide how it's going to be. You could live to work for us again and agree to never accept another job against my family, or I can torture you until you beg for the relief death brings. You choose."

"I know I'm not walking out of here alive. You offer me that compromise, but I'm certain you won't follow through."

"You don't believe I'll allow you to live, but you believe I'll torture you. Do you want to have this over quickly, or will we be here all night?"

He shifts his weight as he twists to look behind him, spotting *Tres J's* for the first time. I prowl forward as though I don't have a care in the world. He and I both know I control the situation. It makes me wonder why this was so easy.

He's a confident man, but not so egotistical as to believe he's untouchable. He must have had some assurances from the Boston Mexicans that everything was going smoothly. Maybe that's why no one here was as on guard as they should've been.

"Who hired you?"

He stares at me for a long moment. "I can't give you an exact answer because I don't know which one it was, but I'd look at Enrique's oldest rival."

I wonder if he means oldest by age or most long-standing enemy. It could be any number of people. I flick open my knife and raise it up to his Adam's apple.

"That's not enough information. How much were you paid?"

"A million."

"What were you supposed to do after you got *Señorita* Bautista?"

"I was to hold on to her here indefinitely."

"Indefinitely?"

"The person who hired me said they'd get her when they were ready."

I glance over at Joaquin, and he nods. Since he's standing behind Mason, he backs away silently. He'll check out the rest of the warehouse. The only way this man would stay here indefinitely is if he had his creature comforts. It makes me think this might actually be his home.

"How were you to get paid?"

"I already got half upfront with a cash drop here. When my employer comes, I'm to receive the second half."

"And you were willing to just wait around, possibly for days, until someone showed up? Did you intend to keep *Señorita* Bautista tied to a chair the whole time?"

Something flickers in his gaze. He didn't pass the test. He planned to do far worse to Flora. When Alejandro sees what I do, he rushes forward. He grabs the man's head, one hand on his forehead and the other under his chin. He snaps Mason's head back, and I draw my knife across his throat.

Jorge and Javier turn surprised expressions at me. It's Alejandro who responds.

"He was going to rape Florencia while he made her wait."

Tres J's aren't triplets, but they may as well be since they're so close in age. They're the same height and practically carbon copies of each other. So, I'm looking at matching shocked expressions before their gazes lower to the ground where

Mason now lies, blood pooling around his head. His eyes stare up to the ceiling as blood splutters from his mouth. I kick him in the balls for no reason other than spite.

I know he's feeling no pain since he's seconds away from death. I rarely indulge in such outbursts, but it makes me feel ever so slightly better after thinking about this man violating my *chiquita*. Joaquin comes back into the main area and barely gives Mason a second glance. It hardly surprises my cousin to find the man dead on the floor.

"He's definitely been living here. It's completely decked out as a home upstairs. Full kitchen, living room, bedroom, bathroom. All of it."

"Then we need our cleaners to go through the entire place."

One team is already at the house in Yonkers. They'll fix everything and scrub it down. They'll leave it cleaner than it was as a new construction. There'll be no hints of the showdown at the OK Corral. Another team will come here to handle the bodies and remove any evidence we were here. They'll also remove any evidence that Mason lived here.

Javier's already on his phone texting the team as my cousins and I climb into the SUV and head back toward Jersey. I think out loud as I consider the little we learned from Mason.

"I ended things because I knew he wouldn't give up anything else. We'd never trust him to do another job for us, and we couldn't forgive him for targeting us. He said to consider *Tío's* oldest rival. I think he means Salvatore. Both Salvatore and *Tío* Enrique have led their syndicates since they were in their twenties, so about thirty years. It's not just Salvatore's age. It's about those years spent vying for the top position in New York."

The Irish and Russians have had their moments. However, before Maks and Dillan rose to their positions, their leadership over the last couple of decades was too weak to truly rival the stability *Tío* Enrique and Salvatore provide their branches.

Alejandro turns toward me from the front passenger seat. "What do you want to do? Do you want *Tío* to address Salvatore or are you going to ask *Tío* if you can lead?"

"I believe he'll ultimately let me decide since Flora and I are together, but if he doesn't allow me to go after Salvatore—if it's him—then there'll be problems."

Javier claps his hand on my shoulder from behind. "There won't be. He won't put you in a position where you must defy him because he understands what Florencia means to you. It's the same as what Maddy means to me and what *Tía* Elle means to him. It's the same as what's between *Tío* Matáis and *Tía* Catalina and between your parents. It's the same as when *Papá* was alive. He'll always defer to us."

It's Jorge who speaks next from the driver's seat. "But I'd listen to any suggestions he has. As well as we know Salvatore, we don't know even a fraction of what he's capable of compared to *Tío* Enrique's firsthand knowledge. They've been enemies and friends over the decades. Take *Tío's* advice."

"You know I will, but before we can decide anything, we need to know more."

Joaquin places his hand on my other shoulder and pats it as he speaks. "I'll start looking up information as soon as we get to your parents' house."

Joaquin has one of his computers with him. He's rarely without one in reach in case there are moments like this where he must do research, so we can make educated decisions before we act. We're a few miles from my parents' house when Alejandro lets us know *Tía* Elle, *Tía* Catalina, and *Tía* Luciana are already there with *Mamá* and Flora. We're almost to my parents' neighborhood when my phone rings. I recognize my father's number. I answer and put it on speaker.

"*Papá*, I'm here with Alejandro and *Tres J's*. We're almost at your house."

"Good. Both of your *tíos* are on the line as well."

This must be serious if *Tío* Matáis has joined the call. *Papá's* in Peru right now, so it makes me wonder why he's the one calling. I'm usually happy to hear from him, but it gives me a sinking feeling. It's *Tío* Enrique who speaks up.

"What have you learned so far? Florencia told your *mamá* you had some meeting to go to with a man she spoke to on the phone, but she knew nothing more than that."

"It was Mason Harrison. He said we should look at your oldest rival. We suspect he means Salvatore."

The three men on the other ends of the call release a slew of curses in Spanish. There're so many that come out so fast I can't tell who says what. When they finally stop, it's *Papá* who speaks up.

"That tracks with what I just learned. Apparently, some *gringo's* been down here poking around."

We knew something was up in Lima, but we didn't know what. My father went down to visit some associates who clued in *Tío* Enrique that someone outside of Latin America's been sniffing around.

"What did you find out, *Papá*?"

"The locals say this man is as handsome as Cortés supposedly was, except rather than golden hair, he has brown. He doesn't speak Spanish, but he practically looks like he could be Latino. Apparently, he was there to set up labs in the Andes."

Papá's referring to the debunked legend. The one about how Montezuma and the Mexica—the Aztecs—thought Hernán Cortés was Quetzalcoatl. He was the ancient serpent god known for his striking good looks and golden blond hair. Apparently, the Conquistador resembled the mythical god.

"He told one of our rivals he has something no one else

does. I assume that's Florencia's formula. At least this man acted as though he already had it."

I'm silently fuming as I listen to *Papá*. I know which motherfucker it is. Handsome, like, a god. That's what he believes he is.

Motherfucking Lorenzo Mancinelli.

Chapter Thirty

Flora

It surprises me how comfortable I am with Pablo's mother and *tías*. All four women have been exceedingly sweet to me, and it makes all of what's happened in the past day easier to manage while Pablo's gone. I was hesitant at first because being around such a loving family is new to me.

Really, it's only been *Mamá* and me for most of my life. I have *tías* and *tíos* on both sides of the family, but we've never been that close to them. Not the way the Diaz family is with each other. It's extraordinary to see the women move around Margherita's house as though it's their home as well. It's clear they spend plenty of time together. Even Elle, who's new to the family, fits in as though she's been a Diaz for decades, not just a few months.

My mind still dwells on how Luciana in particular can overlook my family's past, especially now that her sons are on a mission and in danger because of me.

"Florencia, I can tell you're still apprehensive around me. That's the last thing I want."

I guess the entire family are mind readers, not just Pablo, because Luciana says what I was just feeling.

"It's not anything you've done. You've made me feel extremely welcome. You spent most of your day showing me around apartments and helping me plan my résumé. I just don't understand how you can be so accepting of me when I'm surely a constant reminder of what happened between my father and you. I know I resemble him more than I do my mother."

"That's true. But like I said at dinner, we don't choose the families we're born into. If we could, no one would choose to be part of a cartel. There's more pain and anguish that comes with that than most people would choose. You didn't ask to be caught in the middle of this, but you were. And that's something I will never blame you for."

"*Mamá* won't tell me much about how things were when my father was still alive. She generally refuses to talk about him unless it's singing his praises. I know most of what she says is exaggeration or time softening hard memories. I don't want to open old wounds, but I wish I knew more of the truth."

"Florencia, that's completely fair. There's your family's version, and my family's version, and somewhere in between is the absolute truth. I can only share with you how things were from our perspective. Your *abuelo* was determined to take over parts of Bogotá. He figured he could inch his way into more wealth and more power without my *papá* noticing before it was too late. However, that wasn't the case."

"That sounds entirely like *Abuelo*."

"*Papá* noticed immediately. Rather than back down and save everybody time, money, and lives, Ernesto kept pushing until my father had no choice but to strike back. It was something he disliked because he knew it was inevitable good men would die on both sides when they could've avoided that. There was no way *Papá* would back down from his position since he was *jefe de jefes*. So, he offered a compromise. Domingo's sisters were far too young for Enrique. Luis was already married, and Catalina and Matáis had been together for years and already engaged. It fell to Domingo and me to be the sacrificial lambs."

As Luciana continues, I count my blessings that I got to choose Pablo. It makes me wonder if one day, *Abuelo* would've forced a marriage on me. Likely not since I'm not growing any younger.

"Your father was to get a position high in the Diaz organization. He would've had that to brag about. But he would've worked for *Papá*, which would've kept him in his place. *Papá* was entrusting your father and his family with me, which was a major concession on *Papá's* part. But it gave your father's family status they would never have had on their own. I knew from the very beginning Domingo was unfaithful."

I can't help but flinch.

"I turned a blind eye to it because I knew I'd never love him. We just weren't that compatible. I was fond of him, and I enjoyed spending time with him in the beginning, but we were never going to be a love match. I figured as long as he treated me well, and he loved any children we had, then I could make do. A lifetime in a loveless marriage didn't excite me, but we all have duties to our families and the people who depend upon us."

I didn't feel that way until *Abuelo* backed me into a corner. I knew he was manipulating me when he told me he had people who worked for him relying on the money he'd make from my work. It certainly was never to the extent people depend upon *los Diaz*, but it was enough to guilt me into agreeing.

"War is bad for business for those who depend on the stability leaders should bring them. Ernesto may not have seen it that way, but that's what my parents drilled into me."

"He didn't see it that way until he used that very idea to force me."

I can't help but interject, even though I don't want to interrupt. Luciana nods before continuing. I can see she understands.

"I knew about Magdalena all along. He started dating your mother about three weeks after he proposed to me. That was really just a formality since our fathers had already signed the contracts. We were engaged for a year while I finished school. Once I graduated, everybody started pressuring me to settle on a date. The more time I spent with him once I lived in Bogotá again, the more obvious it became we might not be as compatible as I hoped. It didn't even have to do with his infidelity. When I met Esteban, it's like something came alive within me. I felt things for him I'd never felt before, and I know I will never feel again."

It's my turn to nod. That's how I feel about Pablo. I feel whole now.

"Esteban was a force to be reckoned with."

"I've heard plenty of people say that about you, Ana."

She laughs, but Catalina practically snorts before she speaks.

"You can put it that way."

Luciana ignores her older sister as though the woman never spoke, but I see the humor in her eyes.

"Yeah, well, I'm the easygoing one of the four of us."

I believe her, though the deep-set laugh lines around

Enrique's eyes and mouth tell of a lifetime of laughter. I suppose it hasn't been all horrible for their family.

"Your father never forgave me for choosing Esteban. Some of it was because the peace fell apart when the engagement did, but I never forgave him for being part of the plot that wound up killing my father. He tried to get revenge on me and on Esteban more than once. However, Enrique still considered him useful for some mid-level jobs. It was the same as with *Tío* Humberto, whom Enrique allowed to oversee some of the domestic enterprises since Enrique lived in New York by then. Luis came and went from Colombia a lot, but he was here in New Jersey, just not at this house yet."

It's a beautiful home, and I saw photos of Pablo and his brother as I walked into the living room. This space has plush furniture, including a sofa that invites you to nap.

"Domingo tried killing Esteban more than once, but he always failed because Esteban was three steps ahead of him. When he finally ran out of patience and was too humiliated by his ongoing failures, he eventually turned to *Tío* Humberto. My *tío* suggested he target me, so Domingo did. That's when Esteban could no longer overlook Domingo's bitterness and hostility. I was pregnant with Joaquin when Domingo attacked me. We all knew Magdalena was expecting you, and none of us were thrilled at the thought of leaving a child fatherless, but it was our family or yours."

"I understand that. I can't blame your family for doing what they did. It was necessary to protect you. No one ever told me you were pregnant, and it's only recently that I learned what he tried to do to you."

"Domingo made his own choices, and so did Ernesto. Your *abuelo* was even more bent on revenge after losing your father. He went back to *Tío* Humberto years later when all of his plans for Esteban failed too. It was *Tío* Humberto who suggested Ernesto target Esteban when he was with *Tres J's*."

She pauses for a moment. She doesn't look away from me, so I see the deep sadness that settles in her gaze. I watch her swallow twice before she continues.

"My boys watched their father die that day. He'd gotten them into an SUV when they were under attack. Just as he closed the door with the boys inside, a sniper fatally wounded him. From what I understand, it was very gruesome, and not something boys of eight, nine, and ten should've seen, but they did. It was the first part of their childhood stolen from them."

I think I might be ill. But I force myself not to shy away from hearing the rest of this story. I need to know. I need to know the extent of my family's guilt, and I need to know Pablo's family history if I'm to be part of its future.

The four women watch me, and I feel like I could shrivel under their gazes. Instead, I give myself a mental shake and remind myself that one day I'll be in Elle's position. At least, that's the plan. Since I fully intend to marry Pablo, I can't be weak or squeamish about these things.

"Will you tell me how my father died?"

Luciana hesitates for the first time. Her gaze darts to Catalina before returning to me. Out of the four women around me, Luciana was the only other one living in Bogotá then. Catalina dips her chin, and Luciana visibly inhales. This is the part I really need to understand.

"Your father was a gambler. That's how he wound up in debt to Humberto. My *tío* saw forcing Domingo to work for him as a way to pay off that debt, but also to get an insider within *Papá's* household. *Papá* and *Tío* Humberto had been on poor terms ever since they were kids, but *Papá* tolerated *Tío* Humberto because they were family. However, once *Papá* married *Mamá*—even before they had the four of us—he didn't consider his brother to be part of our immediate family. Two nights after Domingo attacked me, he was coming out of an underground gambling ring, and Esteban was waiting. Esteban gave him a choice. He could leave Colombia for good—go wherever he wanted but never return—or he could die. Domingo pulled a gun on Esteban. He just wasn't as quick as my husband. He aimed at Esteban and missed. Esteban aimed and hit him. I don't know what happened between that shot and the one that killed him. I never asked because I knew Esteban would never tell me."

"So, my father was shot." *Then tortured, then shot again.*
"Yes."

"That's what I deduced over the years, but no one has confirmed it. I even tried looking up police records or any type of story in the newspapers, but it's unsurprising there was no record of it."

"There were mistakes the people of my generation made that have been revisited on our children. My sister, brothers, and I all wish we could undo that, but we can't. Unfortunately, you'll be able to say the same thing one day. But none of us blame our children or our adversaries' children for the decisions their parents made. So, I don't blame you for Domingo's infidelity. I don't blame you for Magdalena's decision to be involved with a man engaged to another woman. I don't blame you for Ernesto working with *Tío* Humberto to murder Esteban. None of this was your fault. Yes, you may look like your father, but that's not who I see when I look at you. Florencia, I see the woman my *sobrino* loves. I see a woman who loves my *sobrino*. What I want to see is a happy future between the two of you. You both deserve that."

We don't have a chance to continue our conversation, and I don't think there's much more to be said when Pablo and the other guys show up. I'm out of my seat and across the living room and into Pablo's arms before I even realize my feet are moving. He wraps his arms around me and lifts me off my feet. We share a kiss other people probably shouldn't see, but neither of us cares.

I hear Javier saying something to Luciana, and I catch him hugging her out of the corner of my eye. He's going home to Madeline, and the rest of the guys will stay to debrief us on what they can. It surprises me when Pablo explains that. I'm certain it'll be a very abridged version, but I appreciate none of them will hide more than they have to. It doesn't take long for them to explain they only made a few steps forward in their progress, but it was better than nothing. They wouldn't tell us who they suspect is the mastermind behind all of this.

Less than half an hour after they arrived, Pablo and I are in an SUV headed back into Manhattan. If only we were in a town car, but for now, Pablo doesn't feel it's safe enough for that.

"I wish you were sitting on my cock right now, but this is far better for us. I'm trying to be responsible, but it's hard."

Pablo's warm breath tickles as his lips practically press against my ear. I turn my head to respond, not wanting the driver or bodyguards to hear me either.

"I bet something's hard, *Papi*."

"I'll show you as soon as the door closes to the outside world."

It's nice to be home, just the two of us. Pablo holds true to his promise. The moment he finishes locking the door, he's backing me against the wall to the right. He crowds me, and I love it. His larger body boxes me in as his forearms rest on the wall beside my head.

"*Chiquita*, the things I want to do to you, the way I want to worship your body."

"Do all of it, Daddy. Whatever you want."

"Oh, I will. Tonight, and in the years to come."

The thrill of that promise courses through me. We gaze into each other's eyes, and I know I want to tell him how I feel. I think he's considering the same thing. I cup his face as his right hand slides from my left shoulder up to my throat. He doesn't squeeze, but the pressure is heavy.

"You belong to me, Flora. Nothing will ever change that. I promise I will spend my life taking care of you and the family we might have one day."

"You belong to me, Pablo. There's nothing I won't do for you and for our family. We're the same, and that's why we fit together perfectly."

We stare at each other for a moment before the words flow from both of our mouths.

"*Te amo, chiquita.*"

"*Te amo, Papí.*"

Two words with a wealth of meaning. Two priceless words. Two words I want to hear and say every day for the rest of our lives.

Our kiss is languid as we revel in our shared declaration. Neither of us is in a hurry, drinking in the emotions that demonstrate the words. His body presses against me as his hand tightens slightly around my throat. The fingertips of his other hand brush against my temple as I wrap my arms around his neck. He presses his thigh between mine. I'm slow to rock against it, but it isn't long before the friction makes me restless for more.

The backs of his fingers trail down my cheek and jaw, over his fingers around my throat, then down my chest until he can cup my breast. I moan as he massages. I arch my back into his hand and ride his thigh as he kisses behind my ear.

"I love you, *chica.*"

"I love you, Daddy."

"I'm going to spend the night inside you."

"Fuck me and make love to me, please."

"You don't even have to ask, little one. I'll fuck you until you're sore, then I'll soothe it as I make love to you."

"I want to remember every moment of it tomorrow with every step, every time I stand and sit. I want to ache for you to do it all over again."

"I want to see my marks on you. I want to know I'm the only man who touches you. The only man you touch."

"Pablo."

He hesitates when I use his name. I offer him a reassuring smile.

"If other people heard the way we talk to each other, they probably wouldn't understand why I agree to most of it. Never once has your possessiveness made me fear I'll lose my independence or that you don't see me as an equal, even when we considered a true D/s relationship. Just the opposite. Your possessiveness makes me feel like I can do anything. That nothing can stop me because you'll always make sure I'm protected enough to do it. It's not a false sense of safety. I understand the dangers we face now and will in the future. But I want you to know how much I appreciate how empowered you make me feel. How desirable."

"I never want you to feel like a possession even when I'm at my most possessive. If you ever do, please tell me. I'm protective by nature and nurture. There will be times when I can't explain to you why I seem over the top. Please trust I will tell you what I can when I decide the time is right. I wish I could always tell you everything, but I never will. Just because I wish I could confide in you doesn't mean I want you to know what I do."

"I understand that."

"I will never lie about how I feel about you. I admit there

will be times when I manipulate you for your safety, my family's, the people who depend on my family, and me. It won't be for my personal gain."

"I get that, but thank you for being honest about it. Daddy, take me to bed."

"Little one, the things I'm about to do to you. I have plans."

Chapter Thirty-One

Pablo

I've often thought of Flora as *la reina*—the queen. From how she stood up to me from the start to how she's handled each crisis thrown our way day after day. But she's always been the queen of my heart. I knew it from the start, and I know it deep into my marrow. Just like there will never be another woman for *Papá*, there will be no one but *mi reina*.

I lead Flora into the bedroom, our fingers entwined. I'm about to tell her to strip when she turns toward me and puts her hand on my chest.

"Daddy, I don't want to move out. I want to stay. Not out of necessity because I don't feel safe. Not because I haven't found somewhere affordable yet. It just feels pointless. I'll want you over at my place every night if I move out. I don't want to be apart from you. I'll only be hoping you invite me to stay here instead of sending me back to a lonely apartment."

"I was planning to talk you out of leaving, so this makes it much easier. If I'd had to, I would've tied you to the bed and refused to release you until you agreed to stay."

"Can you tie me to the bed anyway?"

She waggles her eyebrows at me, and I pounce. I fist my hand in her hair and make her head immobile. I devour her, nipping at her bottom lip before thrusting my tongue into her mouth. It twirls with hers as I unfasten her pants. After what happened today, I'm grateful she didn't wear a skirt like she has. It was colder today than it has been, so she opted for them. I couldn't argue with her since I didn't want her to be miserable. I don't want to imagine what might have happened if all any of those men had to do was flip a skirt out of the way.

"Such a good, *chiquita.*"

She hasn't worn panties since we left Bogotá. I love sliding my hand into her cunt whenever I want. It's why she's worn dresses and skirts so much. But if she had, and any of those men guessed she didn't wear panties...The thought makes me ill. I force myself to concentrate on the present rather than harp on what might've happened but didn't.

"Only for you, *Papí.*"

I growl and pounce again. Hearing her call me that and Daddy fills me with immeasurable happiness. I never imagined it'd be my thing. Not even remotely. But I desire Flora's trust as much as I do her love. It's a sign she does. I pray I do nothing to ever lose her faith in me.

"Strip for me, little one."

She obeys, her eyes averted. She dips her chin, but it's not purely submissiveness. I can tell she doesn't want me to see her smile. It's fucking sexy as fuck.

When she's naked, I point to the floor, and she kneels with her hands on her thighs. I'm certain she's waiting for me to unfasten my pants or command her to, but I have other ideas. I go to the dresser drawer that has all our toys. I withdraw a blindfold and return to her with it. I fasten it over her eyes with a peck on the cheek.

"Don't move, little one. I'm leaving the room, but I'll be right back."

"*Sí, Papi.*"

I leave the bedroom door open and hurry to the kitchen where I grab what I want. I check over my shoulder, wondering if she can hear what I'm doing and figure out what I'm getting. She's attentive when I return, but I see her brow furrowed. I don't think she's guessed. I grab a few more things from the drawer and set up what I have on the bedside table. I return to Flora and help her to her feet before scooping her into my arms. She gasps and giggles as she wraps her arms around my neck. I steal a kiss before placing her on the bed.

"Is there anything you don't want?"

"You stopping. Daddy, can you hurry a little, please?"

I grab the flogger and bring it down over her belly's silky skin.

"Who decides?"

"You, Daddy. But you did ask."

"True, my cheeky *chiquita.*"

I pinch and twist her nipple before pulling. I lean over her and suck the distended flesh. I could do this all night. Her tits are perfection. I push them together, alternating sides until she reaches to press my hands harder against her tits. I pull away and slap each side. Her moan and how she arches until her shoulders are nearly off the bed tells me that was no punishment. I chuckle.

"Needy?"

"*Muy, Papi.*" Very, Daddy.

Fuck. That word.

I'm ready to beg her *to fuck* me.

I reach for a satin band I wrap around her wrists before lifting them over her head.

"Daddy, can we get a headboard you can attach me to?"

"Yes, *chica*. It's going to come with a footboard I can attach you to as well. Do you want to order it tonight?"

"*Sí, Papi.*"

I appreciate how we can switch back and forth between English and Spanish so easily. We spoke mostly Spanish when we met, but since arriving in New York, Flora's asked to speak only English. She wants to get back to feeling fluent since she only used it sporadically in Colombia.

I grab my next implement and attach a spreader to her ankles. I extend the bar nearly as far as it'll go.

"Be a good girl and don't move."

My gaze lands on the labia weights I set on the bedside table. We haven't used these yet. I'm nervous since Flora said she's never worn them before, but she was insistent she wanted to try when we picked out more items last week. I can see she's already wet, and I'm uncomfortably hard.

"If this hurts too much, safe word, Flora."

I clamp the first weight. As soon as the prongs touch her skin, I shift my gaze to her face. Her expression doesn't appear to change.

"How does that feel?"

"Different but not bad."

"Can you handle the other side?"

"Yes, Daddy."

I repeat my actions while I attach the second weight. They're nowhere near as heavy as they could be. They're the lightest ones we found since we're experimenting. She also admitted she wasn't eager to stretch out anything prematurely since she warned giving birth would change things.

When I'm certain she's all right, I move on. I know she

hears me flick the lighter then smells the vanilla and jasmine candle. I set it on the bedside table while I wait for wax to melt. I pop an ice cube I collected from the kitchen in my mouth and settle onto the bed. I let it cool my lips before pressing my mouth to her inner right thigh.

I use my tongue and teeth to guide the ice up her skin. When I reach her pussy, I tongue her clit. She shivers, then lifts her hips to me. Her warm skin and my mouth make the ice melt faster than I expected. I press what's left into her cunt as I work my tongue in and out of her.

Her hands open and close, and I'm certain she wishes she had something to clutch. Her moans remain soft, but they're constant. Her top teeth press into her lower lip. The temptation is too great once the ice is gone. I rise from the bed, which elicits a whimper then a huff of annoyance. I chuckle before using my teeth to tug her lip. It's just enough to make a point without hurting.

I check the candle and see there's enough wax to begin. I press a finger into it to check that it won't harm Flora. When I'm certain it won't scald her, I trickle it between her tits down to her belly, which quivers. I stop just before I reach her clit. She got a Brazilian as soon as we arrived and another three days ago. She shaved while we were in Switzerland, but I know we both prefer this. Her completely bare skin always calls to me since it's easy to spy her clit. I force my attention away from it now and back to her tits.

I grab an ice cube for her left breast, circling it where her skin darkens then over her nipple. At the same time, I pour wax in a serpentine over each breast. Before it cools, I trace the same pattern with the ice, just below the lines of wax. I dribble more wax on her puckered nipples, watching for any sign it's too much over the more sensitive skin.

"Fuck, Pablo. This is the most erotic experience of my life."

"Mine too, little one."

I don't mind when she uses my name. I love hearing it in the breathy voice she gets when we're together like this. It's yet another reminder of how quickly I abandoned the idea of a twenty-four seven. It seems ridiculous now to have even considered.

I wait for more wax to melt, so I press her tits up. I begin on the underside and mark her. I leave love bites all over both, but never where any could show if her clothes shift. I trail my teeth down her ribs to her belly. I suck the skin around her belly button, but I bite the flesh at her waist. It's enough to make her squirm without leaving teeth marks. Instead, I leave more love bites. I straighten to examine my work.

"*Papí, ¿puedo ver también, por favor?*" Daddy, can I see too, please?

"*Sí, puedes.*" Yes, you can.

I slide the blindfold up, and she gazes down at her body before looking across the room at the mirror that reflects how she's spread open to me. She lifts her head as she arches her back to see beneath her tits.

"That's so fucking hot. And I don't mean it as a pun."

I smile before she settles on the bed again. I slide the blindfold back into place. I remove the weights, replacing them with a vaginal spreader. I stare for a moment, a little too excited by the sight. I unfasten my pants and push down my boxer briefs because my *huevos* are about to mutiny. My cock's leaking. I stroke once as though that might relieve some of the ache.

"Daddy, are you jerking off?"

Annoyed.

That's the only way to describe Flora's tone. She doesn't want to miss the sight and doesn't want to miss out on the action. She's made that clear before.

"What can you do if I were?"

She knows I'm taunting her because her hands are bound. Nothing's forcing her to keep them over her head besides her choice. She opens her mouth wide and playfully licks all the way around her lips. Then she flicks her tongue like I do when I'm going down on her.

Tempting.

Instead, I reach for the vibrator she picked out. She says it'll have to do when I'm traveling. I warned her with a spanking that she'll only get herself off when I give her permission and can watch on a video call.

I turn it on the lowest setting and slip it into her. She's breathing evenly, but I know she's waiting for me to turn it up. Such a shame I won't yet. Instead, I strip and grab the bottle of lube before withdrawing the vibrator. Her cream coats it, but I add lube to it. Then, I lift her legs and duck beneath the spreader to kneel between her thighs, the bar resting on my shoulders. I ease the vibrator into her ass, and she yelps. She obviously didn't hear me turn it up.

I pour lube onto my fingers and ease two into her cunt. I work her with slow purpose. I rub her G-spot, my other hand pressing on her belly right where I know she loves it. I know she wants me to fill her more. I ease my ring finger into her, watching it and thinking about what it would be like to see a wedding band on it. I'm not as opposed to that thought as I was a couple months ago when I recognized Javier and Madeline were on their way to an engagement.

"*Papí, por favor!*"

Flora's plea brings my full attention back to her. A wave of guilt hits me for not being entirely attentive to her, but I remind myself I was daydreaming about us. But I want to be present for this and enjoy every hitch of her breath as I edge her. I work my pinky into her, and she shifts her hips. I recognize her unspoken plea for my thumb to rub her clit, but that's not what I want.

I twist the vibrator in her ass, and she practically screams when she feels my fingers press against it through the thin layer of skin separating them. I know the sensation is intense from how her abdomen clenches, and she breathes through it.

"Can you take more?"

"*Por favor!*"

I twist my wrist as I work my fingers farther into her. The spreader helps prepare her cunt for my full hand. I'm careful not to press into her before she's fully ready for me. When I can, I slide in until the heel of my palm is all I see.

"*Ay, Papí. Mucho!*"

My fingers brush deep inside her cunt, and I feel her cervix. I stroke over it, and she bucks. I'm not sure if her conscious mind is even in control of her body anymore as I watch sweat bead along her hairline. She's panting, and her hips undulate to their own rhythm.

"Fuck, Pablo. The urge to pee is supposed to be a warning. I think I'm going to squirt."

"Do you want me to stop?"

"The bed."

I look around and grab my button down. I don't even want to know what the dry cleaner thinks if there's any odor when I drop it off tomorrow. I place it beneath her hips and continue to stroke and slide my hand in and out.

"Don't stop, Daddy. I think it's going to happen."

"Take the blindfold off, *chica.*"

"Yes, Daddy."

She snatches it off and practically flings it across the bed. Her bound wrists don't allow her to use her elbows to prop herself up. She pushes the pillows beneath her shoulders as best she can as she watches.

"Fuck, *chiquita.*"

Her body squirts just like she predicted. Her spray coats my wrist and forearm. My free thumb rubs her clit finally, and she screams.

"*¡Sí!*"

When she falls back against the pillows, I ease my hand out. But I waste no time thrusting my dick into her. I'm almost coming when I'm balls deep. I'm slowly rocking my hips, or this will be over before she gets off with a regular orgasm. I feel the vibrator against my dick, and the pulsating vibrations create a struggle between my balls and my brain. I grind my pubic bone against her clit, knowing that's what she needs to get off.

We've been together over two months, and she hasn't gotten her period. She warned me—or rather reminded me since I took as much biology as she did—that it could mean nothing since she's been on the pill for years, and this has been an extraordinarily stressful month for her. We aren't reading anything into it. But I know I felt her cervix slightly dilated. I want to get her pregnant. I want to have a family with her.

"Daddy, you feel so good. I love that you're bare."

"You love taking all my cum."

"I do."

One day soon, she'll be saying that in front of a priest. My mind flashes to her with a slightly rounded belly. Not so much that anyone else can see it under her gown, but we'd know. I lower myself onto my forearms and pull the satin band from her wrists. Immediately, she reaches for my hips, her hands finding the grooves she loves to hold on to while we fuck and make love.

"Do you want Daddy to fuck a baby into your soft belly?"

"Yes!"

"You're my little cum slut to fuck."

"I am, Daddy. I want it."

"You belong to me, *chiquita*. I'll fuck you whenever I want. I'll breed you whenever I want. Your body is mine to do whatever I want with. I've marked your skin. I'll control your pleasure. I'll claim every part of you when you carry our child. There'll be nothing that isn't mine when my cum takes root."

"Fuck. Keep talking that way. I'm close."

"My little whore's begging for me to breed her."

"Yes!"

"Everyone will know you belong to me when they know I've fucked a baby into you. No one will doubt you're the only woman I want. The only woman I crave."

"Rougher, Daddy. Make me have your baby."

Who knew breeding kink was my thing on top of hearing her call me Daddy and Papí?

The one thing I've avoided since I started having sex is the one thing I want now. If we didn't want a family, Flora would've gone back on the pill. It's odd to think today was the first time we said "I love you." I think we've just known but been nervous to admit it. We accepted weeks ago that we might have a family if we kept having sex without protection. That hasn't slowed us.

A proposal is next.

I know exactly how I'll do it.

Chapter Thirty-Two

Flora

Pablo's words echo in my head as I get closer to coming. I love that most of the time it's praise between us. I love that he doesn't call me a whore or slut in a demeaning way outside of sex or even as foreplay. It didn't bother me in the past when Doms called me those things because it was part of the agreed-upon dynamic. But the emotions I have for Pablo were never part of those previous relationships. It would hurt me to hear him call me that when we aren't in the middle of sex. He gets that, and I think he feels the same way.

We understand each other.

It's how he knows just what I need to hear and feel right now. How he's driving me wild with the need to come.

"Fuck, Daddy. I won't break. Rougher than you ever have been in the past."

"I'll harm you, Flora. I won't do that. I won't lose control."

"Even if you told yourself to let go completely, Pablo, your subconscious would *never* let you harm me. I know that in the deepest part of my soul. More, Daddy."

He slams into me so hard it hurts. Even with the way he stretched me, it's still tight when he's balls deep inside me. It feels like his dick's going to find its way into my stomach with the way he's jackhammering my pussy. I'm going to be so fucking sore tomorrow.

I can't wait.

I definitely never had a breeding kink before Pablo. I would've run naked from the building if any other man told me he wanted to impregnate me. We've agreed we want to be married before any child is born, but I wouldn't mind sharing a pregnancy secret with him during a wedding. I worry though—because of my own baggage, and I know it—a child will one day figure out they were conceived before we got married. I never want a child to believe we only married because I was pregnant.

That worry isn't enough to make me go back on the pill or ask Pablo to wear a condom or pull out. We'll see what happens.

Fuck. What's about to happen is a fucking orgasm.

"Papí, necesito correrme." I need to come.

"Hazlo ahora." Do it now.

In moments like this—when everything is so extreme—English escapes me. I can barely put two words together in Spanish let alone in my second language.

"¡Ay, Papí! ¡Ay!"

I'm certain the men in the hallway—hell the ones all the way in the lobby—probably hear me come. I'll be hoarse in the morning since my throat burns now. My lungs even hurt from how I just screamed. I didn't mean to, but *Holeee. Fuck.*

If our sex life remains even a fraction of what it is now, the novelty will never wear off. It's insane how good sex is with

Pablo. We've talked about joining a club together where he's never been. There are a few, but he wants to make sure none of the other syndicate couples are active members there. He wants to save me the embarrassment, and he acknowledges the other men would like to avoid that for their wives' sake.

"*Chiquita, me voy a correr.*" Little girl, I'm going to come.

"*Quiero hacerte correrte.*" I want to make you come.

He thrusts and growls until he bottoms out, and I watch his abs tense. Sweat slides along his temples, and it tempts me to lick him. I've never done that before. Someone else's sweat is usually gross to me. But not on Pablo. I'd lick *all* of him. Not a sentiment I've had before.

"*Chica?*"

"*Sí, Papí.*"

"*¿Estás bien?*" You okay?

"Yes. I just need to catch my breath."

I'm coming back down to Earth, so I switch to English. I can gather my thoughts enough now. Barely. But I can.

He eases the vibrator out of my ass then reaches up to unfasten the spreader I'd practically forgotten about, but now I'm glad he's releasing me. My legs are stiff, so he helps me bend and straighten. He removes the vaginal spreader too. We roll, and I drape myself over him. He massages my hips and ass, and I could fall asleep. I thought it was only men who passed out after sex.

"Pablo, thank you. This was perfect."

"I'm glad you enjoyed it. Let's take a bath and get all the wax off you."

I'd forgotten about that, but as I shift away from him, some cracks and pinches my skin. We head into the bathroom, which has an enormous soaking tub. If I didn't know Pablo never brought women here because it was and is his sanctuary from the world, I'd wonder if he had it installed to share. He's also a large man who wouldn't fit in a regular oblong tub. His shoulders are far too broad, and his knees would be up to his nose because he's so tall.

He tests the water and adds the bubble bath I like. By the time we're in it, it's practically overflowing. I scoop a handful of bubbles and stick it on his hair. He blows some at me. We laugh, and it's so nice to share something so sweet after something so—dirty.

"What's making your lips twitch, *chica*?"

"I was just thinking about how nice it is to sit here in a bubble bath and be lighthearted after the workout we just had."

"Workout, huh?"

"Vigorous workout at that, *Papí*."

"Yes, it was. Definitely worked up a sweat."

We're sitting facing each other, my legs draped over his. He leans forward and grips my hips beneath the water, pulling me toward him. I make it easier and scooch toward him. Our kisses are light pecks as we run warm water over each other's shoulders. He massages mine, and I lean toward him.

"Mmm. I can't reach that well."

Bullshit. His arms are plenty long enough. I know what he's after, and I'm happy to oblige. I shift onto my knees and lower myself onto his cock. He's fully aroused again, and I'm still slick with his cum. When am I not aroused when he's around?

Our movements now are filled with affection. Some may say I'm warming his cock, but I don't think so. We're not trying to get off, but neither is he ignoring me on purpose to edge me. We're one when we're like this, and I love every moment of it. I'm happiest when we're like this. It gets even better when he wraps his arms around me and tightens, so I lean against him.

"I love you, Flora. I think I have since the very beginning. I knew it was more than lust, even if that was a major part of it."

He tweaks my nipple, and I Kegel.

"I love you, Pablo. I didn't want to admit how sexy I found you. It seemed disloyal to my family, and to want a man like you…I've never been into the bad boy type. It was scary. But I know now you are the man I thought you were, but that's not who I see when I'm with you. You're way, way more than that. I see a gentle and selfless man who makes me happy."

"I can't help the things I do because leaving it behind would put a target on both of us that's bigger than it already is. My family would never let us go unprotected, so it would endanger them too. I have duties I'll never shirk, but I'd walk away with you if I could."

"I know, Daddy. I get it. I know you won't always let me know where you're going, and you won't always know when you'll be back. But will you tell me when you can?"

"Always. I will try to never leave on a trip or mission without saying goodbye and telling you I love you. I can't promise I'll always be able to, but it won't be because I forgot."

"That's all I ask."

He kisses my shoulder and up my neck. I shift to make it easier for him. It allows me to do the same thing until we move to bring our lips together. We stay like this until the water cools. We don't get off. Instead, we hurry to scrub the last of the wax off me. Then we curl up together.

"Pablo's up to something, Madeline. I'm sure of it. You've known him your entire life. Should I be worried?"

Madeline's family already lived in the house next door to Pablo's when she was born. She grew up with him like a brother rather than a neighbor. He used to tutor her in high school science, and they'd hit tennis balls against the side of her house when her older sister and Pablo's younger brother hung out. He made sure Laura and Juan never excluded her when they were little, and all played together. I figured she'd know if Pablo was up to something.

"I don't think so. Pablo's always kept things to himself when he doesn't feel like sharing, but he won't lie to you if he doesn't have to. I know things aren't resolved yet, so it could be that. It could be work. It could be a surprise for you. I don't know anything specific."

"Thanks. I appreciate it."

It's Sunday dinner, and Madeline and I are in the living room with the other women while the men set the table and finish cooking. Margherita and Luis are hosting this week. For twenty-odd years, Madeline's family shared Sunday dinner with Pablo's. They alternated hosting. Shit that happened to Laura because of Juan ruined that. Madeline swears it's not odd to be here with Javier rather than her parents and Laura, but it must be a bit strange.

Javier and Madeline just bought a home in the Switzerland of Queens. It's the syndicate neighborhood where most of the bratva, Mafia, mob, and Cartel families live. It's the one Luciana moved into when she arrived in the States with Javier, Joaquin, and Jorge. Catalina, Matáis, and Alejandro already lived there. Apparently, every time a house comes on the market, a syndicate couple swoops in.

"Do you feel completely settled in?"

"I do. I've been here nearly three months. I wish there was nothing looming over us, but I know not everything happens when I want it to. Hard lesson for an only child to accept." I grin at Madeline.

Pablo and I looked at three houses in the syndicate neighborhood today. There was one we liked more than the other two. Unfortunately, the sellers' agent got really cagey once she recognized Pablo from photos of an event he and I attended last week at the Waldorf Astoria.

Pablo hasn't told me outright, but I figured out *Abuelo* didn't go back to Colombia. I thought I'd be angry or sad, but I was just—nothing. I don't miss him. When I dredge up feelings, it's for *Abuela* who's finally free from the tyrant. It's for my father's two sisters, but there's none for my father's younger brother who's a chip off the old block. I learned that phrase recently from a TV show. Pablo had to explain it.

"You know if you need anything or want to explore more of the city, just let me know. I'm happy to figure out something around my shifts."

Madeline's a midwife at a hospital in Brooklyn. I bet she's fantastic. She's so calm about everything. I experienced Pablo's first mission overseas two weeks after we professed our love for the first time. He left in the middle of the night with a kiss and an "I'll call when I can," which was four days later. I stayed with Madeline and Javier since he didn't go. She and I are growing close, and I've met her sister. Laura was really sweet to me too, which I wasn't expecting given she's married to Enrique's bratva equivalent.

"Dinner will be ready in just a moment."

Pablo wraps his arm around my shoulder as he slips into the spot next to me on the sofa. I sweep my gaze around the room and notice everyone but Luis is in the enormous family room that sprawls into the dining room. I twist to see him walking out of the kitchen. When he joins us, Pablo stands. Before anyone else can, he thrusts out his hand to me. It's not just a gentle offer to help me up but something purposeful. It makes the others watch.

"I got good news while I was in the kitchen."

Once I'm on my feet, he reaches into his trousers pocket to pull out his phone. He unlocks it and hands it to me. I see an email addressed to both of us. I skim it before looking up at him.

"We got the house?"

"We did."

"I didn't know you put an offer on it. I thought the agent said the owners wouldn't accept one from us."

"I made a call. I reminded the agent that who owns the house after the sellers leave isn't their concern."

I glance back at the phone and see how much over asking Pablo offered. It's obscene, but he knows I fell in love with the house. Him shifting catches my attention. I look at him as he lowers to one knee. I drop his phone, which he deftly catches and puts on the floor beside him.

"Flora, we've known since the beginning our path is now one. I knew but didn't understand what the other couples in my family talked about when they said they found 'the one.' Now I do. I want to grow old with you in this house we make a home. I know you're far from what you know, but you're with family. Now and forever. Will you marry me?"

I've been nodding since he got down on one knee, agreeing with everything he's said. He's melted my heart into a puddle beside him. Some couples might prefer a private moment for this momentous occasion, but being with his family is perfect. They've accepted me from the beginning, and this reminds me that in their minds—and hearts—I'm already a Diaz. I feel loved by more than just Pablo. I feel accepted by more than just Pablo. Most of my life, it was only my mother who made me feel that way.

"¡Sí!"

He slides a ring on my finger that could dazzle the space station. But all I want is for him to stand. I tug on his sweater, and he comes to his feet. I throw my arms around him and pepper his face with kisses as he lifts me off mine. We share a kiss that's even more intense and inappropriate for other people to watch than the one after he came home from meeting that mercenary.

Everyone filters into the dining room to give us a moment alone. We rest our foreheads together as we whisper.

"Thank you, *Papi*. All of this is perfect. How'd you know this is the perfect ring?"

"I heard you talking to Madeline a couple weeks ago when you were discussing her wedding plans. You mentioned the style you like. Did I get it right doing it with everyone around?"

He sounds so hesitant that it's adorable.

"You have supersonic hearing, Daddy."

"When it comes to you, absolutely."

"Thank you. I love that you included our family."

I think his eyes water for a heartbeat.

"Do you really consider them your family?"

"Of course."

"*Chiquita*, they consider you family too."

"I know they do. I couldn't ask for more."

We kiss once again before he leads me into the dining room.

"*Chica*, I swear I'll end all this shit still hanging over us before the wedding in two weeks."

"Two weeks?!"

Chapter Thirty-Three

Pablo

I'm grateful to my family for being who they are. Not Cartel. But loving, generous, funny, and accepting. It made last night perfect for Flora and me. I asked *Papá* if it would be a mistake to involve everyone in the proposal. He answered honestly that he couldn't be sure Flora would appreciate it, but he thought it was a nice touch since she has no one else here in the U.S.

Things are still strained with Magdalena. Some phone calls go better than others. People figured out Ernesto fucked around and found out when he crossed Flora. Once people discovered she and I are together, it was a foregone conclusion to most. We've agreed to wait at least six months before we consider Flora going back to Colombia. It'll likely be closer to a year. I want to go a few times on my own before I take her with me. She knows I had to travel internationally, and I think she suspects I went there. I didn't. I was in South Korea.

Today, I'm dealing with fucking Lorenzo.

It's taken three months, but fina-fucking-ly.

Alejandro went down to Peru four times to investigate more. I swear, the man has an invisibility cloak. The way he can slip in and out of places with barely anyone noticing is bizarre since he's nearly six-five and two-forty-five. He's got shoulders wide enough that even our tailor shakes his head with how much material he needs for his suit coats.

Yeah, none of us buys off-the-rack. It's not snobbery. It's practicality. Retail just doesn't fit. To have coats that cover our broad backs and long torsos would mean trousers that would look like clown pants on us. If we bought pants that fit, the suit coats wouldn't fit across one shoulder.

My cousin poked around and learned there was more to Lorenzo's proposed deal than *Papá* discovered. Lorenzo was getting into mining too. Copper and gold are major Peruvian exports. He was going to use the mines as a cover for the labs. Probably blow up half the Andes.

The Mancinellis definitely don't have the sort of people working for them who know what they're doing in a lab condition like that. They've practically set the fucking Amazon on fire before when they've had labs blow up. There are volatile ingredients involved in making our product.

Lorenzo's little incursion into western South America ends today.

He believes he's meeting with a buyer who wants to invest in his doomed endeavor. I've put in a shit ton of work over the past couple months to set this up. I've triple and quadruple checked my work to ensure he hasn't guessed I'm behind all this.

It's no secret Flora and I are involved, and it's no secret I'm the one who got her away from Mason Harrison. I've been fucking the Mancinellis over small time just to keep them on their toes and pissed off. Now we're moving onto the big leagues.

We're meeting in Boston. The Mexican cartel up here understands just how badly they fucked up coming down to NYC and stepping on my toes. They exist just like any other cartel in the States because *Tío* Enrique allows it.

We don't have a substantial Colombian community in Boston compared to NYC, so it's the Mexicans who've emerged up here. It doesn't mean it's a fucking free for all. They know their ultimate allegiance is to my *tío* if they want to survive. They know they shit the bed, and they know they'll be repaying their debt for a *long* time.

Felipe Iglesias is one wrong move away from death. He understands that after my visit up here. I beat the ever-loving shit out of him. Put him in the hospital for three weeks. Intensive care. The pleasure was all mine. Now he's making his first installment by hosting this little tête-à-tête with Lorenzo.

"*El Tigre*, everything is how you wanted."

Felipe's difficult to understand since his jaw isn't healed fully from my breaking both sides. He's also waiting on some dental work. I believe it's a bridge and three crowns. He has at least one false tooth now. A baseball bat to the face a few times will do that.

"Thank you."

He limps away as I look around. My cousins are strategically placed around the restaurant where we're meeting. I chose a public place, so Lorenzo has to behave. He's the most unflappable one in his family. He's the hardest to rile, but when he's pissed...

I can't help but laugh thinking about it. He's going to have a tantrum tonight the likes of which only a cranky two-year-old could match. By then, it'll be more than a meeting not going his way that'll have him throwing his toys and stomping his feet.

Felipe brokered this meeting and made sure the restaurant staff understands they'll be paid well to stay away from our table once Lorenzo and I sit down. He has men scattered around the block as well. I'm certain Lorenzo demanded that too, but I'll take credit for making it happen.

I usually hate having my back to the door, but I'm having a flair for the dramatic tonight. Let his pathetic ass walk around the table to see who he's meeting. *Tres J's* are in position to signal me if something goes wrong. Alejandro can slip out of the crowded space if he needs to get away. He's next in line to inherit after me, so one of us has to survive. He also knows what needs to be done after this meeting to keep the plan going.

"*Él está aquí.*" He's here.

It's Jorge's voice in my ear as I look in my cousin's direction. He flashes me the same grin he's had since he was a toddler. He's the baby of the family, so I was super protective of him until he knocked me out in the boxing ring when he was fifteen and I was nineteen. After that, I learned just how deceptive that smile can be. Never mind all the times he stole my dessert with that smile.

Lorenzo knows he's meeting a Latino, so my dark hair and olive skin won't be a surprise. I'm not worried about him guessing before he has to turn to face me. *Tres J's* blend into the crowd in this Mexican restaurant since they're in jeans and t-shirts for this. I'm the only one dressed in our usual uniform— dark suit, dark shirt, dark tie. I prefer gray tones for my suits and shades of silver or midnight blue for my shirts and ties. Lorenzo likes beige. Suits the *pendejo*.

When in Rome.

Caremonda in Colombia. Penis face.

"Here we are, sir." The waiter shows Lorenzo to his seat.

"Thank you." Lorenzo keeps his voice down as he walks past my right shoulder.

"*Buonasera, faccia de cazzo.*" Good evening, testicle face.

"What the fuck, Pablo? Find your own deal. You're not muscling in on this."

"Too late. Sit."

Lorenzo glowers at me before sweeping his gaze around the restaurant to make sure he's not drawing more attention than his good looks normally do. The two of us together is already getting stares. It's obvious we're both grossly rich, and I'm no troll.

"Pablo—"

"No. In this little come to Jesus, I'm reading the Gospel tonight. Sit."

I gesture to the chair, and he pulls it out as he unbuttons his suit coat. He leans forward enough to ensure I see his gun under his arm. Big fucking deal. I have my shoulder holsters on with a gun under each arm. His balls are not bigger than mine.

"You are higher on my shit list than you ever have been before, Enzo. You done fucked up worse than you can imagine. You meddled in my family's business, and you yanked a woman into our world."

"Your shitbag great-uncle did that. I didn't pick Florencia as his chemist. He did."

"You didn't walk away when you found out he was forcing a woman to work for him. Worse than that, neither you nor your uncle went to mine to tell him what was happening. You used Florencia and didn't care that Humberto would've eventually killed her."

"He might not have."

"I know you—" *only went to Rutgers for computer science* "—aren't the brightest one in your family, but you aren't an idiot."

I'll have to find a fresh set of insults for him now that his lack of an Ivy League or even Top Tier education can't be something to pick on him for. Never mind he went to MIT for grad school in accounting.

"It's not my fault Enrique let the leash go slack, and Humberto fucked you over *again*. For a man who was under house arrest for thirty-six years, he managed to cause a lot of shit from his marble mausoleum."

My eyes narrow at him, and I hear Joaquin mutter through my earpiece.

"I'll shank his fucking *huevos*."

I'm certain Lorenzo's wife, Michelle, would take issue with him coming home a eunuch.

"That's a douche move since you know I'm not alone."

"Did I lie? I know they heard me."

"You're just digging your grave deeper by the syllable. The only appropriate response in this is 'I'm sorry, Pablo. How can I make it up to you?'"

"You've lost your fucking mind."

"You didn't stop when Flora and I left Colombia. You went after her here."

"No, I did not. That was on Harrison. He thought he could impress Uncle Salvatore and make some extra money by taking her. If you hadn't killed him first, my uncle would have for making you think we ordered that."

"I don't believe you."

"I don't care."

"You should." I run my hand through my hair as I lean back in my chair.

"Get to the point, Pablo. Are you here to make a deal or what?"

"Or what."

He assesses me, but before he can speak, his phone vibrates three times then stops.

"You should answer that. It's your family."

The Mancinellis let a call ring three times then hang up as a code. They'll call back in that pattern until the recipient answers. It's the fucking Bat Signal.

Lorenzo eases his phone out and checks the screen. His thumb slides across the screen, and he brings it to his ear as he watches me. I can't see who it is, but they're doing all the talking right now. From his expression, Salvatore's ripping him a new one. He looks more guarded than usual. That's how I know it's his uncle, the don.

"Bad news?"

I gloat as he hangs up and puts the phone back in his pocket. The hand through my hair was my signal to enact my revenge.

"You are *the* most fucked-up of all of us, Pablo."

"It's not like I went after Michelle's dogs. You never kill the dog."

Lorenzo's wife, Michelle, is Laura Kutsenko's best friend. She grew up going over to Laura and Madeline's house all the time. We know each other well. I was the first guy she slept with. We had a summer fling. It's a sore spot for Lorenzo. Laura's Mastiff, Sebastian, is quite the stud. He's sired puppies now owned by couples in all of the Four Families. Talk about a swinging dick. Michelle has two of Sebastian's daughters.

"You fucking killed the deal. Like seriously killed it."

Alejandro gave me the list of Peruvian men involved in the mining and lab deals. They were willing to work for the Mancinellis, knowing it was an operation *Tío* didn't sanction. Each family will get a lump-sum survivor's benefit. Our men rounded them up this afternoon and took care of them ten minutes ago. Salvatore just got the photos.

"You shouldn't shit where you eat, Enzo."

His phone buzzes again. I see the menace in his gaze, and I

laugh. He answers without looking at his phone this time. Once again, it's a one-sided conversation.

"Fall in the jungle can still get exceedingly hot, Enzo. Too bad it didn't rain in Colombia today."

I watch his sun-tanned ears turn red. It's his tell. His temper is slipping. He didn't appreciate us blowing up the five labs his family has in the Amazon. They thought we only knew about three. Those are the ones they had permission to build. There's not a person working in a rival's labs in the Amazon who doesn't get paid by us too. They know which side their bread is buttered.

"What do you want, Pablo?"

"You're going to apologize to Flora."

"Fine."

"And Michelle's going to watch."

"What? No. You are not involving my wife."

"You involved my fiancée."

"She was nothing to you when this started."

"She's everything to me now. You could've reached out the moment you found out Flora and I got together. I know you knew before we even left Colombia. You could've warned me. Not for my sake but Flora's. You didn't. No women and children goes both ways, Enzo."

"I'll give Florencia the apology, but my wife stays away from Mafia business."

He pushes back his chair and stands, buttoning his suit coat. He walks away without another word. Predictable.

He heads to the front door, and I go out the back. I watch him walk toward the corner where his SUV waits. He's looking around since none of his guards materialized like they should have. He reaches for his belt buckle to trigger his tracker, but Joaquin grabs his left arm while Javier gets his right. They drag him into the alley as he fights to break free. The moment he's in the dark and in front of me, Jorge binds his wrists behind his back. Alejandro gags him while I pull out my brass knuckles.

"Count yourself lucky you're the don's nephew. I know I can't kill you."

I drive my fist into his left cheek. He fights not to react, but he can't help but flinch. My next punch goes to his sternum. He'll be lucky if I don't break his xiphoid process. I follow that with a blow to the gut that doubles him over and leaves him wheezing. I slam the fist that doesn't have the brass knuckles into his right eye. I follow it up with a blow to his ear as his head whips away from me.

Joaquin steps up with his knife drawn. I give him space.

"I heard what you said, you *malparido carechimba*. You're lucky I like Michelle, or I'd fucking castrate you. I've heard you fuck like a gigolo, so I won't take your one redeeming quality away from your wife. I'm certain that's the only reason she's with you." Badly born—despicable—face of a vagina.

He rips open Lorenzo's shirt, then pulls his tie extra tight, making the fucker's face turn red. He slices a T on Lorenzo's left ribs and a J on his right. The cuts aren't deep enough to do any real damage, but they'll likely scar enough to remind him for a while that he shouldn't speak ill of our dead.

"Javier, I did a better job than you did. My letters are way straighter."

My middle cousin left the same reminder ten years ago when he and Lorenzo got in a fight during a college spring break trip. They and their groups of friends wound up at the same resort in Ibiza. A drunken fight that Lorenzo lost left him with a reminder of my cousins.

"Yeah, well you're both sober tonight." Javier's mocking tone grates on most people's nerves.

Joaquin steps away, and I take his place. I nod, and Alejandro claps his hands on Lorenzo's shoulders and presses down until the man kneels before me. I grab a handful of his hair and yank his head back. I lean over him, so I'm the only thing he can see.

"This is just the appetizer. Stay the fuck away from my woman, Enzo, or yours will be a widow. I know everyone says I have no soul. Maybe I do. Maybe I don't. What I have is a temper when it comes to Flora's safety. Test me, and I will strike. One day, Salvatore won't be around to protect you. One day, I'll be *jefe de jefes*. I will kill you and piss on your grave."

I kick him in the junk then plow the brass knuckles into his temple. My cousins and I walk away, leaving Lorenzo in the alley. Our men are holding his in a van about two blocks away. We'll release them, and they can deal with his unconscious ass.

We both live to fight another day because I have to let him. But I didn't lie. One day, I'll run this hemisphere. When I do, no place on Earth will be safe for anyone who threatens my *chiquita*.

"*Papi?*"

"*Sí, chica.*"

I slip into bed next to Flora. I showered on the flight back down to NYC from Boston. I had to dispose of the blood splattered suit and scrub myself to make sure I carried none of Lorenzo's DNA evidence on me. My hair's still a bit damp, but I'm presentable enough to be near Flora.

"I'm glad you're home." She speaks around a yawn.

"I didn't mean to wake you."

"It's all right."

She snuggles closer to me, putting her head on my chest and draping her arm over my belly. Her left leg slides between mine. I wrap my arms around her, and my hand rests on her ass.

"It's over, little one."

"Really?" She's a lot more awake now.

"Yes. The man who started this understands what he did wrong. He won't come near you except to apologize."

She pushes up onto her elbow and gazes down at me.

"A syndicate man is going to apologize to me?"

"In front of his wife. Don't be alarmed when you see the bruising. It'll be worse than it looks, but he'll survive."

She stares at me before she nods and settles back into her spot alongside me. She kisses my chest and gives me a squeeze.

"Thank you, Daddy. I love you."

"I love you too, *chiquita*."

Epilogue

Flora

"Damn, Daddy! Let me catch my breath."

Pablo just chased me around our backyard and into the house. Of course, he caught me before I could make it up the stairs to our room. For some reason, he didn't appreciate finding panties beneath my skirt. I took off running out of the living room, and he followed. We've been playing the same games for nine years. I get to see a lighthearted side of Pablo even his family rarely sees.

"You are going over my knee, little one."

"I'm already over your shoulder, and you're already spanking me."

"I know. You're going over my knee, so I can finger you and play with that plug in your ass."

"We'll be late for Josue's birthday party."

Javier and Madeline's little boy turned six today, and they're having a party for him. I doubt it'll rival his fourth birthday when he got a polo pony. That was as much about the little boy following in his father's footsteps as it was prolonging Javier's revenge against Marco Mancinelli.

Josue's the oldest but not the only member of his generation. We're the indulgent *tía* and *tío*. Pablo's taken lessons from *Tío* Enrique, who used to spoil Pablo, his brother, and their cousins when they were kids. Apparently, he brought all the best snacks to games when his brother or sisters and their spouses couldn't make it. It's wild, but all the parents in the Four Families had snack duties at peewee, little league, and high school games since the guys played with and against each other.

"Then you better not come, that way I don't have to punish you for a second thing."

"Pablo, my skirt comes to my knees, but it's breezy today. I'm not going commando around your entire family since the kids will be there. If the wind blows my skirt up—"

"Then you better hold it down. It's never happened."

"But it could."

"If you wanted me to edge you, all you had to do was ask, *chiquita.*"

He grins at me, and lines appear around his eyes and mouth that remind me of his father and *Tío* Enrique. It didn't take me long to call the men and women *tío* and *tía.* I call Luis and Margherita *Papá* and *Mamá.* I thought it might feel odd since I reconciled with my mother in time for the wedding, but I love how close Margherita and I are. She's been a rock for me over the past seven years.

When I didn't get pregnant the first year we were married, we got worried. Margherita and Madeline took me out to lunch since they're both midwives. They discussed infertility with me, and Margherita got me an appointment with an OBGYN she works with. She taught me how to give myself shots during the second year of our marriage when we tried IVF.

She reassured me it wasn't anything I did wrong when I never got pregnant. My "unhospitable womb" and "advanced maternal age" were a combination that's left us childless. Either could've been the reason, but together, it's meant Pablo and I have adjusted our plans.

Pablo insisted he get tested before we did anything invasive on me. He insisted he might be shooting blanks. I know he meant well, but when it was obvious my body was the culprit, it didn't make it any easier knowing he could have kids if he wanted. We've held each other through our tears and grief about the life we thought we'd have but won't.

We're as much on the other side of it as I guess we'll get. It's not exactly a scabbed over wound that won't heal. It's more like a scar that itches sometimes and is numb others. We look on the bright side, which is that I can travel with Pablo whenever I want. I worked in a lab the first three years, but now I represent the three biotech companies we own. I go into an office a couple times a week, and I travel on my own to visit the labs since they're spread across three different countries. Since I work from home more often than not, I can go with Pablo on non-Cartel trips.

We also spoil our nephews rotten. They adore us, and our cousins are forever telling us their children like us better than them. Of course they do. We have all the fun with them, and their parents make them brush their teeth, take their vitamins, and go to bed at a reasonable time.

"Seriously, Daddy. We're going to be late, and everyone will guess why."

"Yeah. It's the same reason we're all late to various events. We're not any different than anyone else, my parents included."

He curls his nose in disgust. We had Sunday dinner at *Tío* Matáis and *Tía* Catalina's last week. *Mamá* and *Papá* arrived just before us. *Mamá's* skirt was suspiciously off center when she got out of the town car. I thought Pablo was going to be ill. I just giggled and hid my face against his arm. *Tía* Catalina came out of the kitchen straightening her hair. *Tío* Matáis called out his greeting from in there and didn't join us for five minutes. Apparently, the *badeja paisa* needed his attention. It's a dish piled high with various meats, plantains, rice, red beans, avocado, and fried eggs.

"Josue will be upset if we're late."

Javier and Madeline named their son after the *abuelo* all the cousins share. From what the older generation says, the little boy is the spitting image of the man when he was a child. I've seen the family photos, and the resemblance is uncanny.

"Then you better not make this last longer than it has to, *chica.*"

That's like saying it better not snow in the Arctic.

He lowers me to my feet as he sits on the end of the bed. He unzips my skirt and pushes it to the floor. He yanks down my panties and holds them up.

"Where were you hiding these? Do you have some secret stash?"

I shake my head, and he narrows his eyes.

"After all these years, have you been wearing panties when I'm away?"

"No. I have a couple pairs as just in case. Windy days, doctor's appointments, things like that."

He considers what I say and nods. "Doctor's appointments only."

"Yes, Daddy."

He pulls out his knife and flicks it open. He shreds the damn things to make his point. There're scraps of satin on the floor when he's done. He puts his blade away and pats his lap. I stretch over it, and he twirls the jeweled plug before pulling and pushing three times. I breathe through it when I want to squirm. His hand lands across my ass, and I yelp. He gives me nine more spanks before his fingers plunge into my pussy. When he withdraws them, I turn my head to look up at him. He licks his fingers and grins at me.

"Better than birthday cake."

"If you say so."

I know I sound petulant, but my ass stings, and my pussy burns. I want to get off more than I want birthday cake—which is saying something because I discovered American buttercream frosting is one of my favorite things.

He slips his fingers into me again, and I do my best not to beg.

I fail miserably.

"*Por favor, Papi. Por favor...Por favor...Papi!*"

"On the way home, little one."

He helps me stand and hands me my skirt. My cunt feels painfully empty, and he knows it. I step forward once my skirt is in place and press my body against his. My hand slips between us and cups his dick.

"However will I make amends, Daddy?"

I bounce onto my toes, give his lips a peck, and spin around. I bolt for the door and toward the stairs. He's right behind me.

"If you can get to the car before me, Daddy, maybe I'll apologize with a blowjob."

There's no way my shorter legs will get me there first. The moment we're in the foyer, and he's certain I won't trip down the steps, he charges past me. He flings open the front door and leaps down the three steps on our stoop. Our driver rushes to get the car door open. Pablo practically dives in. I'm not much better.

Once the door's shut, I'm reaching for his pants. It's only a couple seconds later that his cock is in my mouth. His hand strokes my hair as I suck while I kneel on the seat beside him. He pulls my skirt up and moves on to stroke my ass, which he loves looking at any chance he gets. Just as he gets close, he reaches for me and lifts me. I straddle him and slide down his cock.

"You're going to take all my cum, little girl. It's going to drip down your thighs while we're at the party."

"That's why you didn't want me to wear panties."

"Obviously. Now let me give you an orgasm."

"You're a prince among men, Daddy."

"And you're *mi reina*."

Bonus Epilogue

Pablo

This is one of the best days of my life. Meeting Flora, telling her I love her, proposing to her, and marrying her a month ago are the four highlights.

But today...

Today...

Today is the day fucking Lorenzo Mancinelli stands before my wife and fucking grovels. He truly kisses the ring. He just extended his hand for Flora's left one and bowed over her hand, proffering an air kiss over her four-carat engagement ring and three-carat wedding band. She's looking down at him with such an imperious expression that my cock's hardening. I dart my gaze to Michelle, who's glaring at me. I shrug.

The reception for her son's baptism was a perfect opportunity for this. All of the Four Families are together to witness the momentous occasion. Lorenzo Mancinelli eating crow.

Only the Mancinellis, Laura and Maks—because Laura is Michelle's best friend, and Javier and Madeline—because she's

Laura's younger sister—attended the service. Maks and Javier went for their wives' sake—and safety. Not that the Mancinellis would ruin the day by doing something to Laura or Madeline. It was to guard against any outside threat since the New York Mafia don's entire family was together in a public location.

Other guests haven't arrived for the reception yet. That's more about showing off wealth and brokering under-the-table deals than celebrating the infant receiving his first sacrament.

"Florencia, I'm sorry for the danger I put you in. I'm sorry for embroiling you in syndicate business. I'm sorry for not telling Enrique and his family when I discovered Humberto hired a woman."

"I accept your apology. Thank you. But do you intend to make the same mistake twice?"

Flora knows we commit the same sins over and over. It's why none of us go to church anymore except for family occasions like sacraments. All the men in the Four Families gave up repenting since we know we're just going to do the very thing we'd ask forgiveness for. Each of us got to a point where it felt like we made a mockery of our faith by willfully ignoring the Commandments and thumbing our noses at the sanctity of confession and repentance.

"No. I do not."

"You may not intend to, but will you?"

Michelle shifts to rock her son who's waking up. She clearly wants this spectacle over, but I'm loving every moment of Flora roasting Lorenzo's *huevos*. Watching him squirm in his three-piece suit is priceless.

"No, I will not."

"Stay away from the women in my family, and I'll believe you."

"Thank you."

Flora extends her right hand, and they shake. She turns to

me as Lorenzo walks to Michelle and lifts their son into his arms. The doors to the ballroom open, and guests pour in. Soon noise fills the room as people greet one another. I pull Flora against me and whisper in her ear.

"I don't think I've ever been harder than I am right now. You were breathtaking, *reina.*"

"Thank you, *Papí.*"

I guide her around a set of tables, but rather than stop where I see our place cards, I continue to steer us toward the door.

"Pablo?"

"I'm certain you want to wash your hands after touching his."

"I have hand sani—"

I push open the restroom door and spin her against it, cutting off what she was about to say. I flick the lock as I kiss her. Our hands fumble with each other's clothes as she unfastens my pants, and I inch up her long pencil skirt. I'm fucking throwing this fucking thing in the fucking trash when we get home. Her ass looks too good in it anyway. The possessive beast in me hates knowing other people enjoy seeing it.

Mine.

I hoist her in the air and thrust into her. She Kegels over and over as she rides me. Her legs squeeze my waist as she clings to my shoulders.

"This is going to be hard and fast."

"Yes, Daddy."

"Fuck, you feel amazing, baby girl."

"You too, Daddy."

We kiss to swallow each other's moans. I pound into her until my knees shake. I spin us and walk over to the counter. She presses one hand to the mirror—leaving fingerprints—and the other to the stall wall. I bring her hips to the edge and keep going, my fingers leaving marks on her skin. I kiss along her neck and down to her chest. I let go of her hips to unbutton her blouse.

She's wearing a padded bra to hide the nipple clamps. She was nervous about standing in front of everyone, so I put the clamps on her. The pain was enough of a distraction to keep her mind from spinning. I remove them, and she whimpers as the blood rushes into her sensitive nipples. I suck on each side until I feel her tighten around my cock but not release like when she Kegels.

"May I come, Daddy?"

"Yes, *chiquita.*"

"Fuck, Pablo…Yes…A little more…Just like that, Daddy… Yes! I'm coming, Daddy. I'm coming!"

I know she's speaking barely above a whisper, but her voice fills my ears. Each pant. Each word. Every time she says Daddy. It's pushing me to the edge.

"I'm going to come, little girl."

I feel the first jet of cum as it coats the inside of Flora's cunt. Then the second and third. I pull out and grab between her bra cups. I pull her forward and spray her tits. She'll know I marked her even when her clothes hide it. We're breathless as we share quick kisses. We put our clothes back together after I help her off the counter.

"You look gorgeous, *chica.* You're throwing out that skirt when we get home."

She freezes then steps in front of me when we turn to the door. She shakes her ass as she reaches for the lock. I spank her before wrapping my arm around her waist.

"I'll remind you of that when we get home."

"I know."

I kiss her behind the ear as she unlocks the door. I pull it open, and we come face to face with Shane and Carys

O'Rourke. The women both look away, and Shane and I glare at each other.

"We'll find another one."

Shane mutters as he wraps Carys's arm around his. I smirk. Flora elbows me, and I look down to see her face is scarlet.

"They came to do the exact same thing."

"Yeah, but they hadn't already. We had." Her words are a choked hiss.

"I bet every couple finds a restroom at some point tonight. Hell, even Michelle and Lorenzo will probably slip away. And if any couple doesn't, they'll do it in their town car on the way home."

"It's no wonder our families are huge."

"Yup. Now let's get back inside before *Mamá* and *Papá* notice we're gone."

We arrive at our table, and my parents barely glance at us. They know. I think my face might be the same shade as Flora's.

"It's a good thing I love you, Daddy." I take my seat beside Flora as she whispers to me.

"I love you too, *chiquita*."

Don't miss the next installment

Liesel—He prowls into my boardroom like he owns it—broad shoulders, smug smirk, and the kind of danger that doesn't just whisper, it promises to burn. Jorge Diaz isn't here to do business. He's here to dismantle everything I've built. Arrogant. Gorgeous. Lethal. He looks at me like he knows every secret I've ever buried, and worse—like he wants to strip me down until there's nowhere left to hide. I should hate him. I should fight him. But when his hand brushes mine, I forget how to breathe.

Jorge—She thinks I'm here to invest. She's wrong. I'm here for control. Anneliese Schlossberg is ice wrapped in silk—sharp tongue, flawless skin, and eyes that dare me to push her over the edge. I should walk away. My family's empire is built on blood and shadows, not women like her. But every time she looks at me with that mix of fury and desire, I want to taste what's forbidden. She's supposed to be a means to an end. Instead, she's becoming the one obsession I can't let go.

Sabine Barclay

Meet Jorge and Liesel in *Cartel Rose*.

Thank you for reading

 Sabine Barclay, a nom de plume also writing Historical Romance as Celeste Barclay, lives near the Southern California coast with her husband and sons. She loves her days at the beach soaking up way too much sun, a good Netflix binge, and a strong hot chai. Her heroines are independent women who can defend themselves but love their Alpha heroes who want nothing more than to protect their soulmates in her Mafia Romances. She's Gen Y/Oregon Trail and loves creating engrossing contemporary romances that will make your toes curl and your granny blush.

Subscribe to Sabine's bimonthly newsletter to receive exclusive insider perks.
www.sabinebarclay.com

Join the fun and get exclusive insider giveaways, sneak peeks, and new release announcements in
Sabine Barclay's Facebook Dubious Dames Group

Do you also enjoy steamy Historical Romance? Discover Sabine's books written as Celeste Barclay.

The Cartel Brotherhood

Cartel King

BOOK ONE SNEAK PEEK

ENRIQUE

She's going to fall off that fucking ladder.

I slow my pace to a jog as I approach a house with a woman far too high on her ladder, leaning far too much to the right as she tries to fish something out of her gutters. She's got to be about five-five to my six-three.

I could reach whatever she's fishing around for. She's more likely to fall off and break something. I should mind my own business and keep going with my run, but there's no way I'm doing that. I wouldn't if it were a woman of any age, and I wouldn't if it were an elderly person, either.

If it were a guy my age, maybe I'd let him deal with it, but for her—there's something in how she's reaching. Some frustration I can feel even from here. I approach slowly as I walk up the driveway. I'm only halfway to her when a humongous dog comes bounding toward me.

409

No wonder there's a baby gate across the entrance to her open garage. The massive beast doesn't bark, but he growls. It's a Mastiff, much like the one Laura Kutsenko has, except this one is a different color and easily weighs about fifty pounds more than her giant companion. I wonder if this one is as much of a love bug as Laura's. At least, that's what she's always claimed. The woman on the ladder speaks to her dog, giving him a command.

"Hush, Constantine. Lie down."

The dog immediately obeys, but he inches closer to the baby gate, still growling at me. It's only then that the woman notices me. She grips the ladder as she jerks away. I hurry over and grab the ladder, tempted to demand she come down from there.

"Who are you?"

If anybody's going to do the demanding, apparently it's her. Not that I can blame the woman, since I'm a complete stranger.

"I'm Enrique. I saw you as I was running. You looked a little wobbly up there."

"Well, I was okay until I was startled—but thank you."

Dismissive is the only way to describe her now. I don't blame her for that either. She's a woman in a precarious position with a strange man looking up at her. Now that I'm certain the ladder won't fall over, I step away. I don't need to look like a perv staring up her shorts.

"Would you like some help? I can easily reach whatever you're going for."

Cartel Viper
Cartel Prince

Do you also enjoy steamy Historical Romance? Discover Sabine's books written as Celeste Barclay.

The Ivankov Brotherhood

Bratva Darling
BOOK ONE SNEAK PEEK

LAURA

As I sit across from the four Kutsenko brothers, I press my lips together to keep from drooling. No four men should be so strikingly handsome. Not all from the same family, anyway. I fight a valiant battle against letting my gaze drift toward the eldest, Maksim, whose ice-blue eyes bore into me. After years of negotiating billion-dollar investment contracts while facing countless ruthless businessmen, I've learned to keep my expression studiously blank. But it's a true struggle today. Instead, I focus my attention on the squirrelly lawyer sitting across the conference table. While he's disingenuous with each comment, he's a good negotiator. But I'm better. How cliché am I?

While I feel Maksim watching me, I focus on Dmitry Yakovitch as he continues to argue the merits of the venture capitalist company I represent, RK Capital Group, merging with

Kutsenko Partners. What he means is the merits of Kutsenko Partners acquiring RK Capital Group, then stripping it and making it another money-laundering shell corporation. While most people in New York have little awareness of the Russian mafia, I do. The Kutsenko brothers' names appear on no titles or deeds anywhere in New York City, but it wasn't difficult to determine which shell companies likely belong to them. Their assumption that I'm unfamiliar with them is proving beneficial to me as they continue to whisper amongst themselves in Russian. I think they may even believe they're convincing me that they don't speak much English.

The senior partners of RK Capital Group know who I'm negotiating with, though they may not know I'm aware of these Russians' more nefarious operations. They've given me the go-ahead to agree to a merger with an eventual acquisition, but only for the right price. A price to the tune of twenty billion dollars. Considering an investment firm like Goldman Sachs is worth nearly one-hundred-and-twenty billion dollars, my clients' asking price appears reasonable.

"Mr. Yakovitch, I shall stop you now." I raise my left hand, pen caught between my index and middle fingers. When I have his attention, I lean back in my chair and casually twirl the pen over my index finger and thumb. "Fifty billion is my clients' asking price. You know that. Your clients know that. RK doesn't oppose the merger. What they oppose is the insulting offer you've made. It's nearly noon, and I'm hungry, Mr. Yakovitch. I have a delicious ham sandwich waiting for me. I even have three chocolate chip cookies waiting for me. If we aren't going to make any progress, I shall let you go, so I can move onto my eagerly anticipated lunch."

I cant my head just enough for me to appear as though my gaze rests solely on the opposing attorney's face, but I can see each

Kutsenko brothers' reaction. My face battles yet again against showing my emotions as I fight not to smirk. Their muted but surprised expressions confirm what I already know.

"Please tell your clients to make a reasonable counteroffer, or I will conclude this meeting and enjoy my ham sandwich and cookies."

Dmitry glares at me before turning to Maksim and his three brothers. In rapid Russian, he doesn't interpret my suggestion. Oh no. There's no need for that. I can't catch every word because his voice is too low. But I catch something along the lines of "The bitch refuses to budge. What now? A fucking ham sandwich. More like a stick up her ass."

Maksim swivels his chair to look at his brothers. In Russian, he says, "Fifty billion is ridiculous. She's not so stupid or naïve not to know that. My guess is they'll settle for twenty billion. We offer fifteen."

"That's barely better than what we already offered," Aleksei, the second-oldest brother, argues. "She'll be eating the fucking sandwich and dipping her cookies in milk before we walk out the door. We need the buildings."

"We offer twenty, Maks," Bogdan, the youngest, insists.

As I watch the brothers discuss, their voices barely lowered, I pull my lunch sack from the black leather satchel by my feet and set it beside my laptop. It's a ridiculously pink floral bag with an embroidered monogram, the L and D overlapping. It's an empty prop, but they don't know that. I watch as five sets of eyes narrow. I offer a smile that would appear innocent in any setting other than this meeting. It's patronizing, and I know it.

Bratva Sweetheart
Bratva Treasure
Bratva Beauty

Sabine Barclay

Bratva Angel
Bratva Jewel

Do you also enjoy steamy Historical Romance? Discover
Sabine's books written as Celeste Barclay.

The Mancinelli Brotherhood

Mafia Heir
BOOK ONE SNEAK PEEK

LUCA

This asshole is pissing me off. We've been going around in circles for five minutes, and the longer we stand out here, the greater the likelihood someone will spot us. I have a sixth sense about these things. It's why I'm still alive at the ripe old age of thirty-one.

"Espinoza, enough already. Either sell to us or don't, but we set the price. Your tequila is good, but it isn't nectar from the gods."

I'm watching Carlos Espinoza, some lackey for the Mexican Culiacán Cartel, try to maneuver me into paying more than the agreed upon price. I know it's so he can skim off the top.

"It's as close as you're going to get. You've upped the order, so the price per case goes up."

My uncle, Salvatore Mancinelli, is the New York don. He negotiated this deal, and I warned him it was a bad idea. But what do I know as his underboss and heir? I'm not backing down.

"Haven't you ever heard of a bulk discount? The more I order the better the price should be. No one else around here is buying from you. You know we're your only choice in three out of five boroughs. You aren't going to the Bronx because you won't get more than pennies there. You aren't going to Queens because you don't want to run into the Colombians. You aren't going to Manhattan because then you face the bratva along with us. And what are you going to do in Staten Island? Sell to us anyway? We control Staten Island and Brooklyn when it comes to liquor stores, so take the money and go."

"Luca, there are plenty of liquor stores in Brooklyn that aren't owned by Italians. I'll go there."

We aren't friends. He's patronizing me by using my first name. Fuck him and the horse he rode in on. I have other solutions for this shit.

"And I'll just take what I want from them for free. That's not a half bad idea. The deal's over. Take your shit with the worm in it and go."

"Motherfucking racist. Not all tequila has a worm in it."

"You're selling Mezcal. It's known for the fucking worm. I wouldn't start calling me names, you *penche hijo de puta*."

Fucking son of a bitch.

He has twenty-five crates of stolen tequila that he's trying to offload because he knows he can't sell it at his own liquor store.

"What did you call me?"

Carlos takes what he thinks is a menacing step forward, and his two bodyguards do the same. Not smart. Neither of my two bodyguards nor I react, but the three men in each of my cars open their doors. They won't do more than that. It's just a reminder that the Culiacán can try, but the *Cosa Nostra* still run New York City.

"This is the third and final time I say this. Sell or leave."

Every head turns toward the liquor store's back door as it opens. A gorgeous blonde steps out, and I wish I had the time to appreciate her beauty, but she's about to die. Carlos and his men draw their guns and pivot toward her. My men pull their weapons too, but we keep them pointed at the Mexicans. The woman stands like a deer in the headlights for a second before ducking behind the industrial garbage dumpster like a frightened rabbit. Three shots hit the metal almost at the same moment. That's all it takes for my men and me. The two bodyguards standing with me aim for a guard each, and I set my sights on Carlos. We squeeze our triggers, and the men fall. Screeching tires tell me Carlos's driver takes off. I hear more gunshots as at least one soldier in my cars tries to shoot the escaping vehicle. Glass shatters, but the sedan keeps going. I hear more tires squeal as one of my SUVs takes off and chases the guy. I holster my gun and wave my men to do the same.

I inch forward toward the trash can, but I see the shadow shift. The woman bolts from the other side. She's still the frightened rabbit, but I'm the fox pursuing her. She's fast, I'll give her that. But she has to be at least a foot shorter than me. My legs are a lot longer and cover a lot more ground with each stride.

She weaves among the cars, most likely believing it's harder to hit a moving object. She isn't wrong, but I have no intention of shooting her. I push myself harder and pounce as she darts out and tries to cross the last stretch of parking lot to reach a better lit area near a bus stop. I lunge.

"Stop running, *piccolina*. I won't hurt you."

I wrap my arms around her and pull her back against my chest, but I'm quick to spin her around and put space between us as I grasp her arms. Of course, she fights me.

"If I wanted you dead, I would have shot at you, too."

"It doesn't mean you won't kill me after."

She's breathless as she continues to struggle. I almost let go to take a step back, insulted at what she implied. But I can't blame her. If I were a woman, I'd be terrified of the same thing.

"I'm not going to rape you. I'm going to talk to you."

"Talk? You are not a man who talks if you just killed a guy."

"To keep him and his men from killing you. I told you, if I wanted you dead, I would have shot at you too. And I wouldn't have missed."

She stops struggling against me, but her eyes continue to dart from one place to another, trying to find somewhere to flee. I know I can keep her in place with only one hand, so I release her left arm. I still have a firm hold on her right one, but I haven't held it nearly as tightly as I could.

"I'm Luca. I know you figured out you interrupted something you shouldn't have. Did that man know who you are?"

"Yes."

"What about his driver? Would he know you?"

"Yes."

"Do you have a name?"

"Yes."

"*Piccolina*, we won't get very far if yes is all you can say. Are you willing to answer me with more than one word?"

"No."

I knew that was coming, and I grin. I can't help it. I wasn't wrong about her being gorgeous, but I doubt she wants to know that's what I think. At least, not if I want her to know I won't assault her.

"Fine. I have more than twenty questions I can ask that you can answer with one word. Do you work at the store?"

"Sometimes."

Ah, an improvement.

"Did Carlos know you were still working?"

"No."

"Do you have a car, or do you take the subway or bus?"

She raises her chin and remains silent. Smart but counterproductive.

"The subway or the bus will get you killed. You're too easy to find and follow. Do you have a car?"

"Yes."

"Can you stay with someone instead of going home?"

She refuses to answer.

"If that man knew you and you sometimes work in the store, then he knew where you live. If he found that out, so will someone in his cartel."

"I know. Let me go. The longer I stand here, the more likely someone is to come back for me."

"No one will touch you while I'm here."

"Arrogant. If he shot at me, he would have shot at you."

"And he would have died, anyway. What's your name?"

"Jane."

"Look, I know you won't get in one of my cars and let me drive you somewhere. In most cases, I would say that's a smart move. But you did nothing wrong tonight except for leave work at the wrong time. I know that, and you know that. But the Culiacán won't see it that way, *piccolina.*"

She freezes for no more than five seconds before she trembles so much that I can see it. I don't know what drives me next, but it's the same instinct that's made me call her little girl three times. I pull her to my chest and tuck her head against it. I stroke her hair down to her shoulders, rubbing my hand up and down her back. This is the most inopportune moment to notice she isn't wearing a bra. I will my body not to react.

"What does that mean?"

Her voice is barely more than a whisper, but I know what she's asking.

"It means little girl."

"I should be insulted, but the way you say it..."

"It has nothing to do with your height. I know you're not a child."

God, do I know she's not. She feels amazing. Her tits are soft as they press against me, and I can see she has the most delectable ass. I'd love nothing more than to cup it and squeeze until she goes up on her toes and begs for me to wrap her legs around my waist and fuck her. For fuck's sake. Stop, you disgusting asshole. That is not what you need to be thinking about.

"Why didn't you shoot me? Whatever you were talking about, if it was with a Cartel member, then it wasn't completely legal. Carlos didn't want me alive to talk about seeing you together. Why are you letting me live?"

"I told you. You did nothing wrong but try to leave work. He should have checked the building before starting the meeting. That was on him. The only thing I take issue with is you leaving by yourself and walking into a dimly lit parking lot. I suspect you do that often, and that's too dangerous. Jane Doe, I don't hurt women."

Mafia Sinner
Mafia Beauty
Mafia Angel
Mafia Redeemer
Mafia Star

Do you also enjoy steamy Historical Romance? Discover Sabine's books written as Celeste Barclay.

The O'Rourke Brotherhood

Mob Boss
BOOK ONE SNEAK PEEK

DILLAN

I hate meetings like this. I don't need to wear pants from some shitty off-the-rack suit that are too tight to *try* to make my dick look bigger. I'm secure in my cock size, and I don't need to show how big my balls are for people to know I run this part of the city. I loathe strip clubs too. I'm past the point where naked women make my jimmy do jumping jacks. I can appreciate a hot bod and gymnast level strength, but it does nothing for me. These douchebags? They're practically ready to come in those cheap arse pants. Why am I here? I keep asking myself that. Seamus and Shane are doing just fine with these negotiations. I'm just here to look good. I'm the muscle today. Or rather my name and my position. Who the fuck thought— way, way back in the day —that giving the mob hierarchy nautical names was a good idea? Fucking Skipper. This isn't motherfucking Gilligan's Island. None of these numb nuts are the Professor, even if they think they're fucking Mr. Howell.

But who is that? If this is *Gilligan's Island*, then she's Mary Ann.

I glance at Seamus, but he's focused on the Albanian he's trying not to lose his shite at. Shane smirks at me when I dart my gaze to him. I cock an eyebrow as the waitress walks over. She's definitely not a dancer. She has too many clothes on. But you can barely call the pieces of thread she's wearing clothes. She's got on a bikini top that's barely more than pasties, and the skirt she's wearing would make my Catholic grandmother do somersaults in her grave.

It's the standard uniform for this place, but somehow it doesn't look right on her. Not because she doesn't have a banging body because she does. Not because she's a butter face— but-her-face —as in great bod, not so great face. She's beautiful in a super understated way. That's part of what makes her look out of place. She has next to no makeup on. I think those are even her real eyelashes. The natural beauty is drawing way too much attention.

"'Scuse me."

She tries to step around Zef Hoxha, the *kyre* of the Albanian mafia here in New York. When he reaches out to grab her wrist, I'm out of my seat with my hand around his. He never gets a chance to touch her because my hold is so tight he can't bend his fingers. I keep squeezing until it must feel like I'll snap the bones.

"No touching."

Zef drops his arm as much as my hold allows. I let go and stare at him before I tilt my head toward the waitress. I narrow my eyes, and he knows what I expect.

"I apologize, miss."

"That's all right, sir. Here's your drink."

She's polite as she hands him his glass. Unfortunately, to put down the rest, she has to bend forward, giving everyone a view of her glorious cleavage. Tits and arse are what sell here, and she has them in spades. I'm certain it's why my cousin hired her. If I sit down, everyone will know I'm just as guilty as these fuck nuts because she's made my dick do something that hasn't happened in a strip club since I was like twenty-three. I'm now thirty-three.

Mob Boss
Mob Star
Mob Princess
Mob Saint
Mob Bride
Mob Knight

Do you also enjoy steamy Historical Romance? Discover Sabine's books written as Celeste Barclay.

www.ingramcontent.com/pod-product-compliance
Lightning Source LLC
Chambersburg PA
CBHW020325010826

48973CB00005B/1128